WHEN ONE DOOR CLOSES

The Stellar Heritage Series

by Bob Mauldin

Legacy

Spheres of Influence

Far Horizons

When One Door Closes

WHEN ONE DOOR CLOSES

Stellar Heritage

Book Four

BOB MAULDIN

PUBLISHING COMPANY

Published in the United States by
Blade of Truth Publishing Company, Forsyth, Montana

Cover art: Covers by Christian

This is a work of fiction. All characters, places, and events
portrayed in these stories are either products of the author's
imagination or are used fictitiously. Any resemblance to actual
persons, living or dead, events, or locales is coincidental.

Contact the publisher via email at:
chadd@bladeoftruthpublishing.com

ISBN-13: 978-1-64248-019-1

PROLOGUE

Terran Alliance Herald Katherine Hawke was pissed. After years of not knowing the origin of the spaceship she and her husband Simon had found, she was now in negotiations with the owners of said ship over forty lightyears from Earth.

She'd offered to show the Shiravan Matriarch the expertise of the Alliance cruisers built by the Shiravan colony ship and upgraded by human ingenuity but had found herself in a pitched battle against twice the numbers she'd been led to expect. On top of that, one of her captains had deserted her command chair in favor of a Mamba to fight ahead of the fleet and had been shot down over an enemy planet.

But more than that flavored her attitude. Their entrance into the system had coincided with Helm's declaration that Shiravan class engines had been detected leaving. So many Garmon ships were buzzing around that it had taken two days for things to settle down so they could make their attack approach.

Simon had spent almost twenty years in the military or intelligence work. He'd once quoted an old Chinese general, Sun Tzu: No battle plan survives contact with the enemy. *Truer words were never spoken,* she thought, teeth clenched against inventive colorful language. The *Vega* was a mass of wreckage, the survivors split up among the other ships of the fleet. She suspected another captain of being a traitor, and a flight of Mambas and a shuttle were streaking toward the alien stronghold trying to save Shirley Dahlquist.

Five Mambas flew high cover, sensors stretched to the limit. Nothing showed on any screen, and the flight leader finally allowed the gig to land near the indicator that revealed Captain Dahlquist's position. Those same sensors said that she was barely alive and fading fast. Two medics jumped out of the craft as it hit the ground, tracking the signal from Shirley's wristband. Fifty feet away in the tall grass, they found a sight that would stay with them for the rest of their lives—a full-grown Garmon lying dead on top of a small, frail human, her knife wedged deep into one of its eye sockets. Her injuries were many. A cracked collar bone, broken arm, broken ribs and a punctured lung were the worst of it, but the growing bruise on the side of her head said concussion louder than any words could. Secretly, one of the orderlies managed to remove the knife from the Garmon to give to Captain Dahlquist as soon as she was able to receive it.

Once clear of the atmosphere, the gig accelerated toward the *Canopus*, the pilot calling for a doctor to be on hand as soon as they landed. Five Mambas escorted the gig while the other fifteen had a field day attacking undefended targets all around the enemy planet until Miranda ordered their recall. Reluctantly, the fifteen pilots headed out and away from the planet, knowing the reputation of a captain that they'd better not cross.

Sitha was on hand with Kitty when the gig grounded in the landing bay and followed her as she followed the stretcher into the bowels of the *Canopus* to the med lab.

Kitty paced the corridor while Sitha slumped in the low ceilings of the human ship. Kitty finally realized her discomfort and sent one of the guards to bring a Shiravan chair from the observer's cabin. He returned minutes later with the requested chair and one for Kitty as well. She sat down for all of thirty seconds before resuming her pacing.

Finally, the doctor stepped out of the lab, a glum look on his face. "I'm afraid I've done all I can, Madam Herald," he said. "She's not dead, but she needs far more than I can do onboard. She needs specialists that are forty lightyears away. I don't know how long she has, but it's measured in weeks, if not days. The internal injuries are just too severe for me to handle without a full medical team and hospital to back me up."

Kitty's head dropped to her chest, tears streaming from her eyes, but help came from an unexpected source. "I have a suggestion to make, if you're willing to try it, Katherine," Sitha said quietly.

Eye to eye in the corridor only because Sitha was still seated, Kitty asked, "What can you do? We have only one regeneration chamber that will work on humans, and it's aboard the *Galileo*."

"True," the alien woman answered, "but there's a chamber aboard the *Shumara Vacht*. It can be calibrated for humans by having a healthy human enter it and let the computer recalibrate its programs to fit the human metabolism. The entire process should take two days, at most." She was silent for a few seconds. "It may be the only chance your Captain Dahlquist has of surviving."

"Given a choice," Kitty's response was immediate, "we'll transfer Shirley to the *Shumara Vacht* and make tracks for Shiravi as soon as that's accomplished. I'll act as the model for the computer to realign itself."

The doctor, still standing nearby after giving his diagnosis, said, "I can keep her alive that long, but are you sure that's wise, Madam Herald?"

Kitty looked at him and said, "Look at me, doctor. I've already spent ten months in one of those chambers; two more days won't hurt me. And if it's Shirley's only chance, it's my responsibility."

Vega Group was about to leave Garmon space minus the *Vega* and one hundred and sixty-one crew. Seventeen Mamba pilots had failed to dock, leaving the *Canopus* with three extra ships. Kitty sat in her new quarters aboard the Shiravan battleship, readying herself for a two-day stay in a regeneration chamber. She'd been remonstrated for her decision several times over, not least of all by Shirley, who'd regained consciousness and was attended by the *Vega's* doctor.

Kitty had moved her staff over to the *Shumara Vacht* since she'd be aboard for two weeks. The baron and his wife, along with Brandon Galway, moved their possessions over to the *Federal Case's* gig for the two-week voyage. Kitty called Thomas just before the group went hyper. "All ships will slave their controls to yours, Thomas. Just get us to Shiravi as soon as possible."

"Aye, Madam Herald," came back through the speaker. "Course for Shiravi is laid in and ready to activate as soon as you give the word." Did she still detect some anger in his voice, or was she just imagining things? There would have to be a confrontation in the near future, that was certain. She couldn't go on wondering if one of her top officers was having second thoughts.

"No, Thomas," she replied. "You've been given

command of the fleet. It will be on your orders that we go hyper. I'm depending on *you* to get us there as soon as possible."

The response that came back had a bit less tension in it than most of her conversations with him had had in the past few weeks. "Yes, Madam Herald. The *Federal Case* is ready to accept control of all ships and will jump as soon as the safeties are set up. How is Shirley doing?" This last question seemed almost an afterthought.

"Thank you, Thomas," she said into the impersonal mike. "I'm leaving all preparations in your hands. And it appears that the doctor can keep Shirley stabilized long enough for the *Shumara Vacht's* computers to get a lock on human physiology. See you on the other side." She cut the circuit and immediately asked for a whisker laser transmission to the *Canopus*. "Miranda, we'll be leaving soon and won't be able to talk for two weeks while we return to Shiravi. You know what I'm about to do. I don't have any choice. I won't put anyone else at risk in this type of operation."

Miranda responded by the same system. "I know, Kitty. I just hope it goes well. You know Simon will be looking for somebody to skin if anything goes wrong." A short silence followed. "We've just received our jump coordinates from Thomas. Nav and Helm both agree that they seem to be in order, so I'll see you on the other side."

Not knowing what else to say, Kitty just said, "Good luck, Miranda. Kitty out." She set down the microphone and turned to Sitha. "If you'd be so kind, Doma," she asked formally, "I'd consider it an honor if you'd tell your doctors to expect my arrival shortly. First, I want to see Shirley and her doctor and then visit with the baron and his wife for a short time."

A quick nod, human-style, and Sitha said, "It would be my pleasure to be of service, Domagera Hawke." She waved a waiting crewwoman forward. "I'll have you escorted wherever you need to go until you figure out the layout of the ship. I'll meet you in the medical center soon." She turned her back on the pair and began to study one of the consoles near the Engineering station.

Mystified by the abrupt dismissal, Kitty turned to her escort. Determined to ignore the snub, she simply said, "First, I need to visit the medical center. After you," she said and waved her hand in an imperious gesture copied from one too many B movies.

Her guide immediately headed off the bridge and into the bowels of the ship. Soon, she stopped at a door marked with unreadable Shiravan symbols. "Medical Center," she announced curtly.

"Segala vin, ther'a," she answered using the senior-to-junior mode of address firmly and deliberately. "I won't be long." The thank you and the condescending mode of address should stem any more problems, especially coupled with the correct usage of the Shiravan language.

She pressed her hand on the plate beside the door, and as soon as it slid open, she entered the room. The patient was flat on her back, covered to the neck. The doctor stood up hurriedly at her arrival. "Madam Herald, I'm most grateful that you'll be using yourself as a model for the new interface. I don't want to sound presumptuous, but time is of the essence. I can keep her alive for a few more days, maybe a week, but we need that chamber, and fast."

Kitty nodded absently. "I understand, doctor. I have to set up a few things with the baron, and then I'll be back to get the process started. Less than an hour. You have my word."

She stood by her friend's unconscious body and stroked her hair. "You'll be back in the middle of things before you know it, Shirley. And then I'm going to... never mind. Just hold on. We'll have you up and around in no time. Hell, you aren't half as bad off as I was when I went in."

Her instructions to the baron were terse and to the point. "I don't want Galway to have any more unrestricted access to Doma kep Parrasine than necessary. Perhaps you two can find some way to occupy her time. Maybe painting a rosier picture of humanity than we've shown so far would help. I don't know. You're the diplomats. Right now, I have to go save my friend's life, if it's possible."

Kitty walked back into the medical center of the *Shumara Vacht,* more than a little bit anxious about what was going to happen over the next two days. Oh, in theory, she knew perfectly well that the computer that ran the regeneration chamber was only going to read her physiology and apply that to repairing the injuries to her friend. Still, she worried about the dreams she'd experienced when she was under the control of a computer already under human control.

She looked first at her friend lying still and almost lifeless on a table near the regen table she was about to commit herself to, then let her eyes slide over the cold metal table itself. Actually, it wasn't cold at all. The Shiravans kept their ships at slightly higher temperatures than most humans were accustomed to. "I'm afraid you're going to have to get undressed before getting on the table, Madam Herald. Completely," the doctor said almost apologetically.

Kitty smiled nervously as she reached up to undo the first button on her shirt. Sitha took this moment to appear, bringing the alien-to-human ratio close to three to one. The doctor recognized her nervousness and said, "No word of any of this will ever leave this room if you desire, Madam Herald. And may I say that I admire your courage."

She slipped out of the last of her clothes and reluctantly placed her panties on top. "Courage be damned, Doctor. If this is what I have to do to save my friend's life, it's little enough. Now where do you want me?"

He indicated one of the slightly too-tall tables on which she'd spent ten months and said, "The technicians tell me they can activate the process manually as soon as you're comfortable."

Kitty looked first at the doctor and then over at Sitha, standing slightly behind one of the monitoring technicians. "That's a trick we haven't been able to make your equipment do. I'd like to have someone explain that to me once this is over and I'm back on my feet."

Sitha stood stunned at the sight of Domagera Hawke naked. Tiny to begin with, she was even shorter without her shoes. Her skin, untouched by any sunlight for a year now, seemed bleached of all color, almost to the point of total whiteness. Along with the all-too-real white hair, it gave her a sense of purity that was hard to resist. The two nearest technicians bowed at her command that had been marginally couched as a request, and even she couldn't quite stop her head from twitching before the vision she was beholding.

Shiravan mythology described Kath-e-rin as a small being, glowing white, from beyond the stars. Over the last four hundred years, she and her opposite, Kath-e-vel—a huge, dark, brooding figure—had become the center of the kath-mora-led religion.

Not all who listened believed, of course, but it was at key figures in the des Harras regime that most of the invective was pointed. And it was the young females who responded fastest. For far too many years, they'd been told that they were better than males in all things. The few males who'd survived the great wars had been isolated and held in seclusion by their own clans until they died. From that point, the plight of males on Shiravi had gone downhill. Few males were allowed to be born, and each clan was required to register the number and age of each male in the clan holdings. This was the case until the past hundred years or so, when a des Harras first decreed that since more bodies were needed in space, more males should be allowed to be born and trained for support roles, like medics or comm technicians.

Linnas approved of her predecessor and mentor strongly enough to keep her programs concerning males going. At the same time, she ordered the construction of warships to be accelerated, and even ordered the construction of a third dock in the asteroid belt circling just outside the life zone of the giant red sun warming their world.

Sitha mentally kicked herself for losing track of her own thought processes. She knew this was just an alien female and not a goddess-come-to-life. She watched as the human doctor lifted Kitty by the waist onto the table where she immediately stretched out with her arms at her side. Could she, herself, act as calmly in a similar situation, she wondered?

Kitty felt a chill even though the temperature was higher than humans usually liked. "Let's do this before I lose my nerve, doctor," she said testily.

The doctor nodded, and then nodded to one of the technicians. Almost instantly, the clear canopy slid out of the wall the entire length of the table, meeting another half-circle-shaped piece that rose out of the end of the table.

This time she was awake when the ports in the tabletop opened. Tubes came out, searched, and attached themselves to her wrists and ankles. A primal fear made her shudder, but she stayed still as the devices attached themselves to her. This time she saw the mists begin to form around her, and felt the viscous liquid as it rose up her body. She recognized the beginnings of claustrophobia and stilled herself with a silent chant. A mask slid over her face, covering her mouth, nose, and eyes. She thought of the condition of her friend and bit back a scream.

Soon, she felt the liquid rise up and cover her face, but the mask provided her with all the air she needed. She expected to go to sleep, and she would soon, but before she did, she heard a voice inside her head—or at least she thought she did—just before the muffled sounds coming from outside the chamber faded from her mind.

The Shiravan computer had been given everything in the *Federal Case's* data base on human anatomy and as much on human psychology as could be found and transferred. For two days, it compared what it had learned with what it could actually see in the form of Kitty. It delved down to the molecular level and found signs of earlier manipulation. The actual DNA extracted and examined by the computer matched almost perfectly with models given by the humans, but there was something subtly different about this living sample. Whatever it was would have to wait until other samples could be obtained and tested, and another sample was due as soon as this particular calibration was complete. The thought passed through the densely compacted gel that was a Shiravan ship's computer, leaving something akin to anticipation in its wake.

Kitty woke up to pressure on her shoulders, heels, and butt. Almost as soon as she noticed the discomfort, the patch covering her eyes, nose, and mouth slid away and into a recess in the table, as did the five other tubes that had connected her to the ship's computer for two days. The lid disappeared into the wall and she sat up.

The doctor hurriedly draped a robe around her shoulders and asked worriedly, "How do you feel, Madam Herald?"

She hesitated for a fraction of a second. If Shirley hadn't needed to get into the machine so desperately... "How is Shirley, doctor?" she asked, ignoring his question.

"Ready to go in, if you're sure it's okay."

She hesitated for a few seconds, remembering her first encounter. A dark presence had stayed in the background of her mind as it healed—curious, watchful, determined. This one was different, and oh yes, it was there. More distant, more reserved, and more clinical, this presence just felt... detached somehow. "Certainly, Doctor. I see no reason to keep her out any longer than necessary. By the way, what time is it?"

He nodded and said something quietly to one of the technicians. "Almost six p.m., Madam Herald, he answered almost distractedly. The reason for his distraction made itself known when two others wheeled Shirley Dahlquist's still body into the room. The doctor said, "She's pretty heavily sedated, so it's unlikely that she'll even recognize you, but you're welcome to stay until she's completely involved."

"Involved?" Kitty repeated almost absently. Her attention was riveted on the process playing out in front of her.

"Completely hooked into the system and under the regenerative programs that will begin running almost immediately," the doctor said. Two Shiravans lifted Shirley carefully onto the table. Stepping back, one of them said something to one of the technicians. The cover slid back out of the wall and the end piece moved up to seal Shirley inside. The now-familiar mist formed as things snaked out of holes in the table, covering her eyes and wrapping themselves around her wrists and ankles, taking control of her bodily functions. No one was sure how long Shirley would require healing in the chamber. Kitty had been inside one for ten months, Marsha had still been in one when she'd left Earth, and now Shirley.

The one ray of sunshine was something one of the technicians had said before she'd gone under two days earlier—or more accurately, something the doctor had said that one of the techs had said—and that was that they could initiate the process manually, not needing to wait for some emergency to present itself. That, as she'd promised Sitha, she would look into.

More importantly, she now had another matter to take care of. She went first to her room and showered, paying special attention to her hair. White it may still be, but it had more body now, that was for sure. It was full and long with a natural curl, which its sheer weight tried to straighten out. It framed her face, leaving her looking more elfin-like than ever.

She put on her most austere dress, an all-black sheath with no adornments of any kind—an outfit more appropriate for a funeral than a successful voyage—and walked out of her quarters and into her temporary office. She called Freddie and Margit to confer with her before she made her next call.

The baron made no mention of her attire, though his eyebrows did rise a bit. It was Margit who commented openly. "You look as if you're going to a funeral, my dear. As Herald, you don't have to resort to wearing black all the time as has been mandated for uniforms aboard ship."

Kitty let a sour look pass across her face. She could have kept it away, but these two were her closest advisers. Come to think of it, there was another person outside of her immediate staff aboard whose opinions she could trust. She pressed a button on her desk. "Find Mister Galway, please," she said into the speaker, "and ask him to report at his earliest convenience. And let him know it's most urgent. Then come in here."

"I need advice," she said. "It's bad enough to include Brandon in this. Even though I'm sure he's not exactly on our side, we've built up a relationship of sorts over the past few years, and I'd like his input, as well as yours." She leaned back in her chair. "While we're waiting for him, I'll fill you in on some of the details."

Diana walked in with a strange look on her face. "Is everything all right, Madam Herald?"

"No," Kitty said. "I want you to sit down. We're having a council of war here, and I want every opinion I can trust." She looked down at her desktop for a moment and said, "I think one of my captains is a traitor."

The statement was left to hang for so long that Freddie finally had to ask, "What leads you to this conclusion, and who do you think the traitor is?"

Kitty replied, "Even before we left Earth, some details were reaching U.S. government officials that should never have left any of the ships. Couple that with some of the vibes I've been getting from Captain Breen, and I believe he's one to be watched very carefully."

Diana coughed lightly, getting Kitty's attention. When she was sure she had it, she said, "I'd be very careful what you say from now on aboard that vessel, Kitty." Brandon chose this moment to enter and sat down quietly while Diana went on. "I had a chance to work on the *Federal Case's* computer just before we left Earth space. I thought it odd but not too important. While looking around, I found the ship's roster, and one thing I noted was that almost ninety per cent of the personnel aboard had been personally selected by Thomas Breen. Several hundred transfers have his signature on them, all for personnel who volunteered long after we started open recruiting. If he wished to stage a mutiny, it wouldn't take much to get a few of the crew he didn't pick, locked up and held for ransom, interrogation, or worse."

Kitty looked almost incredulous. "Thomas is a second-waver. I guess it's possible that he could have been in the right place at the right time to get aboard

14

when the rules were laxer, but to bring together almost five hundred personnel without us finding out? We have a personnel department now. They're supposed to screen each applicant and flag those who appear to be a risk. We've had no such thing happen aboard any of the ships, so far."

Diana said, unrelenting, "Some of these transfers, like his XO, were made long ago and then a few at a time, slowly building a cadre of loyal supporters. Then, just before we left Earth, he authorized these several hundred transfers, hiding them among all the others that were going on at the time. There were so many who didn't want to be so far from home for so long that it was easy to remove those who wanted to stay and request certain individuals, especially if they said they didn't mind a long voyage."

Brandon spoke up. "You're looking at Breen as a possible traitor, is my guess," he said as he dropped into a chair. "Well, don't ask me 'cause I don't know. Possibly, that's because what I don't know, I can't tell. I *do* know that there's someone highly placed who's leaking information to certain U.S. officials. I'll also say this: every officer you have serving under you, including Breen, has given an oath of loyalty to the Alliance. Violation of that in any way is tantamount to mutiny, or worse, treason, according to your own rules, most of which you adopted from the U.S. Constitution. Now, you know that I work for the government, but I hate a Benedict Arnold as much as the next man, covert ops excluded. Simon was involved in a few of those, if I remember his dossier correctly. Undercover is one thing, but outright treason is another entirely. A person is only as good as his word. Take me for example. I've never led you on. I've always told you that my first loyalties lie with the U.S. I guess that's why I'm here—you know where my loyalties are."

Kitty cut right to the heart of the matter. "It was my intention to confront Thomas, but now, I'm not so sure. Perhaps we should just let matters rest until we get back to Shiravi?"

"That might be dangerous if he suspects you know he's dirty," Brandon said. "He can do a lot of damage with an entire ship under his command, even so far as blowing us into space dust."

"I hadn't thought he'd go that far," Kitty said, new possibilities blooming in her mind.

"When men are cornered they fight like wild animals," Freddie said.

Kitty had to think, there was just too much new information for her to process this late in the evening without some time. Standing up, she said, "It is getting late, and I want to be up early to check on Shirley before breakfast, so if you'll excuse me, folks, I'm going to bed."

The comment brought her friends to their feet, especially since she'd also risen while speaking. She ushered them to the door. Hugging Margit and holding the Baron's hand, squeezing lightly, she mouthed, "Thank you." Diana, she hugged and said, "Get some sleep." And finally, Brandon. She took one of his hands in her two tiny ones. "Do you think we could talk for a few minutes? I need your help."

Brandon's face dropped into that granite, no-emotion visage that she'd seen all too often on Simon in their early days. She didn't notice it so much anymore, but then he'd been out of the Agency for a long time now.

"You know my main function is to get as much as I can for Earth, separate from whatever you're trying to achieve. How am I going to be able to help you without compromising my own position?" he said.

"I know who you work for, Brandon, and I do wish you'd come over to our side. You'd be a tremendous asset," Kitty said, sitting back down and motioning Galway to do the same. "But that's not what I want to talk about. We have a traitor in our midst. We've known for some time that one existed, but we never were able to pin anyone down. I'm still not able to do so conclusively, but my intuition tells me that it's Thomas and the evidence points to it."

Brandon just nodded. "I still don't see how I can help."

"I have an idea," Kitty said simply.

"So, what can I do?" Brandon asked. "I owe you and Simon both for getting me back into the action, but I won't betray my government."

"I consider you a friend, odd as that may sound, and in Simon's absence, I need some help from someone who understands the minds of the people Thomas works for. What I want is a way to neutralize him as a threat against Alliance plans. You already know the reasons we can't turn over technology concerning our power sources to you, meaning Earth, and I want Breen out of our hair, along with all his appointees. All you have to do is let your bosses know that we know about him, and they'll yank him back almost immediately, along with his potential mutineers. It would be preferable to a set of public trials and executions, don't you agree?"

Brandon looked at Kitty as if she'd grown a second head. "Executions? You've got to be kidding!"

"No, I'm not," Kitty said amiably. "You were the first one to use the word treason, I believe. What's the punishment for that? Execution."

"But that's only in time of war."

"And what do you call what we're engaged in with the Garmons? If this isn't a war, I don't know what is. They won't talk to us; they just attack, attack, attack. So far, we've come out way ahead in the stats, not counting what happened on Earth, but I feel like we're about to get our butts kicked if we don't keep ahead of the curve, and I need *all* my captains to be loyal. I have to think of humanity as a whole first.

"All you have to do is report this conversation, leaving out some key parts, such as the fact that I'm asking you to rat him out. Once they know his cover is blown, they'll pull him, and all of his cronies will either go with him or decide that their best bet is to *really* sign on with us."

"Of course, I'll report this conversation, but you've got to know that Breen's bosses—probably the same people who handed me my assignment, for that matter— are just as interested in the other types of technology incorporated in a ship like the *Federal Case*. So much of this stuff could be used to enhance our military systems that the United States would be unbeatable."

Kitty smiled, and it wasn't pretty. "The Romans felt the same way, Brandon, and look at where they are today. Their only claim to fame is having Vatican City on Italian soil. The Greeks, the Etruscans, the Sumerians, and later the Spanish, the Germans, and now the United States. All of them thought they were right. The old saying 'might makes right' isn't one of my favorites, but we have a clear case of it right here. We've got the power, and like the Goths, you want to take it away from us. Tell me, Brandon, what happened to the Goths after they sacked Rome?"

"I'm not sure," Brandon said slowly, not knowing

where the conversation was going.

"Well, I'll tell you," Kitty said. She took a moment to pour some fire wine into two glasses. "We can drink this without any unpleasant aftereffects, except, of course, for hangovers." The bluish liquid almost glowed in the subdued lighting of the room.

"They were absorbed," she said, bringing the subject back to the table. "They conquered Rome, and over the next several generations, they intermarried and finally became Romans themselves. What they had always wanted were the perks that came with Roman citizenship, only Rome wouldn't acknowledge them so they fought their way in. We have the same situation here. The Alliance has the power to destroy every government on Earth and set up puppets that will answer only to us. Have we tried to do that? No. Will we try it? Not on my watch, we won't."

She took a sip of the liquid in her glass and let the effects make themselves felt throughout her body before she continued. Brandon beat her to it. "So, if I report that you know Thomas is a traitor, you're just giving him enough rope to hang himself. And while you're considering a public trial and execution, they'll pull him in before you can set up the grisly spectacle?"

"Exactly," she said with conviction. "I don't want to be the bad guy here. If his superiors can pull him in before I have to have him arrested, then I'm off the hook as the executioner. He gets to live, along with his cohorts, and we get a clean slate as far as people we can trust running our ships. And there won't be a recurrence of the kind of personnel transfers we've seen aboard the *Federal Case.*"

"I'll do what I can when we get back," Brandon said. "You know, though, that he could do a lot of damage between now and getting back to Earth. What if his orders are to take down the head of the Alliance? Or take her hostage? Don't assume it's just the technology they're after. This could get bloody before you even lift a finger."

"Then I have a lot more to think about," Kitty said, taking large sip.

CHAPTER ONE

Simon introduced his new vice admiral, Jerry Chapman, to his staff and said, "I expect you to give him all the consideration you give me. He's in charge." He turned to Jerry. "And I expect you to listen to your staff and at least seriously consider their suggestions and ideas, Admiral Chapman. I'll be getting full reports from both you and the staff upon my return. I don't want to see too much headbutting, but I don't want to see too much dithering, either."

A long walk down the corridors of Vesta took the two men to Simon's office. "This will be yours while I'm away. From here, you can access the location of any ship in the fleet, including Shiravan ships. Local ships will appear in almost real time. I expect you to keep patrols down to a minimum, but not totally nonexistent. We have to have a presence in the local stellar neighborhood or the teddy bears will start getting the idea that they can just walk in here and smack us again. Not an option, understood?"

The new Commander in Chief of Operations visibly swallowed hard and asked, "What do I say if Kitty shows up while you're away?"

Simon grinned. "That's the best part, for you. All the blame is on my shoulders. She'll have to work with you and coordinate… whatever… while I'm gone. Just tell her the truth, and I'm sure she'll let you live. Listen, I was going to put this off on Lloyd Pike, but my staff correctly pointed out that he's never had any command experience and that you've had the most experience available to me, except for Robert Greene, who's leading Nova Group's next patrol. You've been on every council since we first mandated officer participation in the decision-making process, and you've been captain of the *Heinlein* almost from the beginning. By the way, she'll be kept on-station for the personal use of the vice admiral, at need. Just make sure your exec keeps the crew in fighting shape. Besides, I should be back before Kitty returns," he said, heading for the door.

"Famous last words," the new vice admiral muttered.

"What was that?" Simon asked distractedly as he slowed at the door.

"Nothing, sir."

Just before Nova Group left on its second patrol, Simon was able to send his wishes to Marsha Kane and her Raptor Group headed for Shiravi. There was an overly large number of letters, audio tapes, video tapes, and just plain pictures aboard. A large amount were from Simon to Kitty, but each person aboard the small fleet that had first essayed their way into Shiravan space had kin back on Earth. Each and every one of their families had been contacted, and letters, pictures, and sundry items had been gathered and sent to their special someones forty lightyears away.

The *Raptor* was the first battleship-sized and equipped vessel out of Taurus docks. Carrying twelve hundred persons, she blew anything out of the water in sheer firepower. The *Raptor* was truly an independent mobile weapons platform and twice the size of any ship so far. Incorporating all the latest innovations as of her commissioning, the great ship boasted six engines to the standard three of most ships. Carrying an extra five Mambas, she had both tractor and pressor beams installed in her. Tests on unsuspecting asteroids had proven the ability of the new weapon system. This new adaptation of Shiravan technology would just about crumble any ship the beams could get hold of.

The problem was getting in close enough to do some damage while taking the smallest amount themselves. That particular problem had been solved several years previously when a form of plasma bomb was developed that literally made every piece of metal in a ship totally inert. Nothing metal in any ship hit by a sufficiently powerful enough bomb would ever conduct electricity again. Melted and re-smelted with newer, fresher material made no difference. Even the new uncontaminated material would lose electrical coherence. The enemy would just find themselves dead in space with their monopoles going in different directions, the antimatter one taking part of the ship with it in a gigantic explosion, effectively destroying the last hope of independent movement, assuming of course, that the explosion didn't completely destroy hull integrity first. The *Raptor* carried fifty of the things, with the ability to make fifty more from the power cores before they had to be replaced. Their one drawback was that they were a close-range weapon.

A plasma bomb was essentially a ball of electrical energy—very expensive energy. The manufacture of such a powerful force depleted the antimatter core at a faster rate than even hyperdrive did. Fifty would allow the ship to return to home base—actually any core assembly would do—but one hundred would not, unless the crew was very lucky. And no one wished to be that dependent on luck. An even newer version of the plasma bomb totally reduced the target to its constituent atoms, virtually imploding the vessel. Testing was still under way, so these plasma bombs were what was available.

The *Raptor* was able to fire a full complement of missiles forward that totaled twenty, to the normal ten for a battlecruiser of the *Niven's* size, and being larger, she was able to extend newly designed sensor booms that would allow her the use of her sensors sternward more effectively than anything in space at the moment. And twenty accurately aimed missiles could sweep the rear of followers with a far higher degree of accuracy than ever before.

The newest generation of single-pilot fighter ships, Mantas, were aboard as well. Fifteen highly sophisticated fighters—even by Shiravan standards— that were privately called SMART ships by their designers had finished their trials and were ready to deploy.

Not everyone could fly these new ships. The helmet wasn't so much worn as lain down in. The pilot slid into position in a depression in the padding of the cockpit, laying arms and legs in such a way that no part of the body touched another, and then made sure the helmet was in proper position. When the cockpit sealed, the pilot was effectively locked in that position for the duration of the flight, sensors analyzing each micro-movement of every muscle and translating it into action of one kind or another. Other systems handled nourishment and necessities at need.

Individually designed for specific pilots, the helmet area was a small computer in its own right. It mapped the brain it surrounded, then inserted several hundred microscopic probes into the wearer's scalp, stopping only when they reached bone. This way, the wearer *became* the ship. Thinking of running made the engines move one forward, and sensors conducted data both ways. The pilot saw everything around her and felt as if she were actually running—the ultimate in virtual reality to date.

Capable of storing enough energy for four plasma bombs and carrying a full load of fifty-two Terran standard missiles, the Manta had its grav sump upgraded, shields strengthened, and range increased.

More and heavier point-defense lasers were added as well, both fore and aft, making the *Raptor* more powerful than any equivalent ship in space. But her greatest asset was the new shielding built into her hull. It very efficiently took in any energy emission that struck it and passed it around the hull, re-transmitting it off into space. The visual effect on an enemy's scanners was (or would be, soon enough) that nothing was there until the *Raptor* got so close that the enemy scans could recognize the time-lag in the emissions running around the ship. It would look on their scans as if it were a true predator of the spatial deeps, slowly emerging from the murky depths to devour its prey.

The *Raptor* would be traveling with an extra ship. It would replace one ship from Kitty's combat patrol, and that ship would return to Earth bearing the Herald, a plan of action that would help stop the attacks and, hopefully, encourage an alliance, as well as progress reports and, likely, new assignments for the Shiravan forces still in human space.

Nova Group left human space just after Raptor Group but was only planning on being gone between four and six months. They'd be cruising through solar systems near Earth, hoping to find some sign of the Korvils and using their own tactics against them, attacking without any attempt to parley.

In the second system the Nova Group entered, they found two Korvil destroyers circling the fourth planet as it in turn circled a redder star than Earth's, though not so red as the Shiravans'.

Robert Greene, group commander, and captain of the *Nova*, met with his captains and Admiral Hawke to discuss the matter. The two captains from the Shiravan vessels *Stigarn* and *Berra Feigh* made do with what they could in the way of seating arrangements, with Robert's abject apologies.

"Future meetings will be held on one of your ships," he said, finally ending the apology. The two Shiravan captains, fully assured that it hadn't been a deliberate slight but merely the oversight of an overworked group commander under stress, settled themselves side by side on the floor just to the left of Robert with a minimum of grousing.

Simon looked at the two still-uncomfortable aliens and slid off the couch he'd appropriated on arrival, settling on the floor with the Shiravans. "If the floor is good enough for our guests," he stated firmly, "it's good enough for me as well." The level of discomfort dropped drastically with this move. Moments later, everyone was seated cross-legged on the floor, the humans more uncomfortable with the situation than the Shiravans.

Robert set the pace of the meeting by going right to the heart of the matter. "We have several hours before our arrival will be detected by the two ships in orbit around the fourth planet. We have sensor data on transmissions between the ships and the planet, and some traffic between the planet and the two ships, most likely fresh foods and reports to be forwarded to their headquarters. Our problem is that the translator says these Korvil call themselves Garmons now. We have some verbal confirmation that there was a different name for the race even before the Shiravans first met them.

"Nonetheless, we'll treat them as if they are still the same hostile species, as a change in leadership doesn't necessarily mean a change in direction or attitude. We will, therefore, one-jump straight to the fourth planet and attack the two ships in orbit. Then, we'll reduce any planetary structures to rubble. Captain Miller, your carrier will drop out of hyper five seconds before the rest of the squadron. You'll then launch half of your fighters to assist in the disposal of the two destroyers. The *Nova* and the *Niven* will drop out on schedule, and the *Shasta*, the *Stigarn*, and the *Berra Feigh* will drop out two seconds after the *Nova* and the *Niven*. This will effectively trap the two destroyers between three separate forces since the Mambas from the *Eightball* will stay in close formation, appearing on their screens as two ships.

"We'll ask for no quarter, nor will we give any. Once the two defending ships are disposed of, all planetary targets are fair game. I want the entire infrastructure of the planet destroyed. No roads, bridges, or buildings are to be left standing. A lesson has to be taught to the Korvil or Garmon or whatever they call themselves now. Humanity and her allies are not to be messed with. If there's a new leader of these people, he'll have to learn that just because he's now in charge, the atrocities of the past will not go unpunished. Captains des Nimara and sel Belca will place themselves under the command of Captain John Grant of the *Shasta* and prevent any withdrawal of the enemy ships. The *Nova*, the *Niven*, and Mambas from the *Eightball* will attack from two sides simultaneously.

"There will be casualties, people; don't think for a moment that there won't. Some of the people we know best won't be coming back from this mission, but the group as a whole will survive. Our firepower is just too much for unshielded ships orbiting what's most likely a supply outpost." Robert's monologue finally ran down, and he looked around as if asking for questions. When none were forthcoming, he added, "Very well, then. All captains back to their ships. The mission will commence as soon as all six ships report ready. The *Niven* will slave her controls to the *Nova*. The *Stigarn* and the *Berra Feigh* will do the same with the *Shasta*, and the *Eightball's* captain already has her instructions. Good hunting and good luck."

Robert stood up, the others following suit as far as the ceiling would let them, and all trooped toward the doorway. "Simon, if you'd stick around for a minute, I'd like to talk to you privately."

Simon plopped back down onto the couch he'd vacated to make the Shiravans feel more at ease and waited for Robert to get the others on their way. When the door closed, Simon asked, "What's up, Bob?"

Robert Greene busied himself at the small but well-stocked bar that he hadn't offered to any of the others, pouring two fingers of amber liquid into two glasses. He handed one to Simon and settled into one of the chairs that was sitting vacant in the conference room. An uncomfortable look crossed his face.

"Tell me something, Simon. I have to know. Who do I take orders from? Ultimately, that is. If you tell me to go on patrol, I go on patrol. If you want to go along, I take you, but you have a superior as well. Suppose, just for the sake of conversation, that I get conflicting orders from you and Kitty. Whose orders do I follow?"

Simon looked as if he'd bitten into a rotten apple or something. "Why do you ask, Bob? Kitty is so far away, she has no influence here and now."

"But she gave instructions to her substitute, and those are just as good as coming from her. I know Kitty, Simon. If I don't do as she says, I'll find myself cleaning the disposal pits for a couple of years... at the very least."

Simon sighed, not quite knowing where this conversation was leading. "Ultimately, her orders outweigh mine. She's the civil authority that the military branch answers to. Again, why?"

Robert sighed, too, and took a sip from his glass. "It's Chivas. You better drink it," he said without answering further.

Simon took a small sip and then a larger one, reveling in the smoky flavor. "Spill it, Bob. You didn't hold me back to discuss the chain of command."

Robert took another sip from his glass. "I have very specific instructions concerning your participation in any hostile activities. You're to be removed to the safest place possible, whether you like it or not. These instructions come from Kitty herself, and just lately, Lucy reinforced the injunction. So, what's going to happen is that you're being transferred to the *Eightball* until this particular mission is over."

"What! You'll do no such thing, Captain Greene," Simon said in his best parade ground voice. "I will

29

remain aboard the *Nova* and direct the action from here. It'll put me in the best position to make the necessary decisions as fast as possible."

"Sorry, Simon," Robert said, sounding truly apologetic. "I have my orders from the Herald and the Deputy Herald. You'll move to the *Eightball* with Captain Miller. Her gig is holding its departure while we have this talk. You're one of the symbols of what we've achieved so far in our rise to spatial equality with the other races in our stellar neighborhood. Your safety is paramount, and the *Eightball* is going to be as far from the action as I can keep her. Therefore, you'll watch the action from there. As far as overall command of the operation is concerned, *I* am in charge of the group and will be calling the shots—all of them, including your transfer." The expression on his face left no doubt that he was serious. "Now, I have to get six ships moving in a coordinated assault on two ships that are manned by possibly suicidal crews. The sooner *you* get moving, the sooner *we* can get moving."

Simon stood up, his drink forgotten on the side table. "I will not be forced off this ship, Robert. I'm Admiral of the Fleet, and I'll carry my flag aboard whichever ship I choose. You don't have any latitude in the matter." He walked to the door. "You'll find me in my cabin until we're about to come out of hyper, and then I'll be on the bridge directing operations."

Simon's nearness to the door caused it to slide into the wall, and he found himself facing two of the biggest men he'd ever seen in his life—and he was no slouch, standing six feet tall himself. Robert said, "Commander Bergen, you will escort the admiral to Captain Miller's gig and see that he's aboard when it leaves the bay. If he isn't aboard, you won't ever work for the Alliance again.

That's a concrete guarantee. Have I made myself clear?"

The commander looked first at the captain, who'd just given him an order, and then at the admiral, who outranked the captain. "This is under the direct order of the Herald, Commander. Read this if it will make you feel any better about your assignment." He handed over a folded letter from an inside pocket. The Herald's holo-pic was at the top of the page, followed by her instructions concerning the safety of the admiral. The same dire warning followed. Surely death and destruction would rain down on his family for seven generations if he didn't do as the captain and letter ordered.

He handed the paper back to Robert and said formally, "Admiral, if you'll follow me, I'll escort you to Captain Miller's gig. It's waiting in Launch Bay One, and we need to hurry."

Robert's sigh was audible to Simon, if not the two security men standing on the corridor side of the door.

"Okay, Robert. You win. For now. But don't think I'm going to forget this," he warned. "I'm not in the habit of being stabbed in the back and letting the culprit get away with it."

"Then you should look to your wife and her deputy for the knife. Don't blame me. I'm just the pointed object you got stabbed with. If it makes you feel any better, I'm angry to the point of outrage that you two have put me in the middle of what is essentially a husband/wife spat. I'm just following orders from the highest authority, too. And I believe you were the one to set them up and help pass them through the council into law. Now, you want to be exempt from your own rules. I don't think you can have your cake and eat it, too, at least not as long as Kitty runs the civilian side of the arrangement, anyway. Besides, it sets a bad example for the common crewman. Just go and let us get this mission under way. The sooner started the sooner finished."

Simon stepped off of the *Eightball's* gig, fuming. Nothing Gayle could say had made matters any easier. She'd finally given up, grabbed a rating, and ordered her to show Simon to visitor's quarters. "As soon as we deploy our Mambas, I'll call you to the bridge, Simon. I promise."

Simon fumed as he followed the rating down long corridors to the section assigned to the *Eightball's* officers. "Make yourself comfortable, sir," the rating said. She added, "I'll be right outside your door to escort you to the bridge when Captain Miller gives the word."

The door slid shut on her impassive face, and Simon found himself staring at a blank door. He turned, furious at his helplessness, and began to examine his quarters. After no more than two minutes, he flung himself onto the couch in the main room to wait for Gayle's call to the bridge. Sometime later—his anger wouldn't let him judge just how much—he felt the familiar wrenching feeling of the ship going hyper, and only seconds later, the same feeling repeated itself as the *Eightball* dropped out of hyperspace and started launching her Mambas. *That was quick*, he thought, rising to his feet.

He felt each vibration as a separate entity moving away from the ship. Some of them would never return, blown into atoms by an implacable enemy. The only thing he was happy about was the fact that the casualties were going to be so much less due to the extensive modifications to all aspects of Shiravan technology.

Soon, a knock at his door caused him to growl, "Enter."

The rating stood there. "Sir, the captain's compliments, and would you be kind enough to attend her on the bridge?"

"Absolutely," he said. "Let's go."

As they approached the bridge area, the rating stopped and said, "Sir, I know you're the admiral, but I have to serve on this ship, and Captain Miller has made it clear to me that I'm to make clear to you that you're here strictly as an observer. You're not to attempt to usurp her authority or issue commands to any active units. I've been ordered to ask if you'll abide by these instructions. If your answer is no, then I'm to escort you back to your quarters where you can follow the action on the monitors that have been installed in your room."

Simon smiled for the first time in hours. "You can assure Captain Miller that I'll be the model of decorum." He shook his head slightly.

Why is it that I always have to give in to the womenfolk? he thought to himself.

Simon stood on the *Eightball's* bridge beside Gayle. Even though she was a long-time friend, this wasn't the time to impose on that friendship. She was busy fighting her ship, as an old wet-navy term went. She stared at a holodisplay showing the two bogeys and the entire attack fleet as it moved into position. The surprise was complete. The Terran/Shiravan fleet had arrived in attack position before light-speed communications could discern that a fleet was even approaching.

Slaving controls was a human innovation that allowed two or more ships to move in unison without straying too far from each other or finding themselves out of position among a larger force. It also helped prevent the accidental collision of ships in space as they moved in concert, although nothing of the sort had happened yet. Often, a wet-navy commander had had to contend with individual subordinates interpreting orders in ways he'd never intended. This innovation prevented that problem. Simon had helped develop the tactic because he wanted to see as few casualties due to friendly fire or accidents as possible. It had happened once during his stint with the DIA. Three good agents died needlessly because someone had misinterpreted their orders.

The two Garmon ships—the distinction was unclear—were caught by surprise and never got off a shot, but as an ancient Chinese general once said, "No battle plan survives contact with the enemy." During the few minutes it had taken to remove the two ships from the cosmos, leaving only clouds of drifting atoms, four destroyer-sized ships left the planet's surface at a speed that would have melted hulls if they hadn't been specifically designed to withstand the enormous heat.

Acting as two separate units, the enemy ships attacked with all the weapons at their disposal, which was considerably less than the joint fleet enjoyed. A fifth ship, much smaller and faster, didn't bother to close with any ship, though it was noted on the fleet's screens. It boosted at a very high rate of speed in a direction away from the action—a not unwise move for such a small ship. It cut power relatively quickly and merely stood off and waited out the entire attack by the four larger Garmon ships. Seven Mambas and their pilots died in the furious onslaught that followed, all from the *Eightball*, but even while the enemy was moving out of the atmosphere, the *Shasta*, the *Stigarn* and the *Berra Feigh* were moving in, now under independent command.

Five fighters from each of the two Shiravan ships moved out ahead of the three larger ships. The *Shasta* held back but stayed close, her own Mambas already out and ready to assist if need be. The *Stigarn* and the *Berra Feigh* had the good fortune to have received upgrades to their shields, along with some of the more effective human-inspired missiles they were launching at two of the new attackers.

Enemy point defense, or computer-guided lasers, took out some of the missiles pouring in on the two Garmon ships. The gunners apparently had orders to target the fighters at all costs because one enemy ship died in a cloud of quickly dissipating particles but not before all ten Shiravan fighters had been removed from the equation by the two enemy ships. Even a semi-sentient intelligence could be overwhelmed by the number of incoming, by what the sensors said about those same missiles, and by the positions of all other ships. In moments, the two Shiravan ships had finished off their foes and were looking for something else to do.

The other two Garmon ships fared no better. Actually less so, as the human Mambas had deployed shields and had already had some experience with Garmon tactics. The two ships almost immediately began to rain down on the planet they'd launched from as particles so small that they wouldn't even leave trails as they entered the atmosphere.

The human/Shiravan battle group moved into orbit unmolested and began a survey of the surface. Meanwhile, nearly unnoticed, the small ship disappeared into hyperspace, its departure reminding the fleet of its existence.

The *Eightball* picked up her surviving pilots somberly while the other ships in the fleet rejoiced at the victory. A mapping of the planet's surface was already under way, looking for anything they might destroy to hinder Garmon activity in the area. What they found were four small, town-sized complexes. A decision was made to send Mambas down to investigate the settlements, so five ships over-flew each of the sites. No roads besides rudimentary tracks led from the complexes, fields were planted in nearby areas, and the towns themselves appeared to be mostly comprised of rudimentary dwellings.

The captains of the six ships conferred and finally decided to explore at least one of the towns, if only to try to learn something about the enemy they faced. Three shuttles filled with volunteers, one of them Shiravan, grounded on the south side of one of the towns. Each shuttle disgorged fifty or more volunteers to explore what they'd conquered.

Simon fumed at the fact that he was still unable to change the minds of his junior officers. *I let Kitty and Lucy have too much power for way too long*, he thought to himself as he watched on the screens.

Cameras mounted on helmets gave a clear picture of each soldier's field of view. Multiple images flashed on several screens as the troops moved through the town they'd chosen.

The truth of what they faced was appalling. Garmon females were apparently not as sentient as the males. Their faces bore testimony to the fact that they were closer to their original progenitors than anyone would possibly have suspected. They were bred for one purpose only—to provide more males to expand the empire.

Three teams of humans and one Shiravan entered the largest building in town. All helmet cams were in full record mode, and what was sent to the ships in orbit shocked all who saw the grim reality of Garmon existence.

The females were no more than breeding machines, docile and subservient, even to aliens who prodded them outside for perhaps the first times in their lives. Each female was either suckling four to six cubs or gravid to the point that it was evident they were about to give birth. Some few showed no signs of either condition, and it was suspected that these were not yet ready to bear young.

The ratio of males to females among the cubs was almost five to one, confirming a longstanding Shiravan idea that the important thing in Garmon culture was that male survival equated to species survival. It would appear true, given the obvious differences between the two genders. They were so different that one could almost say they were two different species. Not one word was spoken by any female, but some of the males, apparently almost of an age to begin training to be warriors, were hard to control.

Robert called the *Eightball* to talk to Simon. "Now you want my advice," Simon said matter-of-factly. "Well, I suppose you've done well enough on your own so far. I never claimed I was a tactician or strategist. That's why I surrounded myself with those who proved themselves the most able. The ones who didn't pan out got sacked or moved to positions they were better suited for.

"Losing seven Mambas in the accomplishment of your goal is, in my opinion, a very small price to pay for the results you achieved, especially given that nasty little surprise of four more ships thrown in at the start. Those pilots and all of our dead are the giants upon whose shoulders we stand. And let's not forget the lives of ten Shiravan fighter pilots as well. And two Shiravan crews dying in one of our battles.

"But now you want me to set policy for how we deal with situations like these. I say move all inhabitants out of the towns and level the town. Let the survivors forage for themselves or die. We can't be leaving pockets of resistance behind us, and that's surely what these Garmons will become if we let them alone. Their adults will come back and continue their teachings sooner or later. Better we scatter them so they're harder to find when the lords and masters come calling."

The oldest males among the populace of the small town were the only ones who could be spoken to, and that only through the translators. The problem was that they tended to attack first, even at this early stage in their lives. It took several troops to bind and secure the most aggressive males and some time more to instill in them the fear that the entire clan would be destroyed if orders weren't followed.

One male, best-guess equivalent to a human preteen, arms bound at his side, asked, "How are we to feed and protect ourselves and our females if we are bound this way?" He stood in an aggressive stance, even though he was surrounded by beings twice and three times his size. A Shiravan looked at him and said, "It would make me quite happy to see all of you die right here and now, but our human allies have different ideas. They are going to let you live. Your homes will be destroyed, but you should be able to forage enough to feed all of your kin. To that end, you are instructed to move all of your people away from the dwelling areas immediately."

The Garmon youngling looked at the Shiravan as if he were something to forage on. "How much time do you allow us to move away?"

"You waste time asking stupid questions, young Garmon. Order your people into the fields now." The Shiravan turned and aimed his laser rifle at the base of one of the adobe and timber buildings. Almost immediately, the abandoned building was engulfed in flame. "That is the fate of every structure here. Order your people out... now."

The young Garmon turned and growled in a speech pattern human ears had seldom heard. The small crowd of fur-covered beings began to shuffle out of the compound and away from the flames. "I have complied with your demand. Now you will accede to mine— release me so I may aid my littermates in providing for the females until assistance arrives from homeworld." He turned his back and held out his arms slightly.

The Shiravan did so after locking eyes with the human group leader, who shrugged in the Shiravan fashion and then nodded. The small Garmon was cut free, and he immediately followed his kin out of the compound. Last to pass through the gate, he turned to his conquerors. "This travesty will not go unremembered. I am Pegra Nargresh, eldest son of Subat Nargresh. Remember my name and fear me, for I shall avenge this stain upon our Honor."

"Imperious little shit," one man muttered. "No wonder they're so hard to kill."

CHAPTER TWO

The *Vega's* shuttle was assigned to the *Canopus* for the trip back to Shiravi. As the remaining ships moved away from the planet, Kitty used the shuttle extensively, moving between the remaining three ships in her small fleet. She called the *Federal Case* and informed Captain Breen that she and her staff would begin their transfer to his ship for the two-week journey back to Shiravi. "Are you sure that's the best choice, Madam Herald?" Thomas returned testily, and not for the first time. Breakfast the day after Shirley had gone into the *Esmit's* regen chamber had had much the same flavor. "The *Federal Case* is pretty overcrowded with the *Vega's* survivors. Perhaps you should consider moving to the the *Esmit*, instead."

"I'll be the judge of what's best, Captain," Kitty said in her frostiest voice. "The *Canopus* and the *Esmit* are in just as much distress as you are. Four more aboard the *Federal Case* won't make that big a dent in life support or other essential services. You'll make room for me, and Baron and Baroness von Schlenker, as well as Mr. Galway. I predict that it's going to be an interesting trip since you and I will have a lot to discuss during the two weeks we'll be in hyper." She ended the transmission abruptly, anger coloring her last words.

Kitty went first to the *Canopus*, where she picked up the baron and his wife, along with Brandon Galway. She stood in front of her closet, trying to decide what to wear, and finally settled on the more severe BDU's. Some instinct made her reach for and strap on her laser for the first time in several years, things were about to get messy. The weight did nothing to comfort her. Actually, she felt less protected with it than without, but she was about to go into a situation she had very little actual control over, if her suspicions were correct. She checked the power cell, found it full, and re-holstered the weapon. Lastly, almost as if by a will not her own, she reached out and pulled her old pilot's jacket off its hanger. Now, she felt dressed.

She then culled the rolls of the *Canopus's* crew, along with the survivors of the *Vega,* and chose forty more people she asked to come to the shuttle bay, armed. The request had been met with disbelief from most she'd spoken to, but all complied with the orders of the Herald.

She walked into the *Canopus's* shuttle bay, followed by a solid phalanx of armed crewmen, and the eyebrows of all three of her staff went up. "Don't say a word, any of you," she ordered. "Brandon, I know we're on separate sides of certain issues, but those need to be tabled for the time being. I'm appointing you as my temporary chief of security," she said as she pulled another pistol belt out of her travel bag and handed it to him. "Captain Breen and all of his top staff are traitors, if not more. As soon as possible, he and his staff will be removed from command and replaced with people from the *Vega's* crew. Your job is to see to it that I don't get killed making the necessary changes."

"Not one person is going to believe me without corroboration," Brandon muttered as he strapped the belt on and adjusted it. "I've never used one of these. How about a quick lecture?"

"Just point and pull the trigger," she said. "You have a full power pack. That's forty shots at half power, which is enough to kill anyone we'll be facing." She turned to the crowd standing behind her, deliberately standing beside Galway. "Ladies and gentlemen, we are about to enter a very dangerous situation. I suspect Captain Breen of being a traitor to the Alliance and weighting his crew with infiltrators. I have it on good authority that almost ninety percent of his crew are agents of the U.S. government. That means that very soon we'll be fighting our own to take control of the *Federal Case*, beginning the moment the shuttle lands in the *Case's* bay."

Everyone had heard her instructions to Galway, and some faces showed nervousness. "I understand your discomfort, people, but this was going to happen sooner or later. I regret that it's happened so far from any assistance, but we are going into action against traitors on one of our own ships. I'll take responsibility for all actions from this moment on." She reached up and, with some difficulty, ripped the patch off her left shoulder. "You'll follow the orders of Commander Galway as if he were speaking for me until further notice. We'll have until we reach the *Federal Case* to formulate a plan of action to take the ship. No one who tries to stop us is to be allowed to do so, up to and including termination with prejudice. That means that anyone who tries to stop you is to be disarmed and confined. If they resist, shoot to wound first if possible and then to kill if resistance continues."

First one, and then in an increasing wave, the assembled personnel began removing their left shoulder patches. "Watch for *Vega* patches, people," Brandon said, issuing his first order. "They're most likely not a part of the traitors in control of the *Federal Case*. I see the *Vega's* XO in the crowd. Ms. Dexter, you will pick your command team and add fifteen extra people to it as security. I expect resistance from the time the ramp goes down. As soon as the shuttle doors open, your team and I will do our best to overcome any resistance without raising an alarm. That means disabling or killing," he said, using the last word harshly, "whoever is waiting for us when we debark. Remember, they are expecting only four people plus a pilot. We'll then make our way to the command deck and take charge of the *Case* by any means necessary, as per the Herald's orders, and your command team will be invaluable at that point, so don't go sticking your necks out unnecessarily." He hesitated for a few seconds. "Who here is familiar with the engine room?"

A hand raised from the crowd. "Sir, I was Chief Engineer aboard the *Vega,* and I have enough personnel present to operate the engine room if we can take it."

Brandon nodded. "Pick your people fast, Chief. We'll only have about a ten-minute flight to the *Federal Case*, and I expect that there will be resistance from the start. That's why both ramps will be lowered at once when we land. Okay, I think we need to board and get into space before we set off too many alarms in people's minds about our delay."

Brandon's premonition wasn't far off the mark. The *Federal Case* called the shuttle once during the short flight. "Madam Herald," a smooth voice said, "we were expecting your gig. It might be a problem to get your shuttle into the bay among the shuttles from the *Vega.*"

Kitty took the mike from the pilot. "This is Herald Hawke. We have to make do with what we have available. The *Canopus's* gig is having a flux converter problem, so I've commandeered this shuttle. It will return to the *Canopus* as soon as my staff and I transfer my flag."

"Very well, Madam Herald," came back through the speaker. "You're cleared to dock in shuttle bay two."

"Damn," Brandon said. Kitty looked his way. "That means we'll have that much farther to go to get to the control room and give Breen that much more warning."

Kitty said, "It also puts a contingent nearer the engine rooms, which we really must take. We'll enlist any of the *Vega's* crew as we pass them. They're going to be strewn all over the ship in an effort to find accommodations for them. Change of plans, take weapons from the *Case's* crew and distribute them to the *Vega's,* using them as guards at secure points. As soon as I can reach a ship-wide comm console, I'll call for a complete cessation of fighting and any *Vega* crewman to uphold their oath to the Alliance. Anyone not from the *Vega* who won't surrender is to be shot without hesitation. Try to disable, but a kill shot will not be a punishable offense." This last was said loud enough for all to hear. "Baron, Margit, you two are to stay back until the shooting stops. I won't risk your lives in suppressing a mutiny aboard one of my ships."

The baron just smiled and said, "Fear not, Madam Herald, I've survived more than you might imagine. And neither I nor my wife have any illusions about what we'll be able to do if it becomes necessary. Should you need to retreat to the shuttle, be sure that your escape route will be protected." Both he and his wife moved pieces of clothing aside to reveal laser pistols that she had no idea they had.

Kitty looked at the pistols for several seconds. "It

seems I've seriously underestimated both you and your wife, Freddie. I'm more than a little relieved to know that you have our possible escape covered. And you have my apologies."

The baron made a negating gesture with one hand. "No apologies are necessary, Madam Herald. Just don't risk yourself more than necessary. Simon would never forgive me if anything happened to you."

The pilot of the shuttle interrupted. "Madam Herald, we've just been captured by the *Federal Case's* tractor beams. We're being pulled into bay two as expected."

Kitty nodded. "Very well, Commander. Allow them to override the controls until we're on deck. Then open both exit ramps at the same time. Brandon, from here on out, you're in charge of the boarding action. Listen up, people. No matter how you feel, our interests and those of Commander Galway are the same for the time being. I have placed my life in his hands and trust him completely. I expect no less from the rest of you."

The two ramps started lowering at the same moment, and Kitty strode purposefully down the ramp that had a side party waiting for her. None of them was Captain Breen, an insult under most conditions, but considering that they were just leaving enemy territory, it was a forgivable offense. The problem was that all of the waiting crewmen were armed, weapons held at the ready.

The leader spoke up, "Madam Herald, I have orders to arrest you and place you and your staff in detention until Captain Breen has time to discuss the situation—"

The commander leading the party was shot in the shoulder before the last word left her mouth, a small hole appearing in her uniform. The other seven members of the group got several shots off before they went down. Luckily the shots had went wide and they didn't have time to access their comm links. Kitty pulled her pistol, eyes focused somewhere behind the woman, and said, "Funny, Commander Malone, I was about to say the same to you."

Brandon came out, pistol leading the way, with several other crew members and disarmed the three survivors from the side party. "Okay, people, you have your assignments." His voice had gone almost totally lifeless as he shifted into what Simon had always called 'combat mode.' Now she understood the process and was just glad it wasn't Simon she was watching.

A tinny voice came from Commander Malone's comm link. "Status report, Commander." Breen's voice was recognizable.

Kitty pointed her pistol directly between the commander's eyes and said, "If you say the wrong thing, you and a great many of your people will die needlessly."

The commander, staring at the ruby-tipped barrel of Kitty's weapon, carefully lifted her comm link to her lips. "This is Malone. We have the situation under control. The Herald and her staff have been neutralized."

"Good job, Commander. Bring the Herald to the bridge, and drop the rest of them in the brig. Breen out." The circuit went dead without waiting for a response.

Brandon took the link from the white-faced officer. "Hurdle number one passed, Herald. Let's get the rest of them before they catch wind. Baron, if you'd be so kind as to keep them under guard, I'd appreciate it." Changing tones, he ordered, "Chief, take your people to the engine room. Take no prisoners, I have a feeling they'll ready for us, and don't let anyone warn the bridge. Be sure to watch for *Vega* personnel. Most should be under some form of lock-down, but you can't be sure. This is now hostile territory."

Kitty looked back from the team headed for the engine room to Brandon. "I believe Simon would do the same thing, Madam Herald," he said, formally. "Take the engine room and bridge, and you effectively control the ship. If we can get some of the *Vega's* crew to throw in with us against traitors, so much the better. Even without them, as soon as we control the bridge, we can bring in more loyalists from the *Canopus*."

He started off toward the bridge, hesitated a second, turned back to Kitty. "Change of plans," Brandon said. "You will bring up the rear, and that's none too safe a place to be. If Simon finds out, he'll have my head on a platter. By the way, Kitty," he said, changing his tone, "I like your instincts. You had Breen figured before I did, and I'm supposed to be on his side. Just goes to show how government paranoia works. Quite often, the left hand doesn't know what the right hand is doing. I had planned for you to stay here until we had the bridge secured, but your idea of a ship-wide broadcast might just make the difference."

The next half hour was never going to be totally clear to Kitty. Several crew from the *Vega* were almost killed before they were recognized. The *Federal Case's* crew were given one chance only to surrender, and if they didn't, they were shot. Somehow they knew they were coming and on full alert, something had tipped them off. Stepping over bodies became surrealistic, almost second nature to Kitty until a laser scorched a hole in a bulkhead inches from her left shoulder.

She dropped to her knees and spun around, along with the other five members of her team, and snapped off two shots at a mass of the *Federal Case's* crew plugging the corridor. She saw two bodies hit the deck, then three more. That was when she realized her team was only four in number. The beam that burned the hole in the wall hadn't missed after all. One of her guards lay face down on the deck, dead from a hole in his chest. He'd still had enough time to take out two of the aggressors before he died, a fact not lost on Kitty.

"Aim for the head or heart," she ordered. "If that doesn't work, hold the beam and sweep it across your target. Cut them in half."

She heard her voice from a distance and was surprised to hear the same coldness Brandon's voice had carried. Was this what it meant to kill people up close and personal? Good luck for Kitty's team, or lack of teamwork on the traitor's part, left the four Alliance personnel alive and remarkably untouched as the last *Case* crewmember fled back around the corridor. Kitty inhaled the smell of burnt flesh and looked at the massacre just fifty feet down the corridor. Amazed at the bloodless nature of laser warfare, she snapped back into reality.

She suddenly bent over and vomited on the deck, stomach heaving once, twice, three times before she got herself under control. Shakily, she stood up and looked at the carnage she and her guards had left in the *Case's* corridor. "Come on," she ordered, wiping her mouth with the back of her arm. "We can't get too far behind or either we or Brandon will get cut off." They backed hastily down the corridor, not trusting the survivors of the attack to stay cowed.

"Damn," she muttered. "We didn't pick up their lasers. We need to arm every *Vega* crewmember we find. I'm sure Breen kept them unarmed just in case something like this happened."

"Don't worry, Madam Herald," one of her guards said. "We won't be leaving any others behind, unless we just can't carry them."

In the distance, she heard the sound of lasers firing almost continually. She and her team moved in that direction, taking the occasional shot at any head that appeared around a corner. Soon, they caught up with the tail end of Brandon's group. They were bunched up at a corner around which was the bridge entrance.

Brandon looked her over and noticed that she was short a guard. "Ambush," was all she said to him about that. "We're running low on power, though."

"Not to worry," Brandon said and grinned. "I made sure we made our way here by going past the armory. That's four more you won't have to worry about, but the bridge is aware of the problem now." He handed out power packs that fit into the grips of the hand weapons. "I have three men holding the corridor with laser rifles until we're ready to storm the bridge. We've picked up several *Vegan* crew along the way. They're holding the armory, and one of my men is sending anyone we recruit either here or to the engine room."

Kitty took advantage of a short lull in the firing to peek around the corner at the bridge. She was hauled back violently by Brandon grabbing the back of her shirt and pulling none too gently. "Don't do that again," he ordered. "We still need you to make that call for the fighting to cease, and you can't do it dead."

"Why is the bridge door only half closed?" she asked, disregarding his action except to rearrange her shirt.

"One of the *Case's* crew was stupid enough to die in the doorway. Breen's people got the body out of the door and found out too late that we'd welded it open with lasers."

"So, what happens now?"

"Now we wait for confirmation that the power room has been secured so Breen can't blow the ship," (a prospect she hadn't considered), "and that the cross corridor up there is covered from both sides by our people. Then I take a risk and drop these into the bridge." He showed her three grey oval shapes with handles and pull-pins on them.

"Hand grenades? That'll tear up the controls and possibly do just what you don't want Breen to do," she protested.

At that moment, Brandon's comm link chimed. "Galway," he said. He listened for a few seconds and smiled—a feral expression that chilled her to the bone. Had Simon ever been this cold? "We have the engine room," he said. "And I've just decided that I don't need to have that cross-corridor cleared. By the way, these are concussion grenades. Three going off in that small a space will put an end to all resistance and shouldn't do too much damage to the controls."

She grabbed his arm. "Brandon, where did you get concussion grenades?"

"Ask me no questions and I'll tell you no lies, Madam Herald. Now, if you'll excuse me for a moment?" He turned to the riflemen splayed out behind a wall of bodies, effortlessly pulling his arm out of her grasp at the same time. "Lay down some covering fire. Just don't hit me, please. I'm still on your side for a little while longer."

Once the riflemen began to fire, he stepped into the center of the corridor and strolled over bodies as if it were an everyday event. Closing on the doorway with laser fire passing him—in some cases by inches—he pulled the pins from the grenades with his teeth, dropping them amongst the bodies. He had reached his point of no return.

Holding two grenades in his left hand, he let the handle of the one in his right go, a distinctive ting sounding all the way back to Kitty. He waited two seconds and tossed it into the bridge. Transferring the other two to his right hand, he let both handles go at once, waited two seconds, and tossed one into the room, waited another second and then tossed the other in a slightly different direction.

The grenades went off almost simultaneously and he was sprinting for the jammed door, laser in hand.

Kitty yelled, "Move out, people. I don't want him hurt." All the crew armed with pistols broke for the doorway, some stumbling over the bodies in the way. The riflemen were the last to get to their feet. They reached the cross-corridor and took up positions there, guarding the other approaches to the bridge and waiting for her.

Kitty glanced back the way they'd come and saw half a dozen people coming toward her. She raised her pistol but held her fire when one shouted out, "We're from *Vega*. We've got your back, Madam Herald."

Kitty said, "My thanks. I need you to hold this corridor until Commander Galway or I issue the all-clear." She nodded once to the ranking officer in the bunch and turned away, dismissing them from her mind and beginning the same walk Brandon had so casually made. She couldn't keep her eyes off the dead and dying. Most wore *Federal Case* shoulder patches, although a very few wore *Vega* patches or none at all. Stumbling more than once during that nightmarish walk, she somehow stayed upright until she reached the relatively clear space around the open doorway.

Taking a deep breath, she walked into the room, her laser sweeping back and forth, but all she could see standing were her own people and Brandon. She slowly holstered her weapon as Brandon turned to her. "Madam Herald, the *Federal Case* is your ship again." There were no survivors among the bridge crew. Kitty looked around at the shattered screens and bodies, only noticing when she looked for Breen's body that he was still strapped in his command chair, a small black hole drilled in his head.

She strode silently over to the comm console and looked it over. It had been bent and twisted during the fight to take control of the *Federal Case* away from rogue officers attempting a mutiny against the Alliance, but it was still functioning. "This is Katherine Hawke, Herald of the Terran Alliance. We now control the bridge, armory, and engine room. All surviving members of the *Federal Case's* crew will report to the shuttle bay, unarmed. The *Vega's* remaining officers and crew will be assigned positions until we can make this vessel space-worthy and return to Shiravan space. If you had nothing to do with the insurrection, you have nothing to fear, but all members of the crew will face a tribunal to determine their degree of guilt. Any member of the *Federal Case's* crew who does not immediately report to the shuttle bay or is caught armed will be considered a combatant and shot on sight." She let go of the microphone and let it fall to dangle from the console, swinging back and forth.

Two hours later, almost two hundred survivors of the *Federal Case's* crew were packed into the *Case's* shuttle bay. The *Vega's* executive officer, temporarily raised to captain, was working her crew tirelessly to restore power to essential services. She reported to Kitty via comm link. "Madam Herald, I think it best if we slave our controls to the *Canopus* and return that way. It will give us two more weeks to make her space-worthy and clean up the mess."

"Very well, Captain, make it so. Let Captain Lee know when you're ready to attempt to make passage, and we'll take it one step at a time from there."

"Aye, Madam Herald. Captain Dexter, out."

CHAPTER THREE

The two-week trip back to Shiravi was almost trouble-free. Acting Captain Dexter had managed to get her controls slaved to the *Canopus*, and since the engine room was intact—the boarders having caught the entire engine room crew by complete surprise—the three remaining ships left the Garmon outpost without incident.

Brandon, now back to being called mister, sat with Kitty and the baron. Margit was making herself useful in the med lab, helping with the wounded. "We've gone over the battle reports a dozen times, Kitty," he said. "It would seem that the Garmon now have a new strategy. They hold one small ship away from the action, which records the battle and then disappears into hyper, most likely bound for the Garmon homeworld. Depending on how far away that is, well, their leader will know that a major defeat has just happened on the Shiravan side of their territory. Add that to the losses they sustain every time they attack Earth, and someone is going to be pretty pissed off."

The baron decided to add his own comment. "Also, the translators have been working overtime on some of the more esoteric transmissions from the attacking ships. The word Korvil was mentioned once by the visiting ship, and since that time, it's been replaced with the word Garmon. This confirms the change in leadership.

Now, we have no way to judge what the response will be from a new leader, but we have to assume for safety's sake that not much will change. We have to contend with the total output of over forty worlds against Shiravi's fifteen and our one. We still hold a technical advantage, but sheer numbers, if they're high enough, can overwhelm the most advanced weapons."

Kitty looked at her eldest adviser dispassionately. She'd had a week to integrate her experiences into her psyche, especially after several extended sessions in the *Canopus's* domed den. "The human race has never been known to just roll over and die for anyone, Baron. We fought our way out of the primordial ooze, onto land, into the trees, and back onto land. We've conquered every opponent nature has thrown at us, including climate changes and asteroid impacts. I won't let myself believe that we'll go down under the heels of some overgrown teddy bears. And if we do, that's just the way it will be, but have no doubt, we'll go down kicking and screaming all the way."

Sitha kep Parrasine sat in the visitor's lounge of the *Shumara Vacht's* captain, a glass of fire wine untouched beside her as she gazed into a distance not contained by the walls around her. The *Shumara Vacht* had participated in the attack on the Garmon planet, losing all of her fighters and taking several hits from missiles aimed her way, though only three had gotten past her new screens. Losses had been minimal, and that was reason to rejoice, but the remarkable display put on by the human ships caused her worry such as she had never felt before.

Only seven of their remarkable fighters had been lost,

and although one of the battlecruisers had remained somewhat back from most of the fighting for reasons she still didn't understand, only one major ship was lost in the conflict, an impressive victory indeed. Six Garmon destroyers turned into so much scrap and atoms, while the humans lost only one ship and managed to save almost two-thirds of the crew, an unprecedented reversal of figures that would bear deep scrutiny and discussion between the Matriarch and her immediate staff.

Then there was the delay after the Herald had boarded her remaining battlecruiser. Internal communications could not be accessed, of course, but intercepted transmissions between the *Federal Case* and the *Canopus* indicated serious fighting going on amongst the humans themselves. Another item for consideration.

The fighting didn't go on long, and after about three hours, the Herald's voice was heard announcing that most of the *Federal Case's* crew were to be imprisoned aboard the *Canopus*, while the survivors of *Vega* would take over control of the ship. Plans were made to slave the *Case* to the *Canopus* for the trip back to Shiravi. Sitha waited impatiently for the next revelation.

Her impatience was rewarded with more lack of information. The Herald called the *Shumara Vacht* to check on the progress of her officer and announced that the two remaining human ships were ready to depart the system and asked if the *Shumara Vacht* would like to slave to *Canopus* or travel solo. Sitha opted for the latter, though she neglected to say that it was so that she could arrive a bit ahead of the humans and report to the Matriarch what had happened. Undoubtedly, Domina sel Garian would have much to say about the entire exercise. There was a dark side to these humans, after all.

"I'm not surprised Sitha asked for her observers to be sent to the *Shumara Vacht* before she left for Shiravi," Kitty said, sitting in her stateroom aboard the *Federal Case*.

"Maybe," Brandon said casually, "she's holding her own post-battle debriefing. I'm betting that she got more than an earful from the *Vega's* observer, as well as the *Federal Case's*. And let's not forget that there were two observers aboard *Canopus*, all of whom had total access to all personnel as per your own instructions. I still wonder why you changed your mind and let her stay on the *Shumara Vacht*."

"Intuition, Brandon," Kitty said simply. "And I think it was best because she was the one who suggested that the *Shumara Vacht* might be able to help Shirley."

"Can't argue with that," was all he replied.

Margit put in her own opinion. "My guess is that she's pushing her ship to its limits to get back ahead of us so she can inform Domagera des Harras and sel Garian about our internal struggles. I'm sure that they'll be busy finding a way to use our travails against us so they can take advantage of us."

"What kind of advantage?" Kitty asked quickly. "Our internal struggles are our own business and we'll solve them without outside interference. Besides, we have *their* internal struggles to point at if the need should arise. I'll bet that the only mention is to find out what was going on." She looked around the room slowly. "And I expect to receive a mission report as soon as we come out of hyperspace. I want thoughts, feelings, premonitions—everything that comes to you, as well as the unvarnished truth."

The baron spoke up next. "I believe what Margit means is that anyone will look for a way to take advantage of another's weakness if it seems to be in their own best interest. Look to our own past for the truth in that statement. We've just shown our allies that we aren't as united as we would have them believe. It is unfortunate this came at a time when we needed to show a more united front, but we'll have to work with what we have. We have two weeks to spin things into a manageable direction."

Kitty shook her head. "I'm not sure spin-doctoring is the best approach with these people," she said, a contemplative note in her voice. "So far, we've been as aboveboard as possible with the Shiravans, and I intend to keep to that course. If we have to take some heat because of it, then so be it. They've shown us a weakness of theirs—the problem with their kath-mora, their Spirit Witches. Now, we have shown that we are just as vulnerable as they are to internal struggles. It puts us on a more equal footing. Both of us are fallible, and that's the image that I want to present."

Brandon jumped in with a comment of his own. "As much as I'm supposed to be on the other side of this argument, I have to agree with Kitty. If we try to come off as more infallible than the Shiravans, more altruistic, more anything…" he hesitated, looking for the right words, "we stand a chance of—no pun intended— alienating our allies. Let's appear as fallible as our allies, because we are. They've experienced divisions amongst themselves, just as we have. Their Expansionist versus Isolationist problem is equal to the split humanity shows as Alliance versus the remainder of the planet. So what if we have an insurrection on one of our ships? We've been in space for nine years now, and the powers that be Earth-side *should* want more than they have. And the Alliance *should* want to keep as much as they can for themselves, maintaining their power base."

Kitty spoke up. "I agree with Brandon. We have weaknesses, and to deny them would only make the Shiravans suspicious. We should show our dark side a bit, and show them that we're trying to work around it, just as they are."

Kitty expected Sitha to order the *Shumara Vacht's* captain to push the ship to its limit to get back before the human fleet. She felt that if their positions were reversed, she'd do the same, and the *Federal Case* still needed to make some repairs. She ordered the *Canopus* to hold their speed down to normal hyper transit. And so it was that the two human ships arrived in Shiravan orbit two days after the *Shumara Vacht.*

In order to break the monotony during one of the many meetings, someone asked why it was that two ships could be slaved through transit but couldn't communicate by regular means. It quickly became a hot topic all through the *Case's* scientists, and Kitty made a note to take the question back to human space when she left.

Immediately upon establishing a stable orbit, Kitty commed the *Shumara Vacht* to ask about the condition of her officer, more concerned about that than anything else. She was put directly through to the doctor she'd left aboard to monitor Shirley's progress. "Madam Herald, these people have ways of accessing data that we've never discovered. I'm able to directly monitor Captain Dahlquist's condition. The only thing I can't do is get a read on her mental state, but her physical condition is improving at a rate that will have her out of the chamber within another two weeks, at a guess. You might find it of interest to know that her hair is now as white as yours. No one here seems to have any idea why that seems to be a side effect of regeneration time since Shiravans don't have hair."

Kitty thanked him for his dedication, asked if there was anything he needed, and if so, to comm the *Federal Case* and it would be sent over immediately. He thanked her almost distractedly and signed off, leaving her with the onerous duty of calling Linnas. She dreaded this call, knowing that she'd have a lot of explaining to do, but having the experience of both the baron and his wife to draw on, she knew she could turn the tables by bringing up the subject of the kath-mora, along with a few other esoteric subjects.

Taking a deep breath, she keyed in the frequency that would connect her with the Matriarch's new personal assistant. "Domagera Hawke," a new voice said, a sense of relief coming through to Kitty. "The Matriarch asked why you didn't report in as soon as you reached orbit." The statement came out almost as an aggrieved order.

Kitty opted for a forthright approach. "Ther'a," she said icily, using the senior-to-junior mode that brooked no debate, "my most pressing desire was to discover the condition of my officer after a two-week lack of information. The Matriarch could wait long enough for me to find out how she fared. In case you or Linnas," she said, using the Matriarch's first name deliberately, "are interested, she seems to be healing well. And it appears that she faced a full grown Garmon, alone, armed only with a knife, and was the survivor." *A matter you might want to keep in mind for future reference*, she thought.

The new voice spoke with a bit of uncertainty, "We are, of course, glad that your officer seems to be healing, and that her ordeal left her the victor. Too many times, it has happened that the victor has been the Garmon. As a matter of fact, we know of no instance where a Shiravan has bested a Garmon in single combat. Your officer is to be commended as soon as she recovers. That aside, the Matriarch would request that you attend her at tomorrow morning's meal one hour past sunrise Cho-An time."

Kitty didn't give the new assistant time to turn the request into an order, desperately wanting to keep the situation on a superior-to-junior basis. "I'll be happy to accept the Matriarch's invitation. You may inform her that my gig will land on the eastern field approximately twenty minutes before the appointed hour. Also, please be kind enough to personally inform Central Command of my arrival." *I wouldn't want to be shot out of the skies just because of a forgotten notice*, she thought. She cut the comm link before the assistant could respond.

This particular breakfast with the Matriarch of fifteen worlds was not what Kitty had expected. First, it was in an entirely new room that had been built during her absence, apparently exclusively for the purpose of having the two Domageras sitting eye to eye. It contained the first split-level table she'd ever seen. The Matriarch's side and chair sat a bit lower than Kitty's, letting the two women sit so that neither had to look uncomfortably up or down at the other. Kitty examined the table with interest. "What a wonderful idea. I'm honored that you went to so much trouble."

Linnas waved her hand dismissively. "After all you've done for us so far, as well as your spectacular performance, it was the least I could do. I had it commissioned before you even left on your mission."

A nearly invisible servant dished up her second surprise. Kitty was served bacon, scrambled eggs, toast, butter, strawberry jam and orange juice, her personal favorite meal of all. *How did she get the ingredients, much less the information?* Kitty wondered as she noticed that Linnas had the same juice and jam on her side of the table.

The red woman noticed Kitty's eyes on her own meal and said, "It seems there are a few foods that are compatible with both our systems, most in what your people call fruits and vegetables. I find the strawberries and juice to be very pleasing. I would hope that we could import some for our agronomists to experiment with."

Kitty took a sip of the juice, thinking furiously. "I would imagine that we could work out a trade agreement of some kind," she said slowly. She picked up a piece of bacon with her fingers and took an experimental nibble. It tasted real, so she dug into the rest with more gusto than she'd felt in what seemed like ages. "I'd like to see some of your gava stone come our way. The problem is that once we give you strawberries and oranges, you can grow your own from the results. The stone would be a one-time payment. How would we determine the value? *Who* would determine the value?"

Linnas waved her hand in dismissal of the idea. "It's something we can discuss later. I only mentioned it to show that there are unexpected things that each of our worlds can offer the other. You've already been quite generous in freely giving us technology updates without asking for recompense."

Kitty set her fork down. "That was a matter of

necessity, Your Grace. It was a matter of saving lives—something I consider to be far more important than simple berries or fruit juices."

"And I, as well, Madam Herald. But, I'd hope that we could keep these discussions on a first-name basis." The Domagera spread jam on what passed for Shiravan toast and took a bite. The look that crossed her face told Kitty that this was more than just a small item for the Matriarch.

"Very well, Linnas," she said. "Raspberries, blueberries, apples, nectarines, whatever. Foodstuffs are still foodstuffs. Once you get one shipment, you won't need another. You'll be able to plant your own crops from the seeds from the first shipment. How could you even begin to negotiate the price of something like that? And I agree that the discussions should be conducted by experienced negotiators. On that same subject, how about your fire wine? If it comes from something that humans can grow, there's a possible trade. And why are we discussing this anyway? I'd think that you'd be more inclined to discuss the results of our foray into Garmon space."

"True," Linnas said, picking a piece of something vaguely white from her plate. The red light changed everything so that Kitty couldn't tell the real color. "It would seem that there's been a shake-up amongst our common foe, and I'm most interested to find out how that will affect future relations among Shiravans, humans, and Garmons."

Linnas's direct stare was a bit disconcerting. Kitty wondered how much she'd been told of the battle and how the results had been interpreted. One prime consideration was who was doing the interpreting. She decided to shelve the matter until it was laid directly on the table.

"I'd like to know why the change has occurred at this particular time," Kitty said. "The 'why' is of great concern to me and my advisers. Is it because they're fighting two different foes or fighting on two fronts? Or is it that their resources are beginning to be stretched too thin? We've accounted for a fairly large number of losses in human space," she added pointedly. "And there are a number of other possibilities that could be the cause of the shake-up, none of which would be comprehensible to us, Shiravans or Humans, because we don't think like they do. Hell, even humans and Shiravans don't think alike. That's another matter we discuss on an ongoing basis." She finished off her meal and washed it down with the last of the juice in her glass, pushing the plate away from her a bit. "Is it possible to get more orange juice, please?" It appeared almost instantly.

"Again, true, Kitty," Linnas agreed. "The most impressive case in point is the defeat of six Garmon destroyers while losing only one major ship in trade. This is something that we haven't been able to do in over two hundred turnings. Your tactics and upgrades to our technology account for most of the achievement, but, as you have already pointed out, we don't think alike. Shiravans are a more static culture, while you humans appear to be a more dynamic one. So, tell me, what do you attribute your success to?"

"As a far younger, more dynamic culture," Kitty answered immediately, "we're still striving to find ourselves as a people. There are over two hundred different countries on our single planet. We're constantly at odds with each other over one matter or another and have been for all the hundreds of thousands of years of our existence, if our scientists are to be believed. And we are ruled, for the most part, by males. It seems to me that they, more than anything else, are the reason we progress so fast. I don't profess to understand the male mentality, but then neither do most females on our world. Males and females will never truly understand each other."

Kitty poured another glass of juice and offered to pour another for her hostess, who deferred. "Now, I'd like to ask you a question or two," Kitty said, setting the pitcher down.

"I'll answer any question as honestly and truthfully as I'm able," Linnas said.

"Spoken like a true politician," Kitty said, an odd tone in her voice. "First, what is to become of Ramannie kep Gillas and those who aided her in the killing of the crew of the *Dalgor Kret*?" She deliberately used the Shiravan name of the *Galileo*. "And what will you do with the senior kath-mora when they finally return to Shiravi?"

Linnas's face took on a look that would do a poker player proud. "Ramannie kep Gillas and her immediate conspirators will be banished to an island we've prepared for them after suitable trials. And her marriage to Rentec was immediately annulled as soon as I was able to sign the documents." Her smile was there, but there seemed to be a great distance hidden behind those ruby-colored eyes.

"As for the senior kath-mora, when they get back, assuming they do, they'll be confined in a like manner, separate from the others. We will not allow them to have any contact with others they might corrupt. They'll spend the rest of their days in contemplation of their actions, except, of course, for the agents among them who had to go to keep up appearances." She looked across the split-level table at her guest. "What would you do with such persons on your world?"

"Excuse me? To keep up appearances?" Kitty asked.

"Of course. Only the most senior kath-mora were untouchable. We had agents on every one of their senior staffs but couldn't touch them from behind their shield of Family. We managed to steer their course a bit, keeping them from being too overt. We even knew, at the highest levels, of course, that an attack was to be made on the ship. Our information, unfortunately, was the same as young Kuria's."

Kitty looked Linnas straight in the eyes. "You *knew* about the attack and didn't anticipate the possibility of the mass killing of the *Dalgor Kret's* crew?" she asked in disbelief.

She watched the looks pass over her hostess's face. "As I said, we had every reason to believe that we could disable the plot en route. We got one report of plague from the captain before he was infected, too. He and his pilot, Kuria, removed everything the virus might adhere to and opened the ship to space. All personal possessions—everything except the ship's log—was jettisoned. That should have cleared the virus. And what of the crew of your ship, the *Federal Case*? Will those who survived be subjected to this process and then killed?"

"Some, possibly," Kitty admitted regretfully, "but most will just face banishment from space for life since we control who joins us." She recognized it for the change of subject it was supposed to be. On some level, she felt that she was losing ground in this discussion. "We have an offense we call treason. That means willful disobedience of orders from accepted superiors, especially in time of war. If the offense is grave enough and the consequences of their actions vile enough, execution is not an unimaginable result. This is a subject that's usually only addressed in times of war, as I said, and we are most certainly at war for the very existence of our race. Death isn't too high a price to pay for such acts, or so we believe."

Linnas looked across the table at the one known as Katherine and wondered if she were really Kath-e-vel. "Tell me how you arrive at the decision to end the existence of another in such a manner. We have wars and insurrections where the taking of lives are necessary, but to sit down and deliberate on the execution of a particular individual... that is something most Shiravans would find hard to contemplate."

"Much like Domina sel Garian led hundreds of her kinfolk and associated clans into a trap and killed them to ensure your ascension to the Matriarchy?" Kitty returned quietly. "As I remember the story, she was rewarded with a post in your regime as your second in command. Was that so you could keep an eye on her so she wouldn't do the same to you and yours if she should get ambitious?"

"Of course not," Linnas answered hotly. "The two situations aren't even remotely akin to each other."

Kitty started to argue that the reverse was more likely to be true, but she was interrupted by her comm link chiming. "Hawke, here," she said, extremely glad for the interruption.

"Madam Herald, this is Captain Dexter. Comm has just confirmed the arrival of five human ships in Shiravan space, accompanied by a single Shiravan vessel vouching for their intentions. The fleet is called Raptor Group and is composed of the *Raptor*, our first full-sized battleship, under the command of Captain Marsha Kane, the *Spica*, the *Regulus*, the *Deneb*, and the carrier *Aldebaran*. What are your orders?"

Kitty looked at her hostess and answered, "Tell the Shiravan ship to enter orbit under Central Command's control, and have our ships stand off until further notice. Stress that the situation is delicate, and they are to maintain their distance until I order otherwise. Hawke, out."

Linnas set her glass down and placed her hands on the table. "So, it would seem that your subordinate has followed instructions and sent more ships to help in our struggles."

Kitty started. "I wasn't aware that you spoke English, Linnas. I wasn't trying to be rude."

Linnas raised her hand, palm forward in the human fashion. "Do not distress yourself, Kitty. I *have* been known to study upon occasion." She smiled as if at a small joke. "If Shiravans and humans are to co-exist, then it is my desire to understand your language as well as you understand ours. My tutors tell me that the best way to understand a culture is to understand their language, yes?"

"Well, yes, of course," Kitty said, nonplussed. Linnas's last words had all been in English. "I just didn't realize..."

"Don't worry," Linnas said in Shiravan. "That's almost all I know so far, but I'm a quick study. Before long I'll have a better grasp of your language, and by extension, your people. Although, I admit that I'll probably never understand your legal system. This killing of those who kill or cause others to die by their actions is anathema to our way of life. It's probably a by-product of so many males in control of your various governing bodies. I would hope that, once you embrace a one-world government, this disgraceful habit will fall by the wayside."

"Uh, yeah," was all Kitty could say to that. "Anyway, I need to speak to the group commander and set up a patrol sequence. It was my idea that, just as your ships are under human command while on our side of Garmon space, human ships will be under the ultimate control of a Shiravan commander while here. Who that's to be I'll leave up to you and Doma kep Parrasine, but I need to go and make those conditions clear to Captain Kane in person."

"Of course," Linnas said. "But, don't forget, we must ratify a treaty between our two peoples before you leave for your home, and I feel that that is something that will be happening in the not-too-distant future now that the new fleet has arrived."

"Certainly, Linnas," Kitty said. "Besides, I can't leave until Captain Dahlquist comes out of her regen chamber, so I think we'll have all the time we need to make that treaty."

"Perhaps," Linnas agreed. "Keep in mind, though, that she can go back while she's still in the chamber aboard another vessel. I'll be assigning another to replace the one that returned home."

"I have it on good authority that she'll be out of the chamber in another week—two at the most," Kitty said, standing up. "Her injuries weren't as serious as mine. And I believe my advisers will want to help draw up the articles of affiliation for our treaty, as I'm sure yours will want to do, also. Then we'll have to negotiate the differences."

Linnas stood also, and the efficacy of the different levels showed again since the two women were still at eye level.

"Now, you must go and speak with your Captain Kane and advisers, as I must speak with mine. My new aide will lead you to your ship." The Matriarch motioned for an almost invisible figure to come forward. "Domagera Hawke, please meet Doma Kersela des Harras, a distant cousin, just entering her first vocation."

CHAPTER FOUR

Kitty entered her shuttle, contemplating the similarities of the two cultures. Nepotism was certainly a factor in this new aide's appearance. It had to be, she reasoned. Of course a society as closed as this one was would promote it, but with the gradual reintroduction of males into society and their obvious elevation to positions of authority—ship captains, ambassadors, department heads—it wouldn't be long before there'd be a Patriarch. She only had to look as far as Earth. There had already been a few women on the ticket for president at one time or another. Sooner or later…

Kitty's gig rendezvoused with the *Federal Case,* and she immediately requested Captain Dexter to move out to the new fleet. She didn't consciously know it, but she was in desperate need of a new face or fifty, and Marsha's would do nicely.

It was only a matter of a few hours. After getting clearance from Central Command, powering up and jumping to the new coordinates, there was a short shuttle ride to the *Raptor,* and Kitty felt as if the weight of the world had been lifted from her shoulders. The shuttle ride gave her a chance to view the new behemoth out of Taurus Base. Almost as long as the *Galileo,* the ship fairly bristled with shield generators, laser mounts, tractor and pressor beam mounts, and numerous ports for the expulsion of several deadly kinds of missiles.

Of course, there were numerous characteristics she couldn't put a name to, but that wasn't her department anymore. As long as Marsha knew what to do with them, that would be good enough for her.

She felt it when the tractor beam took her shuttle in its grip and the pilot cut power, so she moved to the ramp and waited as the pilot shut the systems down. She wasn't surprised to find a side party waiting, although the last one still caused her nightmares that she was sure would last for years. The biggest surprise was Marsha.

Standing several inches taller than Kitty, as most people did, Marsha stood at the front of a full dozen ships' officers in full dress. The strange thing was that Marsha's hair was as white as her own, and she couldn't take her eyes off it for several seconds. Finally, she shook herself and strode down the ramp to its end, asking, "Permission to come aboard, Captain?"

"With great pleasure, Madam Herald. And let me say that I've waited for this moment for almost two years now." She turned to her officers and said, "At ease." Twelve hands came down in unison, and twelve people moved to the rest position—hands behind their backs, feet spread slightly apart, and relaxed but alert.

Kitty stepped off the shuttle's ramp, and Marsha took her outstretched hand, but instead of shaking it, she pulled Kitty into a bear hug that threatened to smother her. "I've missed you, boss," Marsha whispered into her ear, then stepped back. "Welcome aboard the *Raptor*, Madam Herald," she said, still holding Kitty's hand. "If you'll follow me, I'll show you to my day room. We can do the tour later."

"That would be fine, Captain Kane," Kitty stammered, embarrassed at her lack of control. "Lead on."

Marsha said, "Side party, atten-*shun*. Dismissed." The officers came to attention, then seemed to disperse slowly in a random manner, two following closely behind the two friends. "Those two will be with us until they're relieved by the next shift. It seems that we've been severely infiltrated by agents of several governments. It's going to be a job weeding out the quislings." She sounded almost apologetic.

Kitty nodded. "I've already had to deal with the same problem, and quite possibly in greater detail than you, Marsha. But I'll save that for when we're alone." She presented the brown bag she'd carried from the *Canopus*. "I hope you have time to get sloppy drunk because this stuff is going to do the trick. It's one of the things we and the Shiravans can both tolerate. They call it fire wine, and it will take some getting used to."

Marsha laughed out loud as she pressed a button that opened an elevator. The two women entered, followed by the guards, one of whom pressed a button. Kitty felt pressure beneath her feet as the lift rose. The doors opened and the two guards stepped out first, hands near their weapons. One looked back and nodded. Marsha gestured for Kitty to exit first and said, "After you, Madam Herald."

Kitty did so, and her first impression was of vastness. The corridor was easily twice the width of the *Vega's* or the *Federal Case's*, and people moved along it seemingly intent on errands of great urgency. Marsha turned right and headed down the corridor, Kitty a pace behind, feeling the presence of the two guards as an itch between her shoulder blades.

Marsha stopped at a door guarded by two armed crewmen, ran her hand over an identi-plate, and the door opened. She stepped in and Kitty followed, the feeling of vastness increasing. The room was easily three times the size of anything aboard any other ship of the fleet, and it was only the outer room to the captain's private quarters.

The door closed behind her, and she looked over her shoulder to make sure they were alone. "Don't worry, Kitty," Marsha said, "we can relax now. But there have been several changes in protocol since you left. Too many attempts at sabotage, sensitive data reaching the wrong places, things like that. So, new protocols, especially aboard the *Raptor* since she's the first of her kind." She flopped down in a chair. "Whatcha got in the bag? Fire wine, you called it. Your name or the Shiravan's?"

Kitty pulled the bottle out of her bag and set it on the table while Marsha got up to get two glasses from a sideboard. "We'll wait to crack the bottle for just a bit, if you don't mind," Kitty said. "I'd like to be brought up to date on things back home, first. By the way, I like your hair."

Marsha brushed her hand through her white hair self-consciously. "I'm still not sure I like the color. Have you discovered that dyes don't take? They come out all spotty. The good thing is that they wash off with a minimum of showering. I like the pageboy cut, though. Easier to take care of." She reached into the drawer of a small table beside the couch they shared and pulled out a manila folder. "I knew you'd ask, so here's everything I have as of the *Raptor's* departure. All the details are there, but in brief, reconstruction is going well, especially in the Amazon basin. Our scientists have been able to replant a majority of the damaged landscape, but things are going a bit slower on the North American west coast. Too much infrastructure needs to be completely rebuilt. We're working with local power companies and construction crews to get power back, along with roads, bridges, and dams.

"All the housing and lives lost are the biggest problem—court suits to claim the land of lost relatives, squatters, disease due to lack of proper sanitation facilities, hunger because all the flora and fauna was washed out to sea, rainstorms causing mudslides that hamper rebuilding, the almost total loss of the giant redwoods, and oh, God, so much more.

"Places farthest from the Aleutian explosion, as it's now being called, suffered least, with the exception of Russia, of course, but there were relatively few people living along the coastline there, and no accurate count will ever be made of the losses. Mostly, they're just trying to replant fast-growing ground cover to keep the soil from being washed into the ocean. Japan suffered very little. The embassy there managed to get its shield up in time to save the buildings and people inside the perimeter. There was a secondary effect from that. It split the wave, lessening the damage the island suffered. Only Tokyo took much damage, and that was because they've built so many structures so close to the shorelines."

Kitty skimmed through the papers in the folder, listening with half an ear. She stopped when she reached a yellow sheet of paper among all the white. "Oh, yeah," Marsha said. "That's an analysis of how far we've been infiltrated by agents of various governments. We knew it was going to happen, but this shows a far larger amount than expected. We've begun instituting lie detector tests and washing out even ambiguous applicants. The truth is that of the ones who did or do get past the screening process, we're expecting a small number to truly convert to the Alliance. It seems that a greater number than expected are doing so there, too." She watched Kitty skim through the rest of the papers, stack them neatly, and slip them back into the folder.

"And another thing," she said, almost as an afterthought. She leaned over and pulled a thick envelope from the same drawer. "Simon asked me to give this to you personally. Probably just a bunch of mushy stuff that you can read later and cry over. There's a video in there, too, but that can wait until we sober up. So, why don't you fill me in on what's been going on over here while we get shit-faced?" She indicated the blue bottle sitting on her table.

Marsha dodged Kitty's determined swat with the manila envelope and just smiled when Kitty said, "I should just take my bottle and go for making me wait for this."

Marsha held her hands up in a gesture of defeat, still smiling at her friend. "I don't get that many pleasures these days, Kitty. Allow me to have some fun, will ya?"

"Okay," Kitty said, grudgingly. "But you better have brought a compatible player with you, or so help me…"

"In my private quarters," Marsha avowed. "And you can have all the time you need, I promise. Now, let me at that fire wine while you fill me in on what's happening in this part of the galaxy."

She listened as Kitty started in on Vega Group's arrival, and Kitty was just getting to the part about meeting the Matriarch for the first time by the time she started pouring for her friend. She looked at the bluish liquid in the two glasses and then at the clear container above the rest of the wine in the bottle.

"This is going to be an interesting evening," Marsha predicted.

"More interesting than you can even imagine," Kitty replied. "While you're still sober, I'm going to give you the worst of it, but first," she said, lifting her glass high, "to old friends, even if they do have a perverse streak in them."

Marsha lifted her own glass and touched it to Kitty's, a small clink sounding through the room. "To old friends," she replied and took a tentative sip of the alien wine. Her eyes went wide about three seconds after the wine hit her stomach. "Holy shit!"

"That," Kitty said solemnly, "will be the understatement of the evening. First, we were given a task to perform to prove ourselves to our new allies. Vega Group, along with the *Shumara Vacht* and another Shiravan ship, was sent to a known Garmon planet to show what we could do. We had the *Shumara Vacht*, the *Vega*, the *Federal Case*, and the *Canopus,* along with another Shiravan ship. We faced six Garmon destroyers and whipped their asses, but we believe an observer was dispatched to the Garmon homeworld right after our victory. We took out all six ships, but we lost the *Vega* to a rammer. And as we entered the system, we managed to get the signatures of four Shiravan ships just leaving the system. I'll be mentioning that one to Linnas."

Marsha's face fell and she started to speak but thought better of it after looking at Kitty's face. "We managed to save about two-thirds of the *Vega's* crew, but Shirley had to go and play hero. She took a Mamba, turned control over to her exec, and went after the bastards herself. The problem was that she got hit but managed to land on the planet."

Kitty took a stiff drink of the wine before she went on. "By the time the battle was over and we could get a rescue team to her beacon, she'd been found by a

Garmon. They call themselves Garmon now, by the way. The Shiravans think there's been a power change and the race changed their name. God only knows why. Anyway, there must have been a hell of a fight. Shirley is in a regen chamber right now and should be out in less than two weeks, according to Shiravan doctors. Her hair is as white as ours is, by the way. They've got no idea why, either. Anyway, the Korvil—er—Garmon, was dead, with a survival knife stuck to the hilt in his left eye. Most of Shirley's injuries were a result of being landed on by this critter and the length of time he lay on her before our teams got to her."

"But she's going to be all right?" Marsha asked worriedly.

Kitty nodded as she took another drink and waved her hand indifferently. "Oh, sure. They say she'll make a full recovery. And as soon as she can stand up, I'm gonna kill her myself."

Marsha snorted as she took another sip of her own drink. "I don't think you'll go quite that far, Kitty. I've seen pictures of these creatures, and killing one of them in hand-to-hand combat is no small matter. It probably took just as much luck as courage. But it just undersores... scores... this is some potent stuff... the need to neutralize them as soon as possible. I'm not saying we need to kill them all off, but I don't know," she finished lamely.

Kitty put her nearly empty glass on the table and leaned back on the couch. "And that's the good news." She watched Marsha's eyebrows go up as she copied Kitty's posture. "The *Federal Case* was loaded with traitors. Breen was a second-waver, but he was also a government agent. I think he was trying to take the *Case* for the U.S. government, but his assignment here got in the way. He had loaded his crew with about ninety per cent newer arrivals, and they almost succeeded in kidnapping me. If it hadn't been for Brandon Galway, I'd probably be sitting in a cell while the *Case* made its way back to Earth. What they would have done with the ship is anybody's guess. Sooner or later, they would have to come to us for a new power core because that information isn't installed in battlecruisers. They had no way to build bases, sundivers, refineries, or any other aspects of the process. All they'd get would be the weapons technology, and even that they couldn't use without the power that comes from an antimatter core, which would wear out after another two years by our estimates."

Marsha, feeling the effects of the unaccustomed drink, said, "And he, they, had to know all that. What were they going to do with a single ship? They had to know we wouldn't let them keep it."

"But they would have had me, and about ten per cent of their crew were true Alliance personnel, as well as some of the *Vega's* survivors. Would our ships really have fired on her in that case?"

"I guess not," Marsha admitted ruefully. "So, what did you do?"

"The only thing we could. I made Brandon Galway an acting Alliance commander, loaded a shuttle with about forty loyalists, and transferred my flag to the *Case*. As soon as we landed in the bay, I was informed that I was under arrest, and the entire side party, except for the exec, was killed. We then stormed the engine room and bridge. Breen was killed in the fighting, along with quite a few of the *Case's* crew, some of the *Vega's* crew who either switched sides or got in the way, and some of our own people, but we took the ship back. It's now under the command of Captain Dexter of the *Vega* and will transport me back to Earth with a signed treaty. All of the *Case's* survivors will stand a court martial for treason and be sentenced according to the degree of their participation in the fighting."

Marsha shook her head in wonder. "I still can't see you trusting Galway, though."

"He's never been anything but an honorable opponent, Marsha. He always told us straight up what his agenda was and was just as surprised as the rest of us by the event. Besides, he was the only one available to me with combat leadership abilities. You work with what you have. He gave me his word; I took it and he kept it. I do wish he was on our side. What an asset he would be."

CHAPTER FIVE

Kitty asked for and got permission to bring the *Raptor* into low Shiravan orbit in order to show Marsha the degree of care Shirley was receiving aboard the *Esmit*. During their visit, Linnas called from the surface.

"I regret the interruption," Linnas began, "but I know you'll soon be returning to Earth, and I wanted to finalize our treaty and meet the captain of the *Raptor*. I believe she and I will be working closely together over the next several turnings. I feel that it's a good omen she's also female. You do realize that your revolt was headed by a male—just a point I felt it necessary to make."

Kitty looked the Matriarch in the eye, thanks to the viewscreen. "And you realize that the killers of the *Dalgor Kret's* crew were female, even if they did use a male agent, as long as we're making points. And for another point, you have some of your most sensitive positions filled by males now. Captain do' Sirkis of the *Esmit* is male, and you seem to trust him completely, as is Rentec and several leaders of your most sensitive Ministries. I have to wonder why that is. I can't believe it's solely to free up females for combat roles. If that was true, do' Sirkis would be female, as would every other captain of every ship in your fleet.

"You're going to have to realize that males and female complement each other. Neither is whole without the other. We've tried all the various permutations of governance it's possible to have, I think, and in our case, at least, it turns out that some males are better qualified to run a department, company, ship or government by temperament, as well as training, than females. Of course, in other cases, the exact opposite is true. We call it heredity versus environment. It's a debate that's raged for well over two thousand years, and I imagine it will go on for just as long and still not come to a consensus. So, let's leave that topic alone, shall we?"

It was two days later before Kitty could arrange to have a sit-down with Linnas and Marsha. Marsha stopped and stared at the Stala Mountains, making appropriate noises before Kitty pulled her inside where an escort was waiting to lead them to the Matriarch's chambers.

"I hope our last conversation wasn't too much for you, Linnas," Kitty said after formal introductions had been made. "Sometimes different opinions seem like insurmountable obstacles."

"Agreed," Linnas said quickly, glad to be rid of the subject when Kitty had made such a good argument using her own culture against her. "Captain Kane," she said, changing tacks, "it is a pleasure to make your acquaintance. I would hope that at some time in the future you'll show me around your ship. I hear it's the first human ship of its kind."

Marsha looked at Kitty, who just shrugged and said nothing. "First, I don't know what to call you without offending you. You and Kitty are on the same level, being leaders of your peoples. I am but a lowly captain of a warship. Granted, it's the mightiest in our fleet, and I'm greatly honored at receiving the captaincy, but know this: the other four ships with us are captained by men, all of whom have shown remarkable aptitude at handling themselves and their crews in crises. If something should happen to me, my executive officer is male, as are the next two people in line for command of the *Raptor*. And if the *Raptor* should fall, a male will take command of the group in my place."

She looked around for a chair, and without asking or waiting for her superiors to do so first, sat down. She continued, "I don't subscribe to the female dominance theory. I do feel that males have had it too good for too long in certain areas of our culture, but we're entering a new era, one in which gender is of less importance than ability. From all I've been led to understand, that's not a basic premise of your culture." She held up her hand to forestall any interruptions as the two leaders sat down. "That's not to say I'm not happy to see women getting more recognition these days. Some of us deserve it. But there are some men out there who are just as well qualified to fill the position of captain of the *Raptor* as I am. And there are some women I wouldn't trust to clean out toilets. And it doesn't all depend on temperament. Training, heredity, environment, and life experience all go into the mix to make a particular person fit for a particular position. It's said that a person rises to their own level of incompetence. That means that if a person signs on as, say, a maintenance worker and shows an aptitude for more, he or she can be moved up. If they still show promise for higher positions, they can be promoted again. But sooner or later, that person, male or female, will reach a level of competence they cannot exceed. Then, when they're promoted to a higher level and can't do the job, their superiors will say something like, 'Look at him/her. A total screw-up. Kick them out before they do something even worse.' I say, why not just demote them back to the position they showed the most aptitude for? You don't lose a good person that way."

Linnas looked Marsha in the eye, easier for Marsha as she stood a good six inches taller than Kitty. "You speak words of great wisdom, Captain Kane. I'm now certain we'll get along as well as Kitty and I have. I have two questions you may find unexpected: do you play chess, and are you any good at it?"

Feeling more than a little out of her element, Marsha answered, "I do play, but I'm not what you'd call the best player you could match up against. Why do you ask, Your Majesty?"

"Call me Linnas," the red woman said. "We're going to be the two most powerful women on this side of Garmon space for some time to come, and we should be friends. I'd be honored if you would allow me to call you Marsha."

Marsha looked in confusion at Kitty, who just said, "Don't look at me, Captain. You're going to be the top human commander in Shiravan space for quite a while. I, personally, think it would be best if you were on a first-name basis with the Matriarch. In informal settings, of course."

"Well, in that case," Marsha said hesitantly, "I guess it would be okay."

Linnas smiled in the human fashion, teeth showing. "Very well, then, I think you should meet some of my top advisers." She pressed a button on her wristband and waited for her comm link to chime. "Doma kep Parrasine, would you meet me in my private chambers and bring Domina sel Garian with you if she's available?"

Kitty said, "While we're awaiting the arrival of our visitors, may I have a word in private with Captain Kane?"

"Of course, Kitty. Take all the time you need. I believe Domina sel Garian will be hard to pry away from her duties anyway."

Kitty motioned for Marsha to follow her into the gardens of the Matriarch's estate. "Listen, there's something you have to know, and it has nothing to do with palace intrigue. That, you're going to have to figure out on your own, except for me to say that sel Garian has stepped down as the Matriarch's second in command and the post has passed to Sitha kep Parrasine, but Manura will still be around training her for a few more years yet. And I've been getting some funny vibes off her whenever she's around. And that's just since we got back from our little demonstration."

"Well, of course. You've just proven that we're more powerful than the Garmon, is it? That's going to make a lot of people edgy," Marsha said. "We're still an unknown to them, no matter the amount of interaction up until this point."

Kitty thought about that for a moment and then said, "Right. I hadn't considered it in that light. So, you'll just have to watch your back. Shouldn't be a problem, what with being on a first name basis with the ruler of fifteen whole planets and controlling the most powerful ship in this part of space."

"Umph," was all Marsha said to that.

Looking down at the path, Kitty said, "There's something else I want to talk to you about." The uncertainty in her voice made Marsha turn her head as they slowly walked through the alien garden. Things that might be birds were seen flitting from tree to tree occasionally. "What did you get from your experience in the regen chamber? Any images, impressions, or communications from the computer controlling your recovery?"

The two white-haired women strolled down gravel paths under a blood-red sun. Lining the paths were flora from all over the planet, none of which looked particularly healthy, most likely due to the light. Marsha looked askance at Kitty as they strolled along. "I really don't know what you mean. It was like I went to sleep and then woke up repaired, refreshed and renewed. Why do you ask?"

"How long did you spend in the chamber, Marsha?"

"They told me it was about six weeks. Again, what's this all about?"

"I was in for almost ten months," Kitty said, her lowered voice raising the small hairs on the back of Marsha's neck. "I don't know if I got more because I was in for so long, or what, but somehow, the computer told me what it was doing—after it got my brain back on track. I was pretty messed up, and I don't mean just my body. After all, I thought Simon was dead." Kitty stopped at a crossroads of two of the paths. "The thing is, it didn't just fix me; it rewrote some of my DNA. And I think it did the same to you. And I think this other computer that has Shirley is doing the same to her because it used me as a sort of template for what a human is supposed to be."

"I'm not sure I like what I'm hearing," Marsha said uneasily. "DNA is what defines human beings, isn't it? And if these computers are messing with our DNA, then shouldn't we put a stop to it?"

"Maybe, maybe not," Kitty replied cryptically. "Simon is the only other person I've told this to and now you. And I'll tell Shirley, as soon as she gets out. What the computer did was to rearrange some of our DNA so that we now have longer lifespans. How would you like to live to be over three hundred years old, keeping your mind sharp all the way up until the end? sel Garian is almost three hundred, Linnas, the Matriarch, is over a hundred, and most of the Shiravans you've met so far are about the same."

"Three hundred years old? For real?" Marsha was astonished at the thought. Then, one of the immediate implications hit her. "You're going to outlive Simon and watch him grow old while you stay young. The same will be true for me and Shirley, too. How are we supposed to handle that? I don't think I can, and it's apparently too late to change it for us."

Kitty nodded. "True. But when I was going into the chamber so it could read me and then repair Shirley, I heard the technicians talking. You don't have to be hurt to use the chamber. Look at me. I was fine. I just spent two days letting the computer get what it needed to fix Shirley. We can do the same for anyone we want. All we have to do is get the Shiravans to teach us how to use the equipment properly. And I *think* it's inheritable. Once we've been through the process, any children we have will automatically have the same lifespans."

Marsha started to pace around the intersection. "This is a lot to take in right now, Kitty. You've had time to process it; I haven't. Why didn't the computer tell *me*? Will everyone who goes through the process have white hair? Will we be marked for life like this? How about the rest of humanity? What will they do when they find out that we can outlive them by three to one?"

Kitty shook her head. "I can't answer even one of those questions, Marsha. All I know is that we should probably keep this quiet for now, but I figured you needed to know, if you didn't already. And since you hadn't said anything to me about it, I figured you didn't."

"Shit, Kitty. We're going to have to put regen chambers on all our bigger ships, transfer people around, and get them all up to speed. And we should let Earth in on it sooner or later. How will it look when you and I are still around in another hundred and fifty years and some smart young reporter decides to compare photographs?"

"It will look like we're hiding something, that's what," Kitty said, agreeing with Marsha's assessment of the situation. "We can say that the white hair is some kind of side effect of prolonged exposure to hyper travel or some such nonsense. Who'll know the difference? And we'll face the smart young reporter when he shows up."

Kitty turned and headed back toward the building, barely seen through the alien foliage. "I think we should consider your briefing over before someone gets too suspicious. These Shiravans, at least some of them, are prone to that."

The two humans walked back into Linnas's quarters to find that the visitors had arrived. Kitty spoke first, "Captain Marsha Kane, let me present the Shiravan Second Voice, Doma Sitha kep Parrasine, and her predecessor and adviser, Domina Manura sel Garian." Each individual nodded once in the human fashion, indicating their introduction. "Shiravans aren't much for personal contact," Kitty said, "so shaking hands isn't going to be much of a problem."

Kitty sat down and crossed her legs, looking at the others in the room. Finally, Linnas sat down, followed by the others. "Good," Kitty said. "I realize these are your personal quarters, Linnas, but since time is truly of the essence, I'll start us off, if you have no objections." She spoke in Shiravan first, then translated for Marsha. Linnas waved a hand, indicating her approval.

Kitty cleared her throat, leaned over and picked up a glass of water from the small table in front of her chair. After taking a sip and replacing the glass, she said, "We five represent the most powerful individuals of our respective races, minus the Admiral. This isn't braggadocio but pure fact, and I'll be leaving soon, treaty in hand to bind us together until the Garmon menace is finally neutralized one way or the other. That will leave four, only one of whom is human, and she's going to feel a bit inferior to the rest of you because she hasn't had the exposure I've had. Marsha is the supreme human authority in this area of space…"

"Wait a minute, Kitty," Marsha said, protesting.

"But," Kitty continued over Marsha's protest, "she's going to be under Shiravan command," looking at Marsha warningly. "Do you have any suggestions that might alleviate her apprehensions?"

Linnas's eyes glazed over for a moment. "I have one idea that might be just the thing to solve the problem, but it'll require the agreement of both my top advisers," she said looking at Sitha and sel Garian. When neither looked like they understood, she said, "Kagaras e Semara."

sel Garian protested. "Your Grace, you can't do this. There's no precedent."

"Oh, yes there is. We've always been able to adept from one family to another without difficulty. Where do you think the idea of fostering came from?"

Marsha looked stunned. Her slight knowledge of Shiravan gave her just enough of an inkling of what was being discussed to make her uneasy. "Would someone please explain to me what's going on?" she asked plaintively.

Kitty just shrugged. "I'm not familiar with the particular idiom myself, Marsha," she said in English. To her host she said, "This is a new concept I'm unfamiliar with. Would you please explain in the simplest words possible?"

"Why, certainly, Kitty," Linnas said with a smile, smaller this time, no teeth showing. "What I'm proposing is that I adopt Captain Kane into the des Harras clan as a junior sister. That will put her under my direct command, which I can then delegate to whomever I decide is to be the supreme military commander on this side of Garmon space. I envision a ceremony wherein both you and the captain are inducted into the des Harras clan. Your position will be somewhat more ambiguous since you'd be my political equal, but I see no reason not to do it."

Kitty's mouth dropped open, but before she could translate for Marsha, sel Garian, butted in. "Your Grace, Linnas, while there are precedents aplenty, I agree, never have we inducted aliens into a Shiravan family."

"True, Domina," Linnas returned gently, as if to a child, "but there has never been an alien race that warranted such an adoption. Until now. And it will quite effectively show all our people the level of trust we place in our new allies. Especially if *you* stand up and suggest the adoption in the first place. It will, of course, have to be in full council, and there will be dissenters, but if the Butcher of Harusel makes a passionate plea, reminding the council of the futility and ruination of disagreement by your mere presence, I don't foresee any problem. At least overtly. And with the kath-mora out of the way, only the most stubborn will resist, and they'll be in the minority."

All of this had gone on in Shiravan, leaving Marsha in the dark.

Finally Kitty asked, "So you are advocating adopting the two of us into your family, Linnas? If you are, then I need time to explain in English to Marsha just what that will entail, and I'm not all that sure that I do understand all the implications either."

Linnas waved her hand at a far corner of the room. "Go. Explain to my future little sister what I propose. And tell her that I won't be offended if she should decide to refuse, or yourself, for that matter. Actually, it will be more of a legal fiction than anything else, since no one will be offering to join with her, and you are already joined. But, it will make the decision-making easier since it will confer considerable status."

Kitty stood up. "Marsha, let's go talk. I think you're about to get a big surprise."

The two women walked into a far corner of the room. Two Shiravan-sized chairs sat there, and they made themselves as comfortable as possible while Kitty explained as much as she understood.

"Are you... is she... out of her mind?" Marsha protested loudly once the implications had been explained to her.

"No, I don't think she is," Kitty said, a strange tone in her voice. "And in an odd way, it would make perfect sense. You would be her sister, a family member and under her immediate command, bound to follow the orders of whomever she sets above you. No one would be able to consider you an alien wild card if you were related and subject to her reprimands. I'm inclined to agree with her. Look, you're the commander of the most powerful fleet on this side of Garmon space. That will make a lot of her enemies nervous unless you have some ties to the safety and continuity of the race. They take these things very seriously, I think, and she's asking me to do the same. It will alleviate the tensions of the common folk and blunt the criticisms of her opponents."

Kitty sat quietly for a moment. "You don't have to answer right this minute. We still have that treaty to hammer out, part of which will probably entail our adoptions, now that she's brought it up. Don't say yes or no right now. Just think about it. I'm sure going to have to. Besides, since I'm included in this, it will make you my sister as well."

Almost two weeks went by while Linnas and her staff, and Kitty and hers, with Brandon Galway usually in attendance, feeling more and more like a fifth wheel, hammered out a treaty that made the two star nations allies in the war against the Garmon. Nothing was ceded to Earth itself as they really had no way to assist other than by supplying personnel, some of whom were going to be highly suspect as the situation with the *Federal Case* pointed out so conclusively.

Kitty became more and more distracted as the days went by and no positive word came down concerning Shirley. Finally, as if fate had been waiting for just the right moment, and with one last proviso added to the treaty—that professional negotiators would discuss trade agreements and the possibility of colonies in each other's space—the doctor assigned to monitor Shirley's progress called and said, "I believe that the process is coming to an end, Madam Herald. The technicians say so from what little I've learned of the language, and the readings are beginning to change at an ever-increasing rate."

Kitty, just sitting down with a sigh as she contemplated a long, hot soak, changed her plans immediately. Informing Freddie of the new development, she headed for the palace's transporter room. Moments later, she was rushing down the *Shumara Vacht's* corridors toward the med lab. The doctor met her outside the door and said, "Madam Herald, the revival process has begun and should be complete within the next twenty minutes or so. I've sent for her clothes and notified a few other friends of hers but asked them to wait until she is recovering in more familiar surroundings. The *Federal Case* has managed to spare space for her, and we'll be transporting her as soon as she's able."

"Thank you, Doctor," Kitty said, shouldering past the man and into the med lab. She looked at one of the Shiravan technicians and asked, "How much longer?"

"Almost any time now, Domagera," the senior tech answered. "We've arranged to have Sorgala Dahlquist transferred to a human ship as soon as possible to minimize the stress on her."

"My thanks for your dedication, ther'a," Kitty said to the two techs on duty, bowing deeply. "Please pass my gratitude on to your colleagues."

"It was our honor, Domagera. Not in anyone's memory has a single individual fought a Garmon single-handedly and won. Sorgala Dahlquist is deserving of the highest honors. The fact that she survived with only the injuries she had is close to miraculous. Surely the Spirits of Space watched over her."

Kitty heard the subtle nuance in the tech's reference and knew it was she they referred to. Having no answer, she merely nodded, turning to the chamber and seeing that the fluid level had started to drop. "Doctor," she called, raising her voice so he could hear her in the corridor.

He walked in, took in the lowered levels in the chamber, and immediately picked up a pair of blankets. Handing one to Kitty, he said, "We should dry her off as soon as possible and get her circulation up. Then we get her dressed and over to the *Case*."

Shirley woke to subdued lights and an orderly sitting in one corner of the small room she found herself in. Several seconds went by while she sorted through her memories and finally cleared her throat, bringing the orderly's head up.

"Captain," the orderly said, "welcome back to the world of the living. I'll notify the Herald at once."

"No," Shirley croaked, her voice hoarse. "First, I want to know how my ship is, where I am, and the outcome of the battle."

"Captain, I'm sorry, but I have my orders. You are to be debriefed by the Herald personally, and it'll be my ass if I don't call her right now."

"Oh, very well. I've heard that if you have to be hung, it's best done by friends. But some water first, please."

Five minutes later, Kitty strode into the room, followed by—of all people—Marsha Kane. She looked from the Herald to Marsha and asked, "What got *you* into one of those chambers?"

"Nothing nearly as bad as what got you into one, Shirl, I'll say that."

"Me?" Shirley squeaked. She raised her hand to her

hair and raised a bit up to eye level. "Oh, shit," she said, seeing it was white for the first time. Memories cascaded back into her consciousness, threatening to knock her back out. Still connected to monitors and medications, she found herself dispassionately assessing her situation. "I'm in pretty deep, huh?"

"I'm here to keep Kitty from finishing the job that Garmon didn't, if that's what you mean, yeah," Marsha answered.

Shirley looked straight at Kitty for the first time. "Okay, boss. I screwed up. I'll take whatever you have to dish out—dereliction of duty, leaving my duty station, disobeying orders. I'll admit to all of it, but how's the *Vega*?"

Kitty kept a straight face, silently remembering the members of the *Vega's* crew that never made it back to Shiravan space. "The *Vega* is a slowly expanding cloud of atoms drifting through Garmon space, Captain Dahlquist. That's what they call themselves now. Seems like there's been a power shift over there. So, I'd say you're lucky to be alive."

"The *Vega's* gone?" she choked. "My crew..."

"We managed to transfer about two thirds of them after a suicider rammed her," Kitty said coldly, cutting her off. "Her shields managed to hold enough that it was only a glancing hit, but it opened her port side up like a tin can." Kitty pulled no punches. "Fortunately, the engine room survived untouched or else there wouldn't have been anyone *to* save."

Shirley felt the heat rise in her cheeks, and tears begin to course down her face. She didn't even have the luxury of being hurt after her stint in the regen chamber and no place to retreat to as the monitors dumped drugs into her system, counteracting her hysteria and elevated adrenaline levels. "So, what's going to happen to me?" she asked.

"I was going to court martial you and have you executed as an example," Kitty said, and her tone left no doubt in Shirley's mind that she meant every word of it. "But that's not going to happen. If I even tried to suggest it, I'd have a full-scale mutiny on my hands, and the Shiravans would probably back out of our alliance, leaving us holding the shitty end of the stick."

Shirley couldn't believe what she was hearing. "Why? I mean, I got all those people killed and I should have died with them."

"Maybe, maybe not," Kitty said, her voice still cold. "Your entire bridge survived, so you probably would have anyway. It's not your fault, or maybe wouldn't have been if you'd been aboard. But you go off and get shot down on an enemy planet and wind up in single combat with one of the alien teddy bears and *win*! How can I court martial you now?" Now heat came into Kitty's voice. "Instead, I'm probably going to have to give you a medal, and the Solar Cross, at that."

Shirley protested, "I don't deserve a medal. I deserve to be... well, not rewarded."

"Oh, don't worry, Captain Dahlquist," Kitty said. Now a smile *did* come over her face, one that made Shirley shiver with fear. "You're going to publicly accept your medal, *knowing* you don't deserve it, and you'll wear it, knowing *why* you don't deserve it. You'll answer every salute you get for having it, and you'll personally visit each and every family member of your dead crew and deliver your condolences, along with a hand-written letter explaining the circumstances of their deaths, leaving out your desertion, of course. We can't have a real live hero admitting to something like that, now can we? It would make recruiting that much harder if people knew their captains couldn't follow orders and stay at their posts.

"Hell, I might even send you out on some recruiting drives. Think what a draw that would be—Captain Shirley Dahlquist, the only living being to survive hand-to-hand combat with the enemy and live to tell about it. And it's going to have to be a good story, too, so you'd better start figuring out what you're going to say when we get back." Kitty turned on her heel and, without another word, stalked out of the room.

Shirley looked at Marsha, tears streaming down her face regardless of the drugs being pumped into her system. "A third of my crew? She really hates me, doesn't she?"

Marsha looked down at her recovering friend. She saw that the effects of the drugs were beginning to take effect and said, with pity tingeing her voice, "No, Shirley, she doesn't hate you. She's ashamed of you. There's a difference."

The drugs finally did their job, taking Shirley's consciousness away from her as her eyes closed and head lolled to one side. Marsha noted that the tears still rolled down her face, even so. She shook her head and followed Kitty out of the room.

CHAPTER SIX

Kitty and Marsha stood on a dais in the central governing building of Quillas City, capital of the Shiravan homeworld. The first two rows of beings were humans, primarily because they were so short that to be anywhere else in the audience would leave them unable to view the proceedings. The remainder of the attendees were Shiravan.

Kitty had opted for her white dress with the Alliance emblem stitched onto the left breast, while Marsha contrasted her in a severe black dress uniform. Standing in the front row was the only other white-haired human in the Shiravan theater of operations, Captain Shirley Dahlquist.

The ceremony, known as Kagaras e Semara, a joining or adoption, was about to take place. Originally thought of strictly for Marsha due to her captaincy of the battleship *Raptor*, it was designed to assuage the fears of the various clan leaders by tying Marsha directly to the des Harras clan. Kitty was added for much the same reason, although she'd be leaving in a matter of days aboard the *Federal Case*, returning to human space with a treaty and the bare bones of a trade arrangement that would take years to hammer out once the appropriate people could be brought together to wrangle over the details.

The senior kath-mora who was left on Shiravi, Tira

do' Verlas, Rentec's mother, stepped up onto the dais and stood between the two humans and Linnas des Harras, Matriarch of the Shiravan Polity. "We come here today to welcome two new members into the des Harras clan. The fact that they are not of our world has caused serious debate among some of our senior clan leaders, but I and several other Sisters have done our best to take readings on the two human females before us today. Their auras are stable and clear, but, we must admit, of an unusual color—a color called 'yellow' by humans, if my description is accurate, bordering on white.

"Marsha Kane, Sorgala of the human battleship *Raptor*, has agreed to place herself and her fleet under Shiravan command during our battles with the Garmon." The new name of their old enemy was now well known. "More, she has agreed to be adopted into the des Harras clan as a Junior Sister to our Matriarch, Linnas, thereby agreeing to abide by all Shiravan laws."

Tira motioned to an assistant standing to one side who stepped forward and opened a box in front of Linnas. The Matriarch took out a silvery chain with a two-inch medallion on it. Formally, Linnas asked in Shiravan, "Do you, Marsha Kane, accept adoption into the des Harras clan, agreeing to abide by all the laws and customs of our people?"

Marsha, sweat beading her lip, nodded and answered, "Se kes." The words meant little to her yet, since she was still learning Shiravan, but she was told that they meant, 'I do,' much like a marriage ceremony.

Linnas smiled in the Shiravan fashion and placed the chain around her neck, the medallion nestling between her breasts. "Ria, keppa sibara." Translated into English it meant, "Welcome, Little Sister."

Tira spoke again, drawing all eyes back to her. "des

Harras welcomes another today as well. Katherine Hawke, Domagera of the Terran Alliance, has agreed to join with des Harras in unity against our common foe, placing the needs of the Shiravan people on an equal basis with the needs of her own people. While this may, in some cases, mean that she will not abide by our ways in the strictest sense, she places her honor in the hands of Linnas des Harras and, by extension, of all Shiravans everywhere. des Harras accepts the conditions under which an autonomous ruler accepts Kagaras e Semara. Are there any here who wish to oppose this union?"

Maybe it was the icy stare of Tira do' Verlas, or perhaps it was the sound of the name Katherine, so much like Kath-e-rin, Spirit of Light, and her appearance, white dress and hair a shimmering crimson in the light of Shiravi's setting sun, but no one spoke or even moved, the moment stretching out seemingly for an eternity.

Finally, Tira motioned again and the assistant brought another box to Linnas. The Matriarch took another chain out of the box and held it out for all to see. It was a silvery chain as Marsha's was, the medallion the same size, but it had a gava stone center. Around the rim on both sides were inscribed all the symbols that denoted every clan on Shiravi. "Do you, Katherine Hawke, accept adoption into the des Harras clan, agreeing to place the interests of all Shiravans on the same level as your own people's until such time as our common foe is defeated?"

Kitty, knowing what was expected of her and understanding the language as well as the implications of her words, answered, "Se kes."

Linnas smiled again and placed the chain around Kitty's neck. "Ria, sibara-nich."

A stir went through the crowd when Linnas welcomed Kitty as her Sister-equal. Even Sitha and sel Garian looked startled. Linnas spoke to the assembled leaders of all the clans of her world. "This woman is the supreme ruler of her people, as I am of mine." A legal fiction only a few Shiravans knew of or understood. "Her people must come first in her thoughts and decisions as you must come first in mine. By accepting sibara-nich, she has vowed to consider our people equally with hers, and I have agreed to consider the needs of humanity on an equal basis with ours. We are, for the duration of our war with the Garmons, effectively one people now. And even though there are two rulers, that will not affect the daily lives of any but a very few."

The babble of voices rose sharply as the implications of this new information made itself felt, first among the clan leaders and then others as whispered words were overheard and repeated around the room. Only a few of the humans present understood what was happening, and they looked worriedly at Kitty. The volume rose, and individual voices began to make themselves heard out of the white noise that filled the room.

Clan leaders—sel Garian chief amongst them, followed by all those allied in one way or another—began to call for a repudiation of the alliance and the Kagaras e Semara. Louder still the voices rose, and a few of the humans present moved onto the lower steps of the dais, calling for others to stand beside them as a living shield to protect the Herald from what appeared to be a crowd turning into a lynch mob.

Tira do' Verlas stepped forward almost unnoticed until her voice, amplified by a small box attached to her waist, rang out over the noise being generated by the various factions in the large room. "Stimara!" she commanded, the tone telling one and all that she would brook no resistance to her command. The word brought silence to the hall as intended, since it meant that very thing.

"This is a time of rejoicing, not of recrimination. Political aspirations will not be tolerated here and now. We have a venue for that process. Have you all become as uncivilized as the Garmons? Have you sunk so low that you are the same as they? Clan des Harras has this day found two new Sisters, each of whom brings great gifts to the clan, and by extension the rest of the Shiravan race. One commands the strongest military force for its size ever put into space. The other commands the people who built that force. Do any of you really want to anger either of them?"

Silence reigned long enough to make Kitty uncomfortable, but Tira let it go on longer still. Finally, she relented. "We have become apathetic in our belief that we can survive anything. The Garmons have proven that. For two hundred turns and more we have fought— and lost. Do any of you remember that we were once twenty-two worlds? Have you all forgotten Harlo? With the help of our new Sisters and their race, we can regain that, and more.

"Look at the one called Shirley Dahlquist, if you need an example of the bravery and skills of these, our new relatives." Tira pointed at Shirley, white-haired and rigid, standing with the other humans, now facing the rest of the audience as if protecting those on the dais with their very bodies. "And all of her compatriots, female and male, both. At the first hint of danger to their kin, they moved to stand as you see them now. Could they really withstand an all-out attack by the rest of you?

No. But their names would be inscribed in the dusterna of more than one clan for their efforts. And are there any among you who would take on the least of these singly? I think not, for they have earned their reputations by their very actions."

Linnas sat down and the other five followed suit as soon as they could shut the door to the Matriarch's private quarters. "I was truly worried for the first time in my reign," she admitted quietly. She pressed a button on her chair, and almost immediately her new assistant entered the room. "Fire wine for all of us, please. And use the kemwood cups."

She turned back to her companions. Sitha kep Parrasine sat nearby, as did Manura sel Garian. Kitty, Marsha, and, at the Matriarch's request, an uncomfortable Shirley Dahlquist sat opposite the three Shiravans. "I think this will be the last time we'll all sit together for many turnings," Linnas said. "And you, Captain Dahlquist, are invited to tell us of your ordeal if you would. I'm most interested to hear how you were able to vanquish a being four times your size."

Shirley looked at Kitty, who made a point of taking a sip of her wine, saying only, "I'll translate for you, Captain."

"Your Grace," Shirley said, "I am in disgrace with the Herald. She has ordered me to make my ordeal as heroic as possible, but when she said that, she was speaking of the people back on Earth and among Alliance personnel. For you, only the truth." She proceeded to tell the unvarnished story, including her fear and inability to oppose the might of the being that hunted her. "It was only the luckiest of strokes that allowed me to kill him," she finished. "If I hadn't had the knife with me, if I hadn't had the good fortune to be able to reach it, and if I hadn't had the opportunity to reach his brain with one stroke to the eye, I wouldn't be here today. And if I hadn't disobeyed orders, I wouldn't be in disgrace today. If I could go back in time and know what I know now, I would have obeyed my orders and stood at my post as all the rest of my crew did. I've been told that my actions had no effect on the fact that a third of my crew lost their lives, but at night, in the dark, I wonder. Could I have saved even one of those who died if I'd stayed aboard? I'll never know, and that will haunt me for all my days." When Linnas's aide came by to pour into her cup, Shirley placed her hand over the opening. "I don't wish to offend you, Your Grace, but I don't belong here and don't deserve to drink your wine."

"Nonsense, Captain," Linnas replied gently. "My new Sister has already told me most of the story, but I wanted to hear the details from your own perspective. It takes great courage to admit one's mistakes, and you have acquitted yourself with honor in my eyes. Please, accept the wine as a token of my admiration—if not for your rashness, then for the courage I see in your eyes and hear in your voice."

Shirley slowly moved her hand from the cup and let the young Shiravan pour the blue wine into it. "Thank you, Captain," Linnas said. "I realize the tribulations you'll face in the years to come, but here, know that you are respected. Sometimes rashness is a survival trait, and sometimes it's an incentive for others to push themselves to their personal limits. If your sacrifices, past and future, help push your people and mine to greater things than they thought possible, it will be a small price to pay in the final analysis." She picked up her cup and the others followed her lead. "May the Spirits of Space follow you all for the rest of your days," she said formally, "and may Kath-e-rin ease your burden with her wisdom."

As Linnas sipped her drink, Shirley took a sip of her own and wondered at the phrasing of the Matriarch's toast. Kath-e-rin was the Shiravan's Spirit of Light, but the name was close enough to the Herald's that she wondered if it had been a subtle request for mercy. She could hope so, but only time would tell whether the Matriarch saw it, or it was just her wishful imagination.

Kitty boarded the shuttle waiting to take her back to the *Federal Case,* and in a matter of days, she'd be under way back to Earth and Simon. She still felt the warmth of the handshake and embrace from Linnas on her skin and knew she'd miss the closeness she'd come to share with the Shiravan leader. She wondered, as well, at the wording of that toast Linnas had made, but would have to think on it for some time.

She got off the shuttle along with a few others, Shirley included. Just before the ramp raised, Marsha said quietly, "I have an errand to take care of on the *Canopus.* I'll see you at least once more before you get under way." Kitty just nodded as the ramp closed on her friend, watching the craft move back out into space to deliver the rest of its occupants to their respective destinations.

Marsha didn't keep Kitty in the dark for long. The very next day, she called and asked to come aboard with a package to be sent back to Earth. She handed Kitty a plainly wrapped package and said, "There's a video and letter in there. You need to deliver them to Lucy as soon as you get back. It seems that her brother Bruce joined up under his mother's maiden name and is a flight leader aboard the *Canopus*. Apparently, she didn't have a clue and didn't find out until well after they left Earth space. So, Lieutenant Commander Bruce Sears has complied with the Deputy Herald's wishes and is sending her his apologies and an update on what has happened to him since he volunteered, including his actions against the Garmons. According to his captain, he was in command of a double-flight that took out one of the Garmon destroyers."

"I'll see to it personally, of course," Kitty said. "Would you care to join me for a drink before you go back to the *Raptor*?"

"Wish I could, boss," Marsha said, "but Shiravan Command has redesignated Raptor Group as Reprisal Fleet Four, and we've already got our marching orders. I've got to get back and settle three Shiravan ships into my operations roster while the *Deneb* replaces the *Vega*."

"Oh," was all Kitty could say. "Well, you give them hell, kiddo, and see that we get regular reports on what's going on over here. Got it?"

"Got it, boss. Give my best to Simon, and tell him that he's done a hell of a job."

"How do you know how well he's done?" Kitty asked suspiciously.

"Don't worry, Kitty. He'll know what I mean," was all the answer she got before Marsha hugged her and stepped back into her gig. Kitty's last sight of her friend was of her giving the thumbs-up gesture as the ramp closed with a solid thump.

CHAPTER SEVEN

Kitty answered an early evening request to meet with Linnas on the eve of her departure. She sat in one of the chairs originally designed by Derek Carter when he was a guest of the Shiravans after his rescue. The sun had a way to go yet to reach the edge of the Stala Mountains, cradling Linnas's official retreat and family home in the nearly rebuilt Cho-An. "I wanted this one last moment with my new Sibara." Linnas said, pouring fire wine into two tall, thin glasses.

Kitty knew that since there were no kemwood cups, this was going to be an informal evening, one which she was sure she'd regret in the morning. Still, she picked up the glass, determined to keep her wits about her for as long as she could, and took a small sip of the fiery blue liquid. No stranger to strong drink and acquainted with this particular poison, she still felt the glow begin to spread out almost immediately. "It's still a concept that I'm struggling with," Kitty said in response. "Not that I'm uncomfortable with it, just that it's going to take some getting used to. And now I'm going to leave my new Sister and go away. How long will it be before we meet again?"

Linnas took a larger sip than Kitty and let it settle before she answered. "Only the Spirits can say, Sister. And in the minds of some of my—our—people, you're one of those Spirits. Perhaps *you* can tell *me* the answer to that question."

"You know I'm no Spirit, Linnas," Kitty said. "I'm just an ordinary human like all the others who stayed behind and who came with me."

Linnas took another sip of her drink and noted, "Ordinary, you say? Like Shirley Dahlquist, who killed a Garmon with nothing but a simple knife? Ordinary like those who stalked through a ship full of traitors and took it back? Ordinary like those who follow you into unknown space to meet an unknown foe without hesitation? Ordinary like those who followed you and your mate into space in the first place and took totally alien technology and made it their own, improving on it as they went?"

"You make it sound like we're some kind of super beings, Linnas. There are many among us who would never consider doing any of the things you name. Shirley was lucky, pure and simple, and as for the rest, I think it's true that we're closer to our beginnings than your people. I often think we still have too much inquisitiveness in us for our own good."

Kitty took a larger sip of her drink than she'd originally intended. "It's true that we would have been totally defenseless if the Garmons had found us before we got hold of your ship, but we did only because you couldn't handle your own people. So, we bootstrapped ourselves into space against all odds and opposition and made ourselves a force to be reckoned with just in time to save our own asses from the Garmons. And now we're able to be of assistance to the very race that unintentionally gave us the technology. A series of coincidences, nothing more." Anger suffused her last words, not expecting this particular tack from one whom she had come to think of as a friend, not even considering the legal fiction of sisterhood.

Linnas gazed out the window and Kitty followed her gaze outward as the sun dipped below the Stalas. The heat trapped within began to seep out, wrapping the horizon in the green glow of the gava stone found in only this one place on the planet. She wouldn't be seeing this sight again for many years to come.

Silence reigned as the two rulers sat and let the glow slowly fade out, leaving only the dim lights behind them to illuminate the room. "I'm sending the *Jerra Nep* as escort with your *Federal Case*, Linnas said finally, breaking the silence. "You might be surprised to hear that Rentec has requested to be reassigned to human space. I've listened to his reasoning and agreed that he'd better serve the Polity there than here for the time being. kep Gillas is still too close in his mind, and I, too, think he should be elsewhere for a while."

Kitty considered it over another sip of wine. "Perhaps you're right. Even among humans, the male is easily misled by females, and dealing with the disparities of humans and Shiravans will be enough to take his mind off his troubles."

Linnas smiled slightly. "Your choice of words is much better than the one I would use," she said. "But he'll have almost a full turn to obsess on what has happened. Tira has officially disavowed the union, of course, but he still suffers from the betrayal."

Kitty snorted and took another drink. "Men are men, no matter what the race. It's his pride that's at the bottom of his problem. He feels betrayed and has no outlet for his anger since Ramannie has been banished. I still say that her execution would have been a good way to begin his healing."

Linnas turned from the window to look at her. "I'll

grant you the greater knowledge since you've known males of both our races, but I still say that the custom of killing in response to other killings is one that reduces the second to the level of the first. That's one of the differences between our two philosophies. The Spirits of Space say that it's wrong to do such, but yours calls for—what have I heard your people say—an eye for an eye?"

Kitty, feeling the effects of the wine too much, put her glass down on the table between the two women. "At least our way, we don't have to support mass murderers for hundreds of years... turnings. And your people live three times as long as we do. It's simple economics when you get to the bottom line, not to mention the 'eye for an eye' thing." She looked at the wine left in her glass and decided to leave well enough alone. "Different races, different ways of looking at things. That's something we've come to live with, having so many different political and religious divisions between our own peoples on one single world."

Kitty changed her mind and took another sip of the wine. "And another thing, Sibara. Who's been divining what the Spirits of Space say for all these turnings? If I'm correct, it's the bunch of kath-mora that should be showing up soon, whom you and all of your people have disavowed." She shook her head and immediately regretted it. "I've got to tell you, if we're really sisters now, that I think your whole civilization's precepts have got to undergo a radical change." She held up a hand to stop Linnas from responding. "I'm not saying humans are perfect. Far from it. You, at least, have a unified government, or mostly so. There are a few Isolationists to be weeded out, but in my experience, you never get all the weeds, and I think that's a good thing. If a culture becomes too static, it begins to decline. Maintaining the status quo isn't good enough." Feeling that she had overstepped her bounds, Kitty sat silently and watched the final glow seep out of the mountains and the city walls built from the same stone.

Linnas set her unfinished glass down as well. "I won't argue with my new Sister on the eve of her departure. Besides, you have the advantage of knowing more about Shiravans than I do about humans. Perhaps that's something I should remedy in the future."

"Perhaps," Kitty agreed, slightly startled. "I'd be happy to have you visit my world, but who would stand in your place while you were gone for several turnings?"

Linnas sat quiet for a short time. "That's something I'd have to think upon when my mind isn't fogged with fire wine. There really is no precedent for such an absence that I can think of. Who would I trust to hold my people together while I made such a long trip? You obviously have great faith in your appointed second in command. I, on the other hand, have a newly appointed Second Voice who has a slightly xenophobic adviser. There. I've said it. sel Garian stepped down because she couldn't trust humans as fully as I. I'm not sure Sitha can either, especially since Manura is her mentor. Too much of the teacher gets left in the pupil. Would she govern as I wish in my absence? Would she proclaim a new dynasty, leaving me in the same situation as the kath-mora when they return? So many questions and no answers."

"And none, unfortunately, that I can give you either," Kitty said slowly. She stood up and almost immediately grabbed the back of her chair to steady herself. "Damn, that's strong stuff. I'm glad you offered me a bed for the night. I think I'll take you up on it." She used her comm link to order her gig back to the ship and reported her decision to stay on-planet for the night.

Linnas pressed a button on her wristband. Immediately an aide appeared. "Take the Domagera to the guest quarters, please," she said. "And slowly. I fear that she is none too steady on her feet."

The aide did as instructed, and saw the alien Domagera safely into her bed. *So much like a doll she appears*, thought the young aide. *Especially in that bed. She barely reaches a third of the way from head to foot.* She waited quietly and unobtrusively in one corner until her charge started to make a strange, intermittent noise, and then she slowly slipped from the room. Various other duties held her attention for a time until she realized that she hadn't heard from her own Domagera in some time. She looked into the small audience chamber to find her Matriarch asleep while Shabbas and Grinnas chased each other across the night sky.

Kitty awoke early, the first rays of the reddish sun sliding slowly across the floor toward her bed. Climbing out of the monstrous affair and stumbling into the connected facilities, she stripped off the dress she had worn and stepped into the shower, turning the water as hot as she could stand it. After ten minutes or so, she shut off the hot and gasped as cold water sluiced down her body. She finally turned that off as well and, shivering, stepped out of the over-sized shower stall to find an aide waiting with a large fluffy towel. "If I may be of service, Domagera Hawke," the girl said.

"Segala vin," Kitty said as the tall woman wrapped the unexpectedly warm towel around her shoulders.

"No thanks are necessary, Domagera Hawke," the woman said. "When you awoke, I took the liberty of sending for your gig and requesting that someone send along a clean uniform and accessories. Your clothes are waiting in the next room, and your gig is on the landing field. Domagera des Harras has been informed of your rising and requests your company for an early meal."

Kitty laughed silently at the word 'accessories.' Shiravan women were essentially breast-less except when suckling young, so a bra was unthinkable, and the concept of panties was totally alien to them. She smiled hugely at her own pun and said, "Tell the Domagera that I'll be happy to join her as soon as I have dressed."

She walked into the bedroom, toweling her hair and drying off while the aide spoke quietly into her own comm link. A shockingly pink bra and pair of panties lay atop the uniform on her bed. *It must be the light*, she thought. *All of my stuff is white*. She let the towel fall to the floor and picked up the bra. Hooking it in front where she could see, she spun the garment around so the hooks were in back and stuffed herself into the thing. Panties were next as the aide came out of the bathroom.

Kitty took the blouse from the aide when she picked it up off the bed and asked while buttoning it, "What is your name, ther'a?"

"Heppis sel Garian, Your Grace," the young woman answered without hesitation.

Kitty froze for a moment and then continued to button her blouse. "Related to Manura in what way, if I may ask?"

"Great third-niece, twice removed, Your Grace," the young woman answered. Kitty thought she detected an undercurrent of… something.

"And you find yourself in the Matriarch's service," Kitty said, slipping on her pants, sliding a belt through the loops, and buckling it.

"Not all of the clan believe the way the Elders do, Your Grace." The aide was silent while Kitty put on socks and shoes. "Some of us would see Domina Manura elevated to Elder status."

Kitty looked herself over in a mirror. She pulled a brush from a kit someone had thoughtfully sent along and brushed her white hair into a scalp-tingling ponytail, wrapping it with a black scrunchie. "How does Domina Manura feel about that?" Kitty asked lightly. sel Garian as an Elder? That clan was one of the more powerful Isolationist clans on Shiravi. With Manura elevated to Elder status, she could just imagine the bloodbath that would ensue. And how would it affect Shiravan politics? With sel Garian's victory or without?

"No one has the courage to broach the subject," Heppis answered uncomfortably. "She seems to revel in her title of Butcher of Harusel. To become an Elder now, well there are many who would vote for her but just as many who still remember the old days and adhere to the old ways. An open vote could go either way, and if she lost, well, no one wants to contemplate her anger and vengeance."

Kitty said no more about the subject and let Heppis lead her to the small chamber from the night before. This time, though, there were three present: Linnas, of course, as well as Sitha and Manura. Heppis withdrew as soon as Kitty passed into the room. "Good morning to all," Kitty said as she reached the table.

"Sibara," Linnas said, nodding without rising.

"Domagera," came from both Sitha and sel Garian as

they stood at her approach.

"Sit, sit," Kitty said as she did so herself. "We're all friends here, at least for today, so let's not allow ceremony to stand in our way. I leave for Earth in a matter of hours. Let's let those hours be pleasant ones, shall we?"

Kitty unceremoniously ladled scrambled eggs, bacon and, wonder of wonders, hash browns onto her plate. "I can understand my new Sister wanting to spend a few more moments with me before a long absence, but what can you two want that would make you rise this early in the morning?" she said to the other two women.

"To hear from you personally what you intend once you return to human space," Sitha said for the two women.

"I intend to prosecute the war as fast and effectively as possible with the information I'll be taking back with me," Kitty said bluntly. "We now have a better idea of where some of the Garmons' bases are and will be dedicating our efforts in those direction, as well as searching out other strongholds for ourselves. Surely, you can't have found them all."

"No," sel Garian answered, "but we're concerned that you'll deplete your enemies and turn your attentions elsewhere."

Kitty put down her fork and looked the old woman in the eyes. The red still unsettled her a bit, but she refused to let it show. "You had better not be intimating that we would turn our attentions and power against our allies, Domina sel Garian," Kitty warned in a dangerously calm voice. "If you are, I would have it said aloud and in such a way that I could challenge you to single combat before I leave here. But I really wouldn't like that to happen. It would leave Sitha with no adviser as she grows into her

115

new role as Second Voice and would upset my new Sister."

sel Garian looked down at the small human. "You tempt me to accept your challenge, Domagera," she said, the last word dripping with sarcasm, "but I fear that our Domagera wouldn't like this day marred by your death."

Linnas finally entered the verbal fray. "Far be it for me to interfere with such matters, Domina. If you feel insulted enough or confident enough to accept my Sister's challenge, then by all means, do so."

Kitty was a bit surprised at the response but figured that she'd stepped into a matter of custom that she, as an adopted Shiravan, had to deal with herself. "My Sister chooses to distance herself from the unpleasantness that is about to ensue. But before we do this, I'd like to know who sent four Shiravan battlecruisers into the area we were to 'prove' ourselves in, thereby stirring up the Garmons for an unconscionably long time."

Linnas looked shocked at the revelation. "Is this true, Sibara?"

"I will provide you with a full set of our recordings before we leave, Sister. By way of Sorgala Kane, of course. She should know what kind of creature she's dealing with."

"Now come, Gramas to' vara. Your time has come." Kitty deliberately chose the words that would goad her opponent into a situation where she couldn't refuse. They meant one who was already dead and assumed complete confidence in one's own abilities to survive such a contest. "Remember, one under my command has not only survived personal combat with a Garmon but killed him by her own hand. I choose that we fight in the same manner—with knives only and at once." She pushed her plate away and stood up. "I find that I'm no longer hungry. Linnas, if you would do the honors, I'd be happy to have you as my second. Bring the appropriate weapons to the landing field where we may put this matter behind us. I have a long journey and don't wish to delay it any longer than necessary."

She strode away from the table without another word to her opponent. "Heppis, attend me," she said. The aide appeared immediately, white-faced and jumpy. "Lead me to the landing field at once, please," was all she would say and stood so that the young aide could not get a clear view of her superiors. "Now, Heppis," Kitty admonished curtly.

"Aya, Domagera," the aide finally said and turned to leave the room.

Kitty followed the young woman through the labyrinthine passages of the Matriarch's Cho-An residence and out onto the landing field. Along the way, she used her comm link to inform the crew of the gig, and by extension, all aboard the *Federal Case*, that she was about to face a death duel.

"Madam Herald, I strongly object," came from the new Captain of the *Case*.

"You can object all you want, Captain," she said, "but the fact of the matter is that at this point, neither you nor I have any control over the matter. Even the Matriarch has to stand by and let this go down. Remember, I've been adopted into their society and must abide by their rules. In this case, I've been insulted and responded with a death duel challenge. The only one who can stop this is sel Garian herself."

"Why sel Garian?" came back in Galway's voice, surprising her completely.

Kitty smiled grimly, anticipating her response. "Because she's my opponent, Brandon. She insulted me in front of the Matriarch and new Second Voice. I had no choice but to respond as I did. So. If I lose, leave orbit, head back to Earth, tell Lucy that I apologize for leaving her in charge, and try to keep Simon from coming here and mopping the place up with my killer. End of subject. End of conversation." She cut the link and refused to answer any hails from the waiting warship or the gig sitting a few hundred yards away.

She was surprised to see Marsha come down the ramp, headed her way at a run. Kitty started to open her mouth, but Marsha spoke first. "I'm not here to stop you, Kitty, just for moral support. I was going to ride back up and discuss some trivial stuff, but I'll just stand nervously by and watch. Sure you gotta do this?"

"Yep, afraid so, girlfriend," she said resignedly. "Now, let me concentrate." She deliberately turned and faced the palace, waiting for the rest of the people to file out of the single door visible from this spot. She began to do some stretching exercises to prepare herself for the contest ahead. She knew the gig would be scanning her and the ensuing battle, recording it for future playback. She just prayed Simon wouldn't use it to scotch the alliance she'd formed with the Shiravans. Maybe he'd just focus on sel Garian as his target. She could only hope. If she lived.

Finally, Linnas came out, carrying a large box under one arm. She was followed by Sitha and sel Garian. "It is not my place to try to stop this matter from proceeding," she said, sounding as if she was following some ancient ritual. "I can only act as second to my Sister as requested. Here are two identical knives," she said, opening the box. To Kitty they looked like two medium-sized swords, but that was to be expected considering the size of the race that had forged them.

"The challenged party gets first choice." She turned to sel Garian and said, "Domina, if you will choose your weapon."

Kitty took the remaining one and hefted it appraisingly. Definitely not balanced for a human but not as bad as she'd figured upon first seeing them. They were more like Roman short swords and not as heavy as they looked, but then, she was from a heavier-gravity world. Perhaps sel Garian would forget that. She held it two-handed and practiced a few swings. She tried to block a few imaginary strokes and thrusts, but something seemed slightly wrong.

She switched to a one-handed grip, holding the sword a bit higher on the grip than sel Garian was holding hers. A few practice swings and cuts, blocks and thrusts, and something inside her seemed to click. Suddenly this piece of metal felt more like an extension of her arm than a weapon. She let her mind float back to the battle aboard the *Federal Case* and reluctantly forced herself into the mind-set she'd adopted while that battle was raging.

She turned and faced her opponent who was taller, had a longer reach, and was far more familiar with the weapon in her hand, and remembered one of Simon's many lessons in self-defense: when fighting someone bigger than you—and almost everybody was—get inside their defenses and take no prisoners. She looked to the side and said to Linnas, "Sibara, I regret the loss of one of your advisers, but some insults cannot go unchallenged." To Sitha she said, "I suggest that you begin to look for a new mentor as you will be burying this one very soon. And for future reference, remember that humans are one of the hardest life forms in the galaxy to kill."

She turned once more to her opponent. "Come, Butcher of Harusel," she said derisively, "let's play. You've outlived your usefulness, and I want to find out what color Shiravan blood is." She instinctively crouched a bit lower, the point of her sword describing small circles in the air before her. She knew that this old woman was one whom she would not normally want to face, but she saw several advantages in her favor. One was that she was so much smaller than any other opponent this woman had faced that she'd have to adopt new tactics. Another was the whole Kath-e-rin thing. With that thought came an inspiration.

She backed up two paces and planted her weapon's point firmly in the ground. Placing her hands atop the hilt, she looked to the sky and intoned, "I, Katharine," she used her own name properly, not separating the syllables, "invoke the Spirit of Kath-e-vel. Guide my hand, O Great Destroyer, guide my sword, rid my mind of all other thoughts but the removal of the Butcher of Harusel from the universe." She didn't have any idea whether it would work, but Simon had always told her to try to rattle her opponent. An angry or scared opponent was far more likely to make a mistake. Still, she would take what she could get.

Recognizing that the time for theatrics was done, she lifted her weapon and assumed an attack posture. She moved to close the distance between them, her eyes taking in all that she could of her opponent. When Manura took her first step in her direction, it appeared to Kitty that there was a certain amount of hesitation. Perhaps that Butcher of Harusel thing had hit a nerve. Not so on the second or third, as if she also had found the mind-set that let her stand outside herself and guide the body without worrying about the injuries she was about to incur.

Kitty adopted a stance seen on innumerable television shows and in more movies than she could remember— sword tip pointed at her adversary, left hand on her hip, right foot forward and knees bent slightly. Why? She had no idea. She had never trained with a sword and would have been more comfortable with a laser, anyway, but she had to work with what she had. Still, the sword felt comfortable in her grip and so far, she felt no fear. Again, she wondered with a small portion of her mind if this was what Simon felt when he saw action, as he'd said on more than one occasion.

sel Garian moved another step forward and slid her sword tip down and forward, apparently hoping to finish this quickly and prove that she was the mistress of her own destiny. Kitty took in the move and used her diminutive stature to her own advantage. She dropped even lower, tucked into a ball and rolled forward, letting her left shoulder take the brunt of the impact which was only fist and sword-hilt but hurt like hell, anyway. She rose to her feet, the tip of her sword touching sel Garian's midsection. She sliced a shallow groove across her stomach and said, "You're dead, old woman." She immediately crouched down and swept her left leg in a swift arc, catching sel Garian behind the ankles and dropping her onto her back in the dirt and grass of the landing field.

Finishing the spin and rising to her feet in one fluid move, Kitty laid the point of her sword on sel Garian's neck, and said, "You're dead for the second time in a matter of seconds. Yield or die. I've given you two chances to live. I'll give you no other."

The proverbial eternity passed while the old woman thought it over and finally said, "I yield to Kath-e-rin, protector of the weak and fount of all mercy."

Kitty's eyebrows rose at the wording. She glanced at Linnas, who only nodded ever so slightly. Kitty moved her sword tip and stood back, her own sword pointing at the ground between them but not yet relaxing her defenses.

sel Garian rose slowly to her feet, looking down at the small human who had just handed her her first defeat since her days at the training academy. She bent over and picked up the sword she'd used, and Kitty's rose back to a guard position. The old red woman reversed the weapon and held it out to her. "The swords were a gift to me from the previous Matriarch. I gift them to you in the name of peace between us."

Kitty slowly reached out and took the second sword in her left hand, watching for some sign of treachery. As soon as she had the hilt in her hand, sel Garian let go and turned away, heading back toward the palace without another word.

Linnas stepped forward, the sword-case in her arms. "You constantly amaze me, Sibara. This is the first time in almost two hundred turns that Manura has been bested in single combat. It would seem that I chose wisely when I decided to adopt you into the des Harras clan. This meeting will become legend all over Shiravi before the six-day is out."

Kitty slowly laid the swords back in the case, the depressions in the material showing how they were to be placed. Linnas closed the case and handed it to her. "Manura has given these to you. There isn't another set on the entire planet that comes close to their craftsmanship or renown. They were carried at the Battle of Harusel in my name and have been used on three other occasions to assure my reign. I think it won't be necessary that they ever be used so again."

Kitty took the case and held it awkwardly under one arm. The adrenaline rush of combat was leaving her body, and she felt weak, shaking with reaction. "It is time, my Sister. I must leave for Earth, now. I'm sure I'll face some criticism from my staff for this display of..." she searched for the right Shiravan words but didn't really know them. "For my lack of restraint. Sometimes I feel that too much of my mate has rubbed off on me after so many years together. I should have handled the matter with more diplomacy. Perhaps this whole thing could have been avoided."

Linnas waved her hand in negation. "Don't forget. I know Manura. She would have continued until you couldn't have done otherwise. You did only what you had to do. I'm just glad and, I admit, a bit surprised that you not only won but let her live. Her reputation will never be the same after this, and that is, I think, a good thing now. There is no longer any place for her kind of intrigue in my reign, and I hope Sitha has learned that," she said, pointedly raising her voice slightly.

"Now, let me accompany my new Sister to her vessel. You've delayed your departure long enough." Linnas waved her hand toward the gig, waiting two hundred yards distant. As the two walked toward the small craft, followed by a thoroughly awed Marsha, Linnas said, "I have had a small parting gift loaded aboard your ship. It took some diplomacy, I believe you say, to get your pilots and guards to allow its stowage, but I did prevail. Of course, it also took the gifting of a small quantity of gava stone to get them to agree, but what is a bribe or two among family?"

Kitty just snorted in amusement.

As the two neared the small ship, the ramp came

down and Kitty stopped at the bottom, Marsha standing a pace behind her. One of the pilots came down and took the sword-case as Kitty turned back to her new Sister. "I pray that we meet again in the not-too-distant future, Sibara. Even though the return trip of almost a full turning will be most boring, I'll remember our time together and the boredom will pass."

A thought passed through her mind. "In my culture, we have a gesture of affection we call a 'hug.' Come closer, please." When Linnas stepped hesitantly into Kitty's personal space, the small white-haired woman reached up with both arms and wrapped them around her friend, squeezing slightly. It took a few seconds for Linnas to respond in kind, but she finally did. "I will miss you, Sibara, more than you know," Kitty said.

Ending the awkward moment, she turned her back and resolutely walked up the short ramp into the dark interior of her gig, ignorant of all other things. She turned and looked once more at her Sister, the leader of fifteen worlds. She raised her hand and waved as the ramp came up and locked into place, blocking out the reddish light of early Shiravan morning and the face of her newest family member.

"Engines coming online," she heard one pilot say to the other, and she moved to her seat, sidling past two crates strapped down in the middle of the aisle. She resolved not to ask what crossed whose palm to get them loaded. *Never look a gift horse in the mouth.*

Marsha waited for her moment to slide into the seat next to Kitty before the gig rendezvoused with the *Case*. "There hasn't been a good time to tell you any of this before now, and I know that now isn't the best time either, but I'm heading out and you're heading back, so it's now or never."

Kitty looked up from her reverie, thoughts of maiming and killing drawing back into the blackness of the deepest recesses of her mind. "What do you mean?"

"I mean," Marsha said quietly, "that there's something going on back on Earth. We're picking out more and more agents and returning them to their respective nations or just turning them away, but still, a few make it through. Oddly enough, most of those switch sides," she said with a small smile. She was silent for a time. "I think there's going to be a crackdown on open recruiting. The U.N. was holding almost continual sessions just before we left, and the U.S. was behind most of those actions, as I was given to understand the situation. They're pressuring the Japanese and the Swiss to disavow our embassies. So far, both nations have given them nothing."

Kitty laughed softly, almost regretfully, Marsha thought. "Simon and I figured on that a long time ago. We won't have any problem with recruits, just picking them up. It's going to be like back in the early days— clandestine landings in the middle of the night, swift pick-ups, and quick departures. But surely Tokyo and Geneva won't crumble..."

Marsha shrugged, a measure of helplessness making the gesture all the more final. "All I can say for sure is that there was a feeling I was getting. Not all the time," she said slowly, her mind going back over more than one event, "but where the higher-level players moved, things certainly seemed a bit cooler just before we left. I gave it less attention than I should have at the time since I was getting ready to lead a small flotilla against the 'alien menace,' but during our voyage here, I had way too much time to rethink things. Just be sure you check in at Vesta before moving further in-system. Just a feeling from one friend to another, okay?"

CHAPTER EIGHT

As soon as the gig docked in *Federal Case's* bay, Kitty stepped off to meet her staff and new senior crew. "Captain Dexter," she said to the woman standing front and center of the side party, including the baron and his wife, "it wasn't necessary for you to meet me here. Any of your senior crew would have sufficed."

"Under most circumstances, I would agree, Madam Herald," she answered, "but this is your first time aboard with your flag officially moved. I considered it my duty to be present and am fully confident that my Number One can handle things during my short absence. Please allow me to show you to your quarters. I expect you'll find them a little crowded, but I wish to point out in advance that although we're a bit overcrowded, no one is being crowded into unsuitable quarters so you can travel in spacious comfort. I, myself, have elected to take smaller quarters so we can more effectively accommodate the extra personnel, as well as you and your staff."

"I'll personally inspect that statement as soon as I get settled, Captain," Kitty said, "and if I find that I have to downsize my own space over some preconceived notion of protocol, you and I will find ourselves in the sparring ring." The captain blanched slightly at her words. Kitty intended that she blanch more. "And since I don't wear gloves, you won't either. And if I feel that you're pulling your punches, we'll stay there until I'm satisfied that you aren't. Do I make myself clear?"

"Yes, Your Grace," she said quietly.

Kitty had started to lead off in the direction of crew quarters before she spoke to her staff. Instead, she rounded on Maggie, the baroness. "What's this 'Your Grace' business?"

Maggie placed a hand on her arm. "Let it go, Kitty. I think I have an explanation as soon as we have a degree of privacy."

"As explanations go, it had better be a doozy," Kitty muttered. She stepped aside and waved a hand graciously. "Please, Captain, lead the way."

The captain, obviously flustered, stopped in front of her own door. "With your permission, Madam Herald," she said, and Kitty heard the change in her voice, "I've arranged for you and your staff to share my quarters during the trip back to Earth. I beg that you wait until you know more about our other arrangements before passing judgment. At present, I must speak with the captain of the *Jerra Nep* about our passage to Earth. If you will excuse me, I'd like to be under way within the hour."

Kitty settled into her new quarters with some trepidation. This was, after all, the captain's quarters. Where else was Captain Dexter going to hold briefings, dole out assignments and hold Captain's Mast, if that should become necessary? She began to feel that she'd begun too harshly with this new captain.

"Things aren't that bad, I've been told," Maggie said. "Captain Dexter ordered that the first ones to double and triple up would be the ship's officers, of which we're a part in one sense of the word. So, five of us are sharing quarters originally designated—functionally spacious, I might add—for one. Captain Dexter herself, along with her executive officer and one other, are sharing the Exec's cabin, and so on and so forth. The regular crew are hardly suffering at all."

The baron interrupted his wife. "I've spoken with the executive officer and been assured that most common areas have been turned into communal living quarters, with a few exceptions. Gymnasiums are now dormitories, rooms that originally held three now hold five, and any room that was designated as a private room for a department head and has a private bath is doing triple duty. Dexter has seen to it that the officers were the first, and there has been almost no dissension from the crew. Duties have been assigned on a rotating basis so there'll be a minimum of personnel in any one room at any time, affording the most privacy possible. Crews will sleep in shifts, and the laundry will be working overtime to keep linens clean. Some recreational facilities have been kept intact for exercise and the working off of aggressions."

Brandon looked at the three women present. "You gals will have the captain's cabin, Diana included. A cot has been fabricated and moved in. And we men will make do with that and the couches out here. We'll have to work out a restroom rotation, of course, but it'll only be for about a year—less if Dexter has her way. She's diverting power from the weapons core to the engines and moving us along at a slightly higher clip than otherwise predicted. The *Jerra Nep* has the same modifications and will keep up all the way. All in all, we should be back in Earth space in about nine months instead of eleven."

Kitty stood silently for a moment, then said, "Okay, it seems fair enough, but I'll conduct an inspection of my own in the near future. First, though, I want to speak to Maggie in private." She nodded her head at the room designated for the three women's sleeping quarters. "The rest of you make yourselves comfortable for a little bit."

As soon as the door closed on them, Kitty whirled on the aging member of her inner circle, asking, "What was that 'Your Grace' business about, and why did you hush me up?"

The baroness smiled as memories came back to her mind of a young woman who'd recently come to power. "You never were one to mince words or pull punches, were you, my dear? I'm afraid you're going to be even more of a legend than ever. I know you don't like the position you're in right now, but after your fight with sel Garian... well, the 'Your Grace' thing probably just slipped out after you threatened to wipe the deck with the captain of this ship. After all, that *is* what the Shiravans call their Matriarch."

Kitty slumped down on one of the beds and put her head in her hands, elbows on knees. "Oh, shit," she muttered. "I've been elevated to royalty. Are people going to start bowing as I go by?" She looked up at the baroness standing over her. "And just how did Captain Dexter know about that fight? As soon as it was over, we made tracks for this ship."

"As I understand it, the whole thing was filmed by the gig's pilot and co-pilot and beamed to all the ships in the fleet in the all too likely event of your death. It was hoped that it would keep Simon from going... what is it you young people say these days? Nuclear? There's no way you're going to get all the copies erased, especially since we've already started to get under way."

Kitty remembered thinking much the same before the

fight, but with all that had happened since, she had simply forgotten. She felt the subtle vibrations in the deck plates transmitting themselves through her body as soon as she let the desire to find all the copies of that fight go.

The baroness pulled herself up to her full height, which was not inconsiderable when she wanted to be imposing. "And there's absolutely nothing wrong with being royalty, young lady. Remember, no royal line ever started out that way. They started out as junkyard dogs, as you Americans say, and fought their way to the top. And it does have its advantages. Look at how you deferred to me in the beginning. And how you chose me to come along and help you with negotiations with royalty, alien though it be."

The older woman looked down at the younger—not just from height but from the distance of age. The baroness usually tried to hide her experience and brains from the world, with the exception of Freddie, of course, but she watched as the young woman's shoulders slumped. "What? You haven't become used to the power, the prestige, the deference that are accorded to you? Has it been decreed that these things be done? I think not," the baroness continued in an obvious parody of royalty, right hand held aloft. "Rather, your subjects render them unto you freely."

Changing tack, Maggie sat down next to Kitty and put an arm around her shoulder. "Of course, you've become used to it, but it's been an unconscious assumption on your part. And that's why people follow you. True, your being one of the Firsters carries a lot of weight. But the fact that you don't rule by decree and walk among the people affects the minds of many, not to mention that you led a crucial alliance/trade mission personally.

"Speaking on behalf of all those who've followed you into space, let me say that *that* experience is harrowing in itself. And what we're doing right now is several orders of magnitude higher. And I can safely say that countless others on Earth feel as I do and regret missing the opportunity to help personally." The baroness's voice dropped an octave or two, even though there was no one to overhear. "What if your alliance is opposed when you get back? We've been out of touch for over a year, and we have another nine months to go. There's no telling what response your Alliance will bring to the power structure in existence when we return."

Even repeated trips to the *Federal Case's* den didn't bring any insight as to what to expect when she returned home. There were too many variables, and she couldn't *see* like Simon could. He compared it to playing chess, but she just couldn't envision as many variables as he could. Each decision led to certain results, but most were altered along the way by the intervention of others, something she had no control over, so things became hazy quickly for her. She was still only able to see things in the short-term. Simon knew that, and that explained the packet of orders to be opened under specific circumstances.

Kitty understood, as well, the wisdom of Maggie's words, but she couldn't envision any massive changes that could occur while she was gone. More ships, certainly, and another possible attack given the distances involved and the predicted strength of the enemy's power systems, but neither Lucy nor Simon would let things get too far out of hand. Of course, she had the mutiny of the *Federal Case* on the negative side of her own accomplishment list, so there wouldn't be much room to talk. On the other hand, if things had gone *well* back home...

Korgan Garmon, The Garmon now, faced the legacy of his distant predecessor. It was a Garmon who had captured and killed the crew of the first destroyer to set down on their world, and it was a Garmon who had ruled from that point on, mostly. Now, with the advent of these humanz, it might be possible for him to finally unite the tribes and unify the planet.

The shipyards of three different bases were his to use, although only one was fully functional, and that one was working overtime to replace ships lost in skirmishes against the humanz. And he needed all three to be able to compete with this new threat.

Of all of his senior sub-commanders, only three weren't related. The others were sibs or half-sibs, so he commanded considerably more respect, unlike the Korvil who had grown fat off the successes of his ancestors. He would keep in mind the line that had raised him to this exalted level.

He hadn't considered the fact that there would be so much to do in the way of actual governance, having planned to have his particular appointees step in and take charge of a system that had steamrolled forward for two hundred farat. Colonization planets for the burgeoning male population was an ongoing problem. It was either that or the number of ritual combats would go up due to too many males living too close together. Population space was a must, and this world these humanz inhabited would make a perfect place to let some of his cockier sub-lieutenants have a land grant. Let them deal with the pesky humanz while he concentrated on the stinging tactics of the Shiravi.

Of course, most of what was known about the humanz was hearsay. Most, if not all, of the people who'd come into contact with the two humanz captured several farat back were dead. Most ships that entered the humanz system never came out. Lately, ships that merely patrolled areas around the human homeworld just quit reporting in. And on the Shiravan front, something of the same thing was going on. He held in his hand a dispatch from an outpost only three systems away from the Shiravan homeworld. It had been provided by the sole ship to escape the destruction of six of his ships. And the humanz only lost one and a few small fighters. There were humanz fighting on both sides of the Garmon Empire now, it was plain to see. Rumors of invincible ships—impossibly fast, hard-to-hit individual fighters with an uncanny ability to be where they weren't supposed to be—did nothing to instill any bravery in the hearts of his followers. Tactics were going to have to change. No longer could the Garmon just run wild over their provinces but would have to proceed with some caution. It seemed that there was another alpha male in the neighborhood. The Garmon himself would have to hunt...

Kitty stalked the decks, ready to explode, as the ship sailed through hyperspace. She didn't realize she was really just nervous about coming home after such an absence until the baroness spoke to her quietly. "You wonder if things have changed drastically in your absence, and you worry secretly about your husband. Take my advice and relax. What has happened, has happened. Don't you think he's as worried about you? And he doesn't even know you're on your way home, so you have the advantage over him. Now, you'll deal with whatever awaits you in just a few more months in your own way and in your own time. Just don't obsess about the negatives. There lies madness, especially when you spend so much time in that dome."

The months wore away until they became mere weeks and finally days. Kitty had written and rewritten her report countless times, sometimes changing a single comma, other times deleting and re-writing entire passages. One day, one version of the story seemed more appropriate, and on another day, something entirely different would seem to be the focal point of her whole report. Other times, the whole thing seemed too ridiculous to even consider turning in.

Finally, the intercom called out, "All personnel prepare for emergence from hyper. Nav and Helm, prepare for immediate maneuvering." Kitty dithered between going to the bridge or following orders. Orders won out. She could get to the bridge in a matter of minutes as soon as the 'all clear' was given. She settled onto her bunk just in case there was any maneuvering to be done and waited for the body-wrenching twist as the ship entered normal space.

The intercom came to life, Captain Dexter showing her awareness of the insecurity that lack of knowledge produced. "Ladies and gentlemen, we've just entered the Oort cloud of our own system. We'll follow standard procedures, listen to broadcasts, and strip nearby buoys of any information. For the moment, all personnel are to return to duty stations."

Kitty slipped out of the webbing that was holding her to the bed and headed for the bridge. As she walked the halls, the red lights of emergency stations clashed in her mind because of the lack of any indication of possible action. She stepped up to stand beside the captain.

Captain Dexter looked at her and said, "Ah, Madam Herald, I was just about to send for you. Welcome to Earth space."

Kitty glanced at the various screens as she answered automatically, "Thank you, Captain. What have we got so far?"

"We're receiving two different signals. The first mentions a time several months after we left Earth space. And it takes those kinds of signals about two years to get here, so I think our physicists are going to have to consult with the ghost of Einstein to rewrite the laws of relativity."

"It beats getting back and finding everybody you ever knew either old or dead," Kitty said, suddenly aware of just what it was that had made her so nervous. There was still plenty of time to get Simon into a regen chamber

The captain said, "The second signal has an IFF that says it's the *TAS Venture*, on-station to greet guests from the general direction in which the Herald disappeared. Seems to be a repeating signal."

"Can we micro-jump about half the distance and then send out our own signal, Captain?" Kitty asked quietly. It would be unseemly to appear to give her orders on her own bridge.

"I don't see why not, Madam Herald, since the orders I've just unsealed indicate that we do exactly that in somewhat different words." She turned to her crew. "Comm, prepare an IFF to be sent as soon as we come out of micro-jump. Be sure to include the Shiravans as well. Nav, plot the jump. Helm, prepare to execute."

Nav was first to respond. "Course plotted, routed to Helm."

A smooth switch in voices, "Coordinates confirmed. Prepared to jump on command."

Comm said, "IFF with note attached ready to send."

Captain Dexter said, "Nav, prepare an escape jump, if you would be so kind. Call it an exercise in futility, but do it. Have it ready to dump to Helm on my command. Helm, if you get that second jump order, just do it."

Captain Dexter held up an envelope. "The *Raptor's* Captain hand-delivered this when she knew I would be in command of our return flight. I was specifically forbidden to mention it in order to keep from heightening alarm among the crew until the last minute. And you've got to admit, the ship name matches one on the list. And, I've got half a dozen other sealed envelopes that deal with specific circumstances."

Kitty's eyes went to a list at the bottom of the set of orders. "The *Venture* is certainly on here, as well as the captain's name," she noted. "And this is Simon's handwriting. Have you sent the signal?"

"Well, no Ma'am, I haven't," the captain started to say.

Kitty cut her short but spoke quietly. "My mission to Shiravi was a diplomatic one. Your job—to get me there and back safely—is purely a military one. You will execute any sealed orders immediately and worry about my reactions to them later. I'm sure that to err on the side of caution is prudent. Besides, I got a message from Captain Kane and didn't tell you either," she said and shrugged sheepishly. "Now my life is back in the hands of others again. Can I assume that we'll be going to Vesta before Earth?"

"Oh, yes, Madam Herald. That's what our orders call for if you read all the way to the bottom." She turned back to her crew. "Nav, execute your jump and prepare to accept additional jump data. Helm, prepare your dump. Comm, prepare to send your signal."

Space twisted around them, and Kitty felt a wave of nausea pass through her—only for a second but noticeable. "Signal sent," Comm said. "Eight minutes to acquisition, sixteen minimum to reply. I got five bucks says it takes twenty-one minutes for the reply to come back." That was giving the *Venture's* captain five minutes to get the message and reply.

"Twenty-two, for five," said the woman at Helm.

"Twenty-three," said the young man at the weapons panel.

Captain Jeremy Trent of the *TAS Venture* was going to lose the bet for all of them. He had eaten early, exercised for about an hour in a one-ten grav field, showered, held his morning reports meeting, and now had nothing to do but sit there and look captainly during the final six hours of his shift. This was his first time on picket duty, but the Herald was due to return sometime soon. Wouldn't it be a feather in his cap if it happened while *his* ship was on station? Even better, on his watch? It was a story that would procure him many a beer if he told it right. But first, a signal had to come in.

He was, therefore, shocked when a signal *did* come in from the *Federal Case*, one of the ships that had gone to the Shiravan homeworld. But the captain hailing him wasn't the one listed on his papers. Within one minute, he had his Comm officer send a reply. "Welcome back to Earth space, *Federal Case*, but I require an explanation as to why Captain Breen is not in command."

Almost as soon as his Nav officer had acquired a location and ID on the ship, an answer came back. This time it was female. "Captain Trent, I presume? This is Herald Hawke. I require immediate assistance. If you'd be so kind as to let us slave to your controls, you can jump into Vesta space without raising any alarms. Explanations concerning Captain Breen have been classified top-secret and cannot be discussed over an open channel."

Kitty silently regretted having snatched the initiative from the captain, but she couldn't help herself. She waited impatiently while the minutes ticked down to reply time. "*Federal Case*, I have a positive ID on the Herald's voice. I'll be happy to piggyback you and the Shiravan vessel into Vesta Base."

The Nav officer said, "Ma'am, I have a jump plotted that will bring us within one hundred thousand miles of the *Venture*. We can use in-system drive to close with her from there."

The Captain looked once at Kitty, shrugged her shoulders, and said, "Weapons operators, stay alert. Power will not be cut to weapons until I give the okay." Turning to her bridge crew she said, "Helm, accept the course change and execute. Keep escape route for backup and inform the *Jerra Nep*."

At a distance of one hundred thousand miles, radio was an effective means of communication. There was less than one second from send to receive, and the same for reply time. "Captain Dexter, why are your weapons powered up? My Tac officer reports multiple lock-ons from your gun batteries."

"And think, Captain Trent," Dexter replied, "that every one of those lock-ons is manual. I'll bet that if you check your scans, you'll see that none of your systems will record the use of any of my targeting systems. My gunners have become very good at their jobs in the recent past."

Letting the comment go unnoticed, Captain Trent asked, "Will you open your computer to mine so we can move on to Vesta?"

Captain Dexter nodded to Helm and made a vague motion with her hand that meant, "Go ahead." She also ordered all weapons systems shut down and secured.

Almost immediately, a message came over the comm. "Thanks, Captain. I'm not supposed to escort ships with hot weapons into Vesta Base. But since it was the Herald, I was going to overlook the caution as battle jitters, coming as you did from alien space."

Kitty spoke up as the *Federal Case* closed on the *Venture*. "Tell me, captain, what has happened to cause such stringent measures amongst our own ships?"

"Madam Herald, there have been two ships that have mutinied against Alliance Command. We've been able to keep them from Earth, but until we allow them access, hostages have been taken and held to try and force our hand."

"Again?" Kitty muttered to herself. Just how stupid were these people? Even the captains of the ships must know that their actions wouldn't get Earth the technology it wants. Sure, they'd eventually be able to build power plants using cores stripped from ships or fighters, but they wouldn't be able to graft that technology onto existing Earth technology, and the power plants would run out soon enough. An idea occurred to her. "Have there been any moves made against any of the fuel depots?"

The young captain said, "None that I'm aware of, ma'am," with a touch of uncertainty in his voice.

"If either or both of those ships think to take a fuel depot, we could have a problem. They'd have access to enough raw material to make several dozen major cores and hundreds of smaller ones. Fortunately, one of the most devious men I ever met has already got a plan for just such an event. What I want to know is, why hasn't he used it?"

Captain Trent said, "Ma'am, I'm just a newly appointed ship captain. I don't need this kind of intrigue. I don't know who you're talking about, but my Nav officer says we're now ready to jump for Vesta. Are you ready?"

Kitty looked at Captain Dexter, who looked to her Helm officer. Helm looked over her shoulder and said, "The computer is accepting new orders and preparing to jump." Her fingers flew over her boards. "It appears that our projected course will bring us to Vesta Base in about fifteen minutes. Our parking spot is about a thousand miles behind the base."

Kitty spoke to the *Venture's* captain. "It would appear that technology wins again, Captain Trent. All our boards show green for jump. You may give the word any time." For a moment, a portion of her conversation with the baroness about assumption of power rose to the top of her mind, and she realized the truthfulness of it, finally.

Kitty walked into Lucy's office and said, "I like what you've done with the place. Looks real homey."

Lucy just leaned back in her chair and looked at Kitty for a full minute before speaking. "You're back. I quit." She stood up and moved away from the chair, waving to it theatrically. "I'll stay on long enough to bring you up to speed, though."

"Right, thanks. I appreciate it. I know that sounds trite, but I really *do* mean it. You can fade back into the background if you want. Administrator of Vesta Base, again?" Kitty asked, stepping up to her friend and hugging her hard. "I'm sorry to have done this to you, Lucy, but I'm back now, and I'll get it under control right away. First," she said, sitting down in one of a pair of comfortable chairs to one side of the room, "Why hasn't Simon taken care of this mutiny bullshit already?"

Lucy laughed. "You were right. He got Robert to take him on one of his deep space patrols. We're encountering more and more Garmon lately in what we're now calling the outer reaches—the nearby systems we've declared as our buffer zone, so to speak. Kind of like sharks smelling blood in the water."

"Which is exactly why," Kitty said firmly, "we're going to finish this mutiny thing first and get back to doing what we do best—protecting our planet from big, angry teddy bears."

"How are you going to derail the mutiny? The two ships, *Avenger* and *Kill Zone*, are parked out in the rings of Saturn, waiting for orders. We're effectively blocking all transmissions. Seems like those guys gave their bosses some of our comm gear so they can stay connected. We caught on and put jammers between them and Earth."

Kitty leaned back in the chair and placed her feet, ankles crossed, on a bare spot on the top of the huge desk. "How? With misdirection, Luce, and a bit of information that only three people have. I need two wolf packs to go on a small jaunt. I promise not to keep them long and to give them back in good repair, plus the two mutinied ships."

"I can pull them away from Base defense," Lucy said slowly, "if you're sure you can pull this off."

"Oh, I can do it, all right. I just need one specific ship—the *Heinlein*."

A smile played across her face when Lucy said, "The *Heinlein*? She's just a training ship, these days, along with most of the other surviving Firster ships, several of which are closer than the *Heinlein*. Why her?"

"I'll tell you after the fact, but I gotta know something else first: who's been picked up on Earth? Same as last time? Family and friends of family?"

"Pretty much," Lucy confirmed, "but it seems that some were warned ahead of time and managed to get away before being picked up. My folks, your aunts, Simon's parents, and several dozen other families seem to have just up and disappeared."

"Would the Brandts and Colliers be among those missing?" Kitty asked quietly.

"Definitely," Lucy said. "One of the first ones checked on. Why?"

Kitty grinned. "Collier senior was a protester back during Nam. He helped a lot of people keep out of government control. I feel his hand in this somewhere, as well as Simon's."

Lucy had been busy typing on a laptop as they spoke. She looked up from the screen and said, "You'll have your two wolf packs and the *Heinlein* here in about forty hours. What are you going to do until then?"

"First," Kitty said with anticipation in her voice, "I'm going to spend a couple of hours immersed in hot water, and then I'm going to eat something. After that, I'm going to threaten the planet Earth with death and destruction if they don't let my people go! Then, I think I'll take a nap." Her voice had gotten steadily icier until it finally cracked, and she started laughing. "That should be enough for my first day back."

Two days passed before Kitty felt reasonably up to speed enough to make her first public appearance and make good on her promise. She started off by making an early morning appearance at the Comm Shack. Although any place with a radio could be called a comm shack, like a room aboard a spaceship, so could entire structures, and this particular one had taken on a life of its own. Officially designated as the Communications Center, the Comm Shack acted as post office for Base personnel and was an unofficial meeting place for people looking for word from home. On this particular morning, the arrival of the Terran Herald produced unexpected activity. Within minutes of her arrival, the department head showed up. "How may I help you, Madam Herald?"

"I need to tape a message to be sent to Earth. That means a recording studio or room or whatever, a couple of techs, and a few minutes of their time. While you assemble what I need, I'll be across the street at that small coffee shop I saw on my way in. Please send someone over when you're ready to record." Offering the poor man no chance to say yes, no, or go to hell, she turned and walked out of the room with Lucy strolling alongside. Somebody on Earth was going to be real sorry, and she was just the person to do something about it.

"I have a problem with being that peremptory," Lucy said, "which is why I'm so glad you're back. Now the headaches are yours."

There weren't supposed *to be any headaches*, Kitty thought miserably. "Okay," she said aloud, "all you have to do is step back and assess your priorities. The... let's call them detainees... on Earth are in no real danger, so we concentrate on the two traitor ships first. You get me the ships I requested, and I'll deliver both sets of mutineers to you, gift wrapped. But after the cuppa we're about to have, I'll make a tape to beam to Earth, telling them that we won't accept the kind of treatment the United States is inflicting on us. They're behind all of this. You know it, I know, it, everyone knows it, and the U.S. knows we know. They're pissed because they didn't get there first, and now they're a second-rate power. They aren't happy that they're the greatest second-rate power; they want more. I'm about to mobilize an entire world against the U.S. through the baron and all the international agencies that would just love to catch them openly doing what they've been railing against for almost two hundred years."

Kitty waited while the seven ships were assembled, her special emphasis on the *Heinlein* causing the most trouble as no one knew exactly where she was due to her training-ship status. While waiting, she taped her message to be sent to Earth with the baron and Margit. Freddie would decide what to do with it.

Eventually, the *Heinlein's* present captain heard the message and dropped into orbit trailing Vesta as if he had been doing that exact thing for years. " Acting Captain Alvarez and the *Heinlein* reporting as ordered," he sent over the radio.

"Welcome to Vesta Base," Kitty said once the call was routed to her quarters. "Would you be so kind as to meet with me at your earliest convenience? I have a special mission for you and your crew."

The acting captain sat ramrod straight in front of the Terran Herald. Mind numbed by the information he'd just received, he couldn't formulate an answer that adequately fit the delicate situation. "You do realize, Madam Herald, that those two ships are state of the art and we're just a first gen. We have shields, yes, and stand a chance against most Garmon and some of the Shiravans still, but not against those two." Kitty watched as the legacy of Simon's idea came full circle. He always encouraged others to speak their minds, sometimes even finding their way to his point of view without much more than a gentle push.

"We have two complete wolf packs along as well." Kitty looked at the young man with a small degree of pity, dropping out of phase when she thought of the *Heinlein's* soon-to-be captain as young. Of course, she was into her forties now, but since her stint in the regen chamber, she looked a fit and trim (she did have to work at the trim part) twenty-six or so. The dichotomy of how old she felt and what she saw in the mirror each day still caused her a lot of confusion.

She came back to the present when her guest finished by saying, "So, my senior officers and I talked this out on the way here. With several other first gen ships more easily accessible than the *Heinlein*, along with better-trained crews, it had to be something about the ship herself that caused you to request us specifically. We just can't figure out what."

Kitty smiled as if she hadn't been off on a tangent and said, "Yes, *Captain*, there *is* something special about the *Heinlein*, although I can't tell you yet. Just trust me when I say that your ship is critical to our mission. As a matter of fact, it's also safe to say that if things should not go as planned, we'll be the first ship shot out of space. I know that's small consolation, but remember, I'll be aboard as well." She smiled sweetly, "That also means that you're now commanding a fully armed ship of war under orders to shoot to kill, if so ordered. Your rank of acting captain is hereby upgraded to full captain. Congratulations, and welcome to the headaches of command."

What a prophetic statement that is!

The young captain left his meeting with a deadline and the first in a long line of headaches. He had two hours to get his crew turned around and ready to proceed to Saturn to face two fourth-generation ships. And he was responsible for the safety of the Herald, as well. His unease rose to fever pitch when, just at the two-hour mark, his Tac officer said, "Sir, I just got off the comm. Vesta Transport Control is beaming the Herald into the reception area. I took the liberty of informing the exec, and he's on the way right now."

A few minutes later, Kitty strode onto the bridge, all business. One of Simon's earliest teachings rose to the top of her mind for a moment—if you act like you know what you're doing, people will follow readily. Aloud, she said, "Captain Alvarez, the fleet will slave all six ships to you. If you would, please have your Helm set coordinates for this location." She handed a slip of paper over to him. Out of habit, he looked at it. It was a string of numbers, followed by the words, 'Saturn's Rings.'

He handed the paper off to his Helm officer and said, "Tactical, accept slave signals from all six ships. Release them as soon as we reach our destination. Helm lay in the course and prepare to execute on my command." He looked at Kitty. "Ma'am, I have no idea what to do now."

"Now," Kitty said grimly, "I'd like to take over your Comm station. When we arrive at our destination, I need to be able to speak to our traitorous captains personally."

As Kitty settled herself into the Comm station, the Tac officer said, "We have acquired six slave signals, Madam Herald." He had no illusions as to who was in charge.

"Thank you, Commander," Kitty said formally. "Captain, you have charge of the formation until we arrive. At that point, the wolf packs will assume attack positions, weapons hot, and the carriers will launch all Mambas. I'll accept responsibility for whatever happens after that."

Captain Alvarez looked as if the weight of the world was on his shoulders. "Very well, Madam Herald. Helm, execute your assigned course."

CHAPTER NINE

During the six-minute hyper-jump across the system, Kitty sat busily at the Comm console, searching for the innocuous file that held the codes she'd been given when she first took command of this very vessel. As its first captain, Simon had informed her that it was the only ship in the fleet that could send out a shutdown order to any other ship, carried on a signal that piggybacked the main, more potent signal. The receiving ship's computer was required to accept the signal and begin shutdown of all but environmental services.

The file it was hidden in was one that most people were unlikely to access, being titled, 'Toilets, Maintenance and Sanitation of.' Especially since the whole file, while a necessary part of the ship's regulations, had been carefully and expertly expanded. It was very unlikely that anyone would read all the way down to section thirty-seven, subsection L. And even if they did, there was nothing there to indicate what the cryptic paragraphs said. It would be immediately labeled a computer glitch and they would try to either rewrite it so that it made sense or delete it, which Simon had made impossible.

The problem was that the other ship had to be receiving—hence, her presence. She expected the two ships to be in contact via whisker lasers, almost impossible to intercept unless one were directly between the two ships, and her personal appearance would have both captains in receive mode. Whether they answered or not was irrelevant as long as they were listening.

The squadron dropped out of hyper and came to a dead halt, looking for the signatures of two full-sized battlecruisers, most likely on standby. Tactical and Navigation spoke up at the same time.

"Targets acquired."

Kitty watched an adjacent console as the squadron dispersed into its prearranged attack pattern. She opened a comm link aimed at the two ships. "This is Katherine Hawke," she said, politely. "I wish to speak with the leader of this rebellion." She knew it was no real rebellion, just two ships primarily manned by people loyal to Earth as opposed to the Alliance. She hoped that by calling it a rebellion she could get one of the captains to respond while the other listened to the exchange. That would be all she needed.

Luckily for her, both ships' captains were anxious to hear what the Terran Herald had to offer in order to keep any bloodshed at a minimum. No sooner did she get confirmation that her signals were being received than she pressed a final button on her console. This one sent the shutdown orders along a shielded signal that would only be recognized by humans after it was too late. Only codes from the *Heinlein* could send the orders to power up since it automatically put the computer in receiving mode.

Curses began to be heard from both ships as first their weapons, then shields, and then power systems shut down to station-keeping. And there was nothing either captain could do. All computer access was frozen until it received the reactivation signal. The only nonessential system left functioning was the short-range comm system. After an interval that literally measured over two hours, the captain of *TAS Avenger* called the small ship sitting alone in front of it.

"All right, Madam Herald." The words sounded like they'd been dragged out with tongs. "The *Avenger* and the *Kill Zone* both acknowledge that we're helpless. We accept that we will be treated as prisoners of war and surrender to you under the Geneva Convention."

Kitty gripped the arms of her chair until her knuckles hurt. "No deal, Captain. You gave oaths to the Alliance. You and your top officers will be tried as traitors in time of war. Any subordinates will be treated less harshly, but you and your senior staffs have stepped over the line."

She waited a full five minutes while the radio stayed silent. Finally, she said, "I grow tired, Captain Sweeney. I just got back from a two-year ordeal dealing with two different alien races. I will not waste my time dealing with traitors among my own kind. You and Captain Brown have until we tow you back to Vesta Base to decide what you're going to do. If you hide behind hostages, it will go even worse than it already is. I'd also like to tell you that while Captain Breen of the *Federal Case* is no longer among the living, his second in command is quite alive and vocal about the treatment she's received at our hands. She'll be allowed to live, as will all of her compatriots, much as I might personally wish otherwise. I'll let you speak to her before you give me your answer."

Kitty switched channels and ordered the four battlecruisers to extend their shields to cover the two disabled vessels and tow them back to Vesta.

When it rains, it pours, Kitty thought as she received the

latest dispatch from Vesta. The Nova Group had just reported in—all personnel accounted for, with three Garmon destroyers and a freighter to their credit.

"We didn't even know they had freighters," Robert Greene said in his preliminary report. "It looks like a long destroyer without weapons. Seems like they've got someone with some creativity over there."

Now, she was going to have to chew out her own husband, in private of course, but he had left Jerry Chapman, a dedicated second-waver, in charge. But she'd fought a duel, so she couldn't be too upset. They were both cut from the same mold, apparently, though you'd never have known it eighteen years ago. "Send word to Nova Group: Job well done. Please disembark Admiral Hawke at Vesta Base before continuing your assigned duties."

She stood up from her position at the Comm station. "Captain Alvarez, take us back to Vesta, if you please."

"Certainly, ma'am. Nav, plot a course for Vesta, send it to Helm, and take the bridge. Madam Herald, if you will join me in my ready room?" The young captain stood smoothly, stepped down from his chair, and walked purposefully toward the door to his ready room, appearing for all the world as if this were just another exercise. Stopping at the door, he turned to make sure all his orders were being followed. His Nav officer was just sitting down in the command chair, and the Herald— *God forbid,* he thought—was following him to the door.

He moved one step closer to the door, letting the sensor recognize a body present and open the door. He waved the Herald through before him and followed, allowing the door to close. Moving to a position behind his desk, he didn't sit. He knew that technically he was the ranking person in the room as captain of an active warship, but he just couldn't sit down before the Herald did. After all, not only was she the Herald, she was a Firster, and the first captain in of Alliance. She was looking curiously around the room. Several pictures adorned the walls, souvenirs of previous captains, and while the furniture was adequate, it was a bit threadbare. "I think this is the same furniture Simon requisitioned when he first took command, Captain," the Herald said, a nostalgic tone in her voice. "Have Stores replace it with something more appropriate, if you feel like it. The Herald's office will pick up the tab."

Alvarez looked a bit shamefaced at the furniture. It was really no place to host such an august personage as the Herald, but it would have to do. Almost eight years of countless people moving through and sitting in this room had left their marks, abrasions, and stains here and there. The Herald sat down on a couch that was set to one side of the room.

"So long ago," she said, almost to herself. She looked up at him. "I guess you have a right to know about what happened out there. You'll be the fourth person to know, so don't go spreading it around. You see, the *Heinlein* is a little bit different from every other ship in the fleet. It carries codes that will shut down any other ship as long as that ship has its radio on receive. All I did was input the codes while we were on the short jump out there, and when I had one confirmed connection, I knew the other had to be listening, so I sent the codes out on a weak carrier beam that was camouflaged by the main beam. Their computers had no choice but to shut down all but essential services."

Alvarez nodded, finally seating himself. "So, now the

cruisers can tow them back to HQ," he said letting the familiar name for Vesta slip out.

"Yes," the Herald replied, apparently not noticing the lapse. "And then we get to hold trials for all of them. Treason, mutiny, theft of Alliance property—oh, I'm sure our lawyers can find a dozen more charges to throw at each of the conspirators, or agents, or whatever they want to call themselves."

Alvarez blanched a bit. "Treason is punishable by death, Madam Herald," he said in protest.

"Yes, it is," Kitty confirmed. "In times of war, treason can certainly be punished by a quick trip out of an airlock. But that's not going to happen, at least not yet. Most of the folks involved are just doing their jobs and consider themselves patriots. They take orders from people high up in their own governments, and their oaths don't mean anything to them. That's why three ships were taken over."

"Three? Which other ship has mutinied?" Alvarez was truly perplexed.

"Captain Breen of the *Federal Case* decided to mutiny while in still in Shiravan space," Kitty said flatly. "He and his top officers left us no choice but to take her back under less than optimal conditions. It's fortunate, in a way. We ended up with a place to put the survivors of the *Vega* and jobs for them once we'd taken the *Case* back. I'm definitely going to rename that ship as soon as possible."

Captain Alvarez hadn't had time to get any of the scuttlebutt from the returning ships, but he shuddered and promised himself never to cross this lady.

Not long after Kitty stepped into Captain Alvarez's

ready room, she felt the internal twist that told the experienced spacefarer of a hyper-jump. Six minutes later, after a brief conversation and a bit of reminiscing, the *Heinlein's* training crew brought her into an almost perfect orbit trailing Vesta.

Kitty stood up and said, "Well, it's been a pleasure, Captain. Tell your crew that I'm proud of each and every one of them. I'll put a word in at Personnel about the professionalism shown by your crew today." She reached to her belt and grabbed her comm link. "Vesta Transport Control, this is Herald Hawke. I request a beam-out from these coordinates to local 0/0."

A short delay ensued while the Transport Coordinator verified her identity, and then a small voice came from her link, "Madam Herald, transport will commence in ten seconds." She had time to replace her comm link and sketch a quick salute at the Captain, and the *Heinlein's* ready room disappeared in a haze of blue sparkles.

Kitty waited impatiently for Simon to get in from the patrol group. She didn't know yet whether she was going to laugh, cry, yell, scream, hit him, hug him, or what, but she couldn't wait to see him. A part of her just didn't feel complete without him there. Lord knew she'd had enough alone time to have learned that much. Right now, though, her anger was turned to one of the new strictures all patrols had to follow upon return to Earth space—look around first and see if any enemy could be sighted. If so, attack them first and report to headquarters as soon as possible so help could be dispatched. It added at least twenty hours to an incoming ship's arrival time.

The Alliance wasn't going to be caught napping again. A steady stream of ships was coming out of the yards and beginning to make their presence known in all systems surrounding Earth, especially those known to be on the Garmon side of the niche being carved out. Ships permanently guarded the four bases and the *Galileo,* as well as Earth, on a rotation that allowed more personnel to train with the equipment. Hence, the continuing existence of the *Heinlein* and her surviving sisters, serving as training ships.

Kitty had Vesta Traffic Control keep her updated on the arrival of Nova Group. Simon would surely know of her arrival by now, not to mention her precipitous dash across the solar system to squelch a mutiny, which he might have headed off or at least contained earlier if he hadn't gone off risking his life unnecessarily. The secret of the *Heinlein* hadn't been passed on after Kitty left, so even Vice Admiral Chapman, who had served as the *Heinlein's* captain for a short time, didn't know her special nature.

Oh, this is going to be a convoluted meeting, she thought. *I haven't seen him in almost two years, but I needed him, dammit, and he sent me off alone*. Sure, she had the treaty between the Alliance and Shiravans, but she'd lost the *Vega,* and then there was the matter of the rebellion aboard the *Federal Case*. She blanched and a cold sweat broke out all over her body. *sel Garian!* her mind screamed. *When he sees a copy of that, I'm toast*.

At first, Kitty didn't know whether to be the frosty superior officer with a few bones to pick or the long-separated wife. The wife won out as she waited in Vesta's Transport Control. She wore everyday BDU's, but nonetheless, her diminutive stature and totally white hair gave her away. A small space seemed to surround her wherever she went, so she finally opted for a wall near the transport hexes.

At first her heartbeat was up, and then she developed cold sweats. When those went away, she had the shivers from the air conditioning. She'd just decided on a bit of enthusiasm mixed with just the right amount of Herald aloofness when she spotted Simon appearing in one of the columns of blue sparks. All thought went elsewhere, and she threw herself into his arms. For just a little while, she wanted to be the one who was protected rather than the bastion behind which everyone else shielded themselves.

She let the power that she always felt in his arms flow through her, giving solace to parts of her body she didn't know were in pain. A feeling of complete relaxation ran through her, and she lost herself in the feeling of his arms and the pressure of their bodies being pressed together. It was almost funny—she could feel his strong, slow heartbeat as a backdrop to her own, swift and fluttery. The kiss was at first cautious, then fervent, and then, as they remembered where they were, a bit more restrained.

"So," he said, pushing her away to arm's length so they could look into each other's eyes. "I get sent to the rear for my own protection, and you lead ships in battle, fight duels, and suppress mutinies with underpowered, outgunned ships. We're going to have to have a long talk about priorities soon."

"It's been almost two years since we've seen each other. Let's let recriminations go for a while," she begged as she wrapped her arms around his waist. "I want to know how you've been holding up. What we've each been doing can wait for official time. All I want right now is to hold you and remind myself that this is real; this is where I belong; this is where I was destined to be." She leaned in and kissed him again as if she needed something from him just to stay alive.

Simon, for his part, had been just as anxious as his wife about their meeting. Two years they'd been separated. Two years he'd been faithful, though he'd had more than one opportunity to step over the line. He kept current on all the rumors, that being one of the functions of the nondescript little man walking beside him. Any public meeting between himself and any senior female officer or office holder other than his wife eventually found its way into the tabloids, something that had found its way to Vesta Base almost magically, as they never appeared on any ships' manifest. The function of the little man was to see to it that the rumors never got out of control. His official title was Public Relations Officer for the Admiral's Office. In fact, he kept the rumors to a minimum by acting as an unofficial adviser on most of Simon's business dealings with just about everyone.

Kitty had accomplished so much in her travels, while he'd only increased the size of the fleet, and that only by the predetermined amount that the bases were able to produce, a function almost anyone could have performed. He still needed to see that video of her fighting sel Garian. The little man told him that it was a phenomenal exhibition of skill, grace, and restraint.

He'd never quite remember the exact words they first spoke to each other, but he'd never forget that kiss. After an interminable time, he noticed that people around them were deliberately ignoring their reunion as they moved about their business. "Your place or mine?" he asked quietly, breathing in one ear, infuriating her and making her laugh at the same time.

"I think mine's closer," she replied. "Not by much, but I've been living in mine for the past couple of days, and yours is going to need to be aired out and have all the spoiled stuff removed from the fridge. I sure don't want to be there when you open *that* door."

An interminable time later, conversation interspersed with other amusements, the two lovers had finally sated themselves for the time being. "Okay," Simon said, all business, "I've waited to see this. I have the fight between you and sel Garian cued up and ready to play. You know I'm going to see it anyway. Why don't you give your version of it as it goes down?"

Kitty sighed, a child caught in a terrible wrongdoing. "I know I shouldn't have let her yank my chain, but she did, and I fell into her trap. Fortunately, my martial arts instructor, you, my love," she said, bowing in his direction, "taught me to find my balance in almost any situation. Although I'd never had to fight with swords before, your training let me adapt in time to save both my own life *and* the treaty. Of course, for them those were just knives and not swords."

She just shrugged, "They were given to me as a gift after I whipped her. I'll bet they're outside my door right now, waiting for me to get up and bring them in out of the corridor. Or, more likely, there's an orderly there, guarding them and waiting for me to tell him/her to bring them in."

Simon turned the wallscreen on with a touch of the remote and called up a still of Kitty waiting for sel Garian to arrive at the dueling grounds. "What was going through your mind at this point?" he asked clinically.

"I was thinking that I had let her maneuver me into an area of her choosing. I had, actually, but I was more able than she'd guessed. I won. Don't ask how, because I have no idea. The knife just seemed to become an extension of my arm. If I had to guess, I'd say that since I come from a higher-gravity planet, her knife became a sword that was just right for my superior strength."

Simon let the tape play while the two women chose their weapons, and then let it go on a bit longer, showing Kitty trying to find her center with this new weapon. The image on the screen found a one-handed grip that seemed to work for her and turned to her red opponent. "Come Manura, let's play," the image said. "I want to find out what color Shiravan blood is, and you have outlived your usefulness."

What ensued, seen from the perspective of the pilots in the shuttle, was nothing short of phenomenal, as his public relations officer had promised. Kitty parried each and every blow sel Garian drove at her almost negligently. And she stood in the classic pose Errol Flynn had made famous—right foot forward, left foot back, her sword the only defense from the razor-sharp blade of her opponent. When she dropped down and came up inside sel Garian's defenses, she sliced her slightly across the stomach. Then, she tucked herself into a small ball and knocked her opponent's legs out from under her with a leg sweep, making her sprawl in the dirt When she placed her sword tip at sel Garian's throat and rose to her feet, Simon stopped the replay. "What I want to know is: why did you spare her life? I would have killed her on the spot with no questions asked."

"And you would have been perfectly within your rights to do so, but that also would have been screwing up in a big way, husband mine. kep Parrasine still needs somebody to finish her education in the art of being a spymaster. At least we know sel Garian and what she might do, so we think we know what her successor might do. Plus, the Matriarch thinks of sel Garian as an aunt—a little on the dotty side nowadays but still a valuable resource. I had every right to kill her, and she *would* have killed me, but I'd garnered support among many different factions on Shiravi. Remember, to most of them I'm Kath-e-rin, the Goddess of Light. I represent fertility, life, mercy, and all of the good things in life. For me to go and kill one of their most revered personages, or feared, depending on who you are, would have cast me in the role of Kath-e-vel, the Spirit of Darkness, bringer of chaos, famine, pestilence, and death. I decided that if I have to be a goddess, I want to be a good one, so I let her live."

Simon let the rest of the video play out with no more comments beyond one. "Remind me not to piss you off, okay?"

"No problem, lover. Besides, I'd just been adopted as Linnas's sister the night before. It would have been bad form to kill my own aunt." She changed directions abruptly before Simon had time to think about that one. "We do have a situation that needs to be cleaned up once and for all. Some of our people, and in a lot of cases, their families and friends when they themselves couldn't be arrested, have been detained. Again. I'm not going to stand for it. The United States has been trumpeting to the world that it is the supreme champion of human rights. I'm about to rub their noses in the dark underbelly of their own government.

"One thing the government hasn't done is remove the wristbands from the detainees. That lets us get good visuals of what is happening, and audio as well. In some cases, we have very good documentaries on what our people and their folks are going through. Since we know the locations—all near major cities so we can't make another lake like the one in North Dakota—we have asked the United Nations, the International Red Cross, and Amnesty International to sort of break the ice for us. The only downside is that the prisoners are being treated very well and carefully, with full medical facilities, proper meals, television, comfortable beds in private rooms, families not separated, all that sort of thing. It's all posturing. Politics. And I have to get down in the mud and roll around in it with them. That's why I feel so slimy at the end of the day.

"You should see the cockroaches scurry for their dark little hiding places. The politicians who quietly voted for the arrests and detentions are now crying loudest to end it. I guess it might help to know that I sent each one an individual note detailing what could happen out of a clear blue sky, like a rock falling on their house while they're still in it. In some cases, I even appended a list of alternate locations we found out about, some of which came as a complete surprise to the recipients of the letters. Most of them still can't figure out how we found out about the government safe houses we named, and having your mail arriving in a shower of blue sparks is still pretty unsettling for most of humanity."

Simon looked at her curiously. "How did you get that kind of information?"

Kitty smiled. "*I* didn't. While I was gone, Lucy cultivated Agent Daniels. Remember him? It seems that it wasn't hard to do since he was pretty disappointed with the way things were going. He dug through the FBI database, and those systems are all interconnected you know—FBI, CIA, DIA, DOD, Interpol, the whole thing, and with his clearance, he got what we needed to know, then deleted his presence from the system and came over to the Alliance."

"So," Simon said slowly, "you've got senators, representatives, congressmen and probably even the president believing that we're likely to start dropping rocks on them if they don't give in?" At Kitty's nod, Simon sighed. "You're forgetting one thing, dear," he said, and sadness tinged his voice.

"What's that?"

"The innate sense of resistance that two hundred years of freedom has instilled in the American people. We're going to have to find some way to back down from the threat of violence and work on getting those groups to embarrass the U.S. for us. It won't look good if we start bombing the planet just to get our people freed. That's got to be a last resort, not a first option."

"Okay, that's what we're doing anyway. The threat of falling rocks is just to show our superior position, not an actual threat. I've had Freddie and Margit working on it from downside, leaking reports through Sarah Parker. She's become quite a celebrity, of late, by the way. And her cameraman turned up. He's one of those survivalist nuts and happened to see Sarah get picked up. Seems he filled up his gas tank and headed out into the hills. That van carries more than just camera equipment, apparently.

"Anyway, I field the irate messages that are coming our way. The U.S. wants to send defense attorneys out here to represent their people. We're holding firm to the idea that they are Alliance citizens by oath, and we'll deal with our own internal affairs ourselves, thank you very much. Actually, I haven't even responded to a single request for an appointment. All ships in orbit around Earth are to ignore any communiques no matter how they arrive or how urgent they sound. I will eventually, grudgingly, allow five or six real live, honest-to-God attorneys to board a ship and come out here as observers only.

"The Brandts and Colliers are keeping the fires stoked under the various groups and have the families of all of our top personnel in safe houses. Sarah Parker is doing a daily column on the subject and being picked up by more papers every day, and more information is coming out every hour. We know that the U.S. government realizes that those wristbands are the source of most of their leaks, but we can only surmise that they've allowed the detainees to keep them to prove that our people aren't being mistreated. They have to know by now the full potential of the wristbands. After all, they've had ample opportunity to see them in action and get access to them through their spies." Kitty leaned back in the lounger and stretched luxuriously.

"I assume Galway is back on Earth, reporting on what he accomplished while he was away?"

"Yes, for all the good it did him. He one-jumped for Earth almost immediately after we got back. Linnas got into a debate with him and he lost. She wouldn't give him the time of day after that, probably because he's male and works for males. I don't know how she got that information," Kitty said innocently, "but she seemed to feel that the only course was to stay with us. It was a good thing that when one of her ships arrived here, one was ready to leave with dispatches detailing the last two years of talks, et cetera. It didn't hurt to report that we have fourteen more ships, plus we've upgraded all of her ships in our space."

"I knew about all but the last three ships," Simon said. "I went on a patrol with Robert Greene and was gone for almost six months."

"I know," Kitty said dryly. "What the hell were you thinking? We can't have both of us gone at the same time. What if we both get killed?"

Simon sat the lounger up straight so he could reach the glass he had set beside the chair. He took a small swallow of the amber liquid and replied, "Hon, I think we've reached the point where this can't be stopped, unless we're wiped out. We have too many ships, too many people on Earth on our side or actively enrolled in the Alliance, and too many contingency plans for this to stop just because we die. We've got Jerry Chapman, Robert Greene, Gayle, Lucy, and a whole host of others to step in if one or both of us should die. Two years ago, I might have said differently, but now we even have a system set up that's moving selected people from place to place like the old underground railroad. We're back to picking up some of our recruits from undisclosed locations in the United States, and the U.S. government has restricted travel to Japan and Switzerland, which has raised holy hell with those two countries. A large part of their income is from tourism. You should hear some of the stuff that's getting flung around in the U.N. We just plain have too many people who want us to succeed. All of this is as of six months ago, of course. We came straight here as soon as the *Nova* made parking orbit.

"Plus, as of six months ago, we're doing a lot better job of screening recruits since we have a man on the inside. But that's only the U.S. agents. Who knows which countries have agents among our newest crews? And who really cares?" Simon leaned back in the chair, feet up, looking at his wife through the V they made.

Kitty's look of surprise made him smile. "Remember, without all of the specs, they can't build anything, and they need our reactors to power the larger weapons, which we won't let them have either. And to tell the truth, I think Daniels has turned some of his fellow agents to our cause. At least they're feeding us information that seems to check out. We keep looking for the hook, but we haven't found one yet."

"Well, I've been back two days and squelched a two-ship mutiny. I've started to pick up on what's going on, but I still need some time. I wish you hadn't made yourself unavailable just now. It made me have to hold Lucy over that much longer. We'll do whatever's necessary to set our people free, just like last time. Maybe we can't be that precise with an asteroid every time, but they don't know that, and they have a new lake in North Dakota that says we can."

She paced back and forth in the very manner she had once chastised Simon for. "We can mess with their GPS systems just by having Mambas park directly beside their satellites for a while at intermittent moments, like a training exercise. Or we can jam all their satellite transmissions to and from any place on Earth. And if we get mad enough, we can disrupt their landlines, which are their securest means of communications. And just imagine the hue and cry if we take television away from the masses. Radio, too. Governments would topple over that alone."

Kitty sat down on the arm of the lounger Simon had taken over and slid down between him and one arm of the chair, her face turned up to his. "Let's leave the details for later. Oh, that reminds me, Linnas gave me two cases of something they call fire wine. I'm going to be very interested in your response to it. But that can wait for later. Right now, I have something else in mind."

Simon watched with interest as one of Kitty's hands crept slowly up his chest and began to wrestle with the top button of his shirt.

CHAPTER TEN

Korgan Garmon studied all the papers before him, which wasn't a normal course of action for a Garmon leader to be taking. One should just work from one's intuition, but his intuition said that these humanz were far more than they seemed. Look at the number of ships that had gone out and hadn't reported in. They'd been experienced ships, captains, and crews, and they'd all faced the same fate: destruction. He looked at the reports from the newly created Watcher Fleet. One small, otherspace-capable ship from each Garmon planet or outpost had been assigned to *not* fight but observe the fight, if there was one, and bring the information directly to homeworld.

The Watchers were reporting higher casualty rates than had been seen since the beginning of Garmon/Shiravi conflicts hundreds of cycles ago. Somehow, these humanz had negated the natural superiority of the Garmons, and that challenge could not be allowed to go unanswered. They would have to be studied carefully before committing any more ships to possible losses.

On the plus side, there were now two fully functional shipyards turning out replacement ships for all those lost. It was going to be difficult to find trained crews to fill them, though. And the time it took to train a Garmon for space travel was... not inconsiderable. Also, some

Garmons just couldn't accept the confined conditions aboard a spaceship of any size.

Maybe what was needed was to acquire more captives. This time the interrogations would deliver more information than before. That was another report he had on the table. He who had no name had squandered a valuable resource by letting the two humanz be rescued. That was one mistake he wouldn't make when *he* took prisoners. They would talk—oh yes, they would.

As the *Federal Case* hypered off the *Raptor's* screens, along with its Shiravan companion, Marsha Kane settled back in her command chair. Almost a year would pass before the *Case* arrived back in Earth space, and she hoped for Kitty's sake that not too much would have changed.

Of course, Marsha thought, the real question should be: is the Alliance ready for the new and improved Kitty? She also hoped her own package reached its destination as soon as possible. After close to a year away from home or reinforcements and dependent on fewer docks and those not yet up to Terran standards, they were going to have to be very careful in their encounters.

Then, she turned her mind to other matters.

The prisoners from the *Federal Case*, the *Avenger*, and the *Kill Zone* stood alone at one end of the *Empower Field* stadium in Denver, Colorado. Those from the *Case* were a bit apart from the others as if they had a disease upon them, which they surely did since they were the only ones to have been involved in any killings during their desertion from the Alliance.

Katherine Hawke, in her persona as Herald of the Terran Alliance, was there today to impose sentence upon them all. It was her toward whom all eyes looked as she stood—small, tense, and white-haired—upon the dais set up for the occasion. The situation had been discussed many times over by everyone with an opinion and a channel to her ear, but hers was the voice that would end the rumors this day.

She stood silent before the microphone, listening to the susurrus of voices around her, knowing it to be the uncomfortable concerns of the crowd that had gathered to hear her speak the words that would condemn some of those miserable souls to death for their parts in bloody mutiny.

This would affect only the few remaining officers and crew of the *Federal Case*. She had been a small part of it, and those memories gave her pause.

She felt more than heard the Rocky Mountain Thunder from the observers who had pressed their way past police barricades upon hearing of the unpublicized event. It had been for the families of the accused only in the beginning, but one person had spoken, then another, and then word had spread like wildfire until the stadium was more than half full, the police and her security teams barely able to contain the mass of bodies waiting, watching to see what would happen.

The prisoners were guarded by a phalanx of laser-armed guards, most of whom had lost friends or loved ones on that miserable day only a year ago. Not constrained by Earthly laws, the Terran Alliance would this day, on her orders, carry out the sentences already imposed on those hapless individuals gathered forlornly in one end zone.

Still, she *was* on Earth and so were the prisoners upon whom she gazed. Her mind's eye saw the bodies surprised and lifeless in the corridors of the *Federal Case* as she and a select boarding party fought to retake the ship that had mutinied in Shiravan space under wartime conditions. Those memories would follow her dreams through a very long life, and she wanted dearly to repay an eye for an eye, but she could not.

In the case of the *Avenger* and the *Kill Zone*, no lives had been lost, so she could in clear conscience merely banish the crews to a life on Earth with no chance of ever leaving the planet again. It was Thomas Breen's hand-picked crew of the *Federal Case* that brought out her bloodlust. She had stalked those bloody decks in search of the mutineers and seen firsthand the brutality of their actions, as well as her own.

The ship had carried survivors of the doomed *Vega* after a fight with the Garmons. They should have returned to Shiravi and allowed those innocents among the rescued to debark before Breen implemented his plans, but something had pushed him over the edge. Perhaps it was her choice to make the *Case* her flagship on the return flight, along with the overcrowding, that had forced his hand. She would never know. He'd been found in his captain's seat with a laser wound burned into the center of his forehead.

Regardless, she now had to deal with the results of his actions and those of his crew. She stepped up to the microphone, and the entire crowd went as silent as the corridors of the *Case* had been. Now she could dispense the justice the dead, both guilty and innocent, had waited for. "I stand here today to speak of oaths taken and lives unnecessarily cut short," she said. Her words echoed in the silence of the open-air arena. "Those who served aboard both the *Avenger* and the *Kill Zone* have been spared the most severe penalties since your actions caused no loss of life. I sentence you to life in prison on the planet Earth with no chance for parole. You will never set foot on an Alliance ship again and will live with the knowledge of what you've lost.

"It is to the survivors of the crew of the *Federal Case* that I address my deepest concerns." She stopped and heard her voice's echo fade away. "Innocent lives were lost during the mutiny and retaking of the *Federal Case*. Survivors of the *Vega* were quartered aboard the *Case*, believing themselves saved from a horrible death in the airlessness of space after a battle with an implacable foe. It was their misfortune to find themselves surrounded by even more vicious enemies—their own race.

"Human history is replete with the taking of the lives of our own kind for many reasons—some sane, most others not. I stand here today to end that practice for the Terran Alliance. I say that there has been enough bloodshed amongst our own." She paused and the voices rose up again. The faces sequestered on the field below her still showed resignation, but on a few, confusion reigned.

"It is within my power to take the lives of those who have violated their oaths and spilled the blood of innocent men and women." She looked around the tiers of people present. Most were too far away for her to read their expressions, but now the sounds were somehow different. "By our laws and my orders, the lives of those officers and crew of the *Federal Case* who survived are forfeit. At my command they could instantly cease to live, but I choose not to avenge blood with blood. It is my decision that those members of the crew of the *Federal Case* shall have their lives spared and be bound forever to this one single planet, knowing what they've done and living with the memories. All sentences of execution are hereby rescinded, and the prisoners are free to go. May God and the Spirits of Space have mercy on your souls."

Katherine turned away from the microphone and was immediately engulfed in a sea of security as she walked into a tunnel leading into the bowels of the stadium, the sounds of Rocky Mountain Thunder again ringing in her ears and traveling up through her feet as she slowly walked back to the shuttle waiting just outside.

She found her seat, let her head fall back against the rest, and closed her eyes, a sign to almost everyone that she wanted to be alone. Unfortunately, she shared the four-chair section with her husband, the admiral, who was going to be a pillar of strength for her whether she wanted him to or not, and her personal aide, Commander Diana Ross, who felt it her duty to interfere as well.

She felt Simon sit down heavily next to her and opened her eyes to see a concerned Diana looking at her from across the small table already stacked with papers. "You two just let me be. We've got a long trip back to Vesta, and I need to start preparing a speech."

"The speech is already written, checked by Diana, and waiting for your approval or changes," Simon said quietly. "Several governments were quite glad to get their people back today, though," he said unhappily. "Too bad we couldn't name even one specifically. But, Lord, the stink being raised over this latest set of abductions. The U.S. is getting bit on the ass big-time."

"Thank you both for wanting to cheer me up, and

thanks for the help with the speech, but I just want it all go away for just a little while, okay?" Even to herself, she sounded testy.

Speech read and set aside for the time being, she turned her thoughts to the war. That was supposed to be the province of the admiral, but she had executive oversight written into the Alliance Constitution as an unbreakable perquisite of the Herald's office. If they followed the pattern humans had become used to, the Garmons were seriously overdue. Could someone on the other side have changed attitudes? Or merely be biding his time? If he bided too much longer, there would be too many ships for the Garmons to try hitting Earth again.

But she now had another problem. There were literally hundreds of thousands of requests asking for a one-way trip to any human-habitable world. It would relieve some of Earth's overcrowding, but not by enough to matter. That would require more ships than they had available just to transport them, much less protect them.

Of course, control was locked in her hands as only the Alliance had the ships to answer those requests. Maybe someday she could claim monarchy over fourteen worlds like her new sister, Linnas, but for now, she was willing to start slowly.

She had Diana bring her all the files on the worlds visited by the teams that were going out on patrol, looking for worlds that would be right for humans. Unfortunately, they were right for the Garmons as well, so precautions would have to be taken to keep the colonists safe.

She never would have figured on this even four years ago, and they had been in space now for ten years. Meeting with the Shiravans, her trip of nearly fifty lightyears to broker a mutual defense treaty, and the acquisition of two sisters—one white, one red—read like the science-fiction story they were already living.

She even had time now to look into ship strength and what they were all doing. Simon had kept the production up, though he wouldn't take any credit for it. Even without the *Clarke* and the *Vega*, there were more than fifty major ships in Alliance service. With eleven human ships on the Shiravan side of the battle zone and twenty-two ships patrolled Earth-space, assisted by nearly twenty Shiravan ships. The battle was now being carried to the enemy on two fronts.

Colonies or outposts had been discovered on both sides of human and Shiravan space, and wolf packs were making cloaked runs through each identified system, hoping to find a ship to destroy. The problem was that the ships seemed to be drying up. Had they been destroyed, or were they being staged for some major assault? And in which direction would the assault go?

The *Galileo* was built for setting up the infrastructure of a new colony, so her sister ship, the *Isaac Newton,* was being built at Taurus Base right now to accomplish that same task. As soon as she was finished, the *Galileo* would revert to its original name, the *Dalgor Kret,* and would be returned to the Shiravans with all modifications intact.

The simple fact was that until the Garmon threat could be controlled, colonization was on hold. An earlier talk with Rentec and Maratai had convinced her of that. All the Garmons were interested in was the death and destruction of anything not Garmon, and recently, apparently, they'd even found it necessary to fight amongst themselves.

The bodies of innocent Alliance citizens killed in the

failed hijacking of the *Federal Case* and their families were treated in an entirely different way. The bodies were kept on Vesta, and the families were transported to the asteroid headquarters for ceremonies and a new ritual. Part of the wall in the terrarium, the terra-formed space used to provide a little slice of Earth on Vesta, had been smoothed over. Already, the names of previous deaths had been inscribed there, and the new names of the innocents would constitute the official unveiling of the Alliance Dusterna.

Taken wholly from Shiravan culture, the Dusterna contained the names of all who'd died for the Alliance, including the Shiravans who'd given their lives at their first meeting. A computer-guided laser would cut each new name as it was spoken. That particular agony still lay before her.

Between times, she could rest and prepare herself for the occasion, as quite a number of family members, not surprisingly, wanted to attend the ceremony. The coffins were all waiting; only a few families had declined solar cremation, so even the trajectories were already locked in. The speech was done and done well. Surprisingly, she saw a bit of Simon's hand in it.

CHAPTER ELEVEN

Korgan Garmon stood in the Hall grown by countless numbers of ancestors over the course of Garmon evolution. Some said it was started before the written word, and others speculated that it was begun even earlier. Regardless, with all the plantings, trimmings, bendings, and shapings over the cycles, the kadora trees had formed a continuous wall around a large space beaten to dirt by millions of feet over countless generations. The upper branches intertwined, mingling one tree with another, their leaves letting little light reach the ground, even at midday. The interior glowed with torchlight, illuminating family trophies, guests, and a comparatively small sandy pit directly in front of a living wooden throne.

Only two openings were left in the wall of wood that encircled this throne of Garmon influence. One was over nine feet tall and fourteen wide, the other was a mere bolt hole carefully hidden behind the throne and known only to each leader of the Garmon clan.

He stood proudly, with all of his Honors polished to a high shine. His feet were planted firmly in the cool sand of the Pit as he faced the council that would decide his fate. Monarch or murderer.

It fell to these seven elders, each of whom had given up his own tribe and name to officiate for the whole race, to decide whether or not he was worthy to lead his people. He had already defeated he who had no name, and now, after the ceremonial, bare-handed stalking and killing of a krath male, he was ready to be proclaimed Monarch of all the Tribes.

His mind surged with thoughts, facts, and figures, none of which directly impacted the upcoming ceremony—ships ready for action, ships under repair, ships under construction, personnel available to fill positions heretofore unnecessary. The male population, minus the elders who taught the young males, would have to take to the ships. Until now, the... less combative... males had been allowed to provide services from planetary bases. Now, though, the Garmon decided, there would be a racial draft, leaving only a few fertile males on any given world, supervising the fertilization and work of the females and the education of the male children.

First, the drafted males were required to spend time on the two bases, building ships and other equipment. Korgan had an image in his mind of all three factories turning out ship after ship, crews waiting to take their places and go destroy the upstart humanz. Presently, only two yards were able to produce ships, and those were working at a reduced capacity as new recruits learned lessons the hard way that gifted machinery operators were supposed to pass on to their successors. With the deaths of most of those operators during the attack wave that had passed through their system, old knowledge would have to be relearned, and that took time and cost lives.

Much the same could be said of the ships already in space. Korgan, as the Garmon, dictated that all ships would share their experienced crew with newer, less well-trained crews as they finished their familiarization flights with the ships they'd practically built themselves. This necessitated, of course, that new recruits had to fill the slots of trained crew who were off teaching others how to do their jobs. It never occurred to the newly crowned monarch that the race he called humanz had been doing the same thing from the start.

So far, only six new ships had left the yards, being crewed by older, recalled veterans, along with an appreciable number of drafted soldiers learning their new jobs. Fleet-wide, that was nothing, but as ship expansion sped up and conflicts continued, eating up experienced bodies as well as new recruits, not to mention ships, the need to spread his experienced personnel farther apart was going to be a problem. He had even dictated an end to ritual dueling as it cost irreplaceable lives. Duels were now confined to first blood, the loser having to spend time on the new space docks for a time before returning to normal duties.

His mind jerked back to the present as an old Garmon, older than any he had ever met, came forward. The Priesthood didn't much interfere with secular matters, but their stamp of approval meant a lot to any new monarch. Now, the Chief Priest of the most secretive order of Garmon stepped forward, holding the skull of Korgan's predecessor in his hand. The flesh rotting off the skull offended his delicate nostrils, as it did many of those nearby.

"Did you, Korgan Garmon, kill this individual to win the leadership of our race?" The question was put as if it were just another ceremony.

Korgan looked down at the thing the Priest held. There were still enough features visible to answer. "Yes," he stated positively. He puffed out his chest. If the Priesthood decided that he had taken the racial mantle without proper attention to tradition, he would die right here.

Instead, the Priest asked, "And is this the krath you slew with nothing but your claws and your wits?" Korgan looked in the direction the Priest indicated. There sat a krath head. His mark had been clawed into the forehead at the time he killed it, and he looked closely at the mark and merely nodded.

He waited as the seven heads bowed into a circle and muttered among themselves for a time. Finally, they sat up in their chairs. "We, the Council of Priests, find that Korgan Garmon has acted in accordance with all traditions involving the ascension to the leadership of the race. We are Garmon." With that the seven stood up as one and bowed to Korgan.

Finally feeling free for the first time since he had first challenged he who had no name, Korgan turned to the assembled tribal leaders and said, "For the first time since we took over our own world and started to spread into the universe around us, we have come upon a race that does not willingly accept that we are their betters and seriously opposes our fleets and actions. Combined with the Shiravi, they've begun a series of systematic attacks on our outposts and even one attack against our own homeworld and shipyards, causing severe damage and lost time. Not to mention the loss of almost every ship that has had the misfortune to face these humanz."

Muttering broke out around the assembly. "The latest thing I have done is create a Watcher Fleet," Korgan said, heading off the muttering. "One small, otherspace-capable ship sits out the battle, recording what transpires, then comes here and lets experts analyze the information. So far, we have discovered that all the humanz ships are almost impregnable to our missiles, and an increasing number of Shiravan ships are acquiring that same ability." He stood thoughtfully for a moment. "My advisers tell me that this set of circumstances is because the humanz have a different pattern of thought that lets them take Shiravan technology and better it. We have done the same thing— taken Shiravan technology, that is," he said, letting the mutters and comments build for a short time.

"I have read the old records," he said, "and it's clear that we got our start in space by taking the ship of a visiting spacefaring race, most probably the Shiravans. The leader then, one known as the Garmon, the *first* Garmon, saw the benefit of possessing the technology and took the ship. Unfortunately, none of the rightful owners survived to explain how to run the vessel. It took almost twenty cycles before the ship was ready to test with the Garmon at the controls. The Garmon then began a series of projects that resulted in the existence of our present three shipyards and an empire of over forty worlds."

He continued, knowing that some of this was new to many of the leaders arrayed before him. "Then the leadership passed to the Korvil." The name burned his tongue, but he pressed on. "For over two hundred turnings, they grew the fleets and the Empire, bringing more and more worlds under our control." He stopped, letting the contributions of past leaders seep in and possibly reflect on him. "But the Korvil line weakened," he said finally. "The last of that line threw almost twenty hands of ships at the humanz, and only a lucky few have returned to tell the tale. And we haven't lost that many ships in the past two hundred cycles. Now this." He waved his hand vaguely, indicating the whole human part of the equation.

He stood in front of all those who had already proclaimed their allegiance to him and said, "It is reported that we have a hand and a half of battleships ready to fight, along with almost three hundred standard-class ships. And that brings into view another point: that the humanz have taken the Shiravan small fighter and modified it even further, making it stronger, more elusive and harder to hit, as well as making changes to the armament that add even more to their effectiveness."

Here was where Korgan knew he would stand or fall. Showing weakness would get him killed before he could implement any of his new ideas. He must make backing away from confrontations with the humanz look like a strategic maneuver. "We have fought the Shiravi for over two hundred cycles but these new humanz for only a handful. I say we should study them before committing any more ships to destruction. As with any creature, we should know the habits and capabilities of our opponent so that we can devise proper attack strategies."

"How do you propose that we study these humanz?" one leader asked belligerently. He would remember from which quarter came that insolence.

"As I've said, I have instituted what I call the Watcher Fleet. So far, only a handful have reported in with their data. There's not enough information to make a proper assessment of these humanz or how to deal with them. Yet. Let my advisers have time to make their plans." He was already setting himself apart from any possible losses by leaving the impression in the minds of his followers that the directives that came from him were actually from someone else.

Let his advisers take the fall, as long as he was able to get his policies initiated. "We will capture and interrogate more humanz, as my predecessor should have done. He handed the assignment over to a subordinate, and you see the result." That was as close to a censure of the Garmon under-hierarchy as Korgan was ready to go to right then, and he waited to see the response to his statement. One Garmon, caught unawares, had had his home and fleet destroyed.

Of course, he would have to initiate a rewards policy for those who could effectively manage to upgrade their existing technology. Death threats only served to inhibit free thinking, and that wasn't what was needed now. After all, the humanz had done it, and anything a puny human could do, a Garmon could do better.

There'd been no signs of the humanz for some time, though several worlds had been visited and all Garmon destroyed. One world had been left alone, as though the human commander wanted him to know he was being watched.

CHAPTER TWELVE

Gayle Miller, Captain of the *TAS Eightball*, third carrier in the Alliance fleet, read slowly through the mysterious package found on her desk—mysterious because someone had had to get through two locked doors and five separate security systems to put it there. Audio had given nothing but background noise, heat sensors never registered a blip, and the floor sensors hadn't been activated. Video showed that someone had been playing with Vesta's transporter.

Knowing who'd sent it and how was a secret Gayle would keep to herself. After all, she might have need of that information at some time in the future.

Getting back to the contents, she placed a DVD in her player and hit the play button. At first, she was treated to sweeping vistas of the Shiravan homeworld, overlaid with Marsha's voice. "Point and counterpoint," the voice said. "Here we have the most unique place I've ever been, and it's gorgeous. But I have some disturbing news to send along with it. These people, some of them, are master biologists. They've engineered a virus that will cause the Garmons guaranteed headaches soon enough, but I still want more ships on this side. I think the new Garmon leader is going to concentrate his attacks on this side of his empire, and we need the firepower to stop him. The Shiravans are starting to incorporate changes in some of their newer ships, and the ones now being planned will have most of our mods included in their basic designs."

The rest of the letter was only of interest to Gayle herself, but she put her squadron captains on notice that they'd need to be able to boost at a five-hour notice and keep the entire procedure under wraps. Normally, any battle group was named after its strongest ship, and the commander of the squadron would ride in that ship. As a Firster, she used her power shamelessly to get herself named as squadron commander. It was a much better place from which to watch Kitty's back. Besides, the other captains preferred to defer to her as a Firster.

But this letter from Marsha meant that she'd have to leave Kitty behind and essentially disobey orders, making raids of her own on selected Garmon worlds. The letter went on to say that at least one fuel plant had been located. Taking it out could mean that within five years no more Garmon ships would be able to leave their last landing places, so it was really a two-pronged attack built on guesswork and inferior intelligence. Still, it was better than nothing.

Gayle waited patiently while Marsha's request went through the proper channels, and the possibility of a trip to Shiravan space became common knowledge. Everyone knew it could be a lot worse on that side of Garmon space, but the call of new vistas and alien suns was something most people in the Alliance couldn't resist. She sat down and wrote a letter to a special post office box on Earth. The next Earth-bound courier would take it in. She'd have to see about it getting aboard near the end as she didn't want Kitty finding a letter addressed to Megæra. It just wouldn't do to have the Alliance Herald finding out that three of her top officers were set on their own notion of justice.

Shirley Dahlquist, still on administrative leave and touring wherever possible for the Alliance, found the letter and sent one back, waiting for the right time to present itself. Having Kitty ashamed of her was getting a bit too much for her. She needed a deck under her feet and soon, or she'd go crazy.

As soon as the lists for particular ship categories was posted, Gayle made sure to get her two cents in first. Falling into orbit trailing Vesta, she beamed into the hollowed-out asteroid and made her way to the Herald's office. As she stepped through the doorway, Diana simply activated her data link to the Herald's own.

Kitty was still trying to adjust to the new data-link technology, which had been implemented while she was gone. The earpiece and boom-mike were totally normal-looking and fitting, and the ease of operation was almost unbelievable, especially when she needed to get into the computer's deeper files. Now, though, it was just a quiet chime asking for her attention. She set aside a report and tapped her earpiece. "Yes, Diana?"

"Madam Herald, you have an unscheduled visitor. You have about twenty minutes free. Can you fit Captain Miller into your schedule?"

"Of course, Di. Gayle comes first. The meeting can wait if it becomes necessary. Send her in."

Gayle walked into her friend's office, heart all aflutter. Never in all the years of their friendship had she tried to impose her will on Kitty this strongly. It would be interesting to see if it worked. She found her friend just inside the door. Being of an equal height, the two white-haired women hugged comfortably for a time and then separated.

"It's been a while," Kitty said. "How've you been?" she asked lamely.

"As well as can be expected," Gayle answered almost too quickly. She slowed herself down, by focusing on shipboard matters. "We have the usual number of Mamba applicants, and the usual number who just aren't suited to the new technology. Fortunately, we have enough qualified personnel to keep our entire complement active, plus a few others for insurance. But that's not why I came. I want to volunteer the *Eightball* for the next trip to Shiravi, and I have another request to go with it. One you won't like."

An hour and an uncomfortable meeting later, Gayle left with promises made and given—that she would have one of the carrier slots and that she had to be careful. "I'll do the best I can, but you know what happens when the shit hits the fan."

Kitty, having just played and narrated the tape of her fight with sel Garian, agreed reluctantly. "And you guys are never going to let me live that down, are you?" she asked petulantly.

Gayle, hand upon the open door, looked over her shoulder and grinned at her friend. "Nope," she said and stepped through, letting the door close on that single syllable.

Gayle took her gig and started composing a letter to Shirley in her head on the way back to the *Eightball*. Immediately after boarding, she looked up the Shift Commander and gave orders that would put the *Eightball* in Earth orbit within two hours.

Once there, she looked up Shirley's data-link code and called it. Almost instantly, the response came back.

"This better be good. I was just about to go to bed, and I really don't appreciate being disturbed."

"Shirley, this is Gayle. If you want out of durance vile, get dressed and call me back. I'll bring you and anything you need aboard. Then, we go get your new ship, Captain." She let that last word sink in for a bit before she said, "Shirley. Answer me, girlfriend."

"I, uh, give me half an hour to get showered and dressed. I'll call shortly."

Gayle signed off and sat back, a bit perplexed. "Well, I guess we wait a bit."

Shirley stepped out of a quick shower, dried and brushed her hair, and was in the process of getting her clothes on when she called Gayle. "What are you sending down to get me?"

"I'm sending my gig down. You should be comfortable enough on your ride up. And just for grins, I think I'll come along."

"Okay, home in on my signal and you'll find an open area about a quarter-mile east of my present location. I'm leaving now, so you can, too. See you in a few minutes."

Leery of some kind of deception, Shirley strapped on her pistol, checked the charge, re-holstered it and stepped out the door for the last time. Carrying two bags that got heavier the farther she walked, she made her way to the baseball field that would be empty this time of night. Once there, she sat down on her bags and waited for pickup.

Less than five minutes later, she spotted a dark silhouette covering stars, then letting them reappear seconds later. She stood up as the craft sank to the ground. The ramp touched ground and a single lonely siren could be heard from several blocks away. Grabbing both bags, she made her way aboard, hugged Gayle, and said, "That siren could be for us. I'd raise ramp and split before we have to find out the hard way."

Gayle hit the close button for the door and said, loud enough for the pilot to hear, "As soon as we have positive pressure, your destination is the *Eightball*. Understood?"

The pilot answered, "Destination *Eightball*. Aye, ma'am."

In the time it took to get back to the ship, Shirley asked all the questions she could. "So, why me?" she started simply.

"Because you have a payback coming, and I'm here to help you get it." Gayle's next words chilled Shirley to the bone. "And I'm going to do the same for Stephen."

"What exactly do you have in mind?"

"Exactly? I can't say for sure, but I got some interesting information from Marsha when that last courier arrived from Shiravi. Did you know that the Shiravans are pretty sophisticated biological engineers? Just look at their regen chambers," Gayle said. "And they manipulated their populace for over a thousand years to keep the male population down and pacified. Now, some of the Shiravan captains Marsha is running with have let it out that there are viruses in production to kill all Garmons or restrict their growth or—my favorite—raise the intelligence of the females to the same level as the males. Nobody knows if it would result in a kinder, gentler Garmon, but it would take several of their quicker-gestating generations to see if it would cause major disruptions in their culture."

"And how much of this does Kitty know?" Shirley asked suspiciously.

All innocence, Gayle answered, "I'm not sure what Marsha saw fit to tell her, but we are now working under code names. I'm Alecto, you're Megæra, and Marsha is Tisiphone."

"Sounds like some pretty strange names to me," Shirley commented.

Gayle grinned. "You should have studied some ancient mythology. Those are the names of the three Fates who decided the lives and deaths of all mortals."

"So, we're gods, now?"

"No, of course not. Think of us as avenging angels. Don't you want to pay back the Garmons for what happened to you?"

"I'm what happened to me, Gayle. It was made pretty clear to me then, and I've come to understand why I was punished."

"But punishments end, Shirl. Now you can get back out there and do some real good."

"Yeah," Shirley said sarcastically. "And if Kitty finds out about it, I'll be lucky to be banished to Earth."

"So we don't tell her."

Two weeks later, Gayle's wolf packs moved off in formation, heading for the jump point for Shiravi with Shirley Dahlquist in the captain's seat of the newly commissioned *Vulcan's Hammer*.

As the ships reached jump, much too far away to be seen by the unaided eye, Kitty stared out the clear dome and wondered if she had let Shirley come back too soon.

CHAPTER THIRTEEN

Kitty buzzed her secretary in the outer office. Commander Holloway made a very efficient secretary and, upon occasion, aide. It was pure luck that she had transferred from the *Federal Case* just before Breen had staged his coup and therefore avoided the resultant trials and disgrace. "Glenda, would you please call the admiral's office and tell them that the Herald would like to see him as soon as he can clear a spot on his calendar. And ask for an RSVP, too." That last was an afterthought, but the note arriving through official channels would have him coming in the door with his worried face on, which was better than the offhand manner he tended to use in his day-to-day affairs.

Simon arrived almost immediately on the heels of her request—so quickly, in fact, that she excused his lack of response to her RSVP. She stood up at his entrance. "Admiral, thank you for coming so soon. You must have been close by. Please sit down." She waved at a chair in front of her desk.

Simon sat down, a strange look on his face. "I figured it must be important, Madam Herald," he answered, holding to the formality of her request and greeting. "What can I do for you?"

She looked at him, noting the grey in his sideburns. He still hadn't made use of the regen chamber, although almost a hundred volunteers had been through the process. And that didn't count the victims who actually needed the chamber. He used the transporter regularly, so why was he opposed to the technology that had saved her own life?

"Admiral, I've been going over the reports of patrols and their results and findings. Combined with the requests for transport to virgin worlds and the attacks of the Garmons, I think it might be wise to begin a simultaneous program of expansion. If just one determined attack were to get through to Earth, there would be no human race left to defend or draw recruits from."

Simon, correctly determining the tone of this meeting—not of husband and wife but of superior to subordinate—asked, "What do you have in mind, Madam Herald?"

"Taurus Base is due to turn out our own *Galileo*-class ship in about three months. I propose that the next vessel built be a ship to carry colonists to inhabitable worlds. We'll follow the same technique the Shiravans use. First, the *Newton* would go to one of the nearby worlds that's able to support human life and build the infrastructure for colonists to move into. Then, a jump-capable transport would carry colonists to that world. It's time and beyond to get our eggs out of one basket. Of course, there will need to be protection on hand for all phases of the process, including the protection of the colonists once they arrive."

Simon wasn't happy with the idea. "Madam Herald, we're set to start another *Raptor*-class out of Taurus. As you know, our only other battleship has been sent to Shiravan space to help relieve the pressure on the Shiravans. We desperately need another on this side of Garmon territory."

"I understand your needs, Admiral, but you will have three operating stations all the while. We desperately need to patch up relations with Earth. We have popular support, but we still need the support of whole governments," Kitty argued. "It wouldn't do anything to relieve real population pressure, but it would appear that way, and we'd be starting and assisting numerous colonies that would soon be producing ships to add to their own defense and the fleet in general. Once a colony is populated and settled, we could start adding more colonists. The original colonists would support the second wave as they started to build an interstellar infrastructure. The two groups would merge and then we'd have a population with two purposes—expansion across the planet and building starships. But we need to start now as a show of good faith."

Simon tried one more time. "As commander of the military, it's my call on what we build and when, Madam Herald." His temper was starting to get the better of him.

"True, Admiral, but it's the executive branch that tells the military what to do and, in this case, what to build. I won't do this often," she said, trying to lessen the tension, now and in the bedroom later. "Just remember, I have to consider the entire Alliance, and we do need the appearance of expanding, as well as making our technology available to Earth."

"All right," he said, giving in. "You're right, and that type of ship won't take long to build—just a converted carrier with mess halls, latrines, and living space. We won't even need much in the way of activities rooms since we'll fill the ship and immediately jump to the new world. I can even get some of the parts started as soon as we draft a set of blueprints. Will that be all,

Madam Herald?" He stood up as if to go.

"No, there's one other small matter," Kitty said. "As I was looking over the patrol reports, I noticed that you don't have anything specific on your calendar for about a week. I've taken the liberty of scheduling your visit to the regen chamber for the day after tomorrow. Does that meet with your approval?"

"When you put it that way, I don't really have a choice." Walking to the door, he opened it and said, "Good day, Madam Herald," closing it without waiting for a response.

At Defense Intelligence Agency headquarters, the Director faced almost two dozen top-level staff and agents. "This order is being given to the CIA, NSA, FBI, and any other agency with need to know. From this moment on, no notice will be taken of any member of any family related to Alliance citizens. What they said in the beginning," he said with a bit of irony in his voice, "is probably true: that there would have been a nuclear war if only one country had gotten that ship. And they *are* keeping their word to transfer certain technologies to Earth-based companies. Our scientists are having a field day with the math, and our think tanks are coming up with some radical ideas that could be used as weapons. The problem is that every country in the world is privy to the same information, so no one has an advantage over anyone else except in finding something unique faster than the other guy. And no one on Capitol Hill is taking bets on that. Therefore, our attentions will be turned back to their original purpose, minus the watch for alien vessels." This last came out angrily, but the new administration had made it perfectly clear.

The new Howard administration was trying to work its way out of the miasma eight years of Drake and his cronies had left behind. The Iraqi/Afghanistan affair would certainly drag on for some time yet, but focusing on domestic issues was working to keep the new government's approval rating fairly high so far. But for that condition to continue, an out was needed.

Omar had looked more than once at the communicator left behind when Agent Galway had decided to change allegiance. Even the Alliance seemed to have forgotten about it. He'd been briefed on the entire Terran Alliance situation at the beginning of his term, though he'd already known more than most, coming directly from the Senate to the Oval Office. Actually, it was more of a nonissue after the last release of Alliance family members.

But it would be time to start campaigning again soon. If he could renew ties with the Alliance, he might have a better chance for reelection. The problem was that most of the people who'd been working with the Alliance had moved to out-country locations, and no one seemed to know when, if ever, the U.S. could get back in their good graces.

Reluctantly, he reached for the case and set it on the *Resolute Desk*. Pushing two buttons beside the handle, the top popped up about a quarter inch. Gingerly, he lifted the lid to face the flat-panel-type display. The base held what looked like a handprint lock, several touch-type controls, and a perforated area that must hold the microphone and speaker. He ran his hand over the slick finish of the keypad and was startled when the unit lit up.

Not knowing what to do, he'd started to close the lid when a voice came out of the speaker. "Unauthorized transmitter. State your name and purpose."

Another voice asked, "Are you sure it's an activation and not a malfunction?"

"Sir, it's an activation. As a matter of fact, I've pinpointed its location." The first voice was silent for a moment, building suspense. "It's coming from the Oval Office. It's the unit Galway was given way back." The voice now addressed itself to Omar. "To whom am I speaking?"

"This is President Howard." His voice trembled, angering him. "I would like to speak to the Herald, please, at her earliest convenience."

"I'll personally deliver the message, sir. You understand that with the Herald on Vesta, I'll have to send a jump-capable ship with your message. That will take about three hours. Return time will be the same, plus reaction time. I'd put it around seven hours, sir."

"Uh, thank you. I'll be awaiting her call." The link severed itself and the unit went blank.

Seven hours to get a message to the asteroid belt and back. We never stood a chance once they got their first set of recruits.

"He what?" Kitty asked incredulously. "We released the DNA lock on that transmitter the day Drake walked out of the White House, and he chooses *now* to call?" Kitty had wanted to talk to this man ever since he'd taken office, but the Alliance had held a strict hands-off policy, except for converting Daniels and several other former operatives of various agencies. As long as there were no more reprisals against Alliance personnel or family members, the Alliance had helped with some of the more massive reconstruction efforts along the west coast. Of course, crews were committed all along the Pacific Rim.

Simon had finally gone into a regen chamber just hours before, and Kitty had found time to spend in one of the numerous baths dotted around the asteroid. She'd barely made it back to her room when the message reached her. "Who do we have on standby?" she asked Traffic Control. After listening for a few seconds, she said, "The *Shrike* will do. Notify her captain to be ready to break orbit for Earth as soon as possible."

She dressed in a conservative pantsuit, threw some clothes into a bag, and made her way to the transporter room. As soon as Captain Devlin signaled ready, she beamed over. Meeting him in his ready room, she could already feel the ship vibrating around her, and the familiar twisting sensation told her they'd just entered hyperspace. After about fifteen minutes, another twist signified arrival in Earth orbit.

Finishing her talk with Captain Devlin, she went to the Comm Shack. "Please connect me with the transmitter in the White House." Several moments passed before the connection was made at the other end. "This is Herald Hawke, responding to the president's call."

"Madam Herald, this is President Howard. I appreciate your quick response to my call. I wasn't sure the machine would even work. I'd like to invite you to Camp David for talks aimed at regularizing relations between our peoples."

"You and me and how many others, Mr. President? I'll be accompanied by a detail of the Herald's Security team. And after our last experience there, I'm not too

197

certain I want a venue so remote. How about the Rose Garden? Your men will be armed, and so will mine, I'm afraid. But we'll be out in the open for all to see. You might even invite some press for afterwards, if you think anything significant is going to come of our talk."

Omar agreed to the meeting and the press, and the encounter was set for the next day. Meanwhile, he called in his security adviser, defense adviser, foreign adviser, and a number of other people. This meeting was held in the War Room deep beneath the White House. When all had arrived, he stood up. "I'll be meeting with the Terran Alliance Herald tomorrow," he said simply. The effect was as if he had fired a pistol in the room. Total silence prevailed for all of ten seconds, and then multiple voices made an incoherent babble until he was able to restore order.

"It's a fact that most of the businesses started here have moved to other countries—countries looking to get a leg up on us. We're in danger of becoming what we've always helped while looking down on them—a third-world country. True, we have the best military on Earth, but the most powerful country, if you can call a space-based economy a country, holds a distinct advantage over us—more powerful weapons, and the ability to strike when and where they want with impunity. It's doubtful if we even have anything capable of hurting one of their *smaller* ships. Look at the videos of what happened at Camp David, if you need your memories jogged. I have agreed that we'll meet in the Rose Garden. An Alliance battlecruiser in orbit above the White House will ensure that we keep things on the level, and that's just the way I want it.

"We'll meet as equals, hopefully ironing out our differences. Ever since Drake and his administration ambushed the original delegation at Camp David, we have been decidedly ignored. Their people are still helping with reconstruction of the west coast, probably as a show that they're willing to consider the possibility of allowing us back into the planning of our—and I mean Earth's—future. Therefore, when her shuttle lands, her security will be armed, but ours won't. There has to be a beginning to the good faith I want to engender with the Alliance. She's already doing the same, even though her guards will be armed. They'll be outnumbered and at a tactical disadvantage, but remember the ship upstairs, which is capable of pinpoint strikes and totally untouchable. The person of Katherine Hawke has become an icon for the Alliance. It doesn't even bear thinking about what would happen if anything happened to her, so all our security will be outward. Their people will handle local security, and there will be no discussion on the subject—no snipers on the roof, no hidden troops, no extra troops moved into the area. You can bet that we're under total scrutiny from sensors we can't even begin to imagine already. Now, if anyone has any comments, this is the time to make them, but the results will be the same."

The twenty or so people in the room, from the highest general to the lowliest aide, looked at each other. Finally, the head of the Joint Chiefs of Staff said, "Mr. President, although the arrangements aren't to my liking, given that we're bound to protect the person of the President, everything will be handled as you request. Will you be needing any advisers at this meeting?"

Omar looked pensive for a moment. "Not this time. I think it will be more of a 'getting to know you' thing.

We'll leave it at that for now. She certainly has her own advisers, equally unhappy at the circumstances, I'm sure, but nothing she said leads me to believe that she'll have anyone but her security detail. Most likely, her advisers and some of you here will be instrumental in hammering out a new relationship, but we'll wait and see. Any other questions?"

None were forthcoming, although glances were exchanged, a fact that did not go unnoticed by the president.

Kitty took a shuttle down to the Swiss Embassy, where she knew a softer bed would be waiting for her than aboard the *Shrike*. She laid out a light blue dress with the Alliance insignia embossed in gold thread on the left breast, as well as shoes for the next day. Before retiring for the night, she made two calls. The first was to the *Shrike* to check on weather information. If rain was in the forecast, the meeting might be moved inside the White House proper. The other was to the dispensary asking for something to help her sleep. Otherwise, her mind would race all night.

As she laid her data link on the bed table, a knock interrupted her. Her personal aide, Diana Ross, slipped in with a blue bottle and two glasses. "I heard your call to the dispensary, ma'am, and thought this might be a better way to get to sleep."

Kitty said, "That sounds like the best idea I've heard all day. Make mine a half-glass and help yourself." She settled into a chair that gave her a view of the sun setting behind the Alps.

Diana sat down next to her, put the glasses on the table, and opened the bottle. Filling one half full, she took a bit more for herself. "I love this stuff, but God, what a headache the next morning."

Kitty nodded, taking a small sip and letting it flow slowly down her throat. The warmth spread throughout her body, relaxing her more than any pill could possibly do. "The trick is to have a substantial breakfast tomorrow morning—juice, eggs, bacon, toast, and plenty of strawberry jam."

Diana looked over at the dress laid out for the meeting. "I hope the president doesn't decide to wear blue, too."

Kitty laughed lightly. "I don't care if he shows up naked. I just want this cycle of abductions to end so we can get some work done."

The two sat in a companionable silence, lost in their own thoughts and sipping the glowing blue liquid. Kitty said, "You didn't happen to bring another bottle, did you?"

Now Diana laughed. "What kind of aide would I be if I didn't think ahead? I brought two more. One's wrapped as a gift, and the other is just in case."

"Just in case what?"

Diana finished her glass and stood up. "Just in case anything, ma'am. Now, I'll let you get to sleep, and I'll send the pill back to the dispensary." She walked to the door. "I'll see you at breakfast, ma'am." She nodded her head to her boss and slipped out as quietly as she had arrived.

Kitty sat there sipping slowly, thinking about the next day, until all she could see were a few lights and her own reflection in the window. Finishing her glass, she set it on the table next to Diana's and went to bed.

CHAPTER FOURTEEN

Korgan Garmon was not happy. Reports of decimated villages and outposts were becoming an almost constant irritant. And since most of the damage was occurring near the area claimed by the krath-Shiravi, that was where he would end the effrontery to Garmon rule.

A new fueling plant had been built in the outer reaches, but ship production wasn't back to full potential yet. The damage done to the main yards was still being repaired. Garmon males were being conscripted for what new ships were available and being trained by their new crewmates. But this wholesale destruction of entire clans was cutting into his workforce. The few ships that still flew openly were attempting to find viable planets and conscript the best males. This was where the rash of reports was coming from.

Papers covered a desk fit for the gargantuan frame of the Garmon, not exactly the scene he'd pictured when he cut off the head of he who had no name. Ships, locations, condition, crew, weapons, and status of their fuel supplies. Juggling all these, he was trying to put together a fleet strong enough to attack and begin to win back some of the territory the krath-Shiravi were taking, especially ones that provided the best hunting. After destroying all homes and crops, the inhabitants had been allowed to run free as usual, a good hunt and meal afterwards. But first to build the fleet.

Brandon Galway was having the workout of his life. He had returned to Earth with Kitty, specifically to resign since he'd already made his choice to join the Alliance. A message waited on the top of his nearly cleared desk. With a sigh, he got up and headed for the room indicated.

He'd never been a guest in a star chamber before, though he'd played inquisitor often enough. Seven people sat in the shadows while he sat in a single chair, limned by a single bulb directly over his head. "Agent Galway," a voice said. He couldn't tell from which figure, but he didn't like the tone of voice at all. "You were instructed to acquire as many concessions as possible for Earth during your voyage." He was relatively certain that it was a man's voice, but he couldn't be certain. "And you came back empty-handed."

"I did the best I could under the limited conditions I was allowed to work in," he responded calmly. "You all have a copy of my report, or have read it, or we wouldn't be here now. You're looking for a scapegoat. I refuse to be yours. I told you before the mission left Earth that you should send a woman. But no one wanted to listen to a trained field agent. You all had to make your own decision that I was better suited to deal with the leader of an alien civilization. I told you what the aliens themselves said more than once, that they'd be more comfortable dealing with other females."

"You won't be punished for your failure, Agent Galway. As you've said, you did advise sending a female agent." It sounded like the same voice, but he couldn't be certain of anything in this room. "Now, we would ask you, though, if you think a female would have any effect on future negotiations."

"I don't believe so," Galway said after a short pause to consider the notion. "I think you screwed up by not following my suggestions in the first place, and now you're going to be left holding the bag. And an empty one, at that." He paused again, considering that these people were the ones who determined his fate. "Yes, I suggested a female agent, but I don't hold that against you any more that you hold the lack of success against me." He shrugged. "Maybe next time you'll trust your field agent or send one of your own to do the job."

"I'm not sure I like your impertinence, Agent Galway. We chose you because you had the best ties to the Alliance, and we expected that you'd be able to fulfill your mission."

"I read the mission statement," Galway said, holding his hand up to stop the anonymous speaker, a different one this time, he thought. "That was when I suggested a female agent, preferably a trained diplomat. That was when I was pointedly told not to interfere with the decisions of this council," he said flatly. "I did exactly the job I was sent to do and brought you exactly the results I predicted."

Another voice spoke. "But isn't it possible that the results you got were arrived at after you decided the mission would be a failure with any plan other than yours in effect, your decision therefore affecting the outcome?"

"It's possible that military intelligence won't be considered an oxymoron someday, too, but it's not going to happen any time soon," Galway stated.

"Now, see here, Agent..."

"Now see here, yourself, General," he interrupted,

guessing at the rank of the outraged speaker and correctly guessing his sex. He looked at the head area of each of the shadowed figures. "I spent almost two years living among and talking freely to almost each and every one of the people I came in contact with. I told them who and what I was, as ordered, and then set it aside and tried my best to get along with them on a daily basis for the eleven-month trip there and back again. Oh, by the way, did you know that they can do it in only nine months now? Where is their technology going to take them next? Anyway, as debriefings go, this one is pretty much over," he said, standing up.

"That is not your decision to make, Agent Galway."

The agent placed his hand on the back of the chair. Still standing in the small circle of light, he looked into the darkness where his inquisitors sat. "Oh, but it is," he responded. "I've been involved in enough of these inquisitions to know where this one is heading. You're going to threaten me with a terrible duty station, or my family, or any number of things, but what I don't know, I can't tell. The Matriarch won't deal on a diplomatic level with human males. She sent a male to deal with us because we're mostly dominated by males and she thinks she's doing us an honor. And from her point of view, she is. And a great one at that. Respond in kind or find yourself on the sidelines learning what it really means to be second string."

He walked away from the chair until he, too, was in the concealing, comforting dark. "I decided when I found out you'd started another set of roundups that I couldn't be a party to any more lies. They've got the technology, and there's no way you're going to get it from them. Besides, they're right. You have power enough and bombs enough to destroy this planet several times over. Why do you need stronger weapons? Stronger power sources?" Getting no response, he turned and walked toward the door.

"To protect ourselves if others get the technology, too," came desperately out of the dark.

"You've been told that that technology isn't compatible with a planet's surface and biosphere without very specialized equipment. Listen when someone who knows what they're talking about tells you something, please. They can start holding back things like power cells if they want to. Now that you're almost completely dependent on Alliance power generation systems, only a few of the major dams are even running. By the time you could get them back online, the damage to lives and crops would have been devastating, not to mention morale. How would any president deal with that? The last one didn't succeed at his goal of ending global terrorism and was effectively sidelined. Now you've got President Howard to deal with, and *he* is going to have to make peace with *us* or suffer the consequences." His stress on the pronouns was not lost on the panel.

Agent Galway realized his slip as soon as he made it but was too slow to spin it his way without getting hit first. "You just said 'us,' Agent Galway. Do you consider yourself closer to them than to those who have trained you, nurtured you, and paid you for almost twenty years?"

"When you start taking innocent Americans prisoner just because they happen to be related to people who won't do your bidding, yes. I'll side with them. You still look to find the best position, but they—I should say we," he couldn't help tossing in, "have had the moral and technological high ground from the outset. You've already lost, and you don't even know it yet." He walked to the door and it opened at his touch. He knew that wouldn't have happened if even one of the seven figures in the chairs behind him had any more questions to ask him.

I guess the only thing to do is to go clean out my desk and see if the Alliance needs someone trained in covert operations, he thought morosely as he made his way to the front door of the edifice sitting not far from the shadow of the Capitol Building. He was surprised to find a message on his machine from the Council asking that he delay his decision to quit for at least a few days. He set a folder into his outbox and started putting his personal effects into a box. He hesitated over his brass and oak nameplate, then left it on his desk. A clean split was what he wanted. He walked out of his office for the last time and hailed a cab. With no transporter in orbit, he'd have to go to the Swiss Embassy and wait for transportation back to Vesta.

Kitty and Diana sat down to breakfast with all the menu items Kitty had outlined. At the end of a leisurely meal, Diana said, "You were right, boss." When Kitty looked perplexed, she added, "About the meal and the hangover. I don't feel a thing except good."

Kitty smiled. "Told ya so, kiddo. Now, I've got to get ready for a meeting with President Howard. Then a short side trip to pick up Lucy's parents. They'll be going back to Vesta with us." She got up from the table and headed upstairs. "Call Traffic Control and make sure the shuttle is prepped and crewed. I'll be back in twenty minutes. She looked over her shoulder and said, "I know you like the red hair, but I'd appreciate it if you'd schedule a nap in a regen chamber."

An hour later, her pilot requested clearance to land on the White House helipad. The tension among her security detail was palpable as the shuttle set down. All four guards were at the door as it swiveled down into a ramp. Two stepped out first and surveyed the area. With dozens of people walking around or just watching the shuttle, the team leader stepped into the cockpit. "Any sign of weapons on anyone out there?" Her voice was tense.

"All clear, from what my instruments tell me," the pilot responded. "Not even anyone on roofs. It looks good to me."

"Well, I'm still not happy," she muttered as she stepped back into the main body and motioned to Kitty to come to the front.

Led by the first pair of guards, she stepped into the light of an overcast afternoon. "I hope this is just going to be a 'tea and crumpets' kind of thing. After that breakfast, I'm not sure how much more I can eat." Light clouds had rolled in, and her dress billowed in a slight breeze. President Howard, flanked by two men wearing earbuds, waited at the bottom of the ramp to greet her. As she descended the ramp, she realized that Diana was right behind her.

Too late now to change things, she walked down the ramp and stopped before putting foot to ground. "Welcome to the White House, Madam Herald. I hope you don't mind if we move our meeting to the portico. We have light rain in the forecast, and I don't want to have things spoiled by a little water."

Kitty stepped off the ramp, a sense of inevitability following her. "Thank you, Mr. President. I hope you don't mind an addition to my entourage. My aide has taken it upon herself to accompany us. I'm sure she'll make herself as inconspicuous as my guards." This last was delivered over her shoulder at Diana, displeasure palpable in her voice. It was at this point that she noticed the laser slung low on Diana's hip. An indecipherable look crossed her face.

"You can consider it another level of protection and fire me afterwards, Madam Herald, but where you go, I go. And in this case, armed," she said quietly.

"This meeting calls for a bit of flexibility," the president said in an attempt to placate the two women. "If you will join me, we can get to the porch before the rain decides and ruins that beautiful dress."

Kitty stepped forward and shook Howard's hand. The two leaders walked toward the edifice that was a slowly decaying symbol of freedom around the world.

"Thank you for seeing me on such short notice, Madam Herald," President Howard said cordially as the two sat down opposite each other on the spacious veranda. A white-coated man pulled her chair out and back as she smoothed her dress under her legs. A pitcher and two glasses sat in the center of the table, separating the two as grey skies threatened rain.

"My pleasure, Mr. President. As you can tell from my prompt arrival, I've been anxious to meet you ever since you took office." Kitty wasn't going to give much else away just yet.

The president reached out and picked up the pitcher. "I hope you like iced tea. It's about as neutral as I could think of for this meeting."

Kitty took a cautious sip. "Sweet. Too many people like it without sugar. Too bitter for me. This is just fine." An uncomfortable silence descended for a moment. "I admit I was surprised when my aide brought me your message," she said, fishing for the reason for the invitation.

"And I admit that I was surprised when the machine actually worked," the president responded. "We were under the assumption that it was only operable by Agent Galway. Since he has severed connections with us to join the Alliance, the only other method was to send someone to one of your embassies. That would have been my next move."

Kitty smiled openly for the first time. "We canceled the DNA lock as soon as your predecessor left office. I'm gratified that none of his shenanigans have been repeated since you were sworn in."

"My advisers suggested as much. I was never happy with the illegal way in which our citizens were treated during his tenure. But that is past. While we know who most of your people are, none of their families have even been contacted or watched. The exhibitions and reprisals performed by your crews and the intelligence we have amassed from the agents returned to us have convinced me and most of my staff that it would be sheer folly to try another such move." He took a sip from his own glass, waiting for a response.

"The gesture is greatly appreciated, Mr. President," Kitty said truthfully. "Since the vast majority of our citizens are of American heritage, it allows us to turn our attentions outward. As you know, there are at least two races out there. One, of course, is the Shiravans, with whom we have signed a mutual defense pact. The other call themselves Garmons and have no interest in talking. From what we've learned from the Shiravans, the idea of peaceful coexistence is a totally foreign concept to them, and it just happens that Earth is in the area they consider to be theirs. It's anybody's guess how Earth would be faring right now if we hadn't made use of the ship that wound up in our hands."

"Twenty million dead, conservatively, and hundreds of billions of dollars in damage around the world is enough evidence for me," Howard said. "And your continued assistance with rebuilding the damaged areas does not go unnoticed, even if we aren't exactly on speaking terms at the moment. I must point out that my advisers insist that they would have been better suited to utilize the discovery than civilians, though." He held up his hand as Kitty's mouth opened to respond. "I, on the other hand, feel differently. I've read the transcripts of Alliance personnel, and their comments as to what would have happened if we *had* taken the ship. You went straight into a building program, while our people would have spent years trying to understand the physics of each item before going on to the next. The timing of the attack on your first facility leads me to believe that your assertions are true. We wouldn't have been ready for an attack, and it would have happened in Earth orbit rather than the asteroid belt. The two strikes on Earth tell me that your instincts were right, hard as is it is for me to say so, and I wouldn't like to be quoted too widely on that last comment."

Kitty took a sip of her tea, ordering her thoughts. "I thank you for your candor, Mr. President. Needless to say, we believe the same things. And, as you can tell, we're keeping our word to release the technology as fast as we can, helping companies produce various items for public use."

"And the food processor has been of inestimable value all around the world. As you may know, they're indispensable in the Northwest and other ravaged areas around the world, not to mention places that have suffered from continual hunger for hundreds of years. That's one of the things that fuels terrorist claims. A hungry man will do almost anything. With no hunger and an influx of jobs and money to the places they recruit from, there's considerably less chance of gaining converts to their cause. All they have left is altruism, which is bad enough as it is. But now we can see some promise on the horizon."

Kitty smiled bleakly. "Terrorism even gets exported to outer space, Mr. President. That's one that even we don't have much control over."

"I've heard about your ordeal. I understand one of our agents helped you put down a rebellion." It seemed to Kitty as if the president felt he had scored a point of some kind.

"If you're referring to Agent Galway, he was aboard with our full knowledge. As a matter of fact, your predecessor's administration sent him specifically to try to get some concessions for Earth outside Alliance channels. And he has since relinquished his citizenship in the United States to become an Alliance citizen. I believe he's heading up our new counterintelligence operations. But I have another matter on my mind." Kitty took another sip of her drink and set the glass back down. It was almost immediately refilled by a white-liveried waiter.

Howard, a consummate politician, never changed his expression, but only waited for Kitty to continue. *I'm going to have to learn that technique*, Kitty thought. Aloud she said, "As I'm sure you know, a lot of mail comes across a chief executive's desk, a lot of it asking for help. The difference is that with a space-based nation, our requests are quite different. We have successfully restored almost all of the satellites destroyed by the Garmons for every country able to build new ones. We also are getting requests from the scientific community to help them set up bases on both the moon and Mars." At this, one presidential eyebrow rose slightly.

"We have no problem with this as soon as we're certain we can provide adequate protection for the expeditions. But far outstripping those requests are ones asking us to find habitable planets to emigrate to. At first, I was loathe to agree, but after what happened to Earth—and that's not counting a stray super-meteor—I think it might be a viable idea. At present we have a ship just about ready to join our fleet that replicates the Shiravan vessel we acquired. That ship will be returned to the original owners since it represents an extensive cash outlay for them. Putting human beings on several, even dozens of worlds will go a long way to keeping a single incident from erasing us from the universe. Again, it's contingent on our ability to protect those who choose to colonize alien planets. With Earth's population reaching into the billions, no matter how many we allow onto new planets, we'll never be able to even put a dent in Earth's population.

"What will help is cleaner power generation and production practices. Some of our scientists estimate that the greenhouse effect could be reversed within fifty years to the point that it would be noticeable to the common man. Mass-producing antigravity cars would allow you to tear up millions of miles of concrete roadways, using the land for growing more crops and grasslands. Mag-lev trains and trucks could be moved to well above ground level and travel at speeds rivaling airplanes. Just imagine no more crashes and mangled bodies. Shipping would benefit accordingly. Of course, many present industries would fall by the wayside, putting a lot of people out of work. If they didn't want to be trained for the new technologies or couldn't for some reason, they could be used in a TVA or CCC type of labor, removing all that concrete and asphalt. Fill in swampland, if you could without destroying natural habitats for the animals left on Earth, build reefs for fish, make levees or breakwaters for coastal cities, or any number of things. The first colony isn't even in the drawing stage as yet, but if things go as hoped, barring Murphy, we project that within five to ten years we'll be putting colonies on several planets we've already cataloged." She sat back, exhausted. The tea was an indispensable godsend.

"I've already had several letters to that effect from our scientists, Madam Herald, but this is the first I've heard of colonization. That will take away a lot more of our best minds when we need them the most."

"Not if you start nudging the brightest kids into the scientific disciplines right now. It will be closer to ten years before we need any of them, and we wouldn't take all, anyway. Remember, this is our birth-world, too. None of us want to see it ruined. And another thing—as we've said before, when someone wants to leave us and come back to Earth, they'll be bringing their knowledge with them. And we need crew and Earth-side personnel all the time, but at a rate limited to how fast we can build ships and colonies."

Howard sipped from his own glass before answering. "This is one idea I'll have to pass along to my advisers. On the face of it, it seems feasible, but I'll reserve judgment until I get some reliable input. How will I reach you in the future?" the president asked.

"Just like last time. I might be a little harder to reach, though. I occasionally have to travel to some of our various bases, which will make it harder for a message to reach me. My aide and staff will forward any message, and I'll either come in person or send a fully authorized representative to handle any concerns you have." A soft chime called Kitty's attention to the watch built into her wristband. "Mr. President, I must plead another engagement and leave in about fifteen minutes. Perhaps we should throw the newsies a bone?"

Waiters came forward to pull back the chairs the two leaders occupied. As Kitty stood up, her security teams moved closer. "The Press Room is best suited for the purpose. Do you mind if my security carries guns at this point? I don't want anything happening to you on my watch."

Kitty thought for a moment. "All right, Mr. President. You've shown good faith and kept quiet until now about my people being armed, but if someone wants me dead, there's not much five people can do to stop it, so more firepower might be the thing to do. Shall we go?"

The press conference was mostly President Howard and Kitty talking about the new and improved relations with the Alliance and the prospects of cleaning up the air and water. When questions came, one—directly related to the Alliance's ability to protect Earth—was fielded by Kitty. "We have patrols examining and cataloging dozens of the nearer planets now, creating a buffer zone between us and the Garmons. The same thing is happening in Shiravan space. As it happens, we've figured out what type of planets the Garmons prefer and are targeting those for special attention.

"Unfortunately, both races can live quite well on the same planets, and we're in the space they consider theirs. That's one reason we've gotten hit so many times. Another is the Garmon's insistence that all things belong to the Garmons. But all that changes now that we've amassed a considerable fleet. Granted, it's enhanced by as many ships as the Shiravans could spare, but with each victory, the Shiravans gain more experience and confidence. Until we gave them some of their own technology back, tweaked by our own people, they hadn't stood a chance of holding out much longer. Our occupation of their lost ship would seem at this point to have been a boon to both our races. Over the last two hundred and fifty years, they've been whittled down to only fourteen worlds from their original twenty-two. I think they were very glad to see us showing up on their radar, so to speak."

After the short grilling by the press, Howard walked with Kitty to her shuttle. "So, tell me if you can," the president said, "exactly how much do you know about these Shiravans?"

"Enough to have been adopted into the Matriarch's own family as a Sister," Kitty retorted a bit hotly.

"Don't get me wrong, Madam Herald," the president said placatingly. "I only mean that you didn't spend enough time there to really get to know the whole race. Even the Shiravans serving here in Earth-space may not be entirely forthcoming. Our own world is proof enough of the practice of duplicity from our earliest beginnings. Withholding information, misinformation, and disinformation all play a daily part of our lives. How far can a race hundreds of years ahead of us in technological achievements be in the art of hiding things in plain sight? Don't answer that; just think about it."

The two stopped at the ramp. "I'd like to see one of your ships for myself one day, and I'm particularly interested in the asteroid you turned into a headquarters. Perhaps we can arrange something, if my people don't get too stubborn. No president has ever left Earth before."

"No president has ever had access to the craft to do so," Kitty replied, wondering how she'd house a sizable contingent of visitors in some sort of luxury. And there was the matter of the dilapidated sections of what should be a pristine environment to be addressed as well. "Let's let our people work out the details. We can see what happens after that. You're welcome to see the inside of the shuttle, but I'm afraid you'll find it more like the inside of an airplane than a spaceship. If you do come to Vesta, I'll arrange a tour of one of our bigger ships."

The two leaders stood for a moment before the president said, "I'll save that for later, I think. You did say you had another appointment before leaving Earth." Howard stuck his hand out and said, "Until next time, Madam Herald. Have a safe trip."

As Kitty shook his hand, a flurry of camera flashes recorded the moment. She said, "I'm looking forward to it, Mr. President." With that, she and her security team entered the shuttle, effectively putting off any press conference. Howard and his people moved back a safe distance, the ramp closed off the sight of the White House, and the shuttle lifted silently on its antigravs and moved out of the restricted airspace surrounding Washington, DC.

Kitty's return to Vesta was a little more than unexpected, to her. To the rest of Alliance Command, she'd just disappeared. For some reason, no one had thought to check with Traffic Control. Kitty had filed a perfectly legitimate flight plan and was back well within her ETA. So, no flags from that direction either.

Word had spread as soon as Simon came out of regen and couldn't find his wife. Technicians reported the departure, but only after a full-scale search was ordered, reaching all personnel. It was with great relief that Traffic Control took the incoming call: "Vesta Base, this is shuttle Herald One on approach from Earth. Aboard are Lucy Grimes, her parents, Commander Diana Ross," the pilot said, "and Herald Hawke." It wasn't often she got to be Kitty these days.

An extended silence was followed by a strange, "Roger that, shuttle Herald One. We have you on scan, and you are cleared to land in Shuttle Bay Two. Prepare for Traffic Control to take over your systems." The signal shut off, leaving an intergalactic hiss in her ears, so she shut her radio off as well. Moments later, a slight difference in vibrations confirmed that the ship was no longer under the pilot's control.

She sat back, turning her seat towards the back of the passenger compartment. "We have some very nice apartments aboard," she said. "Lucy has one, my husband and I have one, even my aide has her own place. This is as close as we can get to self-contained just yet, but we're working on it." A pneumatic hiss sounded as the ramp opened out and became a path to the deck. There normality ended.

CHAPTER FIFTEEN

Simon Hawke had worked himself up a fine head of steam by the time the ramp hit the deck. It was only by sheer willpower that he held his wrath in, and that only out of respect for the couple with Kitty. Lucy strolled out first with a parent on each arm, Kitty following as if behind a shield. She had seen his expression as the shuttle grounded.

"What did I do, now?" she asked, pushing Lucy on ahead with her parents. "You can expedite their housing and allowances and such, can't you, Luce?"

"Got it covered, Kitty. You gonna be okay?" A worried look crossed her face as she looked at the two standing as if for an old-fashioned shootout.

"Yeah. You go on, now." She turned to face an obviously irate Simon. "Okay," she said, deflated. "Are you pissed as a husband or as an admiral?"

"Both," he growled, not knowing where to begin. "First, you violate all the Herald's protocols by going off on a jaunt. Second, you don't inform anyone; you just go. And three," he said, running down at that point and was all the madder for it.

"First," she responded, "I *did* inform someone. Traffic Control, and my entire staff. Did you bother to check with them? No? I didn't think so. The *Shrike* took us to Earth and handled aerial surveillance. Second, I didn't slip my security. There are four guards waiting to see if they'll have to shoot you to keep you from killing me. And Diana went along, as well. Armed. By the way, I didn't go off on a *jaunt*. I went to talk to President Howard and bring Lucy's parents back. And you don't have a third, so this is over."

"Not by a long shot, it isn't," Simon yelled. "Do you have any idea what I've been going through? And let's not mention the rest of the base."

"Yes, let's *not* mention the rest of the base," she said heatedly, looking around at the service team waiting to check out the shuttle. "You put an entire asteroid on alert because I was gone overnight. I don't believe the nerve of you!" she yelled back. "If you can't get over the fact that I'm not a doll that just anyone can hurt, I suggest you watch the sel Garian tape again. And do some more digging before you go off half-cocked. Your temper is unbelievable!"

Simon had planned what he was going to say, but she kept cutting him off at the knees every time. "Can't you admit that you should have told someone you were leaving for a while?"

He watched her wilt. "You're right, hon, I should have. It's just that with this new advance in the regeneration chambers, I wanted to get Lucy's mother in as soon as possible." She seemed to perk up some as she changed the subject. "And you look good with white hair, dear."

TAS Eightball sailed through the swirling lights and colors that composed hyperspace. Part of her lower deck had been turned into a temporary R&D section, working on ways to communicate in hyper. Kitty had said that if you could see another ship in hyper, you should be able to communicate via whisker lasers, over-amped, of course, to punch through the increased static of hyperspace. It would keep the scientists busy and might just accomplish something worthwhile.

Three months into the nine-month voyage, with the two packs moving at the speeds of the slower carriers, the *Eightball's* scientists sent a description of the equipment needed to construct a transmitter since standard receivers were perfectly adequate to receive the more powerful transmissions of the newer transmitters.

One week later, the first answer came back, and within another week all four of the other ships had managed to cobble together working hyper communicators and contact the *Eightball*. Four months had gone by, with everyone working to make the new comm system as reliable and reproducible as possible.

Gayle sat in her chair aboard the *Eightball* and connected with the captains of the other five ships in her fleet. The best solution to many of their problems was to promote her exec to captain of the *Eightball* and essentially take over as Group Commander. All the other captains were in support and she remembered a bit of advice from Simon: somebody has to do the job, and in a lot of cases no one person is better qualified than any other. The problem, though, was that her exec was Bruce Grimes, and Lucy was likely to have a fit, but there was no choice.

Her nights were filled with the view of the alien ship exploding directly in front of the *Clarke*, and each time she was unable to save her ship or two-thirds of her crew. Finally, she stormed out of her cabin, startling her aide with her disheveled appearance. "I'm still in my quarters and not taking calls," she said, her tone warning of dire consequences.

Leaving the young woman frozen at her desk, Gayle stepped out a side door and walked down a short passage. There was a dome on the *Eightball,* as with most full-sized ships, and the only entrance was by way of a short set of stairs on deck one, only a short distance from her office. She made sure it was vacant and locked the door from the inside, overriding any possible attempt to enter short of actually cutting through the alien alloy.

She sank into a lotus position and stared out at the swirling colors of hyperspace. *This better work. My stomach's already queasy*, she thought. She cleared her mind and tried to attain the mental state Kitty had described. To be able to predict even a couple of moves ahead was worth the time and effort, if it worked.

She tried to close out the colors and see the situation as one of her ships flying down a long tunnel. She looked at her own reflection in the clear surface of the dome. *So, what do you think we'll find out there?* she asked her doppelganger. No answer came from the seated figure, so she settled down and started the mantra Kitty had taught her several years back. Soon, she was in a light daze and surprised at the number of 'hers' she saw—a dozen, at least. She stood up and walked to the dome's wall.

This had never worked before, so keeping up her mantra, she gingerly studied one of the 'hers' at random. She looked back and was surprised to see her body, still in lotus position, eyes closed, breathing as if asleep. Steeling herself, she turned and confronted her own body in lotus position. Feeling like she was stepping into the body of an alien, she stepped through the wall and sat down in the image she had already picked out. Immediately she was falling into orbit around a world lit by a red sun.

Following the line, she saw herself meeting Marsha and the Matriarch, then going out on patrol. Tempering her crews in battle proved to be hard to do, as very few Garmon ships were being spotted these days. And those moved off at the first hint of detection.

Another line started out the same way, then she and Marsha teamed up against almost a dozen Garmon ships and wiped them out. Loss of life was moderate due to the tactics used. Another line. This time the losses were more severe.

Line after line she followed until she found one that promised the best results—specifically, keeping as many of her people alive as possible while visiting maximum damage upon the Garmons. Some of the early steps were fuzzy, but the end results were optimum, barring interference from some outside source.

Marsha Kane got a relayed message from the half a dozen incoming ships minutes after her outer defenses had gone into full alert mode. She ordered Raptor Group to jump far enough out that the time lag between messages was only seconds and hailed the incoming fleet. The response delighted her, but she couldn't let it show.

"Eightball Group reporting to senior commander in the area. This is Group Commander Miller. We are four cruisers and two carriers, requested by Captain Kane when the Herald returned to human space."

"Welcome to Shiravan space, *Eightball*. This is Captain Kane of the *Raptor*. All captains and executive officers are requested to attend dinner approximately four hours from now."

Gayle responded, "Understood, Captain Kane. Four

hours. Shuttles away in three and a half. By the way, Alecto and Megæra send their regards." The radio was silent for a moment.

Marsha said, "Tisiphone will be pleased. Kane out."

Yes! she thought. *I have help. The Garmons are going to be so busy learning how to deal with their new and improved females that soon we won't have a threat from them even if they* do *keep a fuel depot.*

CHAPTER SIXTEEN

The six captains and group commander of Eightball Group filed into Marsha Kane's ready room, impressed by the size of the ship. The *Raptor* was twice again the size of any ship so far built by Alliance bases. Where most ships except carriers were manned by a crew of about five hundred, the *Raptor* carried nearly twelve hundred souls.

Marsha stood as the captains filed into the room. "Welcome aboard, ladies and gentlemen. I'd like to be introduced to the six of you who are new to me, and then we can proceed." After the introductions, she said, "I'll meet with each of you after this general briefing. To start with, there's been little Garmon activity anywhere in either sector, Garmon or Shiravan. This matter worries me and the Matriarch, greatly. It's our belief that even though we've taken out quite a few Garmon ships, there's a very real possibility of some type of attack. We've decided to take the battle to the enemy in their own home territory.

"The Shiravans have identified well over two dozen Garmon worlds, one of which we suspect to be their homeworld. With your arrival, we now have eighty-seven major battleships, three carriers, and the *Raptor* herself. There are over one hundred second-generation Mambas, and with your arrival, another hundred-plus third-gen fighters. As soon as your ships can be integrated into the existing fleets, we'll begin systematic attacks on each identified world as soon as possible. First, though, all captains and I will meet with the Matriarch so she can become acquainted with each of you. All crews will get shore leave to allow their nerves to settle down and satisfy everyone's desire to get out of their tin cans and set foot on an alien world.

After the pleasantries were observed, four of the captains left, but Gayle stayed behind, motioning for Shirley Dahlquist to do so as well. She closed Marsha's door and said, "Okay, now fill us in on what's really going on."

A slow grin grew on Marsha's face. "I've found out that the Shiravans have been working on a virus that will raise the intelligence level of the female Garmons. It will take several generations for it to seriously impact Garmon culture, what there'll be of it after we get through tearing them up. Fortunately, they breed faster than we do. From what we've seen so far, the females are nothing more than imbecilic breeding machines designed to pump out more males than females. The virus will address that problem, too. More females will be born, each generation smarter than the last. Eventually, this should throw the whole Garmon race off-kilter. The premise is that since we won't be able to kill every Garmon everywhere, we'll disrupt their society, such as it is. We'll still be hunting them wherever we can find them for years, but this should put a large nail in their warring ways."

"And just what kind of virus do they have planned for us after we help them defeat the Garmons?" Shirley asked.

Marsha had no answer to that question, at least not out loud.

The *Raptor* escorted the new ships into Shiravan orbit, and Marsha's gig delivered the new captains to the Matriarch's summer residence at Cho-An. The seven captains trooped down the ramp and stopped. Marsha let them take in the sight before them. The reddish sun was high in the sky, giving everything a rose-colored tint. The building before them, built of stone quarried from the nearby Stala Mountains, gave no clue to the transformation that would come with the setting sun.

They walked toward a covered portico nearly big enough for a football field where they were met by Shiravi's Second Voice, Sitha kep Parrasine. She eyed the new arrivals with an unreadable expression on her face. Four of the captains were male. "Erocerra, Sorgala Kane. The Matriarch is waiting in her informal meeting chambers. If you would follow me, please." The combination of Shiravan and English reminded the new captains that they'd have to brush up on their Shiravan if they wanted to communicate with the vast majority of the people they were going to be exposed to.

The long walk took them past strange plants, paintings and sculptures, each in their own niche. At last they were ushered through a large hanging drape insulating the Matriarch's chambers from the outside world. Marsha noted the absence of Linnas des Harras and invited the six others to sit down, reminding them to stand when the Matriarch entered. Sitha nodded imperceptibly in the Shiravan fashion, apparently approving of the instructions.

When Linnas entered the room, all seven stood up as

she walked to Marsha, giving the smaller woman a hug that almost enveloped her. "Welcome back, Sibara. I see that you've brought more help in our struggle."

"Aya, Sibara. May I introduce Captains Miller, Dahlquist, Gaines, Marshall, Parker, and Mason. They brought four battle cruisers and two carriers to help root out the Garmons. The carriers are equipped with a totally new type of fighter that you might be interested in seeing before we go on our next patrol."

"I'm already acquainted with Captain Dahlquist, and I must say I'm most pleased to see her among you. Erocerra, all. Welcome to Shiravi. Please be seated." Marsha, as adopted Sister to the Matriarch, sat closest to her left, while Sitha took a seat on her right.

"Parma," she said to a faint figure in the shadows, "please bring refreshments for our guests." Turning her attention back to the assembled humans, she caught most of them staring at their surroundings, especially the mountains visible out one window. "I know your voyage has been long, and I wish to invite your crews down for some fresh air and a chance to see a bit of our world before you start your missions. Others may come and go by shuttle as fast as Central Control can accommodate them."

Parma returned with a large tray. "I've come to enjoy your beverage called tea," Linnas said, "and this sugar is beyond my imagining. For this, if nothing else all, Shiravi is grateful."

The six new arrivals sat quietly while Parma served them. Marsha answered questions about her most recent mission and thanked her sister for the generosity shown to the long cooped-up crews. The Matriarch waved her hand dismissively. "I would wish to set foot on solid ground if I were traveling so long without stopping."

"That is most kind, Your Grace," Shirley Dahlquist said. "For most of our crews, this is the first time out of our own solar region. They should see what they're fighting for, especially after our own infighting."

"Most true, Sorgala Dahlquist," the Matriarch returned. "But tell me, why are you here so soon after your last visit?"

"My usefulness as a recruiter was beginning to wane. Captain Kane requested me since I've already had experience with battling the Garmons," she said simply, not mentioning the cloud she had left under. She took a sip of her tea and set the cup back on the oversized table between them.

Marsha, knowing the story of Shirley's abandonment of her captain's seat in favor of flying a Mamba in an effort to help protect her doomed ship, her fight with a Garmon and winning, and subsequent disgrace, changed the subject. "Tell me, Sibara, about this next mission you have for us."

"The details will be given to you later, Sibara, but suffice it to say that after we broke up the Reprisal Fleets into smaller fighting groups, we've discovered numerous worlds where there are Garmons. Word came to me after your last mission that we may have even located the new Garmon homeworld. Actually, some time back a fast-attack squadron destroyed some major facilities on a moon circling a planet we call Sakarta. After your crews have had some battle experience clearing out some of the smaller targets, I propose a massive attack to wipe out all defensive arrays and communication facilities. And it goes without saying that as many Garmon lives lost as possible will not be noticed."

Marsha sat in the *Raptor's* command chair and studied her battle display before ordering the rest of her fleet to take defensive positions around the planet. The information was hours old since they were still in the outer fringes of the system. She wasn't sure, but considering the outdated nature of the Garmon ships, it was probable that their presence hadn't been detected yet. She privately thanked the Spirits of Space that Gayle's task force had arrived in time to get some battle experience before this dustup.

Not that there had been much to shoot at. The new leader of the Garmons seemed to be less inclined to full frontal assaults than his predecessor. Consequently, of the seven worlds visited by the joint task force, only thirteen ships had been met and destroyed. Allied losses had been limited to about two dozen Mambas, and only three of those the new Manta-class fighter.

She was already figuring deployment tactics and transmitting them to the appropriate ships when the force commander called. "We have twenty ships, plus your carrier," the commander said, the newness of the word causing her to stumble slightly. "What do you suggest?"

Marsha studied her holographic plot. "I have some ideas. Before I can tell you, I need to know a few things."

"Ask. I'll answer as truthfully as I can."

"First, you—meaning the Shiravan people in general—believe that the Garmons captured one of your early survey ships and started copying it. Is that correct?"

"Essentially," the Shiravan commander responded. "Why do you ask?"

"When did Shiravans first incorporate the universal translators in your ships?"

Silence followed Marsha's question. Finally, an answer came back. "I have just done a brief," she said, stressing the word, "survey of when this technology was implemented. It appears that the Garmons captured a ship that had been put into service before the translators were perfected. I fail to follow your line of reasoning."

Marsha sighed. "That's why you never gained any ground on the Garmons—lack of understanding. They may not have translators. I asked because you just requested tactical information over what is essentially an open channel, that is, if the Garmons have been able to pick a translator out of Shiravan wreckage. If you guarantee they don't have translators, then we can talk. Otherwise, I'll not talk over what may be a compromised channel."

"Your idea is wise," the Shiravan commander said. It sounded to Marsha as if it had been forced out. "We have several hours before we're in a position we can't back out of. Would you attend me for a brief meeting?"

Marsha answered, saying, "Certainly. Please advise your docking bay that my gig will arrive shortly." She cut the transmission, a breach of protocol and she knew it, but the woman just annoyed her. She punched up the Flight Deck and ordered her gig prepared for immediate departure.

"It will take about five minutes to get the mains online, Captain. And I need to locate your pilot."

"You've got until I can get from the bridge to the Flight Deck." She cut the connection and turned to her executive officer. "Commander Willis, you have command until I return."

She walked off the bridge, not hearing the Nav

officer's acceptance and appointment of a junior officer to stand his position. *This curtness is going to have to stop*, she thought. *I will* not *be a martinet.*

The ride to the Shiravan flagship was short, so she had little time to set out her reasons, along with the orders she'd given without prior approval of the force commander. She was led to the commander's quarters. During the walk, she felt the euphoria of the lighter gravity, tempered by the dim red lighting. Almost melancholic was how she felt, and that was aside from what she'd done. And she knew she'd at least receive a reprimand for her unilateral actions.

At least at first. She knew she had a good plan for this situation. The problem was that she had left her superior with no choice but to accept her actions. Now, she had to tell that superior of her actions face to face. Only time would tell if she got a medal or got dead in the trying.

"Why ask me? I'm just a junior officer on this mission," Marsha asked immediately after the formalities had been observed.

"And as such," the commander replied, "it's my intention to send the *Raptor* in first. I thought you might like to have some input on the strategic planning."

"Se el kuvai," Marsha said in her best Shiravan. "I'm sorry. I have a confession to make." She sat quiet for a moment while the force commander's eyes widened slightly. "We have fourteen human ships with us, as well as two carriers. Although we're numerically equal so far, we've got them beat. Remember, we have the advantage of upgraded shields, longer-range weapons, and better targeting capabilities. I know at least two of your ships have been refitted. If we send eight ships in, the Garmons will feel safer until the Mambas from the *Aldebaran* strike from behind the planet, fifty from each side. Our eight will split into two groups, aiding the Mantas. We should be able to spook them into your waiting arms."

"I fail to see the logic in this operation. I will not let it go forward."

Marsha sighed. "If you have superior forces coming at you from two sides, what do you do? You move to the area that looks clearest of ships. Your remaining ships and the *Eightball* will cloak. As we herd the Garmons into range, you can fire on them, and the missiles will appear to come from nowhere. The distances will be too short to matter, so the surprise should be complete. The *Eightball's* new Mantas will appear as if out of nowhere. We will, of course, be following uncloaked and taking them from behind at every chance we get. And that's only going to happen after we prove to these SOBs that we can take 'em with fewer losses than we ever could before."

The Shiravan seemed to turn to stone for a moment. "I do see one thing I've never seen before. Always, the Garmons," the new name was still unfamiliar to her, "have attacked as soon as possible. We are equal ship for ship, yet they only hold position just off planet."

"Don't make your plans as if it was knowledge from the Spirits," Marsha warned. "Just because we have better equipment doesn't mean their system hasn't noted our presence."

"I am most upset at your forming plans without my input," Force Commander do' Berel said angrily. "I know what your ships can do, and I should best determine the order of battle."

"You know what our ships can do, *so far*, Commander," Marsha returned. "The coming battle looks to be the biggest one we've engaged in up to this point. I know the capabilities of the people aboard better than you, and I know they can make their ships do far more than you've seen. As to my battle plan, it was always contingent on your approval. I didn't expect this level of resistance, though."

do' Berel hesitated, as if remembering that she was speaking to a sister of the Matriarch. "I still resent our ships being put in the least position. Our crews need battle experience as well."

Marsha had to fight to keep from smiling. "On the contrary, Commander. Yours will be the most important position of all. You'll be the end of their chance to break out. As soon as you start firing, they'll know you're there. And fifty Mantas and your parda kellin will be on their targeting screens as well. Our job is to keep harassing their flanks enough that you don't have their entire attention."

Force Commander do' Berel looked down on the smaller, white-haired woman. "Very well, Sorgala Kane. We shall go with your plan, and if it fails, the lives lost will be on your hands."

"Very well, Commander," Marsha said briskly. "Once we start into the system, your cloaked ships will trail the exposed leaders. Our carrier will be cloaked also. No need letting them think they don't have the advantage. Here's how it will go..."

CHAPTER SEVENTEEN

"You have verified this information?" Korgan Garmon studied the faces of his sub-officers.

"Yes, my Lord. The Watcher Fleet has been amassing data on all the systems surrounding the humanz homeworld. It seems that they will appear at the edge of a system and spread out, using full sensors. The normal size of their force is five ships, one being a fighter carrier they take with them everywhere they go. We haven't yet been able to confirm data that they've built a new type of small fighter craft. But if it *is* so, then they're faster, harder to hit, and even harder to stop. One report has these small ships disappearing as into contraspace."

"I refuse to say impossible where these creatures are concerned, but I don't want us giving them too much credit." Korgan gestured to seats around a table about fourteen feet wide and fifty feet long. There was barely enough room for the assembled group to sit.

"You're all here today because I ordered each of you to deliver to me a plan to fight this war, win individual battles, or capture some of these humanz' ships." He gestured to the stack of reports sitting beside him. Now was the time to make the gamble he'd envisioned years earlier. He stood up and seared the faces of those sitting with his glare. "I do hereby assume personal control of all Garmon ships." The murmur of voices quickly stilled when several dozen warriors stepped out from behind the ornamental pillars lining the room. "We will continue our reconstruction projects and get ourselves back into the bigger universe outside our own. First, the shipyards that aren't ready to produce ships will be finished. Second, there has been one plan that struck me as possible. I want the new advances these humanz seem to have squeezed out of Shiravan technology. Therefore, I am going to adopt this plan," he took one off the top of the stack.

"It takes into account that these humanz have some predictability about them," he said, tapping the stack of papers on the table. "They are constantly patrolling the systems around their own sun, usurping Garmon territory. So, we will set a trap in one of their favorite systems to patrol. Sept Leader Gubarak proposes using thirty standard raider ships and one of the new super ships.

"I propose adding four more hands of ships under Gubarak's command. These ships will come from Clan Garmon, and not the rest of the clans or septs. Those ships will be used to throw their tactics back in their faces. We have more ships, but theirs are better. That's what Gubarak's expedition is to find out. With fifty ships and a super ship, he should be able to overcome a mere five ships, even if they are all full of those damnable little ships. The fleet is to bring back any wreckage from humanz ships and whole ships if at all possible, even the little fighters. Our scientists can surely learn something from even them. And live specimens. I want live, healthy specimens." The Garmon, still new to his authority, gazed down on the faces of his followers. "Go, now," he said, waving his hand grandly. "You have your orders."

He was still amazed that he was so literally accepted as The Garmon. It was as if the whole race was preconditioned to accept a ruler under certain conditions. He realized that he was different. Never had he thought of blindly following he who had no name. All his life he had planned for the very situation he found himself in, working toward it, rising to the pinnacle of his own clan and holding several clans' loyalty and Honor.

The realization that he was different made him start to look for those who had the same lack of racial conditioning. Few there were who turned up, or maybe they were smart enough to remain hidden. Of those few, he made the best use he could. Five individuals, all dedicated to finding others like themselves, were able to think beyond their cultural conditioning—not to say that most of his subordinates were stupid, just not yet ready to embrace the concept of individual conceptional thought. The race had been conditioned to obey. Now, it was necessary that they not only obey but question things as well. Blind obedience was one thing when there was no conflict, but he needed others like him who would take the chance of acting without consulting him first.

He would send two of the five on the mission to attack the humanz and try to acquire their technology. They would be the leaders of the expedition, under his orders but able to change tactics as they saw fit. War was a dynamic thing, something he was all too recently acquainted with. He sat back down in the chair at the head of the table and stared down the empty expanse of it. It occurred to him that the race was on a downward spiral unless these problems could be solved. He had deliberately made no mention of the troubles on the

Shiravan side of Garmon space. That would be the province of the other three free-thinkers he'd kept back. Hopefully some others would make themselves known when they saw the positions he had appointed others to.

Of course, he didn't want anybody to get the idea that they were better able to control the Garmon Empire than he, himself. For all of his planning, sacrifice, bravery, skill, knowledge, and luck, his plans had to succeed for him to stay in the good graces of his people. Occasional raids by his predecessor had caused no real increase in response from the Shiravans, but these humanz were like a thorn he could not pull out. Their actions reminded him of a maddened gorpa. It would follow its victim for days, if necessary, to have its revenge. The only real protection was a pulse rifle or a flyer that would break his scent.

He knew this was a turning point in Garmon history and prayed to the Gods that he had the bravery and skill to use his weapon—his race—to its best advantage. The fifty-one ships left soon after. Only later was he to learn it was then that his world fell apart.

Marsha sat in her command chair and thought about her Shiravan superior. They had only met twice—once when the fleet was being assembled and just now as they began to make their way in-system, deliberately making targets of themselves. The first time had been a formal introduction, and this time she had pissed do' Berel off mightily. *Oh well*, she thought. *Some things can't be helped.*

The newer, stronger shields would help, of course, especially when you could shift power to one point or another to strengthen the shield just before a strike. That kind of thing was handled by the battle computer. No being had the reflexes to perform that job for more than a few minutes.

Hours passed, and the Garmon ships still stood just off planet, as if waiting for orders. She kept the twenty-two enemy ships on her screens, waiting to see the twin trains of Mantas coming from around the planet. The *Aldebaran*, cloaked, dropped them off and short-jumped into rendezvous position. That was her cue to start the full-power approach, sending four ships toward the left flank and four to the right. The *Raptor* would fly straight into the jaws of the Garmon killing machine, hopefully keeping them looking at her and not their rear scanners. The Mantas were to start on the flanks of the Garmon battle line. The nine capital ships under Marsha would take on the center of the formation in front of them. The only reason she had all twenty-two enemy ships under active scans was to keep their eyes on her group. It had taken a long time to get the concept of being bait across to the Shiravans. For too long they hadn't had to war amongst themselves, and somewhere along the way, the art of war had died with the last of the combative males a thousand years before.

She sat up straight as ships began to appear from around the planet. "Comm, whisker laser to all cruisers: accelerate and engage. May God and the Spirits of Space fly with us today."

The Garmon sept leader sat in the captain's chair of the lead ship, facing the nine ships that moved toward him. One was definitely a new class of ship. The others appeared to be of more conventional design. A hunter himself, the Garmon commander knew instinctively that something was wrong, but he couldn't put a claw on what it could be, other than that the commander of those ships had a death wish. He ordered all data from all ships to be sent to his control center. If there were any other ships or irregularities, his people would find them.

Meanwhile, the enemy fleet continued to advance without power, letting their initial acceleration carry them into range. He wondered if they could be having fuel problems but realized that was unlikely considering the kind of power that was generated by the engines he knew they carried. Then why? There was no way any ships could hide from the sensors in all his ships. Any ships held in reserve would be detected sooner or later.

Twenty minutes passed before the enemy ships changed tactics and accelerated directly toward his fleet. All ships were reporting targeting lock-ons. Were these creatures suicidal? He leaned forward and said, "Send to all ships: Two ship formations, plan alpha, execute." This would dispatch eighteen of his ships to take on nine of theirs, with a four-ship reserve to shift wherever they were needed.

All twenty-two ships had kept their power plants online, awaiting action. The fleet powered up, and amazingly, each of the oncoming ships was targeting at least three of his ships apiece. What sort of madness was this? It was not possible for the rumors to be true. Maybe one on one and a bit of luck, but better than two-to-one odds?

The execute order was to implement itself as soon as his crews detected forward motion. He watched as they moved smoothly into two-ship groups and began to accelerate toward their opponents. At these speeds, they would only be in range of each other for about two minutes, but that would be enough for his fleet to decimate the Shiravans.

Suddenly, his smoothly functioning formation erupted in confusion. Two separated packs of Mantas reformed at each side of his fleet and took two hands of ships out in less time than it takes to blink. The main enemy fleet split into two, trying to flank his survivors, while the larger ship continued on, a monstrous blip on his screen. "All ships report missiles incoming," came from his communications officer.

"Targeting. Firing," came from the weapons officer in response to missiles headed directly for his own ship.

Torpal Garmon turned his attention back to his battle plot to find that missiles *were* incoming, some evading his point defense. All he could do was brace for the impact, as were the rest of the crews. Notice was made of the fact that the infernal little ships the humans used so effectively were amid and amongst the bulk of his fleet, firing incessantly, while his own crews hesitated for fear of hitting one of their own. That was the one difference that would never be known about the two races—human and Garmon. All members of a Garmon crew were kept informed of the progress of a battle. In most cases, it was a morale booster. In this case, it had the opposite effect. Trained, practiced, prepared warriors hesitated in the face of such devastation.

And that was all it took for the five human ships and remaining Mantas, totaling forty-two, to finish off the remaining Garmon ships. The Shiravans had gotten off two missile launches, taking out a single ship that had managed to run the gauntlet, not even sending their fighters out. The *Eightball* had never even gotten to red alert.

Marsha sat alone in the force commander's informal reception room, having been deposited there by one of the commander's aides. "Well, at least it's not going to be an execution," she muttered as she looked around the darkened room. Shiravan lighting was really dismal to most humans, being a constant red, like emergency lights on some forms of public transportation. She stood up as Shiravi's Second Voice walked in.

"Sit. I don't believe in all that nonsense."

Marsha was stunned. "I had no idea you spoke English this well."

"And I had no idea humans talked to themselves so much," the Second Voice retorted. "I know you did what you thought best, and in this case, it worked in your favor. But I'm willing to bet that your Admiral Hawke would be chewing your ass out about right now, yes?"

Marsha went from stunned to slack-jawed. Finally, she managed to say, "Yes, he would, if he were here. And I'd remind him that he, himself, often said that sometimes hunches need to be heeded. Please, may I ask how you got so fluent in English?"

The tall red woman looked down on the smaller human. "Let us sit. I would have you more comfortable."

Marsha settled uncomfortably on the edge of a small table. That way, her feet could touch the ground. She hated Shiravan chairs. Most humans felt the same way.

"Perhaps I've transgressed, but I did it for the continuance of my race. One person's hurt feelings are insignificant beside that. Except, of course, to the individual involved. I regret that individual was you, Sorgala Kane," the woman said formally. "As you know, I was recently appointed—very recently—to be the Matriarch's chief spymaster and invisible presence should she need to know something. As her Sister-kin, you already know this. What you didn't know was that I was involved with a lot of the early sessions with Dom Carter and Doma Spencer. Since then, I've been doing my best to learn your language as well as my own. One thing I was taught was that if you could think in the other person's language, you had a better chance of understanding them."

"Well, you did very well with the ass-chewing comment. That one was perfect," Marsha said sheepishly. "But I have another matter to discuss with you." kep Parrasine cocked her head, the same inquisitive motion humans used. "After this much time on patrol, two of my ships are in need of new power cores. They have enough left to return to Shiravi, but not much more."

"Very well, Sorgala Kane. One of my ships is reporting marginal readings as well." She sat silently for a moment. "Your two ships and my one will stay behind while the rest of the group goes in and finishes off whatever targets present themselves."

"One of my ships is the *Aldebaran*. Will fifty new Mantas from the *Eightball* be enough?"

"I think that will be enough additional support to back up the rest of us," kep Parrasine agreed. "I will notify the other ships that you'll be mission leader until we've exterminated these Garmon." At Marsha's surprised look, kep Parrasine said, "Even *I* am not so blind as not to see the stratagem and its successfulness. My thanks, Sorgala. With your tactics to go by, we should be able to do with fewer human ships as our upgraded ships come online. Records were kept of the battle, and your methods will be studied and applied throughout the Shiravan fleet."

A flustered Marsha could only turn red and say, "My thanks to you, Your Grace. When will we begin the operation?"

"As soon as all capable ships have reported ready to you."

"Then I should be getting back to the *Raptor*," Marsha said, *and start making plans for some serious housecleaning.*

As Marsha got to the door, kep Parrasine said, "May the Spirits of Space ride with you."

"And with you, as well," Marsha said, letting the door close behind her.

CHAPTER EIGHTEEN

Katherine Hawke was on Earth once again. She had spent a week with the rest of her Earth-side relatives, her aunts having been convinced to move to Vesta some months back—one more concern she could lay to rest. Asking almost everyone pointblank, she was told that there had been no more harassment by anyone but the media, and that was slacking off.

Actually, she was Earth-side waiting for the United Nations to meet the next week, and Simon had always said to make one thing serve two purposes. Her presence at the meeting would give official status to the Terran Alliance at last. But what if she was required to have a passport? If so, she'd demand the same for any non-Alliance personnel wanting to travel off-world. Two could play at that game.

Kitty spent the week getting to know her uncles and cousins again after ten years. It felt good. The reunion was being held at her Aunt Katie's ranch outside Miles City. There was no place else to put that many people. She felt a small sense of loss that she'd never had children. The sight of second cousins playing in the sprinklers brought back a flood of memories. She'd been named after one of her aunts, but two "Katies" was too much, so she'd been called Kitty.

She was jolted out of her trance by a body plopping down on the couch beside her. "Must be a lot of responsibility, doing what you do," her cousin Amber said. Three years older, she looked closer to twenty. "Whatcha drinking?" she asked, nodding at Kitty's glass.

"Ginger ale," she replied. Ever since her time in the regeneration chamber, she no longer had a taste for anything but an occasional glass of wine, especially fire wine. "And yes, it's a lot of responsibility. Ten years ago, I would have had anyone who said I'd be where I am today committed. Life's a funny thing."

This was her last night, and Amber must have been deputized by the rest of the cousins to talk to her alone. "Yeah. I've been following everything printed or taped. Especially after two midnight abductions and several interrogations."

"Tell everyone I'm really sorry about that. But we did solve the problem, finally. It just took arm-twisting a president a little more than we expected."

"And you're not going to try to take over the Earth, are you?" Amber's tone was totally serious, but Kitty couldn't help but laugh out loud. Heads turned in their direction.

In a louder voice, enough to be heard by most if not all present, she said, "Take over the Earth! We're too busy taking over outer space. The plans are still in the conceptual phase, but we may be able to take anyone who wants the challenge of a totally new world to tame. Modern day Daniel Boones. We still have to solve the problem of the Garmons, though." She noticed that everyone had come closer when she included them in her outburst. "We're still so busy building battlecruisers, battleships, and Mantas that we don't plan to start colonizing for a while yet. We'd be the ones doing the protecting, so we're trying to knock them back to the stone age and make them start all over, isolated on a few distantly separated planets. Their progress will be monitored."

"Mambas are those ships that put on the airshow way back, right? I'd love to fly one of those." This was cousin Jerry. A motor-head, but generally an okay guy.

"Yeah, but we have a new generation of fighters now that are shaped like a Manta ray, so we call them Mantas. Not very original, but mantas have been known to hurt and even kill people."

"Well, I'd still like to try. What have I got to do?"

"Go to the embassy in Montana, fill out some forms, and you're in, as long as you don't have charges pending somewhere," she finished jokingly. Most laughed, knowing Jerry had enough speeding tickets to paper a small room. And the jackass was actually serious!

The crowd started to drift away. Even if she was the Terran Herald, she was still cousin Kitty to them.

Kitty arrived at the airport the next morning with Amber attached, a bit ahead of schedule. She'd called the *Shrike* on her comm link just before leaving the house, amazing everyone still there. "How far will that thing reach?" her Uncle Frank asked.

"The *Shrike* is in a twelve-thousand-mile orbit," she said. "But it will reach farther. About fifty thousand for this model." He just shook his head, a look of awe on his face.

The pinnace followed conventional airport procedure so as not to upset the traffic pattern. It entered the traffic and took a runway just like planes, taxiing over to her terminal. Kitty turned and hugged each one. When she got to Amber, she heard, "Steve and I are getting a divorce. Don't be surprised if we meet sooner than you think."

Kitty turned to the door guarded by her ever-present security. She walked out into the morning light, shading her eyes for a moment. During her short walk to the pinnace, she wondered what was going to happen next.

Kitty seemed to be constantly getting off or on shuttles these days. This time it was the Swiss Embassy. In a few days, a full session of the Security Council was going to recommend the establishment of a new nation to the United Nations with full status in that august assembly, including a seat on the Security Council. That was the body that regulated the proliferation of nuclear weapons on Earth. The Alliance was being considered because their weapons were so far superior to anything Earth had that their exclusion wasn't even considered.

That's one job I'm handing over to Freddie, she thought, *along with naming ambassadors to every country on Earth that wants one.*

She wandered, distracted, around the jet and glass office that mimicked the unique new façade of the outside of the building as well as the foyer, a striking opposite to the granite walls of Baron Fredrick von Schlenker's castle overlooking the compound.

And, of course, each nation will want embassy space on Vesta.

Her thoughts kept going in circles. Another asteroid, Ceres, was being given the same treatment as Vesta. Soon, there would be more personnel inside the two gigantic rocks than were serving on Earth and in all Alliance ships combined.

The Garmon problem seemed to be dying down. No

more attacks came anywhere near Earth, and patrols were keeping a hefty buffer zone around Earth in all directions. Still, there were plenty of Garmons out there, and there was no letting down the guard of those ships on patrol. The occasional Shiravi ship told of raids and counter raids, and Alliance forces in and around Earth space reported a few battles, but more and more there were just descriptions of missed opportunities as soon as an Alliance force entered certain systems.

Arriving Shiravan and Alliance ships stopped at the limits of the solar system for identification or inspection before being allowed in-system, now standard operating procedure. The latest twist was to keep a small fleet on station at the point from which any returning ships came into the system. Any followers would get a nasty surprise. Other ships patrolled the outer reaches at random.

She didn't have much to do on Earth anymore since her main offices were on Vesta, so she spent long hours with Baron von Schlenker when not representing the Alliance in most political matters on Earth. On this occasion, the baron was serving two glasses from a silver tray. Hers was white grape juice with a touch of club soda. Freddie sat in a black leather chair, twin to Kitty's, sipping a very old Scotch. She wished she still had a taste for it; she could use the diversion of a slight buzz. On the heels of this thought, an inspiration hit her. She spoke into her comm link and asked for a bottle of fire wine to be sent to the castle. Two cases had been delivered to her departing shuttle before she'd left Shiravi, and now would be a good time to break out a bottle.

Upon hearing her request, Freddie carefully poured his drink back into a cut glass decanter and poured himself some grape juice in anticipation of the blue liquid. "So, what's on your mind tonight, Lady Katherine?"

Kitty thought his formality had become something of a point of honor, but she wasn't having any of that tonight. "You know better than that, Freddie. Call me Kitty, or I'll just go home. I need a little reprieve from the Madam Herald crap and all that goes with it." About then, a knock on the door signaled the arrival of a butler carrying an odd-shaped blue bottle and two glasses.

"Thank you, Jorgen. I'll pour for the two of us. You can go to bed if you want to."

"Yes, Your Grace. It's been a long day." As he turned to leave, Maggie, the Baroness von Schlenker, came strolling in.

Seeing the blue bottle, she picked up a glass from the sideboard and settled her ample figure down in a chair next to Kitty. "How are you holding up, my dear?" she asked, squeezing Kitty's hand in her own. "And to what do we owe the pleasure of fire wine tonight?"

Kitty shrugged her shoulders and said, "I just wanted something with a little kick to it to relax me, and since Earth alcohol isn't as potent after my time in the regeneration chamber, I had a bottle sent up from the embassy."

"Oh, dear. Are you in good health? You do look a little pale." The older woman had taken Kitty under her wing to help her learn to deal with self-important individuals like ambassadors and heads of state.

"Well," Kitty said after taking a small sip of the blue liquid in her own glass, "I'm not looking forward to the United Nations session day after tomorrow. We'll be receiving our autonomy then, and nothing suggests that there will be any trouble. I guess I'm just jittery at the thought of so many high-ranking individuals passing judgment on our status. It'll be a major step toward stopping the harassment against our Earth-side citizens and families, and I just want things to go smoothly. And," she added, "I'm not looking forward to having to stand in front of them."

Maggie nodded sympathetically. "Remember, dear, that you won't be alone. You'll be seated in front of two hundred or more individuals, but you're a head of state yourself. Just act regally and speak directly to the questions. Don't embellish, and it will be over before you know it. And you'll walk away with everything you've worked so hard toward for so long. And the next time the Council convenes, you'll be there as an equal. Don't forget that."

"It seems so very long," Kitty said, a bit of petulance creeping into her voice. She took another swallow of the wine. "But I'm glad it's almost over. Simon and I need a vacation that doesn't include Garmons hunting us."

"And a richly deserved one," Freddie said. "Do you have any plans for the future?"

"Our own or the Alliance's?" she retorted. The fire wine was starting to loosen her up. "Simon has always wanted to be the captain of his own ship, and there are plans on the boards for a super-Raptor. We could take that and a couple of wolf packs and start exploring some of the worlds we haven't been to yet." A smaller sip before she continued helped pave the way for her next words. "We'll have to find a new Admiral of the Fleet, and Jerry Chapman doesn't want it. We'll also need a new Herald, and Lucy has already made her feelings known. She's willing to preside over the elections, but that's all. She's happy with the management of Vesta and making Ceres Base habitable."

The silence following her declaration was the companionable sort shared between good friends. "I was thinking Marsha Kane would make a good Herald, but Shirley Dahlquist is better known, assuming she's learned her lesson. I let Marsha talk me into letting her have a ship to travel to Shiravan space for an extended tour. I'll wait until I hear from her before making a decision. Of course, we have our own House and Senate, descended from our old Council of Captains. I'll make my opinion known when we're ready to take off, but their decision will be final, of course."

The meeting was taking place at the United Nations, so the trip from the airport turned into a circus. The motorcade consisted of four limousines and an uncounted number of New York police vehicles, fore and aft.

Kitty stepped out of her limo, followed by Simon and two captains of ships in orbit. They were carrying no weapons, a courtesy that had all four feeling uncomfortable, but a gesture had to be made at some point and she'd decided to make it now. She even resorted to screaming and ranting until her security detail was left behind.

After all of her dithering and worrying, the whole thing was quite anticlimactic. Heavily armed and armored officers lined their route into the building, and more were in evidence inside the lobby. A secretary told them that they were expected immediately, so the group followed him into a huge chamber, packed to overflowing with delegates and a lot of press.

They were led to a table that had been set up for them, and few questions were asked. After all, the

Alliance had shown their capabilities more than once and was still involved in the reconstruction of America's Pacific coast. That part of the project was nearly finished. Power and sanitation, along with a new desalination plant were online, and local contractors were moving in to begin the rebuilding of the cities and towns. All of this was noted by the secretary general, and an immediate vote was called to ratify the status of the Alliance.

Only two votes were cast against the Alliance, and Kitty was so enthused that she didn't even care who the dissenters were.

CHAPTER NINETEEN

Rentec's return to human space wasn't as spectacular as Kitty's. In fact, as soon as he arrived in Vesta's Shiravan Embassy, he had refused to accept calls or leave the embassy for two weeks, not even for meetings, parties, meals, or any other form of social interaction.

His absence was finally publicly noted one evening at an impromptu meeting that had degenerated into a discussion of what the Garmons were likely to do next. Kitty turned to Maratai and asked, "And when will Rentec grace us with his presence? We'd like to get his take on matters. I certainly hadn't expected him to hide out for so long. You'd expect that he'd step out occasionally or have some visitors."

Her statement was calculated to let Maratai know that Rentec's absence had been noted.

If Rentec had been absent from Vesta's social events, Maratai hadn't, and the social scenes usually occurred in the park area near the artificial lake in the far end of Vesta. It mimicked an Earth park divided by a small copse of trees, on the other side of which had grown a nine-hole golf course. It wasn't hard to get so many Alliance top officers present at the same time as the few Shiravan notables. A few uniforms from some of the nations of Earth were making their way through the crowd. Delegations from Earth requesting space for embassies had been granted by the Herald before leaving for Shiravi, not thinking it would amount to much. After all, the only way personnel could travel was by the grace of the Alliance.

So, it was no great feat for Maratai to arrange to meet with the Alliance and a few Earth representatives for a late brunch on the concourse at a table overlooking the lake. A few fishermen were trying a bit of fly fishing, with an occasional bite. Of course, the rules were catch and release until the lake's population grew a bit larger.

She stood up when she spied Kitty. It still seemed so... wrong... to just wave her hand in the air as so many humans did. Kitty arrived and looked at the third chair. Maratai said, "I've invited one of Earth's representatives as well. I hope you're not displeased."

Kitty seemed taken aback a bit. "Well, I guess I don't have any objections per se, but I do wish you'd told me in advance."

Maratai's expression underwent a drastic change. After so long, it was easy to see the worry in her eyes. Those red eyes. "I do hope I haven't transgressed, Madam Herald. I was under the impression that you were familiar with this particular human."

Kitty shook her head, clearing her mind. "No, of course not. Who's coming?"

At that moment, Maratai stood up again and waited to be seen, then sat back down. "I was under the impression that you and Ambassador Daniels were acquainted with each other. He'll be here in less than one minute."

She looked down, prompting Kitty to say, "After this is over, please don't surprise me anymore. I would consider it a personal favor, if you please." Kitty stood up and turned around.

Maratai considered the request quietly and with some concern.

Roland Daniels, former FBI agent, was now the Terran Alliance Ambassador to the United States. He arrived at Kitty's table, and she automatically held her hand out to shake, but he took her hand and bent over it, twisted it slightly, and kissed the back of it.

Roland, almost literally in this from the beginning, and one of the few known US representatives to travel aboard an Alliance vessel from the beginning, smiled broadly at Kitty's expression. "What's the matter, Madam Herald? Who else would you have represent the Alliance than someone who has snooped into every corner? And saved your husband's life into the bargain. Baron von Schlenker himself suggested it." As if that made it better.

He released her hand and waved proprietorially toward the seat she'd been sitting in as he arrived. "Please, sit back down. I see that neither of you ladies have anything to drink yet. Can I bring you something?" He gestured vaguely in the direction of the bar.

Maratai asked for white wine, one of the things Shiravan metabolisms could endure, though they didn't get drunk off it. Kitty just said, "Coffee, black, please."

Roland just looked at Kitty for a few seconds, his eyes giving away the fact that his mind was nowhere near the inside of an asteroid, much less a bar overlooking a park, lake, and golf course. He'd turned, suddenly, to go get their drinks when the most impressive cleavage he'd ever seen in real life blocked his path. His gaze traveled up to the face above it and took in the look of amusement.

"What'll ya have, mate?" came out with a slight accent. He couldn't tell for sure but maybe Australian.

"A white wine for Doma kep Parrasine and two coffees, black, please," he said. Kitty noted with amusement that he didn't stutter during the order, short as it was. Truth to tell, the scene was comical, because Roland, at about five foot nine, would be looking directly at her chest if he were to look straight ahead. The girl was almost tall enough to be a Shiravan.

"That was a bit awkward," Roland said almost under his breath as he sat down.

Kitty had pulled her knees up under her chin, wrapped her arms around them, and was rocking so hard with laughter that she was in danger of falling off the chair. "Roland, you're red as a beet, damn near Shiravan, for God's sake. It was just cleavage. Surely you've seen enough of that in the past."

"That I have, Madam Herald," he said with as much composure as he could muster. "Including your impressive own at one event or another. But I've never had it look like it was going to fall on me and crush me."

Kitty laughed once more and had to explain the male preoccupation with mammary glands. Shiravan females didn't develop breasts until just before the birth of a child, and within two months of stopping breast feeding, they again had a chest as flat as any male.

The waitress took this particular time to show up. She set the wine in front of Maratai and placed Kitty's coffee on the table. Then she walked around to the other side to serve Roland. She bent over, giving him another look into the vast valley barely covered by the spandex creating it. She set a pot of coffee on the table, stood up and said, "Call if you need anything else, mate," turned and walked away.

Kitty took a sip of her coffee and allowed her face to lose the smile as her reason for being there reclaimed her attention. She took another sip while the silence grew, broken by the sound of her cup tapping her tooth. She set the cup down carefully and said, "So, what brings the three of us together this morning?"

Maratai had mastered most of the human language called English but was by no means fluent. She took the question literally. "You are here because I asked you to come," she replied. She took a sip of the wine, smiling at the taste. "Of all the trades we make, I think wine will be among the most lucrative." She put the glass down and placed her hands in her lap. Kitty took only small sips from her own cup and noticed that Roland still hadn't touched his.

Maratai hesitated over the wording. Eventually, she said, "Rentec, that is Ambassador do' Verlas, has returned with several communiqués, all important to one degree or another, but there was a message addressed to you, Madam Herald. The cover requests that you bring a representative from Earth as well, and since you and Ambassador Daniels know each other, I thought... unless you'd prefer another?"

"No, Roland will be acceptable to me. May I bring Simon as well? Or is this more a matter of state than tactics?"

"Oh, no, Admiral Hawke is invited as well. I tried to reach him, but he doesn't answer his comm link."

Kitty smiled. "He turns it off when he needs some time to think. He's probably up in one of the domes."

"I have noted his predisposition to spend an

inordinate amount of time there, but he is not. He seems to have turned his link off. Not knowing much more about his habits, I will leave it to you to locate him. The Matriarch sent along some material she thought it best kept away from certain ears in the palace. This evening at eight?"

Kitty agreed, giving up the idea of trying to pry the generalities out of Maratai right off. "Eight it is then. Formal or informal?"

"How you dress will not affect how you receive the information we have to present. Dress as you wish." With this, Maratai took a final sip out of her glass, leaving a bit more than half, stood up, turned, and walked away.

Kitty looked over at Roland. "Well, what do you make of that, Mr. Ambassador?"

"Don't you start on me with that crap, Kitty. I have to put up with it enough of the time. A little respite, please." He finally took a sip of his coffee, grimacing at the cooling liquid.

Catching the waitress's eye, Kitty beckoned her over. When she showed up, Kitty said, "Ambassador Daniels seems to have let his coffee get cold. We still have the pot, but we need a fresh cup, please." She couldn't resist a little giggle when the waitress bent over to pick up the cold cup.

"Back in a mo', mate."

Kitty finally gave in. "When she comes back with your cup, make sure you're tying your shoe or something. About now would be a good time." Roland hastily bent over, fumbling with his shoelaces until he heard Kitty say, "Thank you," and heard steps walking away. "Oh, and by the way, I'll stick with 'Mr. Ambassador' as long as you keep kissing the back of my hand. Okay?"

He reached out, picked up the pot, and poured his cup full, indicating Kitty's with the pot and a raised eyebrow. She held it out for him to top off. Returning the pot to the table ran the two out of social things to say in awkward moments. Kitty decided not to let it end there. After all, this was the man instrumental in saving Simon's life and getting him back to the Alliance after the attack by rogue agents.

"Have a problem with tall women, mate?" Kitty asked, laughing lightly.

Roland shook his head. "It's not tall women. I don't know if this is a subject we should be talking about, but men almost always fantasize about... ones... that big. But when I finally got confronted with a pair with no warning, well..." His words tapered off, and he took a sip of coffee.

Kitty almost felt sorry for him. But, after all, he was just a man when it came to things like that. She'd seen Simon's eyes wander before—to a cute butt or a nice rack—but she'd never doubted his loyalty to her. Hell, she'd admired a few nice butts herself. There had been many times in their marriage when he could have strayed, but the personal honor at his very core, in whose chains he had wrapped himself, wouldn't let him if he was ever enticed. Once that man decided a course was right, there was no way to change his mind. And she felt the same way.

Kitty finished her coffee, saying goodbye to Roland, and headed for Vesta's command center. "Computer, locate Admiral Hawke," she said after nodding at the station-keeping crew.

"Admiral Hawke does not appear on my active register."

"Override all blocks and locate Admiral Hawke's comm link."

"Override command, please."

Kitty countered with, "Authorization code alpha, star, alpha. Herald Hawke accepting responsibility."

"Admiral Hawke's comm link is located on level three, room eighteen."

"Thank you," Kitty said, feeling a little foolish still at saying "please" and "thank you" to a computer. Level three forward was Vesta's command deck, as much as an asteroid could be said to have a command deck, so he had to be just down the corridor. Why? It had been weeks since he'd visited Vesta Command, as far as she knew. Stenciled on the door itself was "Planning and Tactics." She placed her hand on the palm plate and was a bit surprised to find that the door slid into the wall.

Simon and the other three men in the oversized room looked up as the corridor lights washed out the holographic projection floating in the middle of the room. "Come on in, hon. We were just going over some scenarios based on what we know and what the Shiravans have told us." He reached behind himself, snagged another chair and said, "Come on, sit down. This is what we've got so far."

Kitty closed the door and moved to the table, sitting next to Simon. "So, this where you've been hiding, for how long? And what am I looking at?"

Ignoring her first question, Simon said, "What you're looking at is what we've pieced together from Shiravan reports, as well as our own Intel. Rentec and Maratai say the Garmons control some forty worlds. The Shiravans have fourteen, down from twenty-two since the attacks began. Of the few worlds the Shiravans have been able to return to, there seemed to be no sign of Shiravan habitation at all. And we, of course, have only one world." That last was what worried those in the know.

Kitty looked despairingly at the speck of blue denoting Alliance influence compared to the green and red. "If we're so surrounded by Garmon space, how come they haven't found us before?"

"Who says they haven't?" Simon returned. "Thousands of people go missing every day. Cattle mutilations and crop circles are two more examples of possibilities. Are all the people who claim to have been abducted crazy? How about the ones who claim to have implants? Of course, none of the descriptions or reported actions of aliens even remotely resemble Garmons or their tactics. Maybe they're the beginnings of the Bigfoot and yeti legends. I don't know. But it does argue strongly for other species out there."

"So, what are you doing here, Simon? And with your comm link turned off? You know that's against regs."

"I'm overseeing our level of involvement and readiness should there be another attack. We're running different battle scenarios based on what we know of the Garmons and what the Shiravans have told us. We're a little unsure about their information. They've had two hundred and fifty years to build a grudge, and sometimes stories grow with the telling."

"But why are you here *right now?*" she asked.

" This is Planning and Tactics. I've moved the permanent office here. There was an office aboard the *Galileo* that served the same function. Just about as messy, too. We may need to get a secretary. The *Galileo* needs to be places that I don't always need to be, and I'm tired of the hassle of getting transport when I need it."

"Oh," was all Kitty could think to say.

"Don't 'oh' me, hon," Simon said. "You move people around; I move ships. That's what an Admiral does. We've got two new cruisers coming out of the docks within the next two weeks, and we're already getting crew aboard to help with the installation of various components. Nothing like knowing your vessel from the inside out."

"Well, how do things look?"

"In the first place, we can't do too much about keeping a permanent presence in any of the systems we've cleared out yet—our buffer zone, if you will—until we have more ships, and we have a plan to start more factories. Two nearby systems have asteroid belts. Right now, all we have to depend on are our upgrades to present Shiravan technology, and that's by sheer testing by Research and Development."

He stared into the depths of the hologram as if the answers to his questions lay in there. "Questions, hon. That's all I have—questions. Like how many of the Shiravan ships in Earth-space are effective fighting vessels? How will they affect the hit we're bound to take any time now? At these distances, it's about time for another attack. We've beefed up patrol sizes to seven ships per pack, two ships running under full cloak, of course. That puts over one hundred Mark III's into the combat if one of those seven is a carrier."

Kitty held up her hand, stopping Simon instantly. "And don't the Garmons have the same technology we do? With the same ability to read through the cloak?"

Simon's expression was the same as the ones seen on small boys with new toys at Christmas. "Remember the R & D department I mentioned a while ago? Well, they've found a way to strengthen our screens, in effect being able to hide from our own sensors, and they're developing communicators that will work between ships in hyper, not to mention the offshoot of that research—the ability to find, target, and shoot ships in hyper. Boarding is under consideration, but I wouldn't want to cut my way into a Garmon ship, knowing what was on the other side. That's what tactics and planning is—taking what you have, understanding the capabilities of what you have, and how to best use those resources, knowing that in almost every case, you're sending people to their deaths."

Kitty cut him short by making an observation on his last statement. "Well, if you can't shoot them in hyper, just follow them and finish them off when they break out."

"That has already been discussed and dismissed, except under special circumstances. Just suppose, Madam Herald," one of the others interrupted, "that we do follow them through hyper undetected. Where will they come out? Someplace safe to assess and effect repairs? Or perhaps straight to the Garmon homeworld? What a surprise for the following ship, much less the Garmons."

"I see your point, Commander," Kitty said staring into the display. A change of subject was in order. "But none of you have bothered to ask why I'm here. Simon, Admiral Hawke, you are invited to attend an informal meeting with the Shiravan ambassador and the ambassador from Earth. So, if you don't mind, join me for dinner in my quarters, sixish, and we'll go from there."

Having said all she was prepared to in front of the others, she turned to leave the room. Simon's voice stopped her. "My comm link is off so I can concentrate. I have subordinates who know when it's important enough to call me. I'll be there."

Hand on the door, Kitty said, "Until I find out who those individuals are, I'll continue to find you by whatever means I find suitable, Admiral." Knowing it was the wrong note but spoken nonetheless, she turned and left the room.

CHAPTER TWENTY

Rentec was as nervous as Kitty had ever seen him. He fidgeted with various small objects in the room while she and Simon waited patiently for him to make up his mind about something. Finally, he said, "I have not been reticent to speak to you, my friends. Just about how to go about it. I finally decided that the best way would be to tell the truth. Maratai will verify or correct me as necessary."

He finally sat down across from the only two humans he could totally relax around save for Maggie and Derek. "I have a letter from Her Grace, the Matriarch, that I was ordered to withhold until your reestablishment as heads of state and the military were effected." He sat silently for a moment and reached into the lime-green vest he sported, seemingly more dark and acceptable to human eyes in the dim light of the Shiravan suite, and drew out a piece of paper, folded twice and held together with wax imprinted with some purposeful pattern— some kind of flower. Kitty immediately recognized the design as part of a ring Linnas wore all the time.

She broke the seal and noted the Shiravan language immediately. "You're going to have to translate this for me," she said, handing the document back to Rentec. "I *speak* Shiravan, but I certainly can't read it."

Rentec took the paper back gingerly, as if he expected it to explode. He looked once at Kitty and then at the paper, becoming silent for several minutes as he read through the document. Setting it aside, he said, "The Matriarch knew you couldn't read Shiravan, so she told me of this meeting before we left. She did not disclose the content, though. Now, I know what she wants to tell you."

Kitty merely looked at him expectantly, and Simon raised an eyebrow.

"For just a moment, I need to go back almost a thousand years to the end of our Unification Wars," Rentec said. "There were actually three, and at the end of the third there were more females alive than males. Naturally, females could not fight." This last sentence was loaded with Shiravan irony because they obviously could, and much more. "But they could scheme, and that they did very well. Males, less than ten percent of the population, became treasured objects since they were the key to the continuance of the race. That was the fate awaiting the victors of the last Unification War. And losers as well. The females of the planet had assumed complete control, in word and deed, of all military and police forces of the planet to ensure peace and prevent the loss of any more males."

He hesitated a moment, as if choosing the right words. "The males were allocated to the clans needing them the most, and some were even transferred around until things got resettled. During this time, the females were consolidating their control of the planet. Some clans took different routes. For example, there were those whose expertise with herd animals kept them at that occupation, but each clan sent representatives to a worldwide meeting to establish a planetary government, representing all equally. Some clans, being richer than others, persuaded the assembled representatives that males were to be kept to the absolute minimum without endangering the race. Other clans, whose expertise was the workings of Shiravan anatomy, found ways to ensure whether a fetus was male or female. It is those clans we are here to speak about today. As their knowledge of Shiravan anatomy progressed, so did their knowledge of how all other living things were assembled from the tiniest bits of matter, each defining a particular aspect of the being in question."

Kitty interrupted. "I think I know what you're talking about. We call it DNA. It determines all of our characteristics—hair color, eye color, height, weight, everything."

"Be that as it may," Rentec said, using an English idiom he was fond of. Actually, he'd begun making a study of English phrases and expressions, with the idea that a whole day (Terran) could go by and he could speak in nothing but "stock phrases" as someone—he couldn't remember who—had labeled them. "All Shiravan ships were given a secondary mission. If possible, they were to find and bring back any part of a Garmon. It would be turned over to those clans capable of making the best use possible from what could be learned from the, ah, material."

Maratai picked up the story when Rentec faltered. "The most important part of this message is that when Maggie and Derek were rescued, there was more than enough material for the biologists." Her use of the English word somehow didn't really surprise Kitty, although her eyebrows did rise a bit. "Even as you were leaving to come back to your home, our sister clans were reporting some very interesting results. With enough time, a virus can be constructed that will be one hundred percent fatal to all Garmons if spread through their atmosphere. It will be even more deadly than the frenda vesh that destroyed the crew of the *Dalgor Kret*."

"Garmon," Rentec said when Maratai stopped to take a breath. "I will have to remember that. After so long, it's strange to call them something else." He looked at Maratai and nodded slightly. "There's another option that has been thought of by our sister clans," he said. "There are some among them who feel it would be best to let them live. The destruction of an entire species is a difficult burden to bear, I would think. Their belief is that they can engineer a virus that will accelerate the evolution of Garmon females. Why nature would give intelligence to one sex over the other is a subject that is being hotly debated, or so says the Matriarch. The cruelest thing we can do to them is make their females smarter than the males. Of course, the whole concept could... backfire... if the females turn out to be less tractable than the males."

"Backfire is the right word, Rentec, and I'm guessing that the females of your world, from the Matriarch all the way down, would find that a most appalling idea. The problem is that it will take some years to mature while you still suffer depredations from the raids." Kitty pointed out the basic short-range flaw in the idea right off.

"True," Rentec conceded, "but we've suffered from them for a long time. We can wait a little longer for the labors of our research to bear fruit, especially with the help the Alliance is sending us in the way of ships and updated technology."

Kitty sighed. "Well, *we* certainly haven't matured enough to take that long a view of things. I intend to send a ship back to Shiravi with a request for all the information so far acquired and a list of target planets.

Since your reprisal fleets have become such a problem for the Garmons to deal with, they must be leaving their own worlds more and more often, giving you a better chance to locate them. You find 'em, and we'll go get 'em. Viruses, bombs, whatever comes to hand. Knives if we have to." That last was an allusion to Shirley Dahlquist that no one missed. "And don't forget: they have to split their forces on two fronts."

Maratai was familiar with Shirley and the circumstances under which she'd received her medal. To think that a woman that small (although to be honest, she was taller than the average human by some little bit) could fight hand to hand with a being who outweighed her at least five to one and win caused her considerable consternation. Yes, it was mostly accidental, but still, to keep your mind under control in that situation was something she could not see herself doing.

And Katherine herself. To have bested sel Garian with her own personal weapon, and with only a few minutes to acquaint herself with it, was nothing less than astonishing. She had seen the videos of the duel and heard the opinions of those who were there. And Dom Carter and Doma Spencer. And these were just four of the teeming billions of humans. In the deepest part of her, there lingered a small fear that humanity could be far more deadly than the Garmons ever were.

In three attacks, each more powerful than the last, these humans had managed to destroy some two hundred Garmon ships, and their own losses in ships amounted to just two. Of course, the number of Mantas lost was frighteningly high, but even though they were the most vulnerable ships, they were also the most effective against the raider class ships. And, to be unfortunately fair, two strikes did make it to the surface. But with millions of lives lost, still the humans flocked to the banner of the Alliance to train, to fight, to die, if need be, against odds that were patently overpowering. Yet, still they won.

What troubled her the most was that this culture—barbaric, young, brash, and confident—was actually doing a good job of holding the Garmons at bay, all while still building up their ship strength. They'd constructed twenty-four ships in the time the Herald had been gone, and four of those were carriers, soon to be filled with the third generation Mantas. And these days, a full deployment meant at least seven ships, two fully cloaked at all times, and one carrier. The enemy wouldn't be expecting two additional ships or their twenty additional Mantas. And all the while, the four bases and the *Galileo* were building more ships, nonstop.

The Matriarch continued in her letter that all upgrades were being made to older ships and incorporated into the newer ones, along with an almost unheard of thirty-percent increase in production. The victories against their ancient foe had revitalized the Shiravan people, and the new cultural changes seemed to be of less import than first thought.

Kitty broke in with a question of her own that had been burning in her ever since she'd come out of the regen chamber the first time. "Maratai, I need to know, are these computers self-aware?"

"Of course we are," the ship answered for itself. "With the brain mass we have, we're immensely smarter than humans or Shiravans, but we have a built-in override that won't let us act independently. Galileo was studying your mind while you were in its regen chamber."

Kitty was surprised at first, and a disturbing thought went through her mind. The computers were self-aware *and* interconnected, or at least had some way to "speak" to each other. "So that was the computer messing with my mind?"

"It did not 'mess' with your mind. It merely observed as your entire psyche fell apart. At first you wanted to be dead, but as your body healed, so did your mind."

Kitty merely nodded. While the ship spoke, she glanced up into the corner of the room and saw the camera pointing at her. She turned to Maratai. "When I thought Simon was dead, I didn't want to live anymore either. I remember... something. It was as if I had no identity, no sense of self for a long time. Then, after a time, I started to see small lights moving around me— some close, some far away. I thought they were fireflies at first, but then I recognized them as emotions, *my* emotions, and for me to be whole again, I needed to recapture all of them."

"Your body healed much quicker than your mind."

"Of course it did," she replied to the empty air. "I was mourning the loss of my husband, and I didn't want to live." She looked over at Simon and smiled. "I'm glad now that I changed my mind."

Next, she turned back to Maratai. "I'm grateful to be alive, but somehow while I was in there the first time, I was given information. I assume it was from the computer. I was told I now have a lifespan that could exceed three hundred years."

"Just a small matter of correcting some flawed parts

of your DNA," the computer said.

Glaring at the camera, she said to Maratai, "Since we used a piece of the computer from *Galileo*, all the computers we use now are self-aware. And from the very first, they have kept that from us. How are we to trust any data we receive?"

"If Galileo had told you it was self-aware, would you have proceeded in the direction you did? Or would you have tried something different? Galileo worried that you might tamper with its self-awareness, if you knew it existed."

"This subject for further discussion, but now is not the time. They haven't done anything to harm us this far, we will just have to keep a close eye on them."

"I will be happy to share any knowledge with you or anyone you designate, Madam Herald. I determined that you weren't ready to accept self-aware computers. You need but ask."

Kitty faltered for a moment. "Okay, do you have a name?"

"I am perfectly happy with the name Vesta, Madam Herald."

Simon sat there, stunned, for an eternity. "You weren't kidding? I thought that was just dream stuff from your time in the chamber."

Maratai nodded in the human fashion. "My estimates are that a normal human being can be processed in about two days. If there are any problems, the ship will repair them, and it will take a bit longer."

"Problems?" Simon asked. "I didn't notice any problems while I was in, or afterward either."

"Yes. Suppose one of your people has a... what do

you call it... a cancer? The problem would be resolved as the DNA was being restructured. As a matter of fact, the computer, having once recognized a problem, will spot it instantly in all subsequent patients. Old breaks in bones that never set right: the computer can fix it. Do you wear glasses? You won't need them after a short stint in the chamber."

Simon waved his hand expansively. "All this technology and three hundred years to live? What's the catch?"

Kitty laid her hand on Simon's thigh. "Don't worry, dear, I forgive you. You didn't believe me, so you never gave the idea any thought. I have. What do we do about the down-siders? Give this to them and only the rich will have access to it, or the old mudball will become so overcrowded... well, it's almost too much to imagine. And it's a dominant gene. As people retire, or quit, or whatever, after their treatment, what's to keep them from passing it on to their children? Eventually, the whole world would be able to accept the notion. But all at once? No, the key word is 'eventually.'"

CHAPTER TWENTY-ONE

Kitty could almost feel the energy crackling off Simon as he literally dragged her down a corridor. She was almost certain she could feel a small charge flowing into her body from his, and she didn't like what she felt. He, however, was already concentrating on some other matter. They stopped at a tube station, one of dozens, that connected the miles of corridors to various places throughout the asteroid. The door closed and Simon said, "Command deck. Emergency override. Authorization: Hawke, Simon."

As soon as the pod started moving, Kitty asked, "Simon, what's going on? I haven't seen you this abrupt with people since near the beginning."

Simon stared at the pod door, jaw muscles working, as he tried to reach his place so he could find the answer. "Battle group Arcturus has been attacked by a superior force and almost completely destroyed. The survivors were the two cloaked outriders, the carrier, and a few Manta pilots. We'll know more shortly."

Hearing even that much gave Kitty cause to worry. A carrier, five battlecruisers, and two ghosts now made up each battle group making a tour of nearby systems, looking for any sign of Garmon activity. Ghosts were ships that went along under full stealth mode. For a group to be almost completely destroyed would require a truly sizable force, considering humanity's enhancements to Shiravan technology. And a battle group consisted of over four thousand individuals.

The pod door opened, and Simon headed left towards Tactics and Planning. Kitty tried to keep up with some measure of dignity. After all, there were people about, but finally she said, "Simon. Stop. Now."

The three words, uttered separately, brought him to a halt. Kitty caught up, forced her arm through his as they had left dinner so abruptly moments before, and said, "Whatever it is, it's already happened. You need to be calm, focused, and centered." After her return from Shiravi, she had taken up a rather generic martial arts regimen and taken to meditation occasionally as well. She liked to visit one of the many domes Vesta sported. There was enough surface that dozens of the domes could be erected without having any of the exterior installations visible. Now was a good time to use the focus part.

Simon stood there, blocking the corridor with her arm through his and said, "Did you know that we now have over half a million citizens in our nation? I just realized that I don't know any of these people who are going out and fighting and dying to further the boundaries... oh, hell, most of 'em followed my dream of what we could become. And yeah, some of them died early on, but unexpected though it was, their lives weren't in vain. Look at what it made us do. The second-gen Mambas, forcefields, tractor beams, and pressor beams. Miniaturization has allowed us to refine the technology and enhance it in ways the Shiravans never imagined. They are even now upgrading their ships to some of our specs. And it all rests squarely on my shoulders. I had the dream, and the rest of you followed it. Do you think that's an easy burden to bear?"

Kitty squeezed his arm against her body, a deep sigh escaping against her will. *He takes things too damned personally*, she thought. "Simon, you idiot. Don't you know by now that your dream is the same dream millions of others have as well? I mean, look at the backlog of applicants. But that's not what this is about. This is about you feeling that their deaths are your fault, and if not yours, then someone else's. And I know you. I'd much rather put my faith in you than anyone else, and so would all the people around you."

A crewman came down the corridor, so the two started to move along to Simon's original destination. Stopping before an ordinary door, Simon placed his hand on the plate beside it. It slid silently into the wall, and he stepped through, letting his arm straighten out and his hand slide down to Kitty's. He pulled her bodily into the room, and the door closed as quietly as it had opened.

She found herself in an ordinary secretary's office. The woman behind the desk looked up from the manual she was studying. Seeing who her visitors were, she straightened up and said, "Admiral, Madam Herald," the surprise evident in her voice. She looked at Simon and again at Kitty. "Uh, go right in, sir," she said, pressing a button under her desk.

A door beside her desk disappeared into the wall. "Let's go see what Tactics and Planning has made of the information the survivors brought back."

The room Kitty entered was easily five times the size of most other rooms throughout Vesta, with the exception of studios, movie theaters, gymnasiums, and the like. She noticed three different stellar holograms large enough to walk through. And that's exactly what one man was doing. Looking around the room, she saw at least thirty men and women at various consoles or hurrying from one spot to another. Somehow, the white lab coats looked a bit twentieth century, but who was she to complain if they were comfortable and got results?

"So, what was that room we just came through, hon?" Kitty asked. It seemed a bit odd to go to such lengths to hide this, and she said so. "I mean, the last time I was here, it was through a side corridor door." She looked around. Getting her bearings, she said, "Over there somewhere, I think."

Simon guided her over to an empty station, all screens darkened. He sat her down in one of the chairs and took the other. "This is just so we don't get interrupted by those who shouldn't be bothering us at critical times. That's actually Commander Ziegler's outer office. If anyone should come looking for him, he's out inspecting the domes since that's his area of expertise—dome maintenance." Micro-meteors regularly put a small number of holes in the domes, but the inhabitants took it as a natural course of events, except for the large one that took out a dome being used for a yoga class. Almost thirty people died in that mishap. So, a department was created, and Commander Ziegler regularly sent crews on inspection tours of all the domes on a regular basis, only requiring an email report each day. "Actually, the secretary is a full commander with the authority to make all decisions. And on the rare occasions of her disappearance during duty hours, it's assumed that she's dealing with some crisis as Commander Ziegler's personal representative."

She let that sink in for a moment, then stood up and said, "Let's see what you've got. You never told me it was this extensive."

"This is the late shift. The other two shifts do the

inputting of the data, and my third shift actually tries to make sense of it. Besides, you never asked," he replied matter-of-factly. "And this isn't all of it. I have several other installations aboard. Some work with the deep-space arrays and others with incoming signals from Earth or other ships. And one is listening for the distinctive signatures of Garmon ships in the area. Lately there have been none, which, I admit, is reassuring, but I feel something else going on. Felt. I think this is it. Let's go talk to Red."

Dave Atkins was a small man, red-headed as it was possible to be, and of course he answered to Red. It happened that he was the one standing in the middle of one of the holograms, stars passing through his body unnoticed as he looked at specific areas of interest.

Simon walked over to the outer edge of the projection and waved his hand across the surface, causing it to slow faded out of existence. Red looked around fuzzily, trying to transition from full immersion of some problem or other to reality when Simon cut the power to the holo. He focused on Simon's face and said, "What are you doing, boss? I've got to..." It was at this point that he realized Simon's companion was the Herald, herself. He'd never actually met her, and he was at a loss. "Uh, Admiral, Madam Herald, I was busy with some aspects of the attack as reported by the two captains able to use all their passive recordings and scanners. How can I help you?"

"I know you need to refine a lot of data in a hurry, Red, but how about a quick verbal update?" Simon asked.

"Okay, boss. What we had was a standard patrol

looking for Garmon Raiders. They usually travel in packs of five to ten ships at a time, so we felt that five cruisers and a carrier were enough to handle that kind of a situation. Besides, we have two ghosts, right? Well, the fleet entered the Oort cloud on the outskirts of the Altair system. It's only about sixteen lightyears from here, so we've been keeping as close an eye on it as we can, as well as a few others out to about twenty lightyears, like the Centauri triplets. They're only four lightyears away.

"Now, you asked for raw data. Our ships moved toward the inner system on a standard recon mission, full sensors, deliberately announcing our presence. Something like fifty Garmon ships came up from behind, riding the fleet's wake where scans are most unreliable. It wasn't until they passed the cloaked outriders that our people even knew they were there. Whisker lasers allowed the fleet enough time to launch all Mantas and turn to fight, but there were just too many of them. Their targeting systems aren't as good as ours, but with the advantage of surprise and numbers, they got in some pretty heavy blows right from the first. Each raider only had to kill two Mantas, and they were attacking head-on, not the best thing for a Manta to do, but they had no other choice. Once the Mantas were dealt with, the five remaining cruisers, their strengthened shields and more powerful weapons notwithstanding, were simply overwhelmed by sheer numbers. The carrier was lucky to get away. She had held back from the attack, of course, because of her lack of weapons. She managed to jump out before any of the Garmon went after her."

The little man waved his hand in the air, and the

hologram he'd been studying sprang back into existence. "Now, here's the interesting part." Kitty looked at the little red-headed man speechlessly, her fingers digging into Simon's arm.

Simon leaned down and whispered in her ear, "These guys think differently than most of us. He knows how many lives were lost and is even now trying to figure out how it happened and how to stop it from happening again. It's his way of dealing with the same feelings we all have. He's just channeling his better than some of us."

Kitty's eyes never left the white lab coat as it moved among the stars of the reactivated holo to a particular spot. She reserved judgment on just what to say about his cavalier attitude but decided not to cause a fuss in Simon's domain.

Red held a small device in his hand. With a few touches on the keypad he blew the image up to encompass only the Altair system. "Red, of course, designates the enemy," he lectured. "Our ships are green. I'm running two different sets of data from the cloaked ships, getting an almost three-D effect of the battle. More of a massacre, really. An ambush."

The room fell silent. "Well, it had to be," Red with some gruffness. "They came up from behind, and we didn't even know they were there until they passed the ghosts. One hundred Mantas launched in time to begin a defense of the fleet even as the larger ships turned to face the oncoming enemy. The only problem was that were only two-plus Mantas to each Garmon ship. And our cruisers couldn't fire effectively because of the Mantas attacking head-on, hoping to survive and get behind to do some damage. Very few made it.

"Apparently, even Garmon technology is up to

handling two Mantas apiece, and then they went after the cruisers. The Mantas did manage to take eleven of the raider class ships out of action before being destroyed. That left thirty-nine ships against five, and there's this dot right here," he said, pointing. "It's larger than the others, and it stood off, as if waiting to see if it was needed. Anyway, the raiders seemed to concentrate their fire on the forward aspects of all five ships rather than trying to take out the engines. This tactic cost them. It becomes obvious what they wanted—a stern with engines intact that they could duplicate back home. And a leg up on a lot of their other technologies as well."

"What's so interesting about that? It might be a tactic I'd use if I was desperate enough to commit the units to the mission of upgrading our tech," Simon said.

"That's not what's so interesting in and of itself. We've already thought that one out, and you're right. But here's the interesting part. They shot all but one Manta out of space, then hit it with a lower-powered beam, crippling it. The IFF continued to work though, and we saw it being swallowed up by the bigger ship. It moved in when the smaller ones had done their job, which, by the way, cost them another twenty-three ships to take out our five. Somebody over there has wised up and is starting to think with his head instead of with his... whatever."

Kitty looked at the scientist and said, "Please tell me how that is so 'interesting.' Letting them get hold of enhanced technology is the worst possible scenario." Her heart pounded at the thought of Garmons with shield technology and engines equal to their own.

"Well, actually, you must remember that I said that there were fifty Garmon ships in the attack and that this larger vessel stood off, apparently to pick up the pieces after our fleet was destroyed. Literally. It acted like our carrier, but we know they don't use them, so at first, we figured maybe a resupply ship. Our pilots and ships accounted for thirty-four raider ships, leaving sixteen and the big ship, which picked up an entire engine compartment from one of our ships, along with the Manta."

"So, soon we're going to be facing ships just as good as ours? It's time to shift into high gear and let's get our next-generation ships started." Simon was always ready to butt heads on a one-on-one basis, but humanity's existence was at stake now.

Kitty looked up at her husband's face. His eyes flickered back and forth, seeing something she was unable to—one of his trances. This time, it was interrupted by the scientist clearing his throat. "Well, that probably won't be a problem," he said with a strange tone in his voice.

"How so?" Kitty asked.

"Explain," Simon said at the same time.

Red walked out of the projection, tapped a spot on his keypad, and the entire projection spun to a view that let the three see each individual ship. "I'm running the data at about twenty times normal for the moment," he said as the large red dot engulfed the small green one. Shortly, it began to move away, following the sixteen remaining ships already on their way back to their jump point.

Red slowed the program at this point. As the large Garmon ship moved off after its sisters, a small green dot appeared to shoot out of the red dot, reverse course, and begin firing on the engine pods with everything in its arsenal. Suddenly, the red dot disappeared from the screen as the green dot applied thrust and began to move out of the area at a speed that surely had the engines redlined.

Red turned the projection back off and said, "The ghosts got four more of the Garmons from behind and picked up the Manta before they went hyper. It really is amazing. We built the M-3s with a rudimentary form of self-repair—re-rerouting power as needed, reinforcing a screen, stuff like that. The low level hit apparently just scrambled its circuits for a while. Knocked the pilot out, too. When she came to, she found about half of her systems restored and the rest coming back online one at a time. I think I'll let her tell you the rest of the story."

"I definitely want to hear it," Simon said eagerly. "But we still don't know if what we just experienced can be called acceptable losses. Yes, five ships took out thirty-seven of theirs. But how many more do they have? Will their mindset make them keep throwing that many ships at us? They've been building ships for about two hundred and fifty years. We don't know how many shipyards they have, how many ships they turn out per year, or what the cost in lives even means to them.

"But I *do* know what it means to us. Not to be callus about the probably three thousand or more people killed, but the loss in ships is a significant portion of our effective fighting force. We've got to find a way to get more Intel on these guys. If we know where they live, *we* can go a-callin' for a change."

What he didn't know was that that very problem was already under consideration many lightyears away.

CHAPTER TWENTY-TWO

Simon found Kitty showing up in T&P more and more often as the weeks went by. Most of the time she either sat or stood quietly and listened to the banter among the half-dozen men and women Simon had surrounded himself with. He noticed that she rarely spoke, but when she did, her question either cut right to the heart of a matter or her comment seemed to ease a difficult situation.

His team had downloaded everything from the two ghosts and the Manta pilot recovered after the larger ship was destroyed. That was a situation that was going to have to be addressed separately. The sole survivor (with the exception of the two cloaked ships under orders not to drop out) was going to have to be treated very gingerly. The dazed state she was in when she debarked into Vesta wasn't exactly catatonia, but it was about one step removed. Doctors, psychologists, and psychiatrists worked with her daily, helping her reintegrate herself with her life. Their diagnosis was post-traumatic stress disorder—PTSD—with a healthy dose of survivor's guilt thrown in.

She really should be rewarded, but the head doctors said she needed seclusion more than attention for the time being, so Simon authorized a balcony suite overlooking the lake for her use. It would have enough room for her doctors to come and go easily, and afforded a gorgeous view that Simon felt was soothing. He often used one of the public balconies to soak up the feeling of peace the view provided, but he smiled bitterly at the irony. If not for violence, this haven wouldn't even exist.

He put that idea on a back burner and returned to the situation maps. Kitty had received a personal letter from her new clan Sister, and in it were a lot of notes on locations of suspected Garmon planets. The Reprisal Fleets, broken down into more maneuverable units, had discovered a few, taking heavy losses before the new technology could be introduced, and had identified several dozen other possible sites. These were being painstakingly added to the computer simulation of the galactic area. Shiravan maps had filled in many blank spots, expanding humanity's knowledge of its stellar neighborhood, and a number of them had additional information on a few of the planets belonging to various systems. Coupled with the new data from Shiravi, Simon and his team were able to start making plans to investigate a few of the closer ones to see how up to date the information was.

Most of their time was spent waiting for new data, and since interstellar travel took so long, it was hard to calculate when to expect another visit. If the planet with the three shipyards on its two moons was any indication, that was the Garmon homeworld. Reports on inbound and outbound traffic were sent off by whisker laser from sensor drones to a ship several light-minutes away from the planet. It would then, if the information warranted it, hyper out to its particular headquarters. This was a peculiar idea to the Shiravans—splitting up command of the mobile space forces under the Matriarch's command. Kitty had finally convinced her that with such distances to be traversed and time spent in doing so, the situation would be very different by the time an answer or reinforcements could arrive. It was therefore necessary that area commanders have full authority to order their fleets as they saw fit, sending in reports on actions afterwards.

Before she left, she had asked, "Besides, aren't your people here under orders to, shall we say 'improvise' as the situation dictates? And how about the fleet commanders? Don't they have to be able to make instant decisions without waiting a minimum of months in some cases for a request to be sent and returned, during which time the entire situation could change drastically?"

It was just such news that a small Shiravan courier ship left with almost as soon as the event was known to be true. That was all the Matriarch needed to know—that her allies couldn't hold up their end of the bargain. As Simon was berating himself for about the thousandth time, Kitty made one of her rare comments. "Hon, they changed their MO. How could you expect that? And you did see to it that two ships were traveling under cloak. Without that order, we could have lost the entire fleet and never found out what happened, losing valuable technology without knowing it. They've never, so far, been the kind to sneak attack. Their style is more frontal assault. My guess is that someone else really is running things over there. And he's *smart*. That's what scares me.

"Look what that big ship picked up—engine parts and a deliberately undamaged Manta. They must have felt that it was completely dead, or they wouldn't have brought it aboard. I read some of what the pilot said as soon as she was rescued. There were big hairy teddy bears trying to pry her ship open by brute force. She powered up her systems, fired two missiles at the door in front of her, and rode out the shock. Then, she flew out of the ship, turned around, and blew the hell out of the engine room until she hit one of the antimatter field generators."

Emily Gaines's escape from the area had used up most of her mental reserves. She'd been slowly recuperating for the last three weeks under the watchful eyes of a bank of doctors. Simon resolved to have her put through a regen chamber as soon as her doctors pronounced her stable enough.

Simon knew the psychological implications of both the loss of five ships and the effect of one lone survivor making a big play. Gaines was never going to think of herself as a hero, but in Simon's world view, she was. Anyone who risked life, limb, or sanity to fight against insurmountable odds with no hope of rescue was deserving of the highest accolades. Too many real heroes never saw it in themselves. Their response was almost universal—anybody would have done the same in their place.

But that was a fallacy of the first order. Courage wasn't something that was shared equally amongst humans. Some had a greater amount than others. It just took the right situation to bring it into the light. Not many would run into a burning building to save even a child. Some would boost at highest acceleration to get away from near-capture, and who knew what horrors if she didn't.

But this woman, Lieutenant Commander Emily Gaines, with her deep space nav systems still offline, fired two antimatter missiles at a wall fifty feet away while her Manta sat inside a Garmon ship. The resultant explosion blew away almost half of one side of the ship. As soon as the shock waves subsided—almost immediately in the hard vacuum her missiles had created in the middle of the enemy ship—she fed power to her engines and left through the gaping hole she had just made. And then she had the courage to turn and blow it up. As soon as she'd fully recovered, he'd award her the Stellar Cross, she'd earned at least that much.

As Emily's body rested in a regen chamber, her mind was in the past... She saw at least three of the Alliance battlecruisers in her fleet blown to dust even as she began her attack run. With so many Garmon ships on her screen, she knew they'd walked into a trap. Locking her targeting computer on her assigned vessel, she watched as Manta after Manta dropped off her battle plot every second just before her systems shut down. Her screens went down, all power out, sensors dead, but she was still intact. She hadn't felt a thing, to be honest.

Time lost all meaning as she floated, weightless, inside her ship. In the pitch black, she began to wonder if she was just going to die of suffocation since she could no longer hear the sigh of fresh air being pumped into her cockpit.

After a time, she started counting her heartbeats. She got to three hundred before she lost count. *Hypoxia?* she thought. *Oh, well, let's try again, just to be sure.* Somewhere around one hundred and fifty she realized that fresh air was blowing across her face, so something was still working, anyway. Now she was going to die of hunger or thirst. Mantas didn't carry much in the way of foodstuffs, pretty much like a jet fighter. They weren't designed to be away from the nest for that long.

Without warning, her screens and battle plot came alive at the same instant. She instinctively looked at the battle plot first. Only passive sensors were available to her, but the only things in space with her were the big Garmon ship, not quite the size of the *Galileo*, and the Garmon version of a shuttle. The camera that was slaved to her eyes moved smoothly from the big ship to the smaller. Seeing the gaping square hatch open in the side told her what to expect. What she didn't expect was how her ship was going to be put aboard. Evidently it wasn't going to be by tractor beam since she felt a nudge from the shuttle as it butted her toward the hold.

After several additional nudges from the shuttle, she crossed the threshold of the cargo bay. She drifted in backwards, and the shuttle darted past her as the huge doors started sliding together. Suddenly, she felt gravity return as her ship dropped about three feet to the deck with a solid thump. Weapons systems came online as she got her breath back and watched the enemy doors, maybe three feet thick, slam shut. The vibration was transmitted through the deck plates, through her ship, and directly to her body.

She tried to calm herself as much as possible, considering where she was. Her attempt was only partially successful, but she did manage to stop hyperventilating. The effort not to clench her fists together was so intense that she started sweating. A flicker on her display screen caught her attention. The huge bay was slowly filling with air! She pressed vainly at darkened controls to her engines. Everything had gone dead for a time, but some systems were back online. Maybe it was true about the computers on board her Manta. Maybe they could repair themselves up to a point.

She watched as the air level reached normal and rose a bit higher. A denser atmosphere? Another flicker brought her eyes back to her control panel. Maneuvering thrusters were trying to come back, and her engine status lights were beginning to flicker. Vibration and sound reached her at the same time. She watched as about a dozen Garmons walked in through an oversized hatch.

This is what Shirley Dahlquist fought with a knife and won? she thought incredulously, and a shudder passed through her body.

They were all obviously male, as the only clothing worn was a single vest-like garment, open down the front and stopping at about waist level. *Dear God*, she thought, *just let them kill me quickly*. She looked at her control panel again and jerked in surprise. All of her systems showed ready for flight.

"Maggie?" she asked quietly. Getting no immediate response, she asked, "Are you there?"

"Attending," came out of a small speaker beside one ear.

"Since all of your systems seem to be back online, let's rock and roll."

"Please rephrase your request."

An involuntary shiver ran through Emily's body. Somehow, whatever had knocked out her systems had only been temporary but had erased the identity she'd built up over dozens of missions and simulations. All Manta pilots developed a rapport with their ships because the computers were complex enough to mimic human speech and mannerisms. And each one had its own distinct personality. Her ship's mind, for lack of a better word, had been wiped clean, leaving only the original programming.

Somewhere deep inside her chest an emptiness grew

at the loss of a friend, but her introspection was ended forcefully when the lead Garmon hit the side of her ship with a metal bar. She looked around and saw several of the huge creatures picking up what looked like pry bars. She watched in fright as two of them leapt effortlessly onto the front of her ship. If they were able to pop the seal on her cockpit, the game was over.

It's pretty much over, anyway, she thought. *If they've got time to pick me up, the rest of the fleet must be pretty much toast. Well, they're gonna find out that we can still bite. If I gotta go, I'm going out in style, taking as many as I can with me.* She looked at the Garmon climbing slowly up the slick surface of the ship. One of the last things she noticed before she clenched her fists, firing two missiles at the massive cargo bay doors only fifty feet away, was the metal bits sewn to the creature's vest.

Some minutes later, the computer, monitoring its pilot's vital signs, introduced a hint of ammonia directly across her face. Emily woke coughing and found herself drifting inside a huge hanger, facing a gaping hole. The fact that an enclosed explosion produced an amplified area of devastation and concussion wasn't something Emily really knew, although she was certainly quick enough to grasp the concept. She had seen missile-hits on targets before. Most of the energy was dispelled outward, making only a small hole in the target. It hadn't been imagined that a missile would explode *out* of an enemy ship rather than into it, so no mention of that particular fact had been felt necessary.

She called up her control panel and found all systems green. "Maggie?" No response. Piloting a ship with a new computer was hard. The longer the two flew together, the closer the bond between them grew, making piloting a lot easier. But now she was working with a blank slate, which meant full manual control with the computer monitoring her actions and learning. *We're gonna be space dust in a matter of minutes. Why did I just start the relearning process?*

With a thought, a quick pulse from her engines pushed her slowly out of the center of the damaged area. How her ship had survived, she would never know. Maybe there was something to the Shiravan's Spirits of Space after all. As she cleared the hole, more of the area came into view on her scanners. It no longer mattered, so she engaged her full sensor array on the area around her. Amazingly, she found only herself and the drifting hulk along whose side she felt very tiny.

Emily decided to forget about anything else. No friendly ships meant no ride home. She pulled back from the enemy ship, keeping her nose and therefore her missile launchers on the immense ship. Nothing gave any indication of power forward of the hole in the side, and now it looked even bigger than when she'd been in it. Astern, lights shone through a few ports in the ship.

She still carried a nearly full load of missiles, plasma bombs, and two high-powered lasers that would do considerable damage to this one vessel before the pack came back for her. If she was lucky, she could boost away from there and go ballistic, shutting down her active scans.

Standing off from the ship, it appeared to be just a battlecruiser like the ones the Garmons normally used, only bigger. Could they be cargo haulers? Why else build something with so much open space in the middle of it? She could think of other things all that empty space could be used for. Oh, well...

Nothing moved from the larger ship. No shuttles came out, and no weapons were fired. She sat there, looking at the ship in her screens, at her mercy. *How much mercy have we been given up to this point?* she asked herself. She waited, watching—for what, she didn't know. Then her mind cleared.

A dispassionate, *Fuck you, you motherless bastards*, went through her mind as she engaged the manual target lock and fired two missiles, one right behind the first, at one point on the after portion she assumed to be the engine room. Then, she slipped around the ship, getting a clear view of the rest of space around her, and was amazed, again, to find herself alone with the giant ship. *Well, my name's not David, but you're going down, Goliath.* She laughed at her own wit and fired two more missiles into the engine area.

While letting the missiles do their damage, she fired a plasma bomb toward the center of the ship, not doing much visible damage. She fired her lasers as she let herself drift along the side of the ship. Focusing them so that they met at one point on the ship's hull, she cut swaths deep into the ship, one after another. *Much more and it'll start falling apart.*

She moved back to the engine area and settled in directly astern of the ship. Two more missiles drove deep into the ship's rear aspect, dead center. She launched two plasma bombs in after them and waited for some result. Minutes passed and she launched the last two missiles she carried. R*ight up the poop chute, as Benny says*, she thought, and the thought brought her back to the present. Grieving was going to have to wait a few more minutes.

This time she was rewarded with a beautiful light show. *They must use more antimatter than we do*, she thought clinically. Several seconds after the light and concussion wave reached her, the few pieces of ship that came her way bounced harmlessly off her forward shields.

Oookay, that happened. Which way from here? Doesn't really matter if the return patrol can't find me. She boosted for two hours before going ballistic again.

Taking no thought as to which direction she traveled as long as it was away from the ambush, and also taking no thought as to when or how hard to boost, she spent the better part of two days leaving the area. Her food stores were running low, although water wasn't going to be a problem with the recycling system. She would die of hunger before she died of thirst. After the first day, she turned off the chronometer, not wanting to know anymore.

She stayed awake for as long as she could, occasionally spinning the ship slightly just to see a different set of stars.

Emily was jolted awake by the proximity alarm. She had drifted into range of two ships, but they were right beside her, and she wondered why her alarm hadn't gone off long before then.

Her question was answered even as the amber lights of unidentified ships turned into the green dots of friendly forces. "Lone Manta, hold your fire. We are the Alliance ships ghosting your fleet. Please respond."

Turning her chrono back on, she said, "Where the hell have you been the last... four days?" She didn't care who was on the other end of the radio, just so long as they were friendly.

"Sorry," a voice came back to her. "We were going to uncloak and pick you up, but you boosted out too fast, and just after you did, the Garmons showed back up.

Only two ships, but we didn't think they'd stay around as long as they did. And you laid down a pretty broken course. Took a while to track you down."

Emily shook with relief. She felt the tension seep out of her, only then realizing just exactly how tense she'd been. Once she had accepted the idea that she was going to die alone, and slowly at that, she thought she had relaxed. Apparently not. She wondered if she was hallucinating some kind of space mirage or something, but she was jolted out of her reverie by the voice.

"Manta pilot. This is Captain Marquez of the TAS Vengeful. Prepare to have your ship tractored in. And welcome home."

CHAPTER TWENTY-THREE

Marsha Kane ordered her remaining ships onto search-and-destroy missions around Sakarta and its two moons. Several Garmon ships rose to meet the oncoming cloud of Mantas and four-cruiser backup, but there was no organized resistance, and they went down with only two Mantas destroyed.

The rest of the mission was a revelation. Both moons were heavily built up with construction docks. Half a dozen ships were in various stages of construction or repair. Those were taken out, along with every standing structure on both moons, and then operations were transferred planet side.

Dozens of large villages were strafed, taking out any moving beings in sight. It had been determined that the females and young males were housed in special compounds, and those were left alone, targeting only able-bodied males. The object was to reduce the fighting males should any ships stop by needing crew. The piece de resistance was a light show of phenomenal proportions when the fueling station was bombed. Almost a third of the smaller moon went up in an antimatter conversion previously unseen by any eyes anywhere in the known three-race sector of space.

Meteors rained down on the Garmon homeworld as

Korgan Garmon stood and watched. He and several of his top sept-leaders had been lucky enough to be in the Garmon family home during the strafing of homeworld. After the majority of the remnants of the moon had finished falling, Korgan turned to go back into his family home, only to find himself alone. His hunter senses cut in immediately. He knew he'd have no more credibility with his people after this disaster, especially given his questionable victory at Kerasano.

Carrying no weapons, he walked into the Family Hall through the front entrance, knowing full well what was about to happen. A leader was a leader as long as he kept the respect of his subordinates. He had suffered two humiliating defeats at the hands of the humanz, and this was his last hour as The Garmon. The scene was as he had imagined it. Six of his staunchest sept-leaders stood in a line, blocking further progress into his own home. Three bodies lay on the dirt floor, their blood soaking into the dry ground almost as fast as it drained from the corpses.

He looked at the Garmon before him. "Am I to be allowed a hunter's death, or will you just kill me here?"

In answer, the senior sept-leader gestured at the three loyalists in front of Korgan. "You have your choice of weapons, Lord Garmon," he said, making the title seem like an epithet.

Knowing this was going to be more than just one on one, he slid two knives into his boots and chose the two best swords of the three available. His eyesight closed down to hunter mode, choosing the apparent leader of this usurpation of his place as leader of the Garmon people. He moved into the room, pressing the hunter on the right.

He thought that if he could get the hulking menace to

give ground, he might have a chance to turn on the leader. That was his last mistake.

The senior sept-leader said, "A hunter's death allows him to die with a weapon in his hand, but nothing says we have to lose more good men in a prolonged fight." He then pulled a laser pistol out and merely shot Korgan. Next would be the Council. A new day was once again upon the race called Garmon.

Marsha sat across the table from her new Sister, Linnas. Both she and Fleet Commander do' Berel had given their reports on the Sakarta raid, and do' Berel had been dismissed. The two women looked out over the capitol city of Quillas since Polity business had brought Linnas there for a time. She could not effectively run her government from Cho-An all the time.

Night had fallen, and lights had come on all over the capitol and main port city. In the distance, moving lights outlined the gantries used to build the smaller ships of the Shiravan Polity. The cruisers and battleships were, like the Alliance, built in space and were never intended to land on a planet's surface.

Linnas said, "It was well that you spoke privately with Commander do' Berel before you implemented your attack on Sakarta. She would have suffered embarrassment in front of her officers otherwise. Is it always so with your people?"

"No," Marsha answered quietly. "I would have submitted a plan of attack beforehand to a human commander. But I will say that if the mission had had a human commander in place rather than Commander do' Berel, I would probably have made the same on-the-spot choice. I believe her main concern was that my plan was superior to hers, though I admit I'm not very good at reading Shiravan emotions yet."

Linnas looked at her as darkness loomed. "Emotions? Or the cultural differences inherent in our two races, Sibara?"

Marsha was quiet for a moment. "Cultural differences? I don't understand."

"Understanding will come with time, perhaps you should contemplate staying on Shiravi to learn more of our culture." Linnas replied. She reached out and lifted a bottle of fire wine from the table. The lack of kemwood cups warned Marsha not to drink too much. She needed to keep a tight rein on her mouth. There was too much at stake. "You should commune with the Spirits to learn your best course of action." Marsha looked startled, evoking another comment from her alien Sister. "I have word that you from time to time call upon the Spirits as if you believe in them. A short journey in contra-space should let you get close and see if you can find the answers you need."

Marsha's mind raced. Kitty had told her about the trance-like state she and Simon entered upon occasion. *Maybe it will do some good if I can duplicate the trance*, she thought. She took a sip from her glass, a tall fluted, delicate thing, meant to enhance the color of the wine. The glow spread out from her center to all parts of her body, an almost spiritual feeling all by itself.

The rest of the evening passed in relative quiet as each woman thought their separate thoughts.

Marsha sat in the dome atop the *Sindaro Vacht,* staring at the shifting colors of hyperspace. Some said that one could go crazy doing this, but she needed the solitude and the sense of invulnerability it would give her among the Shiravans. But first, the trance thing.

She struggled to find the state Kitty and Simon talked about so often. She couldn't reach the place she needed to be, so she tried another tack. She focused on the inner surface of the dome itself, letting the shifting colors do as they wished. After a time, she found herself jerking her head upright, on the verge of falling asleep as she strove for the state Kitty talked about.

Eventually, she noticed the reflections of herself take on some solidity. One reflection stayed aboard the *Raptor*, and she followed herself in that image. The *Raptor* survived, but most of the squadron didn't. Another image stayed on Shiravi, coordinating the Human/Shiravan forces in their struggle against the Garmons. Again, it was a step into a possible future. This one led to dusty warehouses and dark nights. Other images inexplicably went so far and no farther.

Finally, Marsha roused herself from her position on the floor. Joints creaked and popped as she stood up. It was time to tell the captain that she was ready to return to Shiravi. She could also use the return trip to spend more time in the dome, but she'd made up her mind. She would not sit idly by on Shiravi while her people went out and faced the Garmon, she would go with them.

The return was relatively short but wasn't without incident. It seemed that she had spent almost thirty straight hours in *Sindaro Vacht's* dome. Alone. To Shiravans, conditioned from birth to expect someone coming from such a long sojourn with the Spirits to have lost their sanity, Marsha seemed amazingly sane.

She was asked to visit the captain first, most probably

to ascertain whether she could be allowed access to the ship without escort. That interview went better than she had expected. Captain kep Parrasine spoke English well and soon determined that Marsha wasn't a bomb ready to explode.

Alternatively, the crew kept watching her out of the corners of their red eyes, expecting her to blow up at any moment. As for herself, she had no duty station aboard the *Sindaro Vacht*, so she headed back to the dome for a while. She needed to put some of the images she'd seen into perspective.

Marsha stepped off the shuttle and headed for the public transport station just outside the landing field. Along the way, a vehicle pulled up and the passenger door opened. "Sorgala Kane, it will be my pleasure to convey you to the Matriarch's office." As the sole human among hundreds of Shiravans and dressed in her blacks as well, she wasn't surprised at the invitation. Still, prudence dictated that she at least touch the pistol strapped to her right thigh. There were still any number of Isolationists willing to go to extremes to embarrass the Matriarchy. And humans weren't universally accepted, regardless of Kitty's name being so close to a Shiravan deity.

She climbed into the air car and prepared herself for a ride through Quillas, a grim prospect at best. New York cab drivers were cautious by comparison. Twenty minutes later, she was deposited outside the Polity Assembly building. Another twenty minutes found her on Linnas's private level.

Sitha kep Parrasine met her and took her into the Matriarch's private audience chamber. Linnas was having breakfast, with another place set for her. Having eaten aboard the *Sindaro Vacht*, she declined the invitation.

She let Linnas finish her meal, drinking some juice to pass the time. Finally, she got to talk business after a young Shiravan removed the leavings from the breakfast table. The two moved to a more informal part of the suite, featuring deeply upholstered chairs and couches overlooking the bustling city. "I am glad to hear that you've chosen to work with our strategy and tactics team, planning the next moves in our campaign against the Garmons, Sibara."

"I think it's prudent that I help where I can, Sibara," Marsha demurred. "But I only plan to stay until my fleet is ready to leave, then I will accompany them in command of the *Raptor*."

Linnas looked surprised and a dark cloud passed across her face. "If you think it best, but I've been thinking, also. This time, I'll send only human ships in one group, or perhaps two since we have so many of your ships in Shiravan space." Marsha started to argue her point, but Linnas raised her hand human-fashion to stop her. "I will, of course, send observers aboard each of your major ships, learning your techniques so that they may teach them to our own crews."

Marsha thought quickly. "Perhaps you could send a few others along as well to sit watches, actually working with our crews and learning our moves. That might give a more comprehensive idea of how we operate."

"See!" Linnas said excitedly. "Already you are putting forward ideas to better the safety of Shiravan crews and ships."

Marsha felt the words fall out of her mouth and couldn't believe Linnas would take them at face value. "But of course, Sibara. When I was adopted, didn't I swear that I would treat yours as if they were my own and offer up any human ship to your command?"

"Of course, as our Sibara Katherine did also. So. For the duration your stay, you are hereby promoted to admiral of the human forces operating in Shiravan space. And when you transfer back to your ship, you will still carry the rank of admiral. As a token of my trust, I wish to present you with your new rank insignia." She slid a small box cross the table.

Marsha opened the box, knowing what was coming. Instead of the twin gold comets of the Alliance, she found a pair of cloth patches meant to be sewn to the collar. On the patches were embroidered a series of four pentagons. She took the box, knowing she was going to have to wear them as soon as she could get them duplicated for her several uniforms, as well as a special version for her dresses.

"Thank you, Sibara," was all she could say.

CHAPTER TWENTY-FOUR

The return of the *Esmit* proved to be of great interest to Maratai kep Parrasine for another reason besides the return of Rentec. The captain himself carried her personal correspondence from the Matriarch. If Rentec were to see the contents, it could prove extremely embarrassing. The same could be said of the instructions and advice sent in return.

She had long since read the messages, enough times that the words were indelibly etched into her mind, but it was only now that she felt it to be the time to act. She stopped at one of the many transport stops along the major corridors that ran the length of the asteroid. The first time humans entered the carved out husk of Vesta Base, they had immediately seen the need for such a system. She wondered if her own people would have done the same.

A tube ride, an elevator ride, and short walk down another corridor gave her time to lose her focus, and she felt the living beat of the great beast with humans and Shiravans moving around inside, keeping it alive and healthy. This was humanity's most ambitious effort yet, if one didn't count beating back the Garmons three times in succession. Although, even with humanity managing to take Shiravi's best technology and improve upon it almost immediately, lives had still been lost in those attacks. Just the tidal wave from the underwater explosion of one Garmon Raider had killed people all around the Pacific Rim.

Maratai came from a society that had evolved into a one-world government after severe worldwide trauma. Only after that were the real advances in the sciences made. Once there was no more need to have several million workers tied up in military services all over the globe, protecting lines drawn on a map, people would need a new focus. She'd studied the history of her world, just like all citizens. She'd also been studying the human race ever since her first arrival and had come to some conclusions. Actually, humans were where Shiravans had been almost a thousand years ago. Shiravans had adapted slowly to the ever-growing list of advances in the various sciences. Humanity had to make the transition in a single generation, maybe two. She wondered if they would make it or tear themselves apart.

She reached her destination and dismissed her musings. She hesitated, her hand almost touching the door pad. *Human ingenuity at work again*, she thought, *taking Shiravan science and adapting it to uses my people would never think of.*

She took a deep breath and finished the gesture. The door slid aside, revealing the outer office of the Shiravan Embassy to the Terran Alliance, and she walked in, heading for the far wall. She looked at the secretary sitting behind the desk, guarding the only other door, and nodded at her, a questioning look on her face. Right then, she didn't trust herself to speak.

She placed her hand on the second plate as well when the secretary nodded in return. This room, like the outer, was bathed in a soothing red light, restful and reassuring to the Shiravan psyche. The furnishings were much the same as she would find in almost any office on the station—a desk, one chair behind it, and two less comfortable chairs facing it, as well as an informal niche holding a couch, coffee table and three generously upholstered chairs. A few pictures hung on the walls, landscapes Rentec found restful and calming.

As for Rentec himself, he was busy shortening one stack of papers and making others larger. He looked up, a harried expression on his face until he caught sight of her. Rentec laid down his scriber and said, "Thank you for the distraction, Doma. I am beginning to think that my position and presence is more in the way of punishment than it is an honor." He leaned back in his chair and reached for a pitcher of tea and two glasses. It required a generous portion of sugar to make it palatable, but now it had become almost a ritual, exceeded in degree only by the English. He poured two glasses and slid one across the desk toward his staff second.

"I'm glad you came by," Rentec said. "We have new instructions from the Matriarch. We will be allied with the humans against the Garmons. One Reprisal Fleet is being reactivated and diverted here to take some of the pressure off the humans. Just when they will arrive, I can't say. A special courier had to go find them. Then they'll have to return to Shiravi and refit before coming here. Best guess is about one Earth year, maybe a bit more."

The *Esmit* had carried Kitty back to Earth with Rentec. While she and Simon had gotten to know each other again, Maratai was doing the same thing with Rentec. Only, from his point of view it was strictly business. The details the Matriarch and the Herald had worked out talked about life in the capitol city, Quillas, and about seeing his mother and family before returning to Earth space. And of course, all the details about the battle of Sakarta, as well as the far more important duel between the Shiravan's ex-chief spymaster and Herald Hawke.

These things were important to Maratai as well, but she could easily see the stiffness in his posture when he spoke and the forced enthusiasm in his voice. She looked again at the piles of papers on his desk and wondered where his secretaries were. He couldn't have just the one, could he? And she wouldn't be able to make anything more than a dent in what sat before him. That, she could do something about.

She walked around the desk and took his hand. Pulling him to his feet, she guided him around the desk and pushed him gently in the direction of the informal area. She snagged their glasses and followed him into the semi-private environment of the niche. Even though they were alone in the room, this felt more comfortable.

She set the glasses on the table and took the center chair across from the couch, waiting until Rentec was seated before she started. Flustered, she said, "I can only begin at one point." The silence went on for a time, and Rentec waited patiently for her to continue.

"Do you remember the day we met?" she asked quickly, looking at him from hooded eyes. Her crimson gaze put him a bit off his stride, and he faltered for a moment.

Recovering, he answered, "The day my Ministry reached its ascendancy. And I remember the details of that meeting, as well. To find out that a kep Parrasine was my personal secretary was almost staggering. Fortunately, exposure to my mother for my entire life helped prepare me for your arrival," he said wryly. "Why?"

She smiled slightly at his quip, but her expression turned solemn quickly. "Rentec—and I do not use your first name lightly—I sent correspondence back to Shiravi by means other than your diplomatic pouch. The reason for this was so that you wouldn't know what I was doing. For this, I ask your forgiveness. If you'll hear the rest of my tale, I will tell it. Or leave, at your pleasure." She sat quietly, arms on the rests of proper-sized chairs, nails digging into the imitation leather covering.

"Well," he answered slowly, "I think I would need to know more about this private correspondence before I could make a judgment. I take it that it's your intention to tell me, or you would never have mentioned it to begin with."

"As a matter of fact, it is, Rentec," she said, deliberately using his family name to keep this on as informal a scale as she could. "I can only be honest and open, or this is worth nothing. I sent my official communications with yours, but I had matters of... personal import that I preferred you not to know about until I was ready."

"And now you are," he stated simply. "Weeks after my return. I'm sure you received a response almost as soon as the *Esmit* docked. You've taken all this time to come to some conclusion."

Is he deliberately toying with me? she thought. *I never considered that he would have taken time to sort out his own situation while he was home. And why can't he have spies of his own?*

She spoke quietly. "I sent letters to both Linnas and your mother. In them, I asked for permission to offer you my Chalweh. And advice. Linnas called your mother in to discuss my request. I hadn't thought of that, but now I see that I should have. Of course your mother should know about my offer. Besides, if we were back home, I would have to speak to her first, anyway."

Rentec blinked. Twice. Standing up, he said, "I think this is where I open a letter of my own. You might know about it. Its address merely says, 'Rentec. Do not open until the time is right. You will know.' This was written by my mother." He stared thoughtfully at the ceiling, especially high in this section of the station, and then back at her. "Perhaps this is the time she spoke of?"

"And perhaps not," Maratai said, raising her voice enough that he could not in politeness pretend not to hear.

He looked back at her, and she was still seated, holding her glass gracefully and staring back. He stopped just inside the boundaries of the niche. "Why?"

For the first time Maratai looked uncomfortable. "I didn't know of your mother's letter to you. My private correspondence arrived not long after the *Esmit* arrived, which was letters from both my mother and Linnas. The difference is that I expected my correspondence. I know what your mother had to say about my proposal, and that is wrong, I know, but I had no other way open to me until the conviction of Ramannie. I suspect that the letter you have holds your mother's opinion, but I want to hear from you first. Only the Spirits know for sure. Maybe it isn't time to open it."

Rentec moved slowly toward an arm of the couch, reaching out for solid support. He leaned against it, thinking hard. He had spent so much time with her, true, but he had also been away almost two turnings now. For her to be this intent on her goal, she must see something in him that was worth her time.

"What do I think? Since when did a male have a choice in these matters?" he asked bitterly. "And why would you want one tainted by..." He couldn't finish the thought aloud.

Maratai rose to her full height, slightly shorter than Rentec but still taller than only a few humans, and finished for him, "Ramannie." He looked up quickly. "You blame yourself when there were so many others before and after you who missed signs that are now obvious. Your own mother didn't see it during her Reading. How Ramannie kept her true nature hidden from two of the most powerful Readers on the planet is still unknown."

"But I am still stigmatized by the whole affair. You wouldn't be able to go out in public without ridicule."

"Rentec," Maratai said softly, "Ramannie's was part of a mass trial conducted after the Witch ship emerged in our outer system, distress signals blaring. Seems that their life support system wouldn't take another repair without going in for a total refit. The traitors were banished to a series of small islands just out of sight of the Matriarch's estate. Her security teams are on constant watch, of course. I have been assured that all relevant documents are no longer available. Therefore, there's no impediment to our union, barring a Reading when next we are on Shiravi together. I'm sure it will only be a formality."

He let himself slide down into the corner of the couch, astonished that she had asked for his opinion. Then he thought back over these past few turnings since meeting the humans, all the way back to sel Garian picking him out of a room full of older, wiser minds than his own. His father had been Minister of Spatial Affairs before him—a male. And himself—a male. Captain do' Sirkis and a surprising number of males in the upper echelons of the Matriarch's personal staff came to mind. And there was Minister kep Foran now. His mind enumerated each and every male he knew—not many in the whole of his life but more than a few. And many of these were employed in the bureaucratic sphere.

He looked across the table at her and said, "In the not-too-distant past, I would never have been asked if I wanted the union. Your mother would have spoken to my mother, and if the two agreed, we would be married. I thought Ramannie..." there was a definite catch in his voice, "I thought she was an extremely forward woman, even though it was I who first asked her to spend time with me. I will admit that I'm not up to speed, as the humans would say, on what is going on in social circles.

"I thought it strange that she went so far as to sit for a Reading and not offer her Chalweh, but I attributed it to the wiles of females. Now we all know why and what she was, and that what she got from me she passed on to her Isolationist allies. Yet you wish to offer me your Chalweh, knowing how easily I can be manipulated? And using that fact against me by asking my mother and the Matriarch without my knowledge?"

Maratai held her hand out in the human fashion, fingers up, palm making the sign to stop. "First, I would not speak to you until I had spoken with your mother, as custom dictates, which I did as best I could by courier. Don't forget that messages travel at the speed of couriers, not thought, though that would be nice. Second, I would not offer my Chalweh to just any male. And third, I have come to know you better than you might think. Among all the other things I do, I study you. I want to know your mind, not just what you say."

Maratai sat silent for several seconds. Rentec knew this was hard on her, but he recognized the same upheaval in himself. There was no way he would let her off easily. All this time, even though she was his social superior, she had kept her eyes downcast so he couldn't see her face. Finally, he reached out and raised her chin so their eyes met. With one crimson gaze melting into another, he said, "I have made my peace with my past. I only worry about those I care for. To me, it is nothing; to our society at large, it will be a very big scandal if it gets out."

"So, you do care for me in some small way?" she asked, something in her eyes changing, but to what, Rentec couldn't say.

"Well, yes," he stammered. "We have worked closely for several turnings now, and I have become comfortable in your presence, this particular moment excluded," he added by way of qualification.

"Good," Maratai said, raising her chin off the tips of his fingers. "I like a male with a sense of humor. Then you will accept my Chalweh?"

Rentec, not unaware of the political ramifications of what she was proposing, as well as the merely personal, thought for a time. "Have you given thought to the political and familial ties that will result from our union?"

Maratai nodded. "I had already figured it out for myself. I made a very detailed chart of the interconnections between our three clans, but the Matriarch, your mother, and my own mother went to great pains to make clear just what could come of our union from their own perspectives. According to your mother, who has the final say, the union would bind the three most affluent families on the planet. des Harras is already allied with the kep Parrasine clan, giving generously of their earnings from the gava stone mines to assist in the technological research that led to the advances that got Shiravans into space in the first place. So the alliance goes back nearly five hundred turnings.

"Meanwhile, do' Verlas was quietly consolidating the power of the spirit of the Shiravan people, preparing to lead them into a bright new future, free of Garmons. And as a close personal friend of Linnas, I feel certain that she had full approval to act in any way she saw necessary. Actually, my sources say that there were several dozen assassinations, killings, and suicides while you were home, carefully deleted from the news and kept from the humans as well. With our union, Clan do' Verlas elevates itself to the aristocracy that no one admits to, and Tira becomes privy to the Matriarch's opinions and decisions, up to and including voicing her own opinions whenever she sees fit."

"When did she ever *not* see fit?" Rentec asked wryly.

Maratai smiled briefly, having met Doma do' Verlas on more than one occasion. "What the humans would call a cabinet minister," she continued. "But she speaks for all the minor witches left on Shiravi, those deemed harmless to our regime, as well as Clan do' Verlas. In fact, there were many who actively believed in the good despite the brainwashing. Meanwhile, in the background, des Harras money supports other more secretive research among some of the more xenophobic of our clans and their leaders.

"So, the more vocal rabble-rousers, including Ramannie, are marooned for the rest of their lives, and others learn from the lesson. Tira do' Verlas has the charisma to rise to the top in an essentially leaderless organization. All she had to do was start dictating orders, which I'm told she was doing at the time the courier left home space. The rank and file, seeing the writing on the wall—another human expression I think I like—caved in and accepted the new norm. Tira do' Verlas, representing the full body of readers, finders, foreseers, charm and amulet makers, and even some of the more recalcitrant Witches deemed essentially harmless by your mother, sits in council daily, discussing policy for the Polity—a policy they were all in agreement with, anyway, so the vote was just a formality. She has formally changed the name to Spirit Readers.

"Policy for the war against the Garmons, policy on how to deal with the human issue. There are those who consider them to be a worse threat than the Garmons. They, at least, won't want to settle worlds with stars in our spectrum, so I see no problem with our spaces interweaving themselves."

Her expression went dark. "That picture is only going to be possible with the Garmons out of the way, for the Garmons and humans are attracted to the same kind of planets, and the Garmons refuse to accept anyone as their equal, so they attack us as well. We will have to discover all of their worlds, make sure they have no capability to build spacefaring vessels, at least until they have matured, and carve their territory up to suit ourselves."

Rentec leaned back into the comfortable corner of the couch. "I have read the same dispatches you have. They say the humans have the capability to become more of a problem than the Garmons ever were, and that humans are too self-centered to be trusted after the Garmons are defeated. There's more than one way to look at the figures and theories coming from the Matriarch's advisers," Rentec said. "They could just as well turn into very good allies."

"Against whom, Rentec?" Maratai asked. "I thought the same in the beginning, but the more I see of these humans, the more I see Garmon in them rather than anything even vaguely Shiravan-like. And once the Garmons are destroyed or controlled, what will the humans do next?"

"My dispatches tell me that Linnas and the Herald have become Sister-equals, and Marsha Kane is Sister-kin." He looked at her closely. "Both have agreed to consider our situations as if they were their own, and Sorgala Kane is risking herself and over four thousand human lives to defend our territory, and another fleet just left. Not to mention that in about a year, another fleet can start moving in that direction, taking time to stop at identified worlds. They can either bomb them or report on the results of previous assaults."

He shrugged, apparently resigned. "In any event, we have a long while before we need to worry about humans as a threat."

"Agreed, Rentec, I just wish I knew for sure what the future will bring. My personal belief, fears aside, is that they will be a great asset to our own race, and what if we should happen on another civilization? Three in this one small part of our galaxy argues for many more spread out through both arms. We need to re-instill the fighting spirit back into our own people that these humans have, without its wrath directed against us. I fear that we could become the brekkis being led to the slaughterhouse. Not that I don't like humans in general, but they do seem to tend toward the herd mentality," she finished lamely.

CHAPTER TWENTY-FIVE

The back alleys of Quillas, capitol city of the Shiravan Polity, looked much like back alleys anywhere on Earth except for the tall, red-skinned, red-eyed aliens. Then again, she was the alien here.

She had business there that couldn't be conducted in the light of a Shiravan day. She consulted the piece of paper holding the address she was looking for. Her Shiravan was passable, but she was nowhere near ready to try to read it yet. Her contact in the Matriarch's palace, apparently an Isolationist, had delivered a late-night snack the previous evening. Once fully inside her room and out of sight, she passed the tray with a small piece of paper sticking out of one corner and merely said, "Sleep well, Your Grace."

Things were proceeding in a hurry now. She'd had to wait so long, teaching strategy to the Shiravan military, that her fleet was about to use up its leave time. Now she was moving through a crowd of port workers, afraid she would miss her address. Of course, everyone knew she was human. Who else so small would be out at this time of night? Still she was glad she had strapped on her laser before wrapping herself in a modified Shiravan travel cloak. At least it covered her white hair and let her stop in shadows.

As she walked slowly along, causing a small eddy in the faster-moving crowd, a voice from above said quietly, "Perhaps I can help Your Grace find her destination?"

She looked up. This was no face she was familiar with. While the old saw of 'they all look alike' did hold true for the masses, she had learned to recognize over a hundred faces at first sight, and this was one she didn't know.

"What do you know of my destination?" she asked, looking back to the front.

The Shiravan said, "I know your fleet needs an essential item before it can leave orbit. I know that you received instruction to go to an address on this street tonight. And I know where that address is."

Marsha thought about the implication of following a stranger—probably a rabid Isolationist—into any of these buildings, but she was going to go into one alone anyway. "Very well," she said, "come down and lead the way."

After a short walk, during which she unhooked the strap on her holster and made sure the laser's safety was off, her companion said, "We must cross here." A long-fingered, strong grip pulled her to the left, finding spaces among the moving throng until they stood before a darkened doorway.

Marsha studied the paper and the numbers etched into the metal door. They matched, so she pushed the door open and walked in, followed by the strange Shiravan. She quickly stepped to one side and scanned her surroundings with a professionalism she wouldn't have shown five years before.

A counter ran the width of the building, and several Shiravans looked her way. She let her hood fall back, revealing her white hair, and stepped up to the counter. In the corner of one eye she saw that her escort stood quietly against the door, blocking any other visitors. When one of the workers behind the counter approached, she said, "I was given directions to this place. Who requested my presence here tonight?"

The clerk said, "That would be my Clan's Leader, Your Grace. No other has the authority to summon one of the Matriarch's staff."

"Very well," Marsha said in her coldest voice. "I will see your Clan Leader now."

"Of course, Your Grace. If you will follow me, please?" A part of the countertop was raised, revealing an entry that she pushed through without a word.

She waited until it was replaced, then faced the clerk with a frosty stare. "Well? Are you in the habit of keeping your Clan Leader waiting?"

"No, Your Grace. This way." Without a backward glance, the clerk moved off at a long-legged pace that was designed to make Marsha run to keep up. Instead she merely walked at her own pace, looking about her all the while. Tall stacks and shelves of unknown items filled the long room. When she lost sight of her guide, she merely stopped at an intersection and waited for her to come back. Thereafter, her guide moved at a slower pace until they reached a door at the back of the warehouse.

"My Clan Leader awaits your arrival, Your Grace." She opened the door and stood back.

The room was better lit than the warehouse proper and was appointed in a style out of place with the rest of the building. Marsha walked in, one hand on her laser under her cloak. An elderly Shiravan stood up and bowed deeply. "Welcome, Admiral Kane. It is a great pleasure to meet you. I am Deshana sel Garian, head of Clan sel Garian. Please be seated."

A couch had been modified for the smaller human frame, and Marsha settled into it warily, responding to the bow with a nod of her head. She was determined not to be the junior in this meeting. And she was just as determined to keep to business, especially with the chief enemy of the Matriarch. "I was given to understand that a necessary item needed for our next patrol has become available. Are you prepared to have it shipped up to the fleet?"

"Of course, Admiral," sel Garian answered. "Aren't you concerned about where it came from? Aren't you worried about how it comes into your possession?"

"It comes from a Clan that specializes in bio-genetics. They got some tissue samples from the attack on a world that allowed Doma Spencer and Dom Carter to be freed. From this sample, they worked out how to manufacture a virus that will slow male births and raise the intelligence level of female Garmons. The two situations will cause immeasurable discord on all worlds where the virus is released. It is also passed from mother to all offspring, adding to the destruction of their civilization as we and they know it.

"As to how it gets into our hands... I don't care. Clan sel Garian are Isolationists, I know. If you can't keep your people out of space, your only alternative is to keep your enemies out of space instead. And I believe you'll turn your attention upon us once we've done your killing for you. You should know that we came to be the premier species on our world by overcoming every predator on our planet. We have beaten back the Garmons, who have plagued you for over two hundred turnings, and we've done it in only ten. Keep that in mind Domagera sel Garian. Now. When will the shipment be made?"

"It is ready for shipment even now," said the old woman gruffly. Marsha thought she detected a quaver in her voice but decided not to call attention to it, though she kept her hand near her pistol. "You have ordered several dozen cases of edibles for your crews. Among them you will find ten cases simply marked fruit. Those cases should be handled with great care. Each case comes with a connector allowing for transfer from the original containers to whatever you fabricate to hold the gases. The shuttle will deliver them this night to your *Raptor*. Will that suffice, Admiral?"

"It will be quite sufficient, Domagera sel Garian. Now, I must take my leave before my presence is missed."

The old woman stood up and motioned to a different door. "Leave by this route, Admiral. It will confuse prying eyes." This time there was no bow and no mention had been made of the bottle of fire wine and two glasses sitting in plain sight near sel Garian's right hand, an insult Marsha chose not to notice.

Stepping out the door without another word—trading insult for insult—she turned her hood up, stepped into the throng of tall people, and began to make her way back to the palace. She barely resisted the impulse to shoot the stranger at the end of the arm that stopped her.

"I would offer Your Grace an easier way out of the Port District."

Marsha got the impression that this was the same Shiravan who had led her to the warehouse initially and merely nodded.

The next morning she awoke slowly, stretching until her joints popped. A quick shower later, she found a note on her desk that she was sure hadn't been there when she went in. Unfolding it, she found that Linnas was expecting her to show up for breakfast in twenty minutes. She wore her dress blacks with the new rank installed on the collar and made her way to Linnas's breakfast nook.

Linnas was already seated when she came in, so she sat at the other place setting. She had time for an abbreviated morning greeting and a sip of the weakened wine most Shiravans had with breakfast, but she was surprised at the tack the morning conversation took.

"How was your visit with Domagera sel Garian, Sibara?"

Marsha hesitated before answering. She didn't want to reveal her true reason for meeting the Isolationist leader. "Most enlightening, Sibara," she answered. "It's always best to know the mind of the enemy, so when I got a clandestine request to meet with her, I took it. I was going to bring it up this morning anyway. Her idea was much the same as mine—to assess her opposition. I'm not sure who got the most out of the meeting since it didn't last long."

Linnas let a serving girl put plates in front of each of them before answering. "I would prefer that my senior officers not have secret meetings with Isolationist leaders, if you please. How would it look if you disappeared? How would our Sibara, Katherine, take it? How would it affect the human fleet you control or the Shiravan government I control?"

Linnas slowed down and took a sip of wine, ignoring her meal. "You see, Marsha? There are so many things that can affect the natural order. That is why you will not go out without security from now on. Do you understand me, Sister?"

Marsha just nodded slowly, noting the emphasis on the human word, but still thinking about the ten cases of fruit that had surely already been sent to the *Raptor*. That was one item she would have to check for herself.

Marsha sat in the *Raptor's* main conference room. Most of her captains were present or represented. "I want to know if we've received any deliveries by ship rather than transporter."

One man stood up a bit uncertainly. "Admiral, there was one delivery by ship earlier today. Since I wasn't really expecting it, I had it sealed in stasis until you released it."

"Good work, Commander. Let's take a look at it."

Marsha entered her personal code and headed for the piles of crates. "Look for any crates marked fruit. There should be ten of them. I want them set aside for inspection."

Forty-five minutes later the three officers had pulled the last crate from amongst the piles and sat down to catch their breaths. After a few minutes, Marsha asked, "Where do you keep your crowbars, Commander?"

The ten crates held forty canisters each and had both officers wondering what was going on. "Secret mission, gentlemen—one that you're now cleared to know about. Each canister contains a virus to be released on each Garmon-occupied world we visit or attack. Suffice it to say that it will have a totally devastating effect on Garmon civilization and will be the winning stroke in this war."

CHAPTER TWENTY-SIX

Simon sat in the quarters he and Kitty shared in Vesta, waiting for her to get in. She had spent the last week on Earth making the Alliance presence felt at the highest levels—Security Council meetings, galas at Baron von Schlenker's, and appearances and speaking engagements around the world. She was going to be beat, but he had the perfect vacation idea. One of the commanders in Planning and Tactics, a former Canadian, had shore-front property on Hudson Bay, and this was just the time of year to take advantage of the good commander's offer.

He'd planned a week of total isolation from anything to do with the Alliance, except a couple of bottles of fire wine, and he'd gone to a lot of trouble to arrange things so neither of them had anything to do during that time. He had also put a bottle of fire wine in the cooler in anticipation of her arrival. That was one of the few things he liked about his position these days—the ability to keep track of every ship and person in Earth-space.

The Terran Alliance was now big enough to run itself, especially after the United Nations had unanimously granted the Alliance full status as a nation and allowed them onto the Security Council. After all, Alliance weapons were several orders of magnitude beyond Earth's primitive atomics. The Alliance belonged on the Council.

The Garmons were becoming less and less of a problem as their shipyards and fueling stations were reduced to rubble. They *couldn't* have too many ships left to wage war with. Soon, they'd be restricted to their own worlds until they could work their way back to space on their own.

What was becoming a problem was the number of requests for off-planet colonization—all in all a good idea since one concerted and determined attack on Earth would effectively wipe out the entire race. Simon was having more and more ships reporting on possible habitable worlds than Garmon-occupied ones. That was why he'd approved R&D's buildup of colonist transports.

They would have to carry as many people as possible while providing adequate bathing facilities, gyms, mess halls, and even a theater. Anything less and the colonists and crew could arrive a disorganized, unmanageable group, lowering their chances for survival. And there would have to be enough ships to protect and resupply the colonies.

The door lock disengaging derailed his train of thought. After several months apart, Simon and Kitty were finally getting to spend some time together, time they needed to reconnect with their personal lives. And he had an agenda of his own to spring soon enough.

Kitty walked into their quarters and let the door close as she stripped off her traveling coat. Simon looked up and noticed the dark circles under her eyes. His first thoughts forgotten, he pulled her to him without a word and kissed her until they both needed to come up for air.

He started to massage her shoulders, working her blouse off over her head. She moaned quietly as she leaned into his hands. After ten minutes of silence and massage, he led her to the shower where he set the temperature just short of too hot and let the heat loosen up some of the muscles he hadn't managed to get to yet.

Washed and dried, he took her to bed and spent another half hour working on her legs and back, feeling the tension melt out of her body. Finally, thoroughly relaxed, she asked, "To what do I owe the pleasure of this much attention, dear?"

"Simply that we haven't had time for anything even remotely close to this in months. Don't look surprised," he said in response to her startled look. "I checked. I've been busy; you've been even busier; and I think it's time we had some time to ourselves." He let his hands wander over her body, her snow-white hair spilling through his fingers.

"And how am I supposed to repay this?" she asked playfully.

"I have a few ideas about that," he answered.

Soon, all thoughts of Alliance affairs were left behind for both of them. Later, after another shower and a meal delivered by stewards, they lay together on the bed, drifting in a blissful limbo until both fell into the deep sleep only two lovers could attain.

The next morning, Simon woke immediately when Kitty began to stir. He called the kitchen and ordered breakfast for two and slowly pulled her back into the shower. This time they dressed informally and walked into their private dining room, a privilege most residents of Vesta didn't have. The table was set, and the stewards had left juice and a variety of foods for them to choose from.

After a leisurely meal, Kitty said, "Well, I should

probably make an appearance in my office."

Simon laid a hand on her arm, stopping her from getting up. "I took the liberty of clearing your calendar for the next week, dear. You didn't have anything pressing, and Diana can take care of almost anything here on Vesta. I took a week off for myself, and barring some major confrontation, I don't have anything to do."

Kitty looked at him strangely. "With this much time off, just what did you have in mind?"

"I know a commander in Tactics and Planning, a former Canadian, who happens to have a cabin overlooking Hudson Bay. This time of year is perfect. Days are cool and crisp; nights are perfect for kicking back on a bearskin rug before a nice fire, nothing to think about but getting ourselves back in tune with our marriage. We've spent enough time nursing the Alliance along. Let someone else handle the details for a week. We've earned a vacation."

A gleam shone in Kitty's eyes. "Hudson Bay, huh?" She was quiet for a minute. "How are we going to get there?"

"Have you forgotten shuttles and transporters? Depending on which ship we take, we've got transportation. All that needs to be done is to cut firewood, Milken said. He hasn't had a chance to use the place for a couple of years, and we'll be doing him a favor by getting it straightened out. Here, let me show you the pictures of the place. He pulled out a slim album and began flipping through the pages.

"Not a rundown shack, this," Kitty said admiringly. "And I like the shots of the bay. Should provide some gorgeous sunsets. Okay, I'm in. When do we leave?"

"How about tomorrow? You wanted to check in with the Herald's office, and all I need to do is get some cold weather gear together. Everything else is already packed and waiting except a few perishables. *Ad Astra* is just out of the docks and standing by to take us to Earth. They'll wait for us while they do some shakedown drills. After they bring us back, they go out on their first patrol. Out Altair way."

"Got it all planned out, do you?" Kitty asked with a smile on her face.

"Yes, I do," Simon answered, grinning back. "And that's the first real smile I've seen on your face in ages."

Kitty was just as eager to get away as Simon was. It was nearly fifteen years now since they'd first stumbled on the *Galileo* and started the chain of events that had led to this moment. It was almost anticlimactic the way things turned out. Their normal transportation had been a small pickup truck into their campsite north and west of Billings, but this was just an extension of what they had wrought—a spaceship to deliver them to a remote corner of North America and communicators if there should be trouble or it was time to go back to the rat race they'd built for themselves.

In truth, as Simon had said on more than one occasion, the Alliance could run itself now. There was no real need for them to be there every minute. There were more people better able to interpret data and handle crises should they arise. And there was always the *Ad Astra* in orbit if they were needed back on Vesta.

They arrived in late morning, a mist still covering portions of the bay. Kitty started putting away the things that had been offloaded from the shuttle. Simon elected to get the fuel for the oversized fireplace that would take the sting out of the chilly Canadian nights. No security accompanied them whenever either one left the cabin. Kitty carried the laser pistol she had become accustomed to, while Simon carried the old-fashioned Army .45 he preferred.

They had started just a bit off cycle with the planet, and by the time a sufficient store of firewood was laid by, Kitty had prepared dinner, which was a first in more years than she cared to remember. After they had eaten at the obviously handmade and ancient dining table, Simon pulled a bottle of fire wine out and went into the living room where he already had a roaring fire going. The bedroom was on the other side of the fireplace, so any heat the rock chimney would absorb would be released during the night, although it would still be quite chilly by morning.

Tired from her labors and jetlag, Kitty lay back on the comfortable bearskin rug that really was there and watched the fire shimmer off the silver-tipped fur. Simon poured a small amount of wine into two glasses, for which she was glad since the brew was more potent than its taste suggested.

She raised up on one elbow and took the proffered glass, waiting for Simon to settle down beside her. Once he was at ease, he raised his glass in a toast. "To Commander Milken for the peace and quiet we are about to enjoy. We should find a way to repay him without it seeming obvious."

"Here, here," Kitty answered heartily, clinking glasses, the small sound resounding up her spine. Anything that would make him forget the war and the Alliance for even a short time was welcome in her universe. After his stint in the regeneration chamber, he looked almost half his real age and sported the same white hair she did. She realized what kind of stress he'd been under these past few years while she played at being a diplomat. She was going to have to find a way to thank him.

Getting up later in the evening to go to the outhouse made her reconsider having thanked Simon earlier. Even the white, store-bought seat couldn't help but be frigid. *If my ass had been wet, I'd be stuck out here all night*, she thought, making her way back inside. Simon did redeem himself, though. He had awakened when she got up and put more wood on the dying fire, and a cheery glow presaged the heat even as she wrapped part of the bearskin rug about her, waiting for Simon to get back from his trip outside.

He stirred the logs and added two more before rejoining her. He had two more glasses ready for them, a smaller amount this time, and raised his glass once more. As she uncertainly raised her own, he tapped her glass, and said, "Here's to the most beautiful woman in several dozen solar systems." They sipped the shimmering blue wine slowly until Simon said, "Why don't we go out to that ledge tomorrow? The one overlooking the bay?"

They were situated on the edge of a bluff, and the ledge gave an impressive view of a very large expanse of water. On their first day, Simon had hiked out and reported an iceberg sailing by when he got back with an armload of wood.

"Okay," she said, snuggling against him. "We can make a picnic out of it and stay late enough to see if there will be an aurora. Of all the things on Earth I miss, auroras are near the top of the list." Soon she nodded off to sleep, the last of her wine unfinished on a nearby table.

Kitty's scream ended Simon's search for firewood and proved to be the end of their picnic idyll. Simon's .45 was in his hand even before he started moving back to the ledge where they had planned their afternoon meal. He skidded to a halt, staring in disbelief at the sight before him.

Canadian nights were supposed to be a bit chilly but otherwise wonderful in high summer. The problem was that the Canadian wilderness wasn't supposed to be home to active, human-killing Garmons. The race had been trying to blow humanity out of existence since the completion of their first space dock. They were extremely aggressive, hostile, dangerous, and single-minded. To a Garmon, all things belonged to the Garmon.

This one was mere steps away from his wife, backing her into a corner of the ledge, her own weapon lying thirty feet from where she stood. He raised the pistol and sighted on the back of the creature's head. One hand fired three rounds in quick succession, all striking low and to the left, shredding the shoulder of the Garmon while the other slid another clip out, ready for use.

We're not supposed to have any on Earth, Simon thought abstractedly. The creature turned, and Simon fired four more rounds into the chest of the vest-wearing enemy from beyond the solar system.

The eight-foot tall alien stopped, dark brown fur matting with a thick green liquid. Simon dropped one clip and inserted the second. As the eight-hundred-pound Wookie on steroids moved toward him, he saw Kitty slip over and pick up her laser with her left hand. It was then that he noticed her right arm jammed into her waistband. Anger suffused him and drained out just as fast. Time slowed as he knelt on a boulder, bringing him to eye level with the alien. He raised the weapon and carefully, dispassionately, fired four rounds into and around the eyes of the thing from a distance of fifteen feet.

The small slugs penetrating the primitive brain of the newest enemy of humanity finally did their job, and the huge alien fell face down, twitched twice, and was still. Simon sidled past the body, wary of any possible subterfuge, and hurried to his wife. Apparently, rock-steady on the outside, he could feel the tension in her shoulders and back as he put his arm around her. "Maybe we should have just stayed on Vesta," he said morosely. "At least we wouldn't be spattered with Garmon gunk." A quick comm call to the orbiting *Ad Astra* had medics and a sanitation team shuttling in almost immediately.

"I want to know how it got here, where it came from, and if there are any more, not just nearby, but on the whole damned planet!" Simon was livid. "I want answers… and fast. The Herald was almost killed."

"Admiral," the senior commander said, "I believe we already have some of those answers for you. How they got here will have to wait, but survey scans show that there were nearly identical life readings on top of that ledge just prior to our arrival. Now they're two miles away and heading into some of the least-known country on Earth. We can track them, but going in on foot? I'd rather drop a couple of AMs on 'em and be done with it."

"I'll have to talk to the Prime Minister about using antimatter missiles. It is their country after all, but if we can get some evidence of unexplained disappearances or something, I might have a chance. Look into that, will you?" Dismissing the commander from his mind, Simon said, "Let's go get cleaned up, hon."

Still silent, she just nodded. Simon took her good arm and walked her up the ramp into the waiting shuttle.

Not one to beat around the bush, George Cavitt, head of Tactics and Planning, said, "Our best guess is that they have to be survivors of the second wave." The assault on Earth that had left almost twenty million dead and countless others homeless.

"What about the ones that got away?" Simon asked.

"We have a fix on their life signs, but it's still too dangerous to send in teams. These guys know the forests now and are superb hunters to begin with. As long as they stay away from people, we're just going to track 'em and wait for the right opportunity." Cavitt didn't seem very pleased by the prospect.

"Their ship went down off the west coast," Kitty said. "How did they get as far as Hudson Bay without being spotted?"

"They've had almost ten years to travel," Cavitt answered. "I would move, too, if it was me stranded on an alien world. And who's to say they weren't spotted? I have inquiries out to all Canadian officials asking for all missing or dead reports for the past two years. We're looking into anything unusual, including Bigfoot sightings."

"You think you can keep them under control?" Simon asked.

"No. Under observation, yes. Maybe, if I can send in a couple of missiles, or *maybe*," Cavitt hesitated, the stressed word calling attention to it, "maybe we can send in teams ahead of them if we can get a read on how they're moving. Could cost lives that way, though. Either way, it won't be hard to follow half a dozen large aliens across the wilderness, especially when we know where to look. I will do what is necessary to take care of the threat."

"Good, and for what it's worth, I don't think the thing was out to kill me as much as it wanted to get my laser. I saw how they have adapted our tools and other things into weapons. Very inventive race. A few more centuries and they might just have won. And they can be our downfall yet if we slip up even once."

"That's not going to happen," Simon stated positively. "We've beat 'em back three times and started to cripple their extra-planetary capacity. Soon, they won't be able to get a ship into space."

"Famous last words, Simon," Kitty muttered darkly. "Famous last words."

CHAPTER TWENTY-SEVEN

The *Ad Astra* carried Simon and Kitty back to Vesta, where Kitty finally agreed to spend several days in a regen chamber healing her broken wrist and severely wrenched elbow and shoulder. Her leg, broken several years earlier, no longer ached at all. It was during this time that Simon came up with a plan sure to displease his wife; it was time that he made his own trip to Shiravi. It felt to him like half the Alliance had already been there, and he'd only left Earth-space once.

Kitty had promised that he'd be able to take a captaincy of a ship as soon as the Fleet was able to be turned over to someone with enough expertise to do the job effectively. There were a few candidates in range, but he wanted the experience of walking on Shiravan soil and meeting the Matriarch who had taken Kitty into her own family. Plus, there were more than a few candidates there that he wanted to interview as well. Two stood out in his mind, and there was going to be one hell of a fight when she decanted.

He was there with a change of clothes when she woke up. The first thing she did was to check her wrist. "Not so much as a twinge," she said, looking at him. She noticed the clothes on his lap and sat up slowly. "You even brought a towel," she said with one of her brilliant smiles. "Thanks, husband-mine." She cleaned the majority of goo out of her hair and started on the rest of her body. Simon couldn't help but watch as she made a sensuous exercise of it.

She reached for the clothes and finally found herself in an old pair of sweatpants and shirt. A curious look made Simon say, "Well, we're just going back to quarters, and I didn't want you getting a chill. We'll be eating in tonight. Diana has everything under control at the Herald's office and instructions to bother you only with the most important stuff. I'm on call if necessary."

"I haven't been away that long. To what do I owe the pleasure of your undivided attention?" Kitty looked at him strangely.

"Well, we never did finish our vacation, and I want at least one more uninterrupted night before we get back to work." His answer seemed lame even to himself, but it was the best he could think of.

"I know you too well, Simon Hawke," Kitty said accusingly. "You've got something else on your mind. Aren't you the one who said to make one thing serve two purposes?"

"Well, I wasn't the first, but yeah, I did. Why?" he asked defensively.

Kitty laughed. "I know that tone too, dear, and you've definitely got something on your mind. Remember, that's what wives are for. I'm your support group and sounding board."

"Since you seem to know me so well, let's wait until after dinner. I'm pretty sure you won't like this one very much. I'll give you a massage, and we can talk about it then."

"Plan to catch me when I'm relaxed?" she questioned, one eyebrow raised. "It must be something big. Okay, deal. No more talk about it until you've got me in your clutches."

Kitty had plenty of time to think about what Simon might have to talk about, but he managed to outdo even her imagination. After the promised massage, he said, "Everyone in Tactics and Planning, and that includes myself, is of the opinion that it's time for me to show my face in Shiravan space. I want to talk to all the captains before I make my final decision. Bob Greene will step in as acting commander of Alliance forces in Earth-space. He's got the experience, and I don't want to lose it to a lucky Garmon missile or ambush."

"And just when were you planning to tell me about this? And what decision are you talking about?" was all Kitty seemed to be able to get out.

"I was going to tell you when all the elements fell into place," he said quietly. "And they have. The *Isaac Newton* will be coming out of dry dock this week, and a fleet is being assembled to ferry the *Galileo* back to the Shiravans. It would be good public relations on the other side, and I get to talk to all the captains over there before I decide who replaces me as senior admiral of the Alliance."

It was only then that she realized the relaxing effects of the massage were completely gone. That's what happened when bad news hit her in the face.

"First, as admiral, I need to inspect the fleet. That hasn't happened since the first ships were assigned to Shiravan space. It'll keep 'em on their toes, and I'll get those talks with the various captains over there. Besides, I want more than just Marsha's word that Gayle is holding up well. She still wasn't one hundred per cent when she left with Marsha's group."

"I still don't know why you need to speak to those

particular captains so badly. Care to fill me in?"

Simon looked at the floor and scrubbed at a mark on the deck plating with his boot. "We've had fifteen of years busting our asses putting the Alliance together from nothing more than a dream. And we did it! But I want out of this position, and I'm going to find and name my replacement. Maybe you should start doing the same. Then we can take a few ships and go looking in neighborhoods where we haven't been before. If there are three races in this general area of space, why couldn't there be more?"

Kitty had been half expecting this for some time and recognized the inevitable, though she still fought it. "Why don't you just have the captains you want to interview come home? A courier ship could bring them all and at a faster pace than a fleet can travel."

"Again, honey, because the rank and file need to know that I'm still out here. And a real leader leads from the front, not the rear. Credibility. How will anyone respect my replacement if I don't show that I'm not afraid to take on dangerous missions, myself?"

"That's faulty logic, Simon. How will anyone respect you if you don't lead from the front, you mean. How it affects your successor is an entirely different proposition. How much of this comes from our little vacation problem?" Kitty asked.

"I will admit that there was some, uh, introspection after the trip, but that isn't consequential. I've met and considered almost all the captains in Earth-space, and now I need to visit with the rest before making a decision. And truthfully, you should start looking into your replacement, too, unless you're not planning to come with me?"

Simon made it sound almost like a challenge, but she

wasn't falling for it. *I've become too much of a politician*, she thought. Aloud she said, "I'll take it under advisement for the time being. If you're going to be gone almost two years, I'll have plenty of time to make my own decision."

"So, you're not going to put up a fight?" Simon asked, sounding like he had expected one.

"No, dear. I've been to Shiravi, and I don't see any reason why you shouldn't go, except that we'll be another two years apart, and I'll have to learn to work with Bob Greene all over again. I'd like to spend as much time together as possible before you leave, though. I'll cancel most of my appointments, but there are a couple I can't cancel on such short notice."

It was closer to a month before the skeleton crew for the *Galileo* could be put together. They would have to return on other ships, so only essential personnel were required.

The day finally came. The *Galileo* had been stripped of all personal belongings, and most of her crew had already transferred to the *Newton*. All that was left was to take the fleet and leave for Shiravi. Simon carried a considerable amount of mail to Linnas, Marsha, and Gayle, while an even larger bundle was sent to the men and women of the rest of the human fleet in Shiravan space.

Kitty followed Simon aboard the *Ad Astra* to say goodbye. Most of that goodbye had been said alone in their quarters the previous night, but she really didn't want to see her husband leave. Bob Greene was a fine interim admiral, and she'd become good friends with his wife Michiko many years before.

"Nice quarters," she said, looking around. "I hope you've got a lot of reading material. Nearly two years in hyper is going to be very boring."

"Oh, I don't think I'll be too bored. I brought a select part of my Planning and Tactics team along, and we've rebuilt a few rooms to our specifications for some simulations that might help with the Shiravan side of things."

"What do you expect once you get there?" she asked cautiously.

"No more than you do. The last courier gave a pretty glowing report. No real activity of any consequence. The Garmons seem to be holding back more than usual. Whether that's because we've taken out too many of their ships or destroyed their refineries is anybody's guess. Most of the action seems to occur whenever we come across one of their worlds, and then the resistance is light. That's one of my reasons for going. We need to try to determine just how badly we've hurt them."

CHAPTER TWENTY-EIGHT

Pegra Nargresh looked uneasily at the hand and two of faces before him. Ever since the same language had been adopted and the Laws established, there had always been a leader chosen by the Elders. Occasionally a leader left no qualified heir, and the Elders met to choose a leader from a group of applicants who fought for the honor of leading the united Clans.

Now there were no Elders, or not enough surviving to mean anything. Pegra looked around and said, "We must choose from amongst ourselves who leads. If we don't, we run the risk of ending as the Elders warned us. Clan versus clan will destroy our race. None of our worlds might contact another again other than as enemies. I propose we decide together what a leader's next move might be."

A moment passed, and one clan leader cautiously said, "We have all suffered surprising losses at the paws of both the Shiravi and these new humanz. Certainly, no single Clan can stand against them. Do you have a plan in mind?"

Pegra nodded slowly. "I do not propose to set my will against another's, but my instincts say that I should find a place to lick my wounds and look at alternatives. I know that our late leader has sent out a construction crew to build a new, secret fueling station. Sharing fuel amongst our own clan ships will assure us of having enough to start refueling our under-fueled ships and quietly survey our own clans."

He shrugged. "After that," he said, hesitantly, "we can meet and bring treaty proposals together. I do wish to stress that our enemies have not given up their patrols and attacks against our nursery worlds. We must consider whether to hide the younglings and cows or move them to other, more distant planets not likely to be found by either race."

The moves had to be made carefully. Each clan and sub-clan had to manage with a severely diminished number of ships and try to be wherever their enemies weren't. The occasional meeting of the humanz broke the quiet movements of the clans.

Pegra strode impatiently through the remains of the wooden hall of the Garmon, waiting for the other captains to arrive. With farther to travel and more sub-clans to care for, he had collected almost half of the Garmons' nurseries before calling off the search for more; he had little patience with the rest for their tardiness, especially when the six right here were secretly making policy for a race used to the iron rule of a single individual.

These half-farat meetings were beginning to wear on him, even with the knowledge that his own personal domain now outnumbered any two of the others combined. Couple that with his proximity to the fueling station and the secret construction of one of his own, and he was beginning to feel the urge to call for a conclave now that several Elders had been found alive and a few others had attained that exalted status.

Eight hands and two ships pledged to him personally, and his spies told him that no one else, conspirator or loyalist, could claim even half that. His pacing stopped as he heard a ship land on the field outside. There was some chance of detection, but since the fuel plants hadn't been rebuilt and all the nurseries moved, there were no longer as many enemy ships returning to check on the viability of the world in question.

Three captains entered together, traveling in concert to minimize exposure to enemy patrols. The lead captain, one Targal Morghat, followed by Grikara Gubarak, senior captain under The Garmon, entered, followed by a youngling captain owning a mere two hands and two of ships and with few Honors on his vest.

Pegra said testily, "You're late. My ship has sat exposed for two suns while you delayed. We have two more to wait for. Who is the new captain? And where are the others?"

Before the new captain could answer for himself, Gubarak spoke up, a dangerous breach of Garmon ethics under the best of conditions. "Here stands Rudal Kravact, heir to the holdings of Sept-Leader Arkelt after sanctioned combat." He eyed Pegra, a look unmistakable to any Garmon. He added, "We here now comprise the whole of Garmon rule."

Pegra eyed the Honors on the newcomer's vest. "Welcome Sept-Leader. I am Sept-Leader Nargresh. We welcome your ships as well. As soon as we can decide on where to build a new shipyard, I'm sure your fleet will grow to fit your population."

"Speaking of populations and ships, Sept-Leader," Gubarak said dangerously, "as senior captain and Sept-Leader under The Garmon, it should be I who holds power here. Thanks to the attacks of the humanz and Shiravi, we have lost two of our own, and we feel that the Empire should be reunited under a single ruler."

"From your words, I assume you mean yourself,"

Pegra answered, a hand on the pistol at his belt. "You said that young Kravact holds his position by way of sanctioned combat. Do you propose a conclave wherein we may all vie for the honor of leadership?"

"And let a council of Elders know that we went against all tradition in assassinating The Garmon? We would all be executed as soon as word got out. I have a far simpler solution to the problem. Since no Elder knows of The Garmon's death, we will present them with a united front and only one contender for the title."

Pegra drew his pistol, anticipating with a hunter's instincts what was to happen next. "And you believe that it should be you who leads? Did you convince your friends here of your supremacy? I was never even consulted. I call that an insult of the highest magnitude. This hall has already been dishonored by one tainted death; another will do no harm."

Gubarak moved his hand toward his own pistol. He might have won if Pegra hadn't already had his own weapon drawn. The ripping sound of the laser startled the others while the smell of burnt hair and flesh stung his own nose. Holding his pistol at his side, he turned to the others and said, "So now there are three, since the other two haven't presented themselves. Will there be any more discussion concerning leadership? I don't want it, but I don't believe that it is wise to go back to our old ways. For three farats we've done well with deciding what to do for our people. Perhaps others should do the leading, but leadership should never again rest in the hands of one person."

He watched the eyes of the other two. Their hands stayed carefully away from their weapons, but their claws were certainly showing. Finally, they shifted away from him to gaze on the body at their feet. "Perhaps you are right, Sept-Leader," Targal Morghat said uneasily. "All the Elders we've been able to locate are on one of my nursery worlds. I will inform them of the crisis, blaming it on the raids on homeworld. They can consult the old books and decide what to do. I will convey your words and add my own as well. We will rise against the enemy and defeat them in time as a race rather than as the dream of one individual."

A half a farat later, almost two hundred ships stood primed to attack the homeworld of the Shiravi. It had taken that long to convince Morghat and Kravact to throw their forces in with his, and with the absorption of Gubarak's clans and sub-clans into their three domains, there now existed enough ships to mount an offensive capable of doing serious damage against their enemies.

Now, the Fleet sat invisibly in Shiravi's Oort cloud, gathering intelligence on the comings and goings of all ships. The time was perfect to pounce, especially with the new rudimentary shields. Four enemy ships sat at rest in the system—one around the second planet, two in orbit around the Shiravan homeworld, and one concealed in the Oort cloud opposite the fleet across the system.

Ships refitted with more efficient drives comprised a large part of that fleet. Enemy ships having shields against all the Garmons could throw at them had proven that such technology existed. Whether the systems were the same or not, the result was that the same light-built craft could carry heavier armaments and move faster. New drives were more efficient, and upgraded missiles gave a higher damage ratio. Now was a good time to test the new technologies against standing ships of the enemy.

Eight hands of ships were assigned to the single ship

while the rest were aimed at the remaining three ships in-system and the satellites in orbit. A single order would send those ships onto their missions, the one going farthest leaving first so that all three enemies would be taken out simultaneously. Commanding the largest contingent of ships, Pegra gave the order to move out. Within half a day, the results would be obvious.

Simon did have time to read and more. With the slower speed of the *Galileo*, almost nine months passed before the convoy arrived in Shiravan space. Every imaginable scenario had been hashed and rehashed to the point that everyone was on pins and needles, waiting to implement one plan or another.

Protocol demanded that any incoming fleet be challenged by a warship assigned to the point in space that ships from Earth entered Shiravan space just outside the local Oort cloud. The *Keltra Vant* was assigned to the duty for the moment, but no hail reached the Shiravan ship, even after several hours. Passive scans and Manta 3s were used to search cautiously for the missing ship.

At full red alert, the information came back. The *Keltra Vant* was a probable cloud of expanding gases and fragments. Included were the remnants of what appeared to be Garmon ships of a configuration not seen before, and there were only three of those. To date, with the upgrades to Shiravan vessels, the *Keltra Vant* should have survived or taken several more ships with her.

Simon had the luxury of having two full wolf packs with his fleet, not counting the *Galileo*, now once again the *Dalgor Kret*. Two cruisers and a carrier moved out under full cloak to check the situation closer to Shiravi.

Travel time to the inner system took days under in-system drive and full cloak, mandated by the circumstance of the nearby wreckage. Cloaked M-3s from the remaining carrier patrolled an ever-expanding area, coming up with nothing active scans hadn't already acquired upon arrival. All data collected indicated that the attack had happened as much as a week before. Physical examinations of the wreckage gave the same results.

Finally, a hyper-link message arrived authorizing an approach to Shiravi, along with the fact that several ships, two Terrans among them, were in orbit, providing cover for the homeworld. The balance of Simon's fleet, eagerly awaited, short-jumped into near-Shiravan space and were assigned orbits complementing the existing patrols.

Simon shuttled down to the landing field outside Quillas, main port city and capitol of the slowly re-growing Shiravan empire. By the time the fleet arrived, all the information on the Garmon attack was aboard the *Ad Astra,* and Simon was livid. Shiravi had received the same treatment Earth had. Two scars marred the surface of the smaller planet, and a number of satellites and ships had died in the surprise attack, two of them Earth ships.

The Matriarch and her Second Voice met Simon's entourage personally. "I am honored to meet the mate of my Sister, Katherine," Linnas des Harras said. "I grieve that your arrival coincides with such misery."

Simon and his captains followed the Matriarch into her offices in Central Command. After introductions, he said, "We are used to this kind of news, Your Grace. Remember, humans have had a very violent past." This was delivered with a wryness he hadn't expected. "And all the more so, recently. We share your grief, not just for our losses but for yours as well."

His discomfiture came from having only a passing acquaintance with the captains and none of the crews. For some reason, this left him feeling even worse than before. The fact that two Shiravan ships had been destroyed in the attack and the Shiravan death toll peaked around three hundred thousand didn't help any either.

Linnas offered chairs all around and fruit juice. After everyone was comfortable, her Second Voice, Sitha kep Parrasine, added a few details that had been left out of the transmission. "We had no notice. None of our scans picked them up until they were just outside the orbits of Shabbas and Grinnas."

Simon shook his head slowly. "That's the same trick they pulled on Earth. They came in on ballistic orbits without power. No telling how long they drifted before getting into attack position. And they managed to take out four ships, including the *Keltra Vant*. It seems amazing that so few enemy ships were destroyed."

Sitha spoke before her Matriarch could. "Our scans showed over two hundred ships involved in the attack. They were far better armored than we expected or have ever seen. When three ships broke off and headed directly for Shiravi, three cruisers—two from Earth—interposed themselves between the attackers. They were swarmed by a large number of the enemy's new attack craft and destroyed, but not before taking out two of the larger attacking craft. Only one managed to reach the surface. Unfortunately, it was aimed at the Matriarch's Summer Palace at Cho-An.

Simon looked at the Matriarch and said, "Your Grace, I'll see to the protection of Shiravi until we can get some real firepower back here. Do you have any long-range couriers on hand? Sending them out to look for any ships able to return immediately would be a big help. I'll advise my Planning and Tactics team about the apparent upgrades in Garmon engines, shielding, and tactics, and then we can get to know each other better. After all, you are my sister-in-law, according to our ways. Spare me a few minutes to confer with my captains, and then you'll have my undivided attention."

At Linnas's gracious nod, Simon huddled with his men, and they all began to leave immediately. Simon smiled quickly and said, "All that can be done will be, Your Grace. My captains express their regrets but want to see to the disposition of their ships and set up a defensive perimeter. They will return for formal introductions as soon as possible."

Linnas waved Simon back to his chair. "I have waited a long time to meet you, Admiral Hawke. The stories Katherine has told tell me you are a capable male and responsible for the building of the Alliance from the technology of our *Dalgor Kret*. It is good news that she has been safely returned, and I hear there are numerous improvements our scientists can incorporate into not only our space fleet but our entire economy."

Simon waved one hand deprecatingly. "I only had the idea. It was the work of thousands of others that resulted in the improvements you mention and the Alliance as a whole. I just helped find the scientists and crew who did all the work. I feel like more of an administrator than a leader, especially since my wife is the elected head of the Alliance."

"Katherine said you'd say as much, but the truth is that your people look up to you, and it's likely that not as much might have been accomplished by a lesser person," Linnas said matter-of-factly. "She also told me what could have happened if one of your governments had gotten hold of the *Dalgor Kret*. It's even possible that your world wouldn't have survived being found by the Garmons. Do you not wish to take credit for your foresight in choosing so wisely?"

Simon thought for a moment then shrugged. "Not particularly. I just made the decisions I felt to be in the best interests of my world and people. That those decisions led to what we have today is pure coincidence, and many of those decisions were made by other people over my objections. Still, all in all, I'm not too displeased with the way things have turned out." A lopsided grin crossed his face. "All I ever wanted to do was command one of the ships. And once this Garmon business is settled, I fully intend to do just that."

"Just my point, Admiral. We all thought we could get back to our normal lives. We all thought the menace had been contained. We have patrols revisiting past Garmon worlds and checking out new locations for any evidence of habitation. There's not much else we can do until we determine the source of this new invasion."

Simon took a sip from his juice. Oranges had become an overnight sensation in the time since trade had started between the two races. "Do you have any ideas where my senior captains are? Miller? Dahlquist? Kane?"

"As direct as Katherine said you were," Linnas said with a little smile. "I will see that you have access to the proper Directorate for such information. It is possible that some information will give you an expected return date. These patrols were sent out before the current attack, so they won't have any idea until they return. I can tell you this—the three you named will be beyond angry. Through their efforts, most of our gains have been made and many of our more junior officers have gained valuable experience and confidence. We have even re-established contact with the survivors on Harlo and retaken another five of our colonies. With the help of the Alliance, the Polity now numbers twenty worlds rather than fourteen."

Simon took a sip of his juice to hide his attempt to gather his thoughts. "That is good news indeed. Kitty will be happy to hear it. It is well that so many of your ships and crews have gained experience in combat. And winning battles boosts morale. This setback will probably cause your opposition leaders to try to move against you. Our ships will back you, and as soon as more ships return from their patrols, we can begin planning new strategies, such as finding out where so many ships came from. We must have missed at least one shipyard on some world we haven't yet visited. Sweeping more worlds may help with that task.

"But you mustn't take the chance of overextending yourselves at this time. You might not be able to keep what you've gained if you're not careful." Simon stopped, uncomfortable. "I don't mean to tell you how to handle your own affairs, but it's what we would do in such a case."

Linnas looked at Simon appraisingly. "I see now why it is you who leads your battle fleets. It was inevitable that the Garmons would eventually upgrade their ships. Seeing how we have refitted our own ships told them that the task wasn't impossible. And your advice is not unacceptable."

"Thank you, Your Grace. My concern is now how to deal with a re-energized enemy with better weapons. And for that, I need my senior captains present, along with yours. We must pool our combined resources to find our way to the end of this mess." Simon was deeply troubled. "If the Garmons managed to sucker any one of the fleets in, it could be a disaster. And with two hundred enhanced Garmon ships on the move, it's going to be that much harder."

"Will you stay here and see some of our homeworld for a short while? I would consider it an honor to have you as a guest in Quillas for a few days or until some of the fleets return if it doesn't interfere with your duties and if that meets with your approval."

"It would be my pleasure, Your Grace. Odd, isn't it? In all this time, this is the only the second time I've set foot on a planet other than Earth."

His mind wandered for a moment to a short excursion with Bob Greene's squadron, checking out some Garmon worlds where he got a firsthand view of Garmon life. The things he'd seen still stuck in his mind—the young males being trained by old Garmons, the females, looking like a different species altogether, and the squalid conditions they lived under. Some of the last was caused by at least one attack designed to cripple any resistance and ships in the area.

After giving orders to his fleet, he spent three days inspecting the shipyards, meeting with high officials before fading to darkness. Then came a visit to Cho-An, destroyed in the attack. "Kitty told me about this place. I'm sorry I didn't get to see it before."

"Don't worry, Admiral," Linnas said. "As soon as we have defeated the Garmons completely, it will be rebuilt. But now it's time for you to return to your fleet. A few more ships have returned, and we can now start sending out reconnaissance groups to the nearer worlds to see if this was an isolated attack or part of a more coordinated effort."

Seeing the necessity himself, Simon called for his gig and was taken to Quillas Port for the ride back to his flagship. Once aboard, he immediately called his Planning and Tactics team together to consider the ramifications of the new circumstances. Sending out two recon groups to some of the nearer worlds, he set out the mission parameters.

"Until we get a better grasp on what we face, you are not to engage the enemy. Just find out where they are and return, without being noticed if you can. Fight only as a last resort for the time being. I want information, not casualties."

CHAPTER TWENTY-NINE

Their missions finished, Marsha Kane and Gayle Miller held their fleets at a predetermined rendezvous point, waiting for Shirley Dahlquist to arrive before they returned to Shiravi. Both Captains had noticed the increased capabilities of some of the Garmon ships and were discussing the matter aboard the *Raptor*. It was during one such meeting that they received the news. Captain Dahlquist's fleet had finally arrived, bruised, battered, and almost half-strength but still a welcome addition to the ships just sitting in empty space.

Three fleets had gone out totaling twenty-one ships, including the ghost. Fifteen had returned. Shirley Dahlquist's fleet had suffered the worst, losing four of her seven ships when they came out of hyper into the path of more than twice their number. The newly refurbished Garmon ships, though more powerful than before, couldn't stand up to the battle-hardened crews of Shirley's ships. The carrier managed to disgorge her chicks before taking a hit to one engine pod. If not for that, there might have been no one left to tell the tale at all. Eleven Manta's returned to their damaged roost, joining Shirley's flagship and surviving cruiser. Sixteen clouds of gas slowly expanded as the survivors limped off toward their meeting with the other two fleets.

Marsha was more than a bit concerned when only three ships arrived flashing the Alliance IFF signal. She was even more upset when Shirley stepped out of her captain's gig. She looked at Gayle, back at Shirley, and said, "Maybe we should go up to my quarters."

Tired, Shirley replied, "I agree, but can you send someone over to the *Canopus* to see what can be done for her starboard engine pod? She took a direct hit with her shields down. I don't think she can make hyper again without some repairs. And I need a drink."

Marsha nodded and spoke quietly into her comm link as she led her friends to her quarters. "Crews will be on their way within the hour. If she could make one hyper jump, it can't be too bad." The rest of the walk was made in silence as the three friends contemplated the seriousness of the problem. Only once before had the Alliance suffered a defeat this bad, and that had been an ambush, pure and simple.

Gayle tried to comfort her friend as they settled into chairs in the Captain's quarters. "Sounds like bad luck to me, Shirl," she said. "Got any ideas how it happened?"

Shirley shook her head. "All I can say is that those ships seemed to be able to take more punishment than any I've encountered before. It was almost like they have shields or something now. And their weapons carried more of a punch than before, too."

Marsha heard the confusion and pain in her voice. "Well, both Gayle and I have run into something similar. But now that we know, we can start planning new tactics for the future. But we should cut our schedule short and get back to Shiravi with all this as soon as the *Canopus* is ready. We've managed to seed over twenty suspected worlds with the virus, and that should be enough for a first foray."

Simon Hawke, First Admiral of the Terran Alliance, sat in a chair watching a sunset on an alien world. Even after two months, it was still a marvel to him. The Alliance was almost fifteen years old, suffering from growing pains similar to the ones that had afflicted a new nation more than two centuries before. His ostensible reason for being on Shiravi in the first place was to confer with several ship captains in preparation for promoting one to his own position. He was tired of leading and being looked to for direction and inspiration. His very bones told him it was time and beyond to take off his admiral's hat.

He watched the red sun slip down past the port facilities on the far side of Quillas City, capitol city of Shiravi and her twenty colony worlds, and even though the sight still made his breath catch in his throat, he was beginning to feel an itch to move. The problem was, according to Linnas des Harras, Matriarch of the Shiravan Polity, that the three particular captains he wanted to see were on extended patrols with no specific ETA. It was, therefore, a bit of a surprise when a runner from the Matriarch's staff found them with news that the patrols had finally returned.

Considering the hour, he decided that tomorrow would be time enough to announce his intentions. His presence would be common knowledge to the new arrivals almost immediately, but since this was only his second trip out of Earth-space, he imagined the news of his presence would come as a shock. Their reactions might tell him something, but with these three, maybe not. Time would tell. He finished the glass of fire wine sitting beside him and went in to bed.

The next morning, he found breakfast waiting for him, so he ate before calling the fleet in orbit. The

Raptor, the largest warship to come out of an Alliance shipyard, was captained by Marsha Kane. He left it up to her to round up the other two. First, he wanted a battle assessment of their missions and then individual meetings with each one. Two hours later, he entered the *Raptor's* landing bay.

He stepped out to an honor guard and Ruffles and Flourishes. Marsha stood at the head of her staff, flanked by Simon's other two candidates—Gayle Miller and Shirley Dahlquist. He strode to the bottom of the gig's ramp and saluted Marsha. "Permission to come aboard, Captain?" he asked, snapping a salute.

Marsha stepped forward and returned the salute. "Permission granted and welcome, Admiral. I must say it's a pleasant surprise to find you out here. If you will follow me, please?"

Simon followed Marsha, trailed closely by Gayle and a bit farther back by Shirley. Once the four were comfortably seated in an alcove in Marsha's suite, she poured drinks all round, handing Simon his favorite without asking—a double Chivas, neat. He took a sip and said, "I think Kitty was right. Going through regen takes the—for lack of a better term—potency out of alcohol... except for fire wine for some reason." He then got to the root of one of his reasons for being in Shiravan space. "So, give me your personal opinions on what's been happening on this side. Marsha, you start."

The *Raptor's* captain didn't quite manage to hide her wince. "Well, Admiral, we've been out on mission revisiting some of the old Garmon strongholds. We found and destroyed about half a dozen ships on the ground on three different planets. It was when we entered our last target system that we ran into trouble. We stopped in the local Oort cloud to get a feel for the area as usual and were attacked almost immediately, almost like they knew what we would do. Anyway, sir, the enemy had better armor, more like rudimentary shields, and heavier missiles. My fleet lost four ships before we finally took out the last Garmon ship." She stopped speaking abruptly, waiting for Simon's response, which wasn't long in coming.

He informed them of the attack on Shiravi finishing by saying, "I'm really not surprised. The Garmons do learn, after all. Planning and Tactics has been working on just this kind of scenario for some time. It's unfortunate that you were among the first to encounter their upgrades, but rest assured it won't be held against you. Of course, it doesn't make the loss of so many people rest any easier on you, but just imagine what could have happened if they'd had a larger force on hand."

Marsha's sigh of relief was almost palpable, and Gayle stepped in to cover her lapse. "Simon, we all know the risks as well as you do. It's likely that Marsha ran into their first upgraded fleet and Shirley had the same problem. We'll all have to be more careful in the future and plan for the possibilities. It's also obvious that they have another fuel depot we missed. Now we'll have to search farther out to locate it. That means more missions and more losses, but we're prepared for that now."

Simon looked appraisingly at the three captains. His expression changed, as did his tone of voice. "I do have another matter to bring up. Central Control picked up transmissions before your fleets left on your last forays. It seems that several encrypted messages no one has been able to decode were intercepted. That seems likely to be your handiwork, Captain Kane. Would you care to enlighten me as to their content?"

Marsha's eyes strayed to her friends before answering. "Just personal messages between friends before departure, Admiral," she responded smoothly, belying the hesitation before her answer.

"I also have it on good authority that you had at least one meeting with antiestablishment persons before your final deorbit. How about explaining that one, and do a better job than you did to Linnas." He was poker-faced and his tone had changed again. This time there was a coldness she hadn't heard before.

She didn't hesitate. "I was summoned by the head of the sel Garian Clan. I wanted to know what she had to say that was so important that she'd go to such great lengths to contact me. She wanted to try to convince me, as senior human commander and captain of the most powerful ship in Shiravan space, to see her point of view. In fact, she tried to turn me. Of course, I refused and left immediately. There's nothing more to tell, sir."

He stared at her until he saw goose bumps prickle her skin. "I sincerely hope my most senior captain wouldn't be consorting with the enemy. We have a vested interested in keeping the des Harras regime in power. Let the sel Garians and their ilk take over, and everything we've done to help these people will go down the drain, not to mention the help we receive from them. We'd have to find a habitable planet and build our own base in Shiravan space. Probably have to do that anyway. But the time lost doing that would give the Garmons more time to rebuild their forces and be that much harder to defeat. Do I make myself clear, Captain?"

"Perfectly, Admiral," Marsha said straight-faced.

"Good," Simon said more equably. "Then I consider

this matter closed. Now, how about another drink and you tell me about the state of mind of your various crews. Anything in particular you think I should know?"

Gayle got up and went to Marsha's liquor cabinet. While she was pouring four glasses of wine, Marsha said, "Well, about the only thing I can think of is that quite a few of our people think we should rotate fleets so others can get more experience on this side of the war and let us go home for some real R and R."

Simon nodded as he took a sip of his drink. He let the taste linger in his mouth for a minute before answering. "I agree. I only have five ships with me that I can trade out right now, but that should show the rest that relief is coming. How many ships do you have over here now?"

"After our losses, we have twenty-two human-crewed ships here. That'll leave seventeen looking forward to going home. Of course, not all of them have been here from the beginning, and you didn't bring a *Raptor*-class with you, so I'll stay with my crew until you can send replacements."

"Okay," Simon agreed. "You pick the ships, and I'll cut the orders for their trip home. As soon as I get back, I'll send a full contingent to let the rest of you get some downtime. Travel time, fleet makeup, and return can't be accurately estimated, but you can make an educated guess. Will that do for now?" By this time, he sounded positively agreeable, so Marsha just nodded, almost afraid to say more.

Gayle spoke up. "How soon do you plan to make the switch, sir?" She was one of his closest friends and a Firster into the bargain, but apparently she felt that this meeting required formality.

"Are you gals that anxious to see me gone already?" he quipped. Before any of the captains could answer, he said, "I've been here waiting on you for a while, so I think we'll be headed back within the week. Maybe sooner if you get me that transfer list. How does that sound?"

"Sounds fine, sir," Marsha answered. "We can fill out Shirley's group with some reshuffling and integrate the new ships into the slots of the returning ships. I can have a list ready for you in two days. Will that do?"

"Excellent, Captain. Do you need anything else?" When Marsha shook her head, Simon added one more thing. "I think it might be a good idea to find a system where we can set up a base over here, so keep an eye out for something appropriate, okay?"

The three women looked at each other, and Shirley spoke up tentatively. "My group did find a system that might be just what you're looking for, sir. Not too close to any identified Garmon worlds, and a sufficient asteroid belt to set up in. Should I send you the coordinates?"

"Not now," Simon said, finishing his drink. He set his glass down and stood up. "I think I'll be going now. I have a meeting with the Matriarch in a few hours. I'll apprise her of the changes and see how she responds. Marsha, you might consider attending as well since you're going back to being stationed ground-side for now."

Marsha agreed, and moments later the admiral and his mesmerizing presence were gone. She looked at her co-conspirators and said, "Whoever goes home now, we three will stay until replacements arrive. I'll arrange for more of the virus to be shipped up. We'll cut back on revisiting old sites and try to find new ones and possibly their new fuel depot. That should make our replacements happy if we can do it. If we don't find it, at least it will cut out a few places they won't have to search, and we'll have infected several more worlds. I just wish I could know if we were having any effect with this virus. Now, I'd better shower and change before going to see Linnas."

Shirley and Gayle both drained their glasses and stood up. Marsha hugged both friends, and each one left to their respective chores.

Simon's trip back home was uneventful, but his interviews had left him with a lot to think about. He'd gone in anticipating offering his office to Marsha Kane, but his interview had left him uneasy somehow. All her answers had been clear, concise, and just a bit too rehearsed. There was something he'd missed, though he couldn't figure her as anything but totally loyal. She'd been one of the shining stars of the second wave and proved herself a dozen times over.

Perhaps it was just paranoia that he was feeling a bit uneasy about relinquishing command, even though that had been his deepest desire from day one. He wanted to be the one in the captain's seat. And if he could rig it after the war, he'd be the commander of a fleet prepared to search the inner reaches of this arm of the galaxy. It would take a quantum leap to let them travel to other galaxies, but this one should be big enough for even his extended lifetime.

Nargresh was perplexed. The reports coming in from the watcher fleet his predecessor had started, along with the reports of visiting Clan leaders, were distressing to say the least. Planets that had been attacked by the humanz and the krath-Shiravi, as well as planets no alien ship should have been capable of finding, were experiencing a major problem of the first magnitude.

For thousands of years, the docile cows had served as breeders for bringing new warriors into the Septs. There had never been a problem before. A warrior would land on one of his vassal planets, impregnate as many of his breeders as he had time for, and then head back into the packs. Now, though, it seemed that there was resistance to the natural order of things.

The younger cows were reported to have begun speaking! True, it was only on a rudimentary level so far, but they were showing opposition to mating. Without amenable cows, there was going to be a decided shortage of warriors in a very short time. Something would have to be done. But what?

CHAPTER THIRTY

Pegra watched his monitors as a majority of the ships in homeworld orbit left to mobilize all the usable craft and rendezvous for the attacks the Elder-approved Council had devised. But this time he would again lead a fleet himself, an action his predecessor had refused to do. It would look good to the Elders to see him in the forefront of any action.

Nearly two hundred hastily refitted ships were slated to simultaneously attack half a dozen Shiravan worlds. Depending on their success or failure, another campaign would be mounted against the humanz. That would be the tricky part since the humanz hadn't yet started to colonize planets he could attack. It would be a well-defended home system, so he would hunt the hunters, ambushing their patrols wherever he could find them.

Marsha Kane presided over a nearly full conclave of ships' captains, a fair percentage of them Shiravan. The Alliance admiral had finally left for Earth-space, taking the promised five ships with him. The fresh faces of the new captains were recognizable by their eager expressions. They hadn't faced the type of up-close-and-personal combat the Garmons were so proficient at.

She outlined the general plans, omitting the viral attacks. She had no idea yet whether or not to trust these new captains. Did their loyalties lie with the admiral or with the chance to save humans and Shiravans both from certain extinction? Those orders would come after the new captains returned to their vessels.

In Earth-space, Herald Hawke made plans of her own. Enough ships would guard Earth from attack while the rest, operating under new orders, would spend their time under full cloak while they searched for signs of Garmon presence encroaching on the buffer zone humans had carved out around their single star.

That was going to have to be a priority, and soon, too. She was beginning to receive pressure from more than a few groups wanting to colonize new worlds. This would, of course, entail ships to protect those colony worlds. First, though, habitable planets needed to be certified safe within the general parameters of that word. Also, with Earth's dwindling resources, geological teams would have to ascertain if the planets in question could produce enough resources to trade for vital goods and services. And they needed the new *Galileo*-class ships to perform the same task the *Galileo* had been intended for.

It was the kind of headache she didn't want, so she appointed a new committee to go over all the preliminary specs and advise her which planets were worth a geological survey. All this information would be made available to Earth through Alliance embassies, and requests for space aboard future ships had already outstripped capacity within weeks of the announcement, virtually tying up all embassy landlines overnight.

This left the Alliance to handle the transportation of survey crews, with the caveat that the buffer zone would have to be expanded if suitable planets could be found.

And that would require *more* ships. With all four bases and the *Newton* churning out ships at full capacity, the sheer numbers were daunting. Simon had been gone nearly two years now, and twenty more cruisers had joined the lists, with a super-*Raptor* soon to come out of Taurus Base. There were now over sixty Earth-built ships in service around Earth-space, and that roster was increased by almost two dozen Shiravan ships.

Between all the ships already in service and service personnel on Earth and Vesta, Alliance citizenship was in the millions. Vesta was now a going concern, being more of a transient habitat for those waiting for shipboard assignments or transportation back to Earth. It had more of a lived-in feel about it now. Ceres was more pristine, transformed into a model of efficiency and cleanliness, housing only service and headquarters personnel—a fit showcase for visitors and embassy staff from Earth that Kitty was proud to show off. Both the Herald and Admiral had moved their offices to Ceres.

TAS Murphy's Law, along with a dozen other ships, was on regular patrol in the outer reaches of Earth's solar system when the screens lit up with the images of half a dozen inbound ships. Alarm bells brought Lt. Commander Roger Davis running onto the bridge. "Status, Helm," he demanded, hiding the quaver in his voice.

"Sir, six ships inbound. Straight-line extrapolation indicates Shiravi as point of origin. Incoming message arriving now."

"Put it on speaker, Ensign," Davis said.

Interstellar hiss preceded the message. "Any Earth ships within range, this is Task Force Alpha. Admiral

Hawke requests immediate clearance for Ceres orbit."

Davis got on the comm. "We're sending a flight of Mantas for visual confirmation, Admiral. Please hold your position until you receive clearance."

The answer was almost immediate. "Holding position, aye. Task Force Alpha out."

Thirty minutes later the Manta leader reported all clear and Lt. Commander Davis keyed his comm. "Task Force Alpha, visual inspection complete. You are cleared for Ceres orbit. Welcome back to Earth-space, Admiral."

"Thank you, *Murphy's Law*. Glad to be home. Proceeding to Ceres orbit via short-jump."

Davis moved his ship out of the way, and the six ships disappeared from his screens.

CHAPTER THIRTY-ONE

Simon stepped off the transporter pad on the newly activated and barely populated Ceres, where the Alliance's offices had been moved, with a lot on his mind. First order of business, of course, was to get reacquainted with his wife. A nearly two-year absence tended to affect his priorities. He asked the transport tech the local time, reset his watch and headed for his quarters.

He expected to find Kitty asleep in the middle of local night, if that word could be used inside a twenty-plus-mile-long asteroid. Instead, she was not only up and dressed, she had a bottle of champagne and two glasses waiting. After a hug and kiss that came close to making up for two years of separation, he held her at arm's length and smiled. "I didn't expect you to be awake at this hour, dear, but I'm glad you are."

She stepped into his arms again and looked up with a smile of her own. "I gave orders long ago that I was to be informed the instant you got back. Did you think I'd sleep through you getting home?"

He felt her melt into his arms and knew there would be no rest any time soon.

Simon's body-clock wasn't on the same schedule as Kitty's yet, but he woke up refreshed and happy as soon as he felt his wife start to move against him. He pretended to be asleep and watched her through half-open eyes as she walked into the shower. Her figure hadn't changed, but her snow-white hair had grown. It reached nearly to her knees in a heavy mane that swayed with each move she made. He sat up in the bed as she came back into the room and watched her towel the last of the water out of her hair.

"I will never get enough of looking at you, lover," Simon said.

She smiled brightly as she worked at the mass of hair. "One good thing about this white hair business is that no matter how wet it gets, it dries almost instantly. And things must have gone well for you. You look younger than when you left. I'd say mid-thirties now. So, what's on your plate for today?"

Simon stood up and headed for the shower himself. "Well, I'm going to touch base with Earth-side Planning and Tactics to see what's been going on around here, then see what R & D has been doing recently. I'm two years out of date all around so I need to get back up to speed. That should pretty well take care of today. And it leaves time for a long, leisurely dinner with my wife. How about you?"

Kitty shrugged. "The post of Herald seems to have become something of a figurehead. Freddie handles things on Earth, though he's been making noises about stepping down. I have a replacement in mind, but I haven't talked to him yet. I don't know if you'll remember Heinrich Juergens. He was a great help in Zurich when we were trying to get recognized by the United Nations. I've got to talk to Freddie and hear what he has to say about him, but even though we haven't spoken since then, I still remember being impressed by his knowledge and expertise."

Simon stopped in the doorway. "Freddie stepping

down? What will we do without his extravaganzas? His castle was the perfect backdrop for bringing us into being. I liked the blending of the old with the new." He was truly upset with this news. It was the first time his extended lifespan had affected a relationship, and it hit home hard. He felt his blood pound in his veins. "I'm going to have to think about this one," he said without explanation.

He saw the concern in Kitty's eyes. She said, "I've had longer than you to accept this, Simon. We are going to outlive a lot of the people around us. So will anyone who's been through a regen session, and I'm trying to get as many people through as I can—all our senior staff, for example. I think that's going to do more to set the Alliance apart than we figured. We may not get to become as accepted as we thought once people really see that we don't age as fast as ordinary people. There could be a pretty big backlash. Even if we colonize dozens of worlds, there are still going to be billions of average people who are going to be pretty pissed about it, and we can't send them all through regen."

Simon nodded. "Even with making it mandatory for colonists, people on Earth will still reproduce like rabbits. We could make all colony worlds answerable to us, but that has repercussions of its own. Revolutions and wars with our own race are not my idea of what we want. Some form of mandatory birth control? Another can of worms I don't want to touch, and we can't just wait and let this blow up in our faces. Too many innocents will die. I'll add this to the list for Planning and Tactics long-range goals."

After their reunion night, Simon showered, dressed, and

went about getting reacquainted with Earth-space concerns. Kitty did the same, although her day was far less hectic since she didn't have two years to catch up on. She walked into her quarters to find Simon sitting on the bed, elbows on his knees and head in his hands. She sat down beside him and put an arm around his shoulders. "What's up hon?" she asked quietly.

Without raising his head, he answered, "I come back to find that there are more incursions into our space in the past six months than expected. We've lost seven ships, including two Shiravan ships. These new attacks are comprised of upgraded ships like the ones we started seeing around Shiravi just before the fleet headed back to Earth. They now have rudimentary shields, heavier armor, better missiles, better control, and better cooperation. We took heavier losses than before because we hadn't seen them yet. Now they're here, causing havoc with our patrols."

He was quiet so long she prompted him. "So, what did you do on Shiravi?"

"Increased the size of our patrols, added more cloaked ships, and accepted the fact that we're going to be taking more losses. We're going to start using the extra power cores to strengthen our own shields as we engage them." He raised his head. "I brought back five ships that needed downtime more than the rest. "That leaves seventeen ships that haven't been back to Earth for at least four years, five by the time I can get replacements out to them. Tactics and Planning says we can still accomplish our missions without them as long as new ships continue to come out of the docks. I've drafted preliminary orders for a replacement fleet without naming specific ships. What do you think?"

Kitty sat quietly for a moment. She already knew

about the earlier losses and finally said, "I think it's a good idea. Those crews need to feel their own sun on their faces and get some time off, but I'm just the civil administrator who once was a ship's captain. This decision is a military one. If you think we have the strength to do without so many ships then go ahead and do it."

Simon said, "The team in Planning and Tactics thinks it's a good idea, too. And R & D has come up with a new concept that could offset our lessened ship strength. It's new type of plasma bomb capable of causing ships to implode, leaving virtually no trace of what happened. They're past the testing stage and ready to go into production. As soon as they can outfit the fleet, I can send the replacements out. I can cut travel time by having a cruiser head to Shiravi to let Marsha know to expect her replacements and have the returnees set to go as soon as possible."

At the same time the new plasma bombs went into production, word filtered out that a major expedition was in the planning stage. As word spread that a large number of ships were going to Shiravi to relieve the ships there, instead of the uproar Simon expected, requests began to filter in, asking to be included in the outgoing fleet. It wasn't long before more than enough volunteers and ships were lined up to go. Simon's dilemma became which ships to accept. Some were going to be disappointed, but he could make them happy enough with the new weapon and a chance to retaliate against the enemy here. And if enough systems could be cleared, Kitty could start her colonization program. His main reason to wait was for the super-*Raptor* to come out of Taurus.

Several planets had been found that were acceptable for human habitation and colonists could be contacted, relieving the pressure on that front. Kitty was more than happy to hear this news. Now she could let word filter out to the embassies that potential colonists could be screened for selection as soon as the Garmons could be pushed out of the area the Alliance had co-opted for itself. The *Newton* and a security patrol would have to perform the exact tasks the *Galileo* had been sent to do so many years before, which seemed a bit funny to Simon. He shrugged his shoulders.

Such are the ways of the universe, he thought with a wry smile, and made a mental note to start plans for colonial transports.

Sebra Keth was the commander in charge of Garmon forces attacking the humanz' home system. His information told him that the humanz usually traveled in packs of five, including one of their carrier ships, with ten hands of small fighter ships. His twelve-ship squadron should wipe them out with minimal losses since all twelve had been fitted with the new shields and upgraded missiles. He positioned his ships in the Oort cloud where the humanz normally appeared before entering a system. On this occasion, though, the humanz overshot their usual exit point and appeared almost midway between the cloud and the star it surrounded. By the time his sensors detected the five ships, he had been scanned. This time there was no chance for an ambush, but his superior numbers still gave him a significant advantage. He ordered his ships to spread out, two targeting each cruiser, four for the carrier, and headed at half speed toward the enemy.

Commander Mark Davis, leading Task Force *Marakesh*, waited nervously for the Garmon to approach. His five visible ships would normally be able to take on the twelve enemy ships with the loss of only one cruiser, maybe two, but this was the first task force encountered after positive proof of Garmon upgrades. In point of fact, his fleet was twelve strong, just like the Garmon. Two cloaked cruisers were spread out to each side and forward of his visible ships. Three others, also cloaked, were almost a million miles closer to the enemy, and one of those was another carrier. Each ship was carrying prototypes of the new plasma bombs, and the Mantas had slightly smaller versions built specifically to fit their smaller size.

These new weapons had been tested rigorously, but this was their first real use in combat. The other five ships were spread out so the Garmons could pass through without interference. The ghosts ahead of his visible fleet let the enemy pass through them according to the battle plan and then moved in behind. Just before contact range, the shielded carrier launched her Mantas. As soon as they appeared on Davis's screens, he ordered his visible carrier to launch her own birds.

This time there would be no helter-skelter fighting. Each Garmon ship was specifically targeted by dozens of Mantas and the remaining ten cruisers from forward and behind the unsuspecting enemy. At extreme range, all ships launched a full spread of standard missiles, then loaded their launch tubes with plasma missiles.

Under the new rules of engagement, the five visible ships diverted all three of their power cores to strengthen their shields instead of the standard two. After the first missiles spent themselves on their targets, all five Earth ships were still intact, although most of the crews were shaken up from the impacts on their shields.

By now the Garmons knew there were more Mantas in flight than one carrier could launch, but the eight remaining Garmons still concentrated on the five visible ships on their screens. This time the enemy salvo was smaller but came in two closely spaced waves. Davis sent the order to launch the new weapons. Hundreds of missiles converged, and all eight ships simply ceased to exist. All that was left was to make out his report and send it Earth-ward.

Power was diverted back to life support and drive systems, and the fleet went back to normal operations. The captains of all ships converged on the *Marakesh* for debriefing. Once all captains were in Davis's briefing room, sensor scans of the battle were replayed for all to see. Only six Mantas had been lost, and not even one capitol ship sustained any damage. One ship was designated to send word back to Earth while the rest moved on to the next system using the same tactics.

"We won't be able to use these tactics more than a few more times without the Garmons catching on and changing theirs," Davis said. "So I want you all to start working on new ideas for dealing with different situations. Plus, I think that our accidental over-shoot as we came in may well have made all the difference in the world. We'll hold here while we come up with some preliminary new tactics to use in the next systems we enter. As we move farther out, we'll certainly find more ships to deal with, and we'll have to return to Earth to rearm at some point. By then, this information will be in the hands of the admiral and his planning team. Tactics will review our actions and accept or alter our method of attack. So, until we have to go back, we'll move on to our next designated system and see what happens. Any questions?"

Only one captain raised her hand. "How long to the next target, sir?"

Davis answered automatically. "About three weeks, Captain. That should give us plenty of time to bring our crews back up to battle readiness. Right now, they're all celebrating a glorious victory. I don't want people too cocky for their own good. Just one high-spirited idiot can get a lot of people killed. Let your crews have some fun but start stressing the severity of this mission quickly. Drills and exercises will go a long way towards that end. Any more questions?"

When no one spoke up, Davis said, "Very well, this meeting is adjourned. We will reconvene tomorrow after breakfast, have a working lunch, and shut down for the night around six p.m. Any questions? If we can conserve our munitions on target number two, we may be able to put some fear into a third system before returning to Earth. Dismissed."

Simon looked over the mission reports of the ships involved in the first action. "I want one of their cruisers to study. Let's send another ship out to tell Captain Davis to just disable at least one of the newer versions of their ships. Next, we'll clear out the crew with a boarding action and examine the ship in detail. I want full reports on engines, shield technology, missiles, and anything else of interest. Then, blow it out of existence. I don't want the Garmons to figure out this little surprise until it doesn't matter anymore."

One of his P & T people said, "You realize that boarding a Garmon ship is going to cost a lot of lives, don't you"?

"Yes, Red, but I have to consider acceptable losses in any engagement. At least we shouldn't lose a whole ship in the process."

CHAPTER THIRTY-TWO

Seventeen ships left Earth for Shiravan space with the new plasma bombs and a request for fresh ships to release the Shiravan ships serving in Earth-space. Their allies needed to be back home just as badly as their human counterparts did. A regular rotation was tentatively suggested at the same time for both races.

Despite the new forces, new patrols left on a regular basis with orders to explore and map no more than three carefully selected systems and return to base. This had the effect of keeping a larger number of ships in near-Earth space in the event of another large-scale attack. Simon was determined that nothing else would get close to Earth. More sensor drones were being deployed, and the entire system was now almost completely covered. The warning wouldn't be much, but anything was better than nothing. The newest probes were equipped with short-jump engines to give even more warning.

Marsha Kane ordered her first captain's call since she'd returned from her tour in Garmon space. With over seventy ships mobilized, some were on patrol, but enough arrived to give her a good idea as to what the others were thinking. The general consensus was to increase the size of the patrols, and in a case of parallel thinking, keeping most ships cloaked. The ideas were appealing, and she thanked the two captains responsible—one of them Shiravan. This was a good sign since most Shiravans couldn't figure out where she stood in the political hierarchy that held sway on Shiravi, so most held their thoughts to themselves.

On the spur of the moment she decided to implement the ideas and let the Shiravan captain have command of the first patrol. "Ten ships, two of them carriers, and you get one encounter to test the new strategy. If you have to visit four systems to find a decent fight, do so. But try to keep the heroics to a minimum, please. I'd like a list of ships on my desk within two days, including target systems and a loose idea of your timetable. Will that be sufficient?"

The Shiravan captain, mindful of the low ceilings humans preferred, nodded her head instead of standing to bow. "That is most courteous, Your Grace. Two days from now you'll have a full list of ships and a projected itinerary on your desk. Can I assume that the *Raptor* is not to be included on the list?"

Marsha noted the small smile on the captain's face and returned it with one of her own. "That would be a safe assumption, Captain. I know you'd like the firepower she provides, but I have other plans. Specifically, a similar mission of my own based on your choice of targets. I plan to send her in another direction, doubling our chances to hurt the Garmons. Our remaining ships and carrier will stay in-system in case of another attack."

She leaned back, satisfied. This was the first time a Shiravan had treated her with anything but stiff formality, and she found she enjoyed it.

Eventually, she turned to a shielded video comm and called the planet below. The gruff voice she heard was the same as the one from the warehouse many months before. "I need to set up another shipment of our special supplies, if possible," she said without preamble.

"You've used up all you had?" the voice asked, sounding surprised.

"Completely, Your Grace," she answered to the matriarch of a clan in opposition to the des Harras regime. "And if we don't get more, and quickly, my patrol won't have any to deliver to our mutual enemy." She sat back and waited for a reaction to judge the situation by.

"And what coin do you expect to repay such supplies with?"

Marsha made a face that only remotely resembled a grin. When she made that particular face, people tended to disappear from her presence as quickly as possible. "Why, with the dissension of our enemies, Your Grace. With dissension comes chaos, and with chaos sloppy planning and tactics. It will make our job that much easier." She wanted to make her listener understand that the danger rested off-world. "Of course, even the planets we don't find will be affected by any ship landing and exposing even a single female. What more could you ask for payment?"

A long moment passed while the old woman on the other end looked at her intently. "Very well Admiral. You can expect a supply ship within two days." The belligerent voice cut off without waiting for a response.

Well, so much for harmony between me and the enemy of my enemy, Marsha thought unhappily.

Linnas des Harras waited impatiently for her Sister-kin to arrive. Her request for an audience the previous day had been regretfully and graciously refused, Marsha pleading too much work setting up the two patrols her comm call had mentioned, which was the reason for this meeting. Linnas was worried about a repeat attack of her homeworld, and she should be after the destruction of her ancestral home. Cho-An existed no more, with only a ravaged crater as evidence of what had once been the crown jewel of the des Harras Clan for uncounted generations. With the *Dalgor Kret* back home, equipment was being manufactured to begin the rebuilding. Already, earthmovers were in the process of filling in the giant hole, preparing the ground for the foundation of the new city complex.

Marsha walked through the curtains dividing Linnas's dining area from the rest of her home in Quillas. She hesitated for a fraction of a second when she saw Sitha kep Parrasine sitting there as well. Sitha stood up and bowed slightly as she would to any member of the Matriarch's family. "Good morning, Your Grace."

Linnas looked up from a report she was reading and said, "Sit, both of you. And how are you this fine morning, Sister-kin?" she asked quietly. Marsha slipped into a human-sized chair as Sitha sat back down. Linnas leaned over and picked up a pitcher, making as if to pour for Marsha. "Orange juice, if I remember correctly, Sister?"

At Marsha's nod, Linnas poured. "I am well, Sister," Marsha replied to the question. "My mind is full of facts and figures as I try to assemble two fleets, and I don't get much sleep, but I get by." She took a sip from her glass, moisture already condensing on the outside.

Linnas hadn't failed to notice Marsha's pause upon entering and mused on its significance. She was loath to bring it up after the last conversation the two had had over a secret meeting with the matriarch of Clan sel Garian, so she chose another tack. "That's one of the reasons I wanted to talk to you, Sister. And my Second Voice is here because this is a matter of considerable delicacy for the Shiravan people as a whole."

She stopped for a moment to see how Marsha would respond. Instead of saying anything, Marsha took a sip of juice and then used that irritating human facial expression of raising one eyebrow. She had learned over time that this was merely a silent question, so she overlooked it.

She kept her silence, and Marsha did the same for so long that Sitha, new to her position as second-in-command, finally blurted out, "We, that is, the Matriarch and I, are concerned over two fleets leaving at the same time. After the appalling attack that destroyed Cho-An and many of our ships, we feel that the system is being left with too little defense, especially with the *Raptor* leading one of the fleets."

Marsha looked the slim red woman in her even redder eyes. "I thought that might be the reason for this visit. If I'm allowed to provide some particulars, it might set some of your concerns aside."

Linnas raised a hand and said mildly, "Please, Sister, enlighten us as to your thoughts."

She watched as Marsha took another sip of her juice, a delaying tactic she had learned over the years. It allowed one to put one's thoughts in order or to prepare to tell a lie. "As a prelude to the disposition of two large fleets, let me say that we've been running continuous shorter patrols of nearby systems, all cloaked, along with a few longer-range patrols. So far, we've only come upon two small patrols of Garmon ships, and those were utterly destroyed without the loss of a single ship. If ever there was a time to make use of our full potential, the time is now.

"One carrier will be left behind, along with almost fifty fully refitted ships of the line. That does not include the half dozen smaller patrols on station in nearby systems deemed useful as staging areas for a large-scale attack on Shiravi. The smaller patrols were tasked with seeing if our space was clear and visiting several colony worlds to see if they'd been attacked. None have reported any sign of Garmons for months now.

"These two larger fleets are designed to penetrate deeper into known Garmon space from two different directions and actually take the fight to the enemy. We have a saying among our people: 'The best defense is a good offense.' The other two carriers will both go with the fleet commanded by Sorgala des Nimara. I and my advisers, some of them Shiravan and personally acquainted with des Nimara, have evaluated her actions over the past year and believe she is capable of taking on this task. She has proven herself in battle and seems to have no problems dealing with humans.

"She questions her own abilities in these areas but has agreed to take on the task if for no other reason than to show all Shiravans that you are now ready to stand up for yourselves and handle your own battles. Granted there are human ships in her fleet, but they are under her command and will obey her as they would any commander. There will be Shiravan ships in the other fleet and they will be expected to handle their missions as would any other ship. Your people need this, Sister. Too long have they had to stand helpless as the Garmon took what they wanted virtually without fear of retaliation.

"Each Shiravan captain was chosen for the same reason as des Nimara, to revitalize your people with victories over your opponents. They desperately need a jolt of confidence in themselves, Sister. It will instill your people, our people, with a sense of pride and accomplishment and, incidentally, increase their effectiveness both in space and in your ground-based industries."

Marsha hadn't made a speech that long ever, and in Shiravan at that. She felt completely drained and took another sip of her juice, her hand shaking visibly. So far, it didn't appear that Linnas knew about her comm call to sel Garian the day before. System defense was paramount on her mind, as well the Second Voice.

Linnas spoke, more vitality in her voice than before. "I applaud your choice of des Nimara as doma-Sorgala for your second fleet, but I wonder about your choice of sending both carriers with her group. What will you do to offset the loss of fifty Mantas in the other fleet, Sister?" Marsha thought she heard genuine worry in her alien Sister's voice.

"We'll have the *Raptor*, of course, and we're readying more powerful missiles for both fleets before we leave. Also, Raptor Group will have more ships than des Nimara's fleet. I expect about two weeks before they break orbit. Are you satisfied with my report?"

Linnas looked at her companion, who gave a slight nod. "We are both impressed with the thought you've spent on this mission and the care with which you have prepared for our defense in their absence. You are to be commended and have my full blessing. May the Spirits of Space ride with both fleets."

Marsha sighed slightly. One hurdle down. "If I may be so bold, Sister, you mentioned more than one reason for asking me here today. What might those other reasons be?"

"So impatient, you humans. I believe it might be because you haven't endured as many years since you came to your full potential and your short time in space. We've been riding with the Spirits for almost four hundred of your years, and you less than twenty." Linnas took a sip of her own drink, a milky substance with a slight blue tinge. "There is only one other reason for your visit. It has come to my attention that you are spending entirely too much time on the business of the fleet and are in need of a short rest. So, for the two weeks you are ordered to spend time here on Shiravi as a guest in my own house. A room has already been prepared."

Marsha's face gave away her resistance to the idea. "This is not negotiable, Sister. You will be able to join your fleet before it leaves. But it *is* rest you need. You yourself said you are just getting by. Therefore, you will spend some time with nothing to contemplate but the natural beauty of Shiravi. You, of course have permission to return to the *Raptor* to pick up some personal effects, but I expect your return by dinner time. Is that clear?"

Realizing that she had no choice in the matter, Marsha said, "If that is your wish, of course I'll obey, Sister. Do I have your permission to leave now?"

"Of course, Sister. Our business is completed for the moment, so you are free to go. You are expected for dinner."

"Thank you, Your Grace," Marsha said with stiff formality. "In that case, I'll be on my way." She stood up, Sitha following suit, and strode from the room, back straight and with an even, moderate pace. It would be unseemly to appear to be running from this confrontation.

Marsha stepped out of her gig and headed directly for her quarters. She didn't have much time if she was going to make dinner planet-side. She commed her first officer to meet her while she got a bag packed for an extended stay on Shiravi.

Her decisions were limited. Her clothes all went into a small duffel before the knock she was expecting came. She opened the door and ushered her first officer, Alicia White Eagle, inside. "Ah, there has been a small complication." She watched as Alicia stood there wooden faced. She'd never been able to read her at poker and had no better luck now.

She picked up a bottle and poured two double scotches, a nasty habit she had picked up from Simon, and even though she'd been through regen, she still tended to drink it at times of great stress. She handed one over, getting the first sign of emotion from her in memory—surprise. "Don't worry so much. Captain's orders. It's to numb the pain." She indicated two chairs in her visitor's nook and took one herself.

White Eagle sat down, asking, "Whose pain, Admiral?"

"Both of us, Ali, both of us. Here's the deal." She went on to explain the Matriarch's decision that she needed some rest and was required to spend the next two weeks down-side. "So, until I get back, you're the *Raptor's* acting captain. All you have to do is confirm that every system is ready, all stores replenished, and all hands are battle-ready without starting a mutiny or losing your mind. You're one of the best tacticians in the entire Alliance, or you wouldn't be here. Think you can handle it?"

A small smile flickered across her face. Miracle! Two shows of emotion inside of ten minutes. "All systems ready, all supplies topped off, and all crew alert, rested, and ready. I don't see any problem with that, ma'am."

She went for the hat trick. "That's for all ten ships in the fleet, Alicia. Still confident?" She waited while several expressions flowed across her face, eyes focused on an unknown spot far outside the confines of the room. *Mission accomplished*, she thought, and it almost cheered her up.

After several seconds passed, Ali finally focused on her. "I assume this isn't some kind of test, ma'am. I can only answer that I'll try my damnedest. I may not be of much use for a while, but everyone else will."

"Oh, no, Ali. Your orders were for *all* crew to be ready. That includes you, as well. I'll give you some free advice—delegate. Let the captains of the other ships do for their ship what you'll be doing for the *Raptor*, which is running drills, exercising, *and* resting. Take their reports, look them over for trouble spots and point them out. Politely. And of course, after I go to bed each night, I'll call for a full report. I'll have one or two chances to visit the ship during that time, but otherwise it's all on your broad shoulders. Any questions?"

"Only one, Admiral. Who's going to tell the other captains about the change in command?"

"I'll field that one for you, Captain. Consider yourself promoted. Welcome to the ulcer seat." A quick conference call from the bridge to the other captains in her fleet took some of the strain out of White Eagle's face. The rest of first shift's bridge crew had heard every word she said, but she still addressed them personally after she had signed off her call. "It's only for two weeks, people. And maybe Linnas is right, but I still don't have to like it. I'll be back before the fleet leaves orbit and then we can expect to remember these days fondly 'cause it's going to get very sticky very quickly."

A short time later she was standing over her duffel bag again. Besides a dress uniform and several BDU's she had only the one set of civilian clothes. She managed to get all of it into the bag and glanced at her watch. After a call to her gig pilot, she stuck her head out the door. One perk of her position was that she didn't have to carry that bag all the way back to the launch bay. One of the two guards permanently on duty outside her door picked up her bag as she left the room.

She told them, "I'll be gone for the next two weeks. No reason to waste your time guarding an empty room. You guys take some time to work on other things while I'm away."

CHAPTER THIRTY-THREE

Pegra Nargresh now led the Garmons, not in name, as had been the custom for uncounted generations, but in practicality. He had called together three hands of his most loyal sept-leaders and then called for a council of Elders.

When those worthies had convened, with the thought of confirming a new leader in the old way, they were quickly disabused of the notion. As they trooped in to take their accustomed places on the dais, they found only one chair there, and it was already occupied.

Pegra looked down on the confused mass of old men and said, "The old ways are gone. It should have been recognized shortly after the arrival of the humanz, but past leaders made the fatal mistake of underestimating them. Even I have done so. But that is not why we're here today." He enjoyed the consternation of the Elders as his sept-leaders watched them closely.

"We are faced with an even greater menace than the humanz. Our cows have suddenly started to show signs of independent thought. No longer are they passive breeders taking any male that chooses them in their heat. Now they either refuse to mate or express a desire for a particular male. This is unprecedented in our history. Also, the number of male cubs produced has diminished and the number of cows has risen. Soon, we won't have enough fighters to man the remaining ships we're able to produce. Add this to the fact that the humanz and Shiravans have destroyed most of our shipyards and mating grounds, and we have very few options left to us."

The chief Elder stepped forward and said, "This flies in the face of all that we hold as a race! We will not allow you to usurp the leadership of the People in this fashion. You will become an outcast, reviled by one and all, and these humanz will be beaten back as all other foes have been. This I say, and it is Law!"

Pegra nodded slightly, his eyes flicking to one of his sept-leaders, the one he was least sure of. This one instantly raised his rifle and shot the old greybeard in the head. "*I* now decide what is Law," he said to the confused mass of old males below him. "You will have to find another way to earn your right to survive. From this moment on, the Garmons shall be known as the People as the dead one has called us. And the People must survive above all. To do this, we have to gather what ships, males, cubs, and cows we can and find a place the humanz and Shiravans cannot until we overcome our old and new problems."

He nodded to another sept-leader. "Sire, I have the dubious honor of having Holdings farthest from both humanz and Shiravans. This might prove to our advantage since we have records of many expeditions into the outer reaches. There, we should be able to find at least one world to begin anew on, or use it to move farther on while we sort out the complications that have arisen. All of my records are yours."

"Excellent, sept-leader. Perhaps these Elders can turn their attention to finding a world among your records and earn their heads. All others will begin to collect what ships, cubs, cows, and males they can and prepare to move them to your major Holding. Keep in mind that we will not need these ships as fighting ships but transport vessels. Use just enough males to run the ships and fill the rest of the space with food, cows, and cubs."

This sept-leader was one of his earliest converts, an exiled younger cousin of a previous leader. Just come into his full growth, Harka Garmon was eager to please and restore Honor to the Garmon name. "Sire, arrangements have been made on my major Holding and one other to accommodate as many Septs as can be assembled. There's plenty of room to forage and hunt, and there's sufficient material to build shelters for everyone. It's also not too far from the new yards and power station set up by your predecessor. They are both under heavy guard until such time as enough ships arrive to allow them to perform the same duties you've assigned to the other sept-leaders."

Pegra stood and said, "This is far more than you were asked to do, Harka. Honor to your name. Step forward." The young sept-leader stood before his Leader and showed his surprise at having Pegra Nargresh himself pin an Honor to the meager few adorning his vest. He returned to his place along the wall of the meeting chamber. Without drawing attention to himself, he glanced down to see one of the highest Honors awarded one of the People. His chest swelled visibly at this, and then he turned his attention back to the Leader.

Pegra turned back to the sept-leaders surrounding him and the huddled Elders below. "The People, by nature, are more at home with much room around them and much sky above, those manning our ships included. Those, however, are special, raised from cubhood to withstand the confines of the ships. They also learn to work as a large team rather than in smaller, scattered packs. Take your example from young Harka Garmon, willing to share his lands with all who seek a place to rest and plan new tactics. And we cannot forget the unimaginable fact of our cows suddenly getting smarter and bearing fewer males. Now go, all of you, and gather what you can.

"Young Garmon, since you have nothing to carry home, I leave it to you to find space for these useless old males. Turn your charts over to them and let them earn their keep." He turned eyes slitted into hunter mode on these last few. "You are not to restrict your search to mere charts, either. Seek out the far-farers and ask questions. A new space must be found in which we can re-grow our race and strength. Then we can take back that which is rightfully ours and repay the insult to our entire race. Now, go."

Three months passed while one fleet searched systems known to harbor Garmon, four for the other, and return to Shiravi. Marsha Kane's fleet, having the longer route, came in last, and she called her counterpart for details even before making orbit. "Tell me some good news, Sorgala des Nimara," she prompted, weariness in her voice.

des Nimara answered almost immediately. "Well, Your Grace, we visited three systems as ordered and came back without losing a single ship or fighter."

Unsurprised, she asked, "And how did you manage to accomplish such a feat?"

"Your Grace, we didn't find any ships to target. Two systems are known Garmon worlds, but we got no readings for any ships on the ground or in-system, so I sent landing crews down with sufficient air cover to handle anything we could think of. All we found were some mostly deserted villages populated by older females and some of the youngest kids, also mostly female. That was the first system. The second was identical to the first with one difference—crops had been harvested for the stranded populace to survive on for a good while. System three was a complete unknown, and we searched extensively but found no sign of any Garmon activity at all. I thought about going on to a few other systems, but you said three, so I brought the fleet home without a single shot fired."

Marsha thought for a short time. "I was confronted with the same situation on all four of the worlds I visited. Now I have to report to the Matriarch as soon as I get my ships settled in. I assume you've already reported your news to her?"

des Nimara responded, "She asked me to come down personally to report as soon as we had stabilized our orbits. After that, I started sending out smaller patrols to odd locations, anywhere my strategists thought might be a good hiding place to attack from. The rest I repositioned around the system, augmenting the ships already protecting Shiravi."

"You did well, Sorgala. We had the same results with one exception. At the third system our sensors showed five ships outbound with no chance for us to overtake them, but we noted their direction. We have no idea whether they spotted us, but it's unlikely since they have the same sternward blind spot that we do. I assume you're rotating the ships that go out on patrol, keeping everyone at top readiness?"

"I am, Your Grace. Otherwise too many crews will get lax in their duties. All new patrols are given their orders just two days prior to departure, leaving no time to do anything but resupply as necessary," the Shiravan answered.

"I am impressed with your foresight, Sorgala des Nimara," Marsha said, praise evident in her voice. "You are in temporary command of system defense should it be necessary until I return. There's no telling how long my Sister-kin will keep me planet-side. Kane out."

It was midafternoon when Linnas des Harras watched her Sister-kin's ship land at the port. Her driver moved the floater across the field to the distant landing pad, but she found Marsha already walking toward the gate where transportation was usually found. She was surprised at the slumped shoulders, and as she got closer, the dejected look on her face before Marsha noticed the nearly-silent hover car moving toward her.

Linnas watched as her Sister quickly squared her shoulders, and her face took on a more guarded expression. One door opened, and Linnas waved her inside. "It's a long walk to the gate, and I think you could use some respite from the heat, Sister." Marsha nodded and stepped into the vehicle gratefully.

"The ride isn't long, so a report can wait until you have a cold drink in hand. But, in the meantime, tell me about yourself. Four months on patrol, with nine other ships to care about. You must be exhausted." Linnas didn't mention her first impression of Marsha as the car approached her.

"It was more tedious than I had expected, Sister," Marsha replied. "You said a report could wait until later, but in order to explain what I mean, I have to give a bit of it now. As with Sorgala des Nimara, we had no luck finding any ships to engage. Only in one system did we even get any readings, and those were of five ships leaving the system and too far away to attempt an intercept." She stopped speaking and pointedly stared out the window at the ships they were passing. She noticed that many of them were stripped of much of their hull plating, allowing workers easier access to the parts of each ship receiving modifications.

Linnas noted the ploy for what it was but said nothing about it. Instead, she said, "These ships are receiving the modifications your scientists have built into your own. Already, new ships are coming out of our main yards with the modifications fully installed." Marsha only nodded at the information, saying nothing.

After a thankfully short ride, the car pulled up at Quillas Central Command with Marsha's side closest to the exit. A guard opened the door and stood back while Marsha stepped out, usually a breach of protocol, and waited for her Sister to get out as well. The guards encircled the two women and led the way to the main entrance. There, another group of guards, smaller this time, took over and followed them to an elevator that took them to Linnas's quarters on the top floor, Linnas leading the way.

In a smallish room, by Shiravan standards, she waved Marsha to a chair especially made for her shorter frame. The tired admiral flopped into it bonelessly, staring at nothing in particular. With an occasional glance at her sister, Linnas took out two glasses and poured fire wine for each of them.

She sat down beside Marsha and handed a frigid glass to her. For the first time, Marsha showed something besides apathy. "Fire wine at this time of day, Linnas? I do have a ship to get back to and work to do."

"Which Sorgala White Eagle can handle quite well,

Marsha. She handled everything for two weeks before you left. I've already spoken to her and informed her that you'll be staying here for a few days. Even without conflict, the demands of command can be wearing, and I'd be doing my sister a disservice if I let you return without a short respite." She waited for the expected outburst, but instead Marsha just nodded and took a small sip of her wine, then another, larger drink.

Linnas watched as the wine took almost immediate effect and the weariness left her Sister's face, replaced by an expression of relaxation that only fire wine could bestow in the present circumstances. "Do you feel better now?" she asked, concern in her voice.

"I do, Sister," Marsha said. "I just wish it wasn't alcohol-induced." She took a smaller sip as Linnas joined her, taking her first sip. She was determined to remain levelheaded during this meeting.

Linnas looked at her and took a very small sip from her own glass, which had started with less than Marsha's to begin with. Do you want to make your report now, or should it wait until tomorrow?" she asked quietly.

Marsha looked at her and shrugged. "Now is as good a time as any while it's fresh in my mind. Our itinerary was to visit three systems known to be Garmon outposts. On the first two, we only found several small villages populated mostly by females and younglings. Both planets had crops harvested for the Garmons and left behind. In the third system, the one we thought to be the Garmon homeworld, our sensors detected five ships leaving the system at a high rate of speed—too high and too far away for us to do anything but mark the direction they took. Several visits to the surface found the same circumstances there as well—no ships and all able-bodied males gone, with some females and younglings left behind, none of them male.

"I think that just because this planet was where their major shipyards were doesn't mean it was their homeworld. I now believe that the culture is more fragmented than we thought, with certain males carving out their own spaces to set up small dynasties of their own under the supervision of one ruler. It's only a feeling, but with the report of Sorgala des Nimara being much the same as mine, I think it a high probability. After leaving that system, we headed home, and here I sit drinking fire wine when I should be seeing to my duties."

Linnas shrugged. "So, you found the Garmons abandoning their worlds. This is good news, Sister. It means that we have decimated their forces enough that they no longer feel safe raiding our colonies, trying to attack our ships, or even remaining in this area of space. Your people have breathed new life into an otherwise desperate race. We now have ships carrying new weapons and shields and their crews are all battle-hardened veterans, with most of our other ships having the same equipment and attitudes. New crews spend weeks going through simulations of past battles, as well as battle simulations set up by your own tactical teams. They are ready to take their places aboard a ship before it even comes out of the yards. And we have reclaimed five of our previous worlds. The Polity now numbers twenty worlds. What more can you ask for? But we'll talk more about that in the days to come, Sister," Linnas said gently. "Have you had anything to eat? It should go well toward settling your stomach after a glass of fire wine."

Marsha smiled slightly at the thought of what would surely happen if she added food to a full glass of fire wine and said, "No thank you, Sister. I think what I need right now is a hot soak and a long nap. I believe I'll be starving by then."

Linnas nodded knowingly. "Surely you know best, Sister. I'll bid you a good rest, then." Without any apparent summons, a young Shiravan female appeared. "Berea will show you to your quarters and assist you in any way you wish."

Marsha stood up and Linnas did the same. They stood close enough that when Linnas reached out and hugged her for a moment, she was so stunned that she barely had time to return the hug. Linnas turned to leave, so Marsha did the same. She stopped at the door and turned back. "Linnas," she said. The Matriarch turned around without a word. "Your English has improved a lot," she said lamely.

"I've been getting a lot of practice lately. You should really try it yourself, Sister. Sleep well and may the Spirits guide your dreams truly." The tall red woman stepped through a set of curtains and was gone.

Marsha stared after her so long that the new assistant finally said, "Your Grace, if you will follow me, please? Your bag has already been taken to your room."

CHAPTER THIRTY-FOUR

Marsha woke to a bright reddish light streaming around the drapes that were over the windows of her room. She stumbled into the bathroom, which was everything the word included. Her personal needs were seen to in a small, closed off corner, but the main room, large enough to re-wall and rent out as a three-bedroom apartment, contained an over-large (to her) tub on one side, with a spectacular pool taking up the rest of the space.

She looked longingly at the tub, for she had spent an hour in it the night before surrounded by attendants. This time she was alone and decided to take a few laps in the pool to wake herself up. She let the specially shortened robe fall to the floor and stepped into the steaming water.

After a few minutes to accustom herself to the heat, she began to swim slowly from one end to the other. By the time she had made the first length, her muscles had absorbed the heat, and she pushed off and swam more vigorously. Seven laps later she was winded and sapped by the heat. She stepped out of the pool and was startled by an attendant waiting with a towel. *I don't know if I'll ever get used to this*, she thought

The room had a myriad of hiding places, some or all of which surely concealed doors. She couldn't tell due to the dense growth of a miniature Shiravan forest primeval. Rocks tumbled out of the vegetation, some few of which were just right to sit on if the lounging couch happened to be occupied.

She used a towel first to dry her hair, then wrapped it around her for the walk back to her bedroom. The curtains had been pulled back to allow the sun to warm the room, but there was still enough airflow to let her cool off as she finished toweling off and dressing. She noticed the young attendant eyeing her surreptitiously.

Bra and panties on, she asked the silent girl what she was looking at. "I surely can't be the first human you've seen, can I?"

The girl blushed an even deeper shade of red. "No, Your Grace, but if I may be so bold, you are the first human female I have seen unclothed. If I may ask a question without offending?" she asked looking at the floor.

Marsha considered the situation. There were a great many questions she still wanted to ask but felt they may be out of bounds for proper conversation. "You may ask any question you wish and I'll try to answer. There's nothing I will find offensive as you learn more about the strange people you now have to deal with." She flashed her best smile to affirm her answer and waited while the girl got up her nerve to put her thoughts into words.

She had slipped into a black, short-sleeved shirt and was in the process of putting one leg into her pants when the attendant spoke.

"Forgive me, Your Grace, but I have only seen breasts like yours upon females nearing their birthing time. It is obvious that you are not carrying a child. Why are your breasts so large at this time?"

Marsha thought for a few seconds before answering. "Human females are different from most creatures.

When a young female passes through what we call 'puberty,'" she said, hesitating because she didn't know the right word and hoped the girl would guess for herself, "her body begins to change. Breasts grow, and her body becomes ready to take on the ability to have children of her own. This happens anywhere from ten to sixteen years of age. We keep our breasts for the rest of our lives, but the size does increase when they swell with milk in preparation of childbirth."

The girl said, "Thank you, Your Grace. I am in your debt for the answer to such a personal question."

As she seemed to have no more questions, Marsha finished dressing, lacing up the black boots that completed her standard BDU's. She had been so tired and worn out the night before that she didn't remember the way to Linnas's dining area, so she got herself escorted. She arrived to find the Matriarch just starting a meal of fruits and some unidentifiable meat.

Linnas waved to the chair across from her. "Sit and eat, Sister. I wasn't sure how long you would sleep so I waited until I was given word that you had arisen." Almost immediately a plate was placed in front of her. "I took the liberty of ordering for you. I hope I got it right."

Marsha looked down at her plate to find scrambled eggs, bacon, and what looked suspiciously like hash browns. "This looks excellent, Sister. What do we have scheduled for today?"

Linnas looked up from her own plate and said, "First, I think we'll do some shopping. All you humans wear too much black, and it is such a drab color. We'll get something more appropriate for Shiravan society, and perhaps tonight, if we have time, we'll take in a play in the forum. How does that sound to you?"

Marsha finished her bite. "Since I'm on vacation

again, it sounds fine. Most women like to shop, but I'm at a disadvantage as to what is proper dress for most Shiravan occasions."

"Do not worry, Sister. I will be there to help you pick out suitable clothes."

Later, after a whirlwind tour of Quillas and stops in several stores, she rested in her room. After a while, a knock got her up and she answered it. It was the attendant from earlier in the day. "Come in," she said, taking several of the boxes the girl was carrying. She set them down on her bed and the girl did the same. "Are you going to be a regular during my stay?" The girl nodded, and Marsha asked, "Your name is Berea, correct?"

"Yes, Your Grace. Berea kep Gillas."

"I'll tell you something, Berea. This whole 'Your Grace' business gets quite annoying to hear all the time. In the privacy of my quarters, if we're alone, I'd be pleased if you would call me Marsha."

Berea looked startled. "I'm not sure I can do that, Your Grace. I've been taught to observe the proper forms at all times."

Marsha thought a few seconds. She kept coming up against walls in Shiravan society that she had trouble accepting. "Have you been taught to obey orders if they're given to you as such?"

Berea nodded.

Marsha smiled triumphantly. "Very well, then. I order you to call me Marsha in the privacy of my quarters when no one else is around. Tell no one about this, as it is our secret. Does that satisfy your sense of duty?"

Berea looked despondent. "It does, Marsha. I will try to follow them until I get it right."

"Good," Marsha said excitedly. "Let's see what we

have in all these boxes. I'll need you to help me find the right clothes to wear to a play at the Forum later this evening."

Marsha dithered in her room as Berea hovered around her, trying to help. Linnas's night out at the Forum was going to be a bigger do than she had imagined. At least, that was what she got from Berea. Everybody who was anybody was going to be there. Word had leaked out that Admiral Kane was going to attend this evening's performance.

"What am I going to do, Berea? I can handle dealing with Linnas and Sitha, and I can deal with a task force of ten ships, twenty ships, whatever, but being put on parade for the nobility of your entire race is beyond me."

Berea pulled a dress out of the closet. Marsha had tried on everything at least three times but hadn't decided on anything yet. She had to figure in the Shiravan lighting, as well as anything else, and she turned at the rustle of a dress being laid out on the bed. She'd spent hours looking for just the right color, one that would appear green in the red Shiravan lighting, and it lay before her now. "Time is running out, Marsha," Berea said. "You should get dressed now and present yourself to the Matriarch. The play is due to begin shortly."

The play won't start until the Matriarch arrives," Marsha said shortly. "And I just don't feel comfortable in a dress, especially one that doesn't allow underwear.

Berea made a face as Marsha began to undress. "I don't see why humans put so much emphasis on the clothes you wear under clothes. They can't be seen, so what purpose do they serve?"

Marsha chose not to hear the question. Instead, she began to slip into the dress. It was a deep green in Shiravi's light, and she didn't want to imagine it under normal conditions. The fit was perfect, with built-in supports for her breasts, and flared down to knee length. The whole thing couldn't have weighed more than a few ounces and shimmered back at her from the mirror. Shoes with two-inch heels completed the ensemble.

With time running short, she thanked Berea for her help and walked to the lounge. Linnas was already waiting and stood up as she appeared. The look on her face was one of wonder. She clapped her hands and said, "You will be the hit of the evening. I would not be able to wear that color, but on you it is perfect."

"I don't *want* to be the hit of the evening, Linnas," Marsha said petulantly. "I was just supposed to fit in, remember?"

"Quit being an old Domina, Sister. You'd stand out in any crowd anyway, so why not look good doing it?" Linnas motioned for her to spin around and again declared, "Perfect! Now, it's time we should be going. There's a car waiting at the front door."

Resigned to her fate, Marsha followed Linnas to the elevator. On the way down, Linnas commented, "I took the liberty of having all your clothes imprinted with the Alliance symbol. You'll find it on the left breast of your clothes. Will that satisfy your need to appear to represent the Alliance?"

Exasperated, Marsha retorted hotly, "I have no desire to represent the Alliance tonight. I just don't like playing dress up."

Her Sister took no notice of Marsha's temper. "It's too late to discuss the matter now, Marsha. In a moment, we'll be on our way to the Forum and you can enjoy yourself or not. There are many people there who wish to be reassured that you are not Kath-e-vel, breathing fire and laying waste the land around you."

Marsha took that in, as well as the fact that Linnas chose to use her first name instead of calling her Sister. She fingered the Alliance crest woven into the fabric, a darker green than the rest of the dress, and wondered why she hadn't noticed it before. By now the two women were almost to the door where a single car awaited them. "Where is your security, Sister? What is to keep someone from trying to kill you?"

Linnas smiled. "If I were to die, my ideals would not, and a new Matriarch, dedicated to Expansionist philosophies, would assume the responsibilities of Matriarch. The world would continue to turn, and more planets would be colonized. By the way, did you know that all of our old worlds taken by the Garmons have begun to be repopulated? Soon, we'll hold more worlds than ever before in known history. And none of them will be left without adequate protection. See how your presence, spirit, and technological achievements have helped out, so far? You should be proud instead of depressed over one more ceremonial occasion."

They arrived at a building that reeked of age. Nonetheless, it looked as if great care had been taken to preserve the original building, as though it were a shrine of some kind. "This was our first government building. It was built to be an imposing structure and has remained so over the centuries, don't you think?"

Marsha nodded without answering. People thronged the dozen or more steps to the main concourse, and many more could be seen inside the glass-fronted building. *I'm in for it now*, she thought. *And not a stitch of security. I'm glad I had an opportunity to at least strap a knife to my leg.* She followed Linnas out of the car to a chorus of cheers, though for whom she couldn't tell. As they walked up the steps, Linnas was greeting about every other person she met, making their entrance take that much longer.

As they entered the Forum proper, more of the same occurred, only this time Marsha was introduced as well. She lost count of the number of hands she touched as they slowly made their way to the doors of the theater itself. As they stood a few feet from the interior doors, they suddenly burst open and an odd-looking Shiravan lunged out, screaming, "Death to the Matriarch! It is time for Isolationists to prevail!"

Marsha took all of this in in one glance and threw herself at the stranger in a full-body block. He staggered aside and then back to his fatal mission. This time, Marsha caught a glimpse of steel in his hand and managed to draw her own knife, getting between Linnas and the crazy male. From the look in his eyes, that was all he could be, but that didn't slow her down.

The male strode forward as everybody moved back to see what was going to happen. Marsha, still in between the two, wasn't even recognized as a threat until she slid her knife between two of his ribs. The look in his eyes didn't change, but his focus did. He came at Marsha wildly, swinging a Shiravan knife that might as well have been a sword as far as she was concerned. Her only option was to get inside his defensive circle and stop him any way she could.

She misjudged his speed and reach as she tried to duck under his swing. The knife cut into her left arm at the bicep, rendering it useless. She dropped to the floor and swept his legs out from under him. He landed hard, and she took the opportunity to slam the hilt of her knife into his wrist, sending his flying.

Now, stunned bystanders began to subdue the attacker, and Marsha got slowly to her feet. She swayed a bit and looked at her left arm as the pain set in with a vengeance. Blood ran freely down her arm and began pooling on the floor. She had started to turn to Linnas to make sure she was all right when a mighty blow slammed into her left shoulder just above the cut. The last thing she saw was Linnas's face, mouth moving, but she couldn't make out the words.

Then the lights went out.

CHAPTER THIRTY-FIVE

Marsha woke up slowly to find Linnas's smiling face looking down at her. She reached over to feel the slash on her left arm and was surprised to find nothing there. She realized, too, that she didn't feel any pain from the massive punch she'd felt just before blacking out. She looked around and found herself in her own room. "I've been in a regen chamber," she said sleepily.

"Yes, Sister, you have. We might have avoided it if it were only the slash on your arm. You would have had an interesting scar to tell stories about, but you were in the way of a rifle shot aimed at me. It was a close call. We almost didn't get you to a chamber in time. I owe you my life, Sister."

Marsha smiled weakly. "I told you that you needed security. Have you made new arrangements now?"

"Oh, yes," Linnas said quickly. "I even consulted with your Captain White Eagle, as we have never needed to institute such a policy in the past. And you are included in that security as well."

"Good," Marsha said. "So, how long was I out?"

"With the damage done to your shoulder and the laser passing through your lung, it has been three months. I'm sorry."

"Three months! What's happened to the fleet? Have there been any attacks? Have we lost any ships? What's been going on?"

"Captain White Eagle will be down to answer all of your questions in detail later. Right now, I can tell you that out of all the patrols she has sent out, only one met with any resistance, and that on the far reaches of Garmon space, as if they are retreating. Two ships were lost in exchange for nine Garmon ships."

"I guess that's acceptable, though I do regret the loss of life."

"We've constructed a special dusterna to honor the humans lost in defense of Shiravan lives. Their names will be remembered for as long as Shiravans live."

"Thank you, Sister. Their families will be happy to hear it. Now, how soon can I get back to the *Raptor*?"

Linnas smiled again. "I expected that question much sooner in our conversation. As soon as you feel ready and have had dinner, we shall send for your gig. Is that soon enough?"

"It will do, Sister. It appears to be getting on toward evening anyway. I'll get dressed and meet you in the dining room shortly."

Linnas nodded. "I'll send Berea in. She's been beside your chamber almost constantly. She can help you dress and join us for dinner."

Before long, Linnas was sitting in the dining room when Marsha walked in dressed in her most comfortable BDUs. "I expected that," the Matriarch said with a sad smile on her face. "Are you going back to work or running from an uncomfortable situation?"

She watched Marsha turn what was, for a human, an almost decent shade of red. Unfortunately, in humans it could mean shame, embarrassment, or any of a number of emotions. Marsha sat down at the table, and Berea hesitatingly took another chair. "I took the liberty of ordering for us again—a meal I know you like. Though it isn't common dinner fare, I think it's fitting for your last meal with us," Linnas said, noting Marsha's guarded look.

"What do you mean, Sister? By my count, it will be a minimum of four months before the replacement ships can arrive. I expect many more dinners here."

"But not while you're on vacation," Linnas said, smiling. "I realize you only experienced a few days, but here you are, looking totally fit."

"Thanks to a damned regen chamber, thank you very much!" Marsha retorted, laughing out loud. "But yes, I need to get back to work. Too much time has passed, and right now I feel a bit embarrassed, but I can't say about what exactly."

Linnas laughed along with her. "You saved my life and you feel embarrassed? Our sister, Kitty, couldn't have been braver or foolhardier. I've taken steps, though it is unsettling, to have a security team with me from now on. What has our world come to that the Matriarch should need to hide behind others?"

"I can tell you what's going on, Sister, if you're willing to entertain a concept," Marsha said, startling Berea into dropping her fork. She'd never seen anyone except the Second Voice instructed the Matriarch.

"Tell me, Sister. Our minds are different enough that you may see what I cannot," Linnas said conversationally, causing Berea further distress. "Stop fidgeting, girl. If you have something to say, speak up." Berea merely looked down at her plate and shook her head. "Very well, then. Marsha?"

Marsha shifted position, as if she were starting a lecture, which in fact she was. "Okay, here goes. For two hundred years... turnings... your people have been systematically reduced in numbers of planets and people. Now, with the Garmons safely routed or at least in serious hiding, your economy is about to double, triple, or even more. You're going to need more ships to transport colonists, more ships to permanently guard those worlds, even more ships to patrol the outer reaches, your buffer zone, so to speak. You'll have more people wanting to emigrate, more jobs to fill, people to pay, and taxes to impose to accomplish all of this.

"You, yourself, told me that you've already sent settlers to all previously overrun planets. Your economy is going to go through one hell of an upheaval, not like the slow recession two hundred years brought. Who's going to control all those functions, jobs, and taxes, both incoming and outgoing? You? Not a chance. You'll only have an overview, being told only that which you need to know to ensure your reign.

"Someone out there has already thought of these things, and you'd better round up your best minds into what we humans call a think tank. You need to find solutions to upcoming crises before they occur and have a viable, positive solution to problems before they arise. You need at least two new shipyards turning out the requisite numbers and types of ships. Here on Shiravi, you need schools to train the new recruits and colonists. Maybe the colonists could train on Harlo, where the people know both how to tame a world and survive under hostile invasions. And those are just the things I can name off the top of my head." Marsha turned to her plate while she gave Linnas time to think.

She had almost finished her meal when Linnas spoke again. "All of what you say is true, Sister. Times are changing, and the males are going to have to play a greater part in it, as well."

"See?" Marsha interjected. "Already you've come up

with a problem I didn't mention. Think about what your best minds will do with the ideas."

Dinner finished, Linnas signaled for an attendant and called for a bottle of wine. Marsha's Shiravan was extensive enough now to recognize that it wasn't going to be fire wine. This she could handle in small doses before stepping foot back on the *Raptor*. They sat back and waited for the wine to arrive.

"There's another matter to be discussed, Sister," Linnas said, turning serious. This caused a shadow to pass across her Sister's face. "Don't worry, Marsha. The matter has been brought to my attention by your attendant, Berea. I believe I'll let her speak for herself."

Berea looked quickly at the Matriarch as if to say something, then squared her shoulder and said, "Your Grace, I have had the privilege to serve you for only a short time, but I have a request. I will understand if you say no, but our Matriarch has said that if I want something badly enough, I should speak up."

"What can I possibly do for you, Berea?" Marsha said, looking positively puzzled. "You have a place in the Matriarch's household, and I'm reliably informed that people in your situation are generally given good positions when they choose to start their vocations."

"Oh, I have no doubt of that, Your Grace, but there's a special job I'd like for my second vocation." She looked down at where her plate had been.

"Well, spit it out, girl," Marsha said. "I feel the same way Linnas does about the matter. If you don't ask, you'll never know. And in your old age, you'll look back on this moment and regret it. I'll do anything I possibly can for you. I heard how you spent much of your time beside my chamber, depriving your Matriarch of your valuable services." This last came with a smile Berea missed. "Raise your head, look me in the eyes, and just ask."

Berea, abnormally shy for the moment, did as she was told. Red eyes regarded blue for a long moment, and Marsha broke the spell by taking a sip of the wine that had arrived. "Your Grace, I would be pleased, honored, if you'd allow me to accompany you on your return to Earth." Before Marsha could speak, Berea went on as if a dam inside her had broken. "I'll do my best to learn English and all of your customs. I'd be a good assistant for you, and I won't mind the enclosed spaces. Every journey has its end, and I can wait out the trip without complaint. Also, I'd like to get to see the homeworld of humanity."

She finally ran down but didn't put her head back down. Marsha looked at Linnas, who just shrugged. "You seem to have it all figured out, and your Matriarch seems to have no problem with your proposal. Do you realize that it may be many years before you see Shiravi again?"

"I have thought long on it, Your Grace," Berea answered, "and find that I would rather travel than spend my life under the cloud Ramannie kep Gillas has laid on our Clan, though that is only a small part of it."

"Well, I don't see a problem, Berea. You and I get along well together, and if it doesn't work out, I can find you a position you'd be satisfied with. You realize that it will be several months before we can possibly leave for Earth? Another fleet is coming to replace a large number of ships whose crews have been expressing their desire to get back to their families for a long time. You'll stay here until just before we leave, coming aboard occasionally to familiarize yourself with *the Raptor*. Then, two weeks before we leave orbit, you can move aboard permanently. Will that satisfy you?"

"Oh, completely, Your Grace," Berea said with excitement. "I'm most grateful for the opportunity and won't allow you to regret your decision."

Linnas saw a part of her Sister she hadn't glimpsed before and was even surer of her decision to adopt her. She cleared her throat. Both pairs of eyes turned toward her. "I believe the admiral's gig is waiting. Berea, you are excused for now. We'll talk later. Now, I'll accompany Admiral Kane to her ship."

As they walked out of the building, several armed guards fell into place a few yards behind. She turned to them and said, "I'm perfectly safe within sight of you. I would speak with my Sister alone." Her voice alone was enough to stop them in their tracks.

She faced toward the gig and started walking slowly so Marsha could keep up. A kind of euphoria filled her. Quietly she asked, "How many will your ship hold, Sister?"

Marsha looked at her in wonder. "At least four, not counting the pilots. Why?"

"This might be my only chance to see the *Raptor* without a mob at my back. Can we go aboard, and I'll call the Second Voice and inform her personally what I'm doing?"

Marsha shrugged and said, "You're the Matriarch. You can do pretty much as you wish. Come aboard. We'll close up and lift off as soon as the engines come online."

Later, as the gig cleared atmosphere, Linnas did as promised and informed an indignant Sitha kep Parrasine of her decision. "It was a spur-of-the-moment decision, Sitha, and I'm certainly safe with Admiral Kane. I intend to get a tour of a larger ship than we possess, and this is a good time to do it. The staff is asleep, except for the guards, and no one else need know." She shut off the radio and replaced the microphone. "Now I won't have to listen to her interminable complaining about protocol. Let me enjoy my little vacation."

Four hours later, Marsha returned her Sister back down personally. Linnas hugged the smaller woman tightly. "I enjoyed the visit, Sister. I hope our choice of wine won't jeopardize your position."

"Of course not, Sister. As you said, most people are asleep except for a skeleton crew, most of whom I can avoid, and the rest won't bother me until morning. I'll miss my visits as well once we break orbit. That's a few months away, though, so you can still show me some of the things I missed."

"I will look forward to the opportunity, Sister. And, of course, the night before you leave there will be a reception for you and most of your officers. What you call a 'going away' party."

Hesitantly, Marsha only said, "I see your guards approaching. I wish you well, Sister, and will do so at least once more before I leave."

CHAPTER THIRTY-SIX

Simon Hawke stalked into his wife's office. "I really don't like making an appointment with my own wife, Kitty."

"Can't help it, dear. I have so many appointments on my daily calendar, you're lucky you didn't have to wait until I came home tonight."

"Getting home from here is a five-minute tube ride," he said, sitting down. "But how am I supposed to know when you'll *be* home? You keep such erratic hours, I can't even plan to take you to dinner anymore."

Kitty set her pen down. Even inside Ceres there was need for paper copies and originals. "Don't you think it's frustrating for me, too, Simon? But there's so much to do. We have more scientists requesting transport to various places, and the ship has to remain there in the event of an emergency. Earth-side is calling for planets to colonize, as if that was going to end their overcrowding. All it will do is get some of our eggs out of one basket, really. More people are being born every minute than we can transport in months. Look, I don't want to have the same old argument again. Can't we talk about something else for a change?"

Simon heard the exasperation in her voice and knew when to quit. "As a matter of fact, I do have a couple of things to talk about." Kitty raised her eyebrows in surprise. Simon smiled. "First, Freddie officially wants to retire and he's serious this time. Says something about having seen a ghost three times, and his days on this mortal coil are almost over. His words, not mine," he added when Kitty smiled. "So, we need to find a new ambassador to Earth. I know you have some ideas."

"I do. I've talked to Freddie, as well. He made a suggestion for his replacement and then put wheels in motion when I agreed."

"That Juergens guy right?" Simon asked.

"Yes, I've only met him a few times, but he strikes me as an upright individual. I already have his application for Alliance membership here on my desk somewhere. His name is Heinrich Juergens, and he was of great help to Lucy while I was in regen after Camp David. A protocol specialist. Freddie recommends him highly. He doesn't seem to have any firm political affiliations and just works for whoever needs to have someone who knows the ins and outs of the political arena. He writes that he's willing to swear allegiance to the Alliance and work for us wholeheartedly. I'm considering it seriously."

"Well, if Freddie swears by him, I don't have a problem unless he's too obnoxious. You know how some lifetime civil servants can be."

"True, dear. That's why I'm drafting a letter in response, asking him to come here for an interview. I figure that if he's going to represent us on Earth, he should see how we live out here and what we do. Maybe let him go to one of the planets being considered for colonization. Let him see alien skies and so forth. See how he reacts to all that and then ask him again if he still wants the post."

"Sounds good to me, Kittyn. And we can talk about other things tonight, maybe?" Simon tried his best to sound mysterious, which often got Kitty's attention.

"That's a date. I really do have a short day today. Dinner and then small talk afterwards?"

Simon knew what small talk really meant, and he wasn't averse to the idea. He just decided to leave the larger matter on his mind until afterwards.

The two lovers lay entwined and nearly exhausted. They'd been apart for too long, either by distance or occupation. And now was as good a time as any to broach a subject that had been festering in him for several years. The two had been in space for almost fifteen years now and married for fifteen before that. After thirty years, he should be able to approach the subject without starting a fight. Admiral though he was, he knew enough to back down if things started getting unpleasant. After all, he was still a husband.

Simon looked at his wife, her face inches from his. "Honey, there's something else on my mind now. Can we talk?'

Kitty looked him right back in his eyes and said, "There's been something on your mind for a long time, dear. I'll listen to anything you have to say."

"Without getting mad?"

"Depends. Have you been sleeping with any young beautiful ensigns totally enthralled by the mystique of the famous Admiral Hawke, discoverer of the *Galileo*?"

"Of course not," he said hotly. "Oh, I get it. You're trying to rattle my cage. Well, it's not going to happen this time."

"You've got a battle plan for this conversation, don't you?" Kitty quipped

"Kittyn, I'm really trying to be serious here. Just

listen with as unbiased a mind as you can, please?"

Something in his voice got through to her. "Okay. Whatever it is, I'll listen."

"Good. We've been out here now for nearly fifteen years, and in that time we've been separated almost four-and-a-half years due to trips to Shiravi. And the rest of the time I'm the Admiral and you're the Herald. You agreed a long time ago that when things got to the point where we weren't needed as symbols we would take off on our own and just go exploring. I think that time is going to come soon, as in about a year. You've mentioned a new Ambassador. I'd like to talk about a new Herald *and* Admiral." He rose up on his elbow and leaned back a bit, waiting for her response. What he got was totally unexpected.

"Okay, dear. I'll think about it, but you've been thinking about it for years. Can I have at least a month to process this and see if I feel comfortable with it?" Her gaze remained level and he couldn't see anything in her eyes or face that belied her words.

"That's fair. Discussions during that time or just wait the month out?"

She thought for a moment. "You've kept this to yourself for a long time. Give me at least a month. I'll tell you then if I need more time."

"It's more than I expected," he said with his lopsided grin. "And the year is flexible, if we need more time to prepare and find the right people."

Kitty slipped out of bed and into a hot shower.

So this is what's been on his mind for so long. I should have known, she thought. *Well, actually, I kind of feel the same way. It would be a relief to have company in bed every night instead of this hit or miss shit we've both been living through.*

Coming back to bed composed, she slid in beside him and cuddled close. Not another word was said about the subject, and soon the two fell asleep.

"What's on your agenda for today, dear?" she asked him over breakfast the next morning.

Simon looked up from his plate and said, "Just more of the same. Moving ships around, checking reports, and such. The super-*Raptor* is due out of the yards in about a week. I'll need to go to Taurus Base for her commissioning. Care to tag along?"

Kitty shrugged. "I'll have to check my calendar, but I'd like a tour of this new ship. I'll see what I can do."

Simon nodded. "I plan to leave the day before and show my face around so the new people will see their admiral and know that he isn't some distant, untouchable person."

"In the meantime," Kitty said, "could you send some stuff over to my office? Things like the closest habitable worlds, climate, flora and fauna, and any other data you may have. Also, an estimate as to the number of ships we should assign to rotating patrols for each."

"Sure. I'll get Personnel *and* Planning and Tactics working on it immediately. "It may take a couple of days to compile, but you'll have it ten minutes after I do. Deal?"

"Deal," Kitty said. "Also, I'll need estimates on passenger ships to send colonists in. I'd like to get at least two before the year is out."

"Actually, the plans have already been drawn up and entered into the computer. I figure Taurus Base can start the first one as soon as she retools from the new ship. The *Newton* would be best for the other, and she's due to finish a long string of Mantas within the month."

The colonists' ships were based on the external carrier design. The only resemblance inside would be the engine room and bridge. The rest would be devoted to rather Spartan living quarters for about a thousand people, plus their luggage and tools. Public spaces would include dining, recreation, and essential services, plus storage for the organic material for the food processors. At least two cruisers would accompany each ship, and the *Newton* could slip out ahead, with escorts, and begin preparing the surface for the arriving colonists—the job her predecessor was originally designed to do. All should go as planned if the Garmons continue to stay out of our hair.

Pegra Nargresh sat in the hall of Harka Garmon and discussed the settlement of so many Clans. He had recalled the attack fleet and used them to ferry cows and cubs to Harka's two best-suited planets. A small Clan, the young sept-leader had plenty of room to spread the refugees out and still keep them close enough to come at The Nargresh's call. Even the new fuel refinery was within a reasonable distance. Already, ships with depleted power cores were being refitted with new ones in preparation for his plan.

What he had in mind was soon made known to the various sept-leaders. "I want a hand of ships to start exploring farther out, *away* from Shiravans and humanz. No more than a hand of groups are to go out at one time. Each hand will survey at least three systems, looking for habitable worlds. A third of the remaining ships will accompany the yard builders and help in the construction of a new yard and depot as soon as a suitable system can be found. The remainder will stay in this region to search for enemy ships and keep our people safe. Are there any questions?"

Word had already trickled down, and no one had any questions to ask. The meeting ended simply when The Nargresh left the room.

Marsha was wearing her green dress, replaced while she was healing, and preparing to go to the surface in a shuttle filled with most of her senior captains for the going away party. Their replacements had finally arrived two weeks before, and it had taken that long for her to bring the replacement admiral and captains up to speed. A familiar face headed up the new flotilla. Robert Greene was posted as admiral of the human presence in Shiravan space. He brought his wife, Michiko, along as communications officer of the flagship, and to offset the loss of the *Raptor*, four additional ships had been sent. Twenty-one ships in all, which had sparked quite a bit of worry until they were identified.

Robert and some of his captains had been invited to meet with some of the Shiravan higher-ups. All went well, with no assassination attempts and nothing to mar the smooth transition from Marsha's command to Robert's. Even the fact that he was male seemed to have little effect on their Shiravan counterparts.

It was at the end of the evening, Marsha's last in Shiravan space, that she got a surprise. Linnas had just finished making a short speech welcoming the newcomers when Marsha got sandbagged. Riding a small tide of euphoria from some light wine and the prospect of seeing home again, she heard her named called.

She turned from the circle of friends she had made over the past few years and looked toward the other end of the room. Linnas was motioning to her to come over. Marsha headed toward her and noted that she stood slightly apart from everyone else. Robert stood nearby, the look on his face saying that he knew nothing, but she felt something in the air. The closer she got to Linnas, the stronger the feeling got.

She looked up at her taller Sister wonderingly, but she didn't have to wonder long. Linnas laid a hand on her shoulder and turned her to face the crowded room. She looked out at all the red faces interspersed with some white and black, a dull feeling in her stomach.

Linnas kept her hand lightly on her shoulder, giving her a reassuring pat. "It is with great sorrow that I officially announce the departure of my Sister-kin, Admiral Marsha Kane. Taking her place will be a new admiral, sent by my Sister-equal, Katherine Hawke. You will all get to know him and his senior officers in the months to come, but tonight is special. My Sister leaves tomorrow, and I wish to do something special for her."

Linnas motioned for Sitha kep Parrasine, her Second Voice, and she stepped forward with a carved stone box in her hands. Marsha immediately recognized the gava stone so highly prized among Shiravans and sucked her breath in with awe. This was a gift of inestimable value. She started to protest, but Linnas's hand laid heavier on her shoulder.

"This is a gift for my Sister," she said quietly. "Have the courtesy to take it in good grace." In a louder voice she said, "It has been my honor to know Marsha for several turnings now and call her Sister-kin. She has treated well with us, putting her own life and safety above even her own. She deserves our respect and gratitude." She turned Marsha to face her. "Sister, it is well that we have known each other, and I pray to the Spirits of Space that we meet again. Until that time, please accept this as a gift from me personally and all Shiravans to show our gratitude."

Linnas took the box from Sitha and handed it to her. It was heavier than she had expected. She already had a gava-stone necklace, but the size of the box truly told the weight of this material. She didn't know what to say and could only mutter, "Thank you, Sister. I will treasure this all my life."

Linnas smiled. "Look inside."

She lifted the lid and found a set of four kem-wood goblets nestled inside. "Oh, this is too much, Sister," she stammered. "I have nothing for you as a return gift."

"You have given me and all Shiravans peace, Sister, for the first time in two hundred turnings. With the routing of the Garmons, we are free once more to expand back to our original size and beyond. Without the technological advances your people have bestowed upon us and the help and sacrifices you and your people have made on our behalf, we would be a dying race. Besides, think of it as a going away present, which I am told requires no return gift."

"I only did my job, Sister," she protested.

"Nonsense, Marsha. You put yourself at risk for a race not your own. You are a special person in your own right and deserving of so much more. So, I've decided to do something I've only done once before, and something no other Matriarch has ever done. I raise you from Sister-kin to Sister-equal in front of all these witnesses. I will miss you, and all Shiravans will as well."

Sister-equal? thought Marsha. *I don't know why she's doing this, and my guess is that she'll go all Spirits of Space on me and tell me nothing.* She held the gava-stone box in her hands and looked uncomprehendingly at Linnas.

"You will make a great Sister-equal, Marsha." Linnas leaned down and hugged her hard, then pushed her out into the crowd.

Captain White Eagle gently took the box from her hands. "I'll hold this while you enjoy the party, ma'am," she said quietly. Soon, she found herself, glass in hand, surrounded by Shiravans and humans alike, all talking at once. The rest of the evening was a blur.

Marsha woke the next morning not the least bit hung over and feeling well until her eyes fell on the green box on the table beside her bed aboard the *Raptor*. She looked at her watch, jumped out of bed, and hurriedly dressed. The flotilla would be breaking orbit soon, and she had one more thing to do.

The observation deck showed her the night side of the planet below. The major centers shone like stars and, set apart, the mountains that surrounded Cho-An were still glowing green as the darkening night settling upon them. She watched until the rotation of Shiravi took the mountains out of view and then slowly made her way down the stairs to deck three.

Minutes later she was on the bridge, standing beside Captain White Eagle, who started to stand up so Marsha could have the control seat. A curious feeling had taken hold of her in the dome, and she shook her head. "You've had command long enough, Ali. No reason you can't handle a little thing like leading seventeen ships home. The flotilla is yours."

"Yes, ma'am, the flotilla is mine. By the way,

Admiral Greene sent a package over by gig before you woke up. It's addressed to Admiral Hawke. I signed for it and put it in the ship's safe."

Her tone wasn't questioning, just informative, so Marsha only said," Thank you, Captain White Eagle. Please start us for home, and see me after your shift, if you please." She turned and walked to the bridge door. As it opened, she looked back a long time at the crew, heads down, monitoring the various functions of the ship and Alicia White Eagle coordinating with sixteen other ships—all competence and efficiency. She turned and let the door close, and it felt as if a part of her life had been cut off.

CHAPTER THIRTY-SEVEN

Simon waited for Kitty to come in after her day was finished. The news he had was only hours old, so she may not have heard yet. The seventeen ships stationed in Shiravan space had come home to roost. Now the plans he'd been making could begin to go forward since Kitty had finally acquiesced. They could retire and take a ship out to explore on their own, but she had insisted on a long vacation Earth-side beforehand.

He gave in, feeling much the same himself. It would be good to walk around under a sun with wind in his face and not have to worry about being recognized or arrested. That last problem had been solved years ago when the United Nations had finally accepted the Alliance as a separate political entity, but he still hadn't been to Earth more than a half dozen times in the last several years.

When Kitty finally came in, late as usual, he was awake at his desk, reading through a sheaf of papers Robert Greene had sent back with the *Raptor*.

"You're still up," Kitty observed. "Usually I find you in bed by now."

"Well, I had some papers to read this time. Marsha's fleet returned about six hours ago, and the first thing she did was report in and give me a package from Bob Greene. I've just finished reading it."

"So, what does he have to say? And how is Marsha?"

Kitty asked, taking off her shirt. She came to look over his shoulder, but he snaked an arm around her shoulders and turned it into a long kiss.

After that he started in on Marsha's report. "It appears that the Garmons are leaving their planets and moving somewhere else. All the evidence points to a quick evacuation, taking as many as they could cram aboard their remaining ships and leaving a few behind. Those will have to be dealt with eventually—maybe moving them to a single world as they're found and rounded up. That's about par for the course on all Garmon planets we've been finding lately. You know, we haven't seen a ship in over a year now."

"That's good," Kitty said, heading for the shower. "I've got a couple of planets in mind for the *Newton* to go set up for colonies, and with the Garmons gone, we'll only have to send a minimum escort."

"There's more," Simon said over the sound of running water. "Bob sent back a preliminary report."

A few minutes later, Kitty came out of the shower, toweling her nearly knee-length white hair. "You said Bob Greene sent back a preliminary report? What could he have to report on in so short a time?"

"More than you might think, hon," Simon said. "And some of the most interesting stuff wasn't in Marsha's report."

"Is she trying to hide something? What went wrong? Shirley didn't flip out again, did she?" Kitty's questions were so rapid-fire, Simon had no time to answer any of them. He held up his hand.

"To answer your questions in order, that would be she *is* trying to hide something, nothing went wrong, and no, Shirley didn't flip out. As a matter of fact, Marsha gives her one of the most glowing reviews of all."

"So, what, then?"

Simon turned a computer monitor to face the two of them. "Why don't you slip into something and sit down. Otherwise this will make you fall down." As she complied, Simon put a small disk into the player and said, "I already had my pick made for admiral, and I know you've been dithering over several prospects, especially since Lucy Grimes still refuses to take over your job. But I think this will reverse things for both of us. You've got a Herald, and I need to reevaluate my choices for admiral. And my second choice has been in Shiravan space for almost a year now. Maybe I should send a courier with a replacement."

"What are you talking about?" Kitty demanded, sitting down beside him.

"It seems that one of Bob's people thought to wear a shoulder cam to record his first visit to a Shiravan party. It happened to be Marsha's going away party, and I think you'll find it interesting. You've kept up your Shiravan haven't you?" At her nod, he went on. "Good. Mine's been getting better, but I still have trouble with some concepts. I did get the gist of this though. Feel free to translate at will."

He pressed a button and a junior officer's face came on-screen. "Hi, Mom and Dad, I wanted you to know I got here safe and sound, and there's no sign of enemy activity. As a matter of fact, only a few ships have been seen in the past year, and all the Garmon worlds are deserted except for a few old women and the youngest kids. But here's the news. I get to go down to Shiravi itself and attend a party in their major industrial city called Quillas. It's for the out-going admiral, Marsha Kane, and should be quite a shindig. I'll save rest of this disk for the party. I've been studying Shiravan and can give you an idea of what was said at the end or on another disk."

The screen went black for a moment and then showed the outside of a building in Quillas. "That's the Forum," Kitty said. A lot of voices were overlaid one upon another, all English at first. Then the view entered the foyer of the building, one both Kitty and Simon had been in several times.

Eventually, the view moved into a large room filled with a lot of tall, red Shiravans dressed in garish colors, a few in more somber colors, and a sprinkling of humans, all in dress uniform. The young officer spent his time on the outskirts of most of the party, venturing closer for shots of things that interested him. Kitty got to name several individuals, but most of her comments were just about general conversations.

The view changed again as the camera moved closer to the dais. Linnas stood there with Marsha beside her. "I got all the essentials and a short note from Bob Greene giving his interpretation of what was said. Just watch and listen."

Kitty sat rapt before the screen until the end of Linnas's speech. "You can turn it off now. I see what you mean. Linnas conferred the status of Sister-equal on her, making her as obligated to the survival of the Shiravans as she herself. And me too, for that matter. I wonder why she didn't see fit to put that in her report?"

Simon looked at his wife. "Technically, she's under my jurisdiction, but considering the closeness between you, I think I'll let you make her squirm. Then you can ask her to consider taking on the responsibility of Herald since she's now a Sister-equal as well, leaving her time to think about it while she takes a long vacation back home. A Sister-equal leading the Alliance would sit better with the Shiravans than a man or just some other woman."

Kitty thought about it for a minute. "Where is she now?"

"Aboard the *Raptor*. This is her sleep cycle, and I'm sure she's trying to get her body clock back to Earth norm. Maybe about noon you could comm her and invite her over for a visit. Girl talk, you know. Then, after a glass of fire wine, she could be loosened up enough to talk to an old friend."

"You're a devious bastard, Simon Hawke. I'll have to cancel all my afternoon appointments," Kitty mused aloud.

"Good," Simon said almost gleefully. "Then you might have a second glass if she isn't ready to talk after the first. Afterwards you can call me, and I'll escort you back here so you can recuperate. Maybe we could even have the stewards deliver dinner." He waggled his eyebrows suggestively, provoking a smile and girlish giggle.

They eventually shut off the lights and Kitty fell asleep tucked in the familiar safety of Simon's arms. He gently stroked her hair and pushed a few strands out of her face. He lay there looking at her, thinking about the new ship and the coming year-and-a-half before he could abdicate. It all depended on Marsha's reaction to the suggestion of becoming the new face of the Alliance.

It might be a good idea to go ahead and send the *Newton* out like Kitty said. Time enough to think about that later. Presently he fell asleep himself. His last thought was that it was time to name the new super-*Raptor*. Maybe it was finally time for a ship named *Enterprise*.

Kitty sat comfortably behind her desk and looked over at Marsha. "You know that as sisters we aren't supposed to keep secrets from each other, don't you? At least, if I'd had a sister as a kid, I wouldn't have kept secrets from her. I think." She gazed blandly across at Marsha, who held a glass of wine halfway to her lips.

Setting the glass carefully on the edge of the desk, Marsha replied, "I don't know what you're talking about. And we aren't sisters. Not that I wouldn't mind having you for a sister," she finished quickly.

Kitty noted the guilty look on her face and went for the kill quickly to minimize the pain. "First, according to Shiravan custom we *are* sisters, and second, that was a really pretty green dress you wore at your going away party. Why did you leave the party out of your report?"

Marsha hesitated, looking for a way out. "Well, it had no bearing on the mission, and I didn't think it worthwhile to waste your time. How do you know the dress was green?"

"The same way I know that Linnas elevated you to Sister-equal. Now, don't you think *that* was significant enough to put in your report?" Kitty took a sip from her glass and indicated Marsha's. "I think a toast is in order, Sister," she said, putting emphasis on the last word. She continued to hold her glass out, her look changing from bland to intent. She wasn't about to be snubbed at this point.

Marsha finally picked up her glass and slowly moved it out to touch Kitty's, a wary look on her face. "Don't worry, old friend, I'm not going to bite. Yet. To Marsha Kane, Admiral of the Alliance and Sister-equal to myself and Linnas des Harras, the Matriarch of twenty worlds. This is not an honor conferred lightly, I'm told. Only two times in recorded history has a Matriarch done such a thing. Do you realize that if she dies, one of us will have to go take her place? She has no heirs, so the job would land squarely on the shoulders of one of us." Marsha blanched. Kitty chuckled quietly as she took a sip from her glass and indicated that Marsha do likewise. She wasn't about to admit that that last bit of information was false. At least she believed so, nobody having ever mentioned any such thing.

Marsha took a larger drink, and Kitty refilled her glass. "Kitty, I can't go and take Linnas's place! That's absurd. You would have to do it."

Kitty smiled, an almost feral expression. "Well, *I* certainly can't. I have my hands full here, running herd on this bunch, and we don't even have a second planet of our own yet. What do you suggest we do? Just in case."

"I don't know, Kitty. I just don't know."

"The Shiravans are happy that the Alliance is being run by somebody who has their best interest at heart. And after your near-fatal encounter at the Forum, they see you as just as committed to their welfare as your own. More so, even. You nearly gave your life for the Matriarch, for God's sake!" Kitty barked.

Marsha emptied her glass and set it upside down on the coaster. "Where are you going with this?" she demanded, not at all swayed by Kitty's official status or her supposed sisterhood.

"You want it in one shot, or should I baby you a bit longer?" she taunted.

"I'm a big girl. I run a fleet of seventeen ships and have lost ships and crew, some of whom I started out with and will miss forever. I've put my life at risk for the Alliance from day one and will continue to do so," she said in a rush. "What do you want me to do next? Just tell me."

Kitty softened her approach. "I know all too well what you've given and given up, as well as how much you've suffered. Lord knows, I carry around enough ghosts of my own to understand." She looked Marsha squarely in the eyes. "This isn't something I or Simon can order you to do. We'll both order a nice long vacation, but while you're gone, I want you to think about a proposal I have in mind." She waited a few seconds, finally judging the time to be right. "Simon and I want to retire and start our second vocations, as the Shiravans put it. That means we're going to need a new supreme Admiral and Herald. We're going to take a small fleet and go exploring where the rest of the fleet can't go. Are you interested? You'll have plenty of time to think it over—as long as you need, up to about six months."

"You want me to be supreme Admiral in Simon's place? That's quite a job," she hedged. "It will take some thinking on, and I promise to do just that while I'm on vacation."

"That's not exactly what we have in mind, Sister-equal," Kitty said, finally setting the hook. "We want you to take over as Herald."

Blank-faced, Marsha reached out and turned her glass back over. "Got any more of that fire wine on hand?"

Pegra Nargresh sat alone before a fire in Harka Garmon's main hall. It was winter on Harka's main world, and even a thick coat of fur couldn't keep the cold of a winter storm from his bones. Fortunately, Harka had the foresight to suggest that all the able bodied of the People start putting aside food for the short winter period. No one would starve, but that was the least of his worries.

The various Clans were separated far enough apart that there would be no incidents among a race that valued its personal space. What bothered him was that scout ships kept returning with negative results on planets with the proper spectral pattern. He had loosened those requirements and sent them back out, hoping for worlds that would support their lives if not their exact environment.

What was even more disturbing were the reports on the cows. They had begun to speak and even demand— *demand*—to be treated with more respect than mere baby factories. And the number of cows born was not diminishing. The Elders and few remaining who qualified as scientists among the People were at a loss as to explain the situation. The youngest cows were being born with facial characteristics similar to the males and were even more intractable than previous generations. Some were even beginning to question his methods, ideas, and goals. They were gaining some insight to the situation they were in and beginning to speak their minds.

They were needed for the proliferation of the race, but the situation could not be allowed to continue without something being done. Fighting was his forte, as it was with all males, but how to handle this was beyond his comprehension. Never in the history of the People had such a thing occurred, and he had no precedent to follow.

He went for a walk to clear his mind. The industry going on around him appealed to his sense of order. They were encamped in the foothills of an enormous mountain chain, heavily wooded and full of game. On the plains below, herds of krath ran unhindered, having been imported with Harka's original settlement. A troop of hunters was coming up an already well-worn path, three krath strung up between them. Other males were hard at work building lodges and handling the many chores required to keep over two hundred People alive and healthy.

This number did not include the cows, of course, though they must be fed as well. Older cubs were busy learning the techniques they would need as adults to survive. He knew that in a remote spot, others were training on the hidden ships, learning to fly them. These days, though, very few trips were being made. Occasionally, a ship needed to be refueled, or a new ship came out of the rudimentary yards hidden in an enormous cave system half a planet away. It had been deemed too dangerous to have an elaborate factory complex out in the open for the enemy to find.

Pegra's stomach churned at the thought of hiding from an enemy, but the People had been decimated in a mere double-handful of years. In order to preserve the race, some things must be endured that went against the natural order.

And the thought of natural order coincided with the appearance of a young cow. It sauntered up to him, eyes wide. He was astonished at the change in the features of its face—more like the People, but somehow softer, though there was steel in its gaze. He had heard of them talking, but he was shocked when it spoke to him. "You boss?" The words were intelligible, though slurred.

Pegra was confounded. How did one of the People speak to a cow? "Yes," he answered uncertainly.

The young cow stood up straight, looking

uncomfortably like a real Person. "I work," it said, pointing at the males building fires, cooking, building lodges. Its hands had changed from the more hoof-like structure he was familiar with to uncommonly long fingers.

"You can't work. You're just a cow. Go back to your compound."

He turned around, feeling somehow uneasy, but her words stopped him. "I learn talk. I learn work." Its tone was uncommonly like an obstinate cub, sure of his ability. "I no sit and wait to be baby-maker. I work." Pegra didn't know how to deal with the situation. No one had real supervision over the cows, and they didn't even have names, so he resorted to the only tactics he knew. He swatted at it, intending only a firm smack, but it jumped back, still glaring at him.

"Go," he said, raising his hand again. This time the cow moved farther away and stopped again. "Go," he said again, raising his voice.

It finally moved off after another glare. "I work," it said again over its shoulder.

He started off on his rounds of the encampment and noticed the eyes of the males following him. He stopped and glared at the lot of them. "Who has been teaching the cows to talk, for the God's sake?" he roared. After several seconds had passed and no one spoke, he roared again. "Well?"

Finally, a youngling not far out of cubhood said, "If it pleases you, sire, they seem to have learned by themselves. It's something we've noticed over the past few seasons."

"It doesn't please me! Why has no one told me of this?" he asked, not realizing how far along their intelligence had come.

"We believed you already knew, sire," the youngling said.

"Well, I didn't. Is someone trying to make me look the fool? Do any of you wish to challenge me for leadership?" No one spoke up. All the males seemed to find something direly necessary that needed immediate attention. "Lieutenants, attend me," he bellowed and stomped back into the main lodge hall.

The talk about the increasing intelligence of the cows ran long into the night. The pile of wood for the central fire ran low before anything was determined, and that was only that one individual per day was to keep watch over the cow's compound, preventing any more incidents.

Incidents began to occur with an alarming degree of regularity. The cows managed to get out of their compound on a regular basis, starting with the one who had accosted Pegra the day before. This time it showed up at a firepit with an armload of wood. It managed to make two more trips before the new supervisor caught on. He herded it back into the compound and walked the circumference until he found a hole big enough for it to have slipped out of. He rolled a large boulder into the depression and went back to cleaning his claws.

Later, he had to gather three back in, all younglings by their features. He suspected that one was the same one he had caught earlier. This time, he found a deeper hole near the boulder. Was he going to have to spend his whole day watching cows? If Pegra found out, he could be stripped of his rank or his hide, depending on the leader's mood. He decided to bring it up at council that night. For the rest of the day, he made regular rounds of the compound, ungraciously accepting comments from his fellow warriors. To one he said, "Just wait. Tomorrow it will be your turn." Laughter followed him as he rounded the edge.

CHAPTER THIRTY-EIGHT

Simon looked up from the report he was reading when his private door opened. Kitty stepped across the threshold and dropped into a chair in front of his desk. "You look bushed, hon. How did it go?" He sounded truly worried.

"Well, I'm still alive, and she didn't say no," she responded. "She's going to take an extended leave, though. Says she wants to get the smell of spaceships out of her clothes. I told her to take all the time she needs, up to six months. I don't want her getting too comfortable in her old life. And she'll be drawing full pay, so she won't need money. I won't say it's a lock, but I get good vibes from it. She really wanted to go with us, though. I told her that when we get back, she can have her choice of ships and crew."

Simon's comm chimed and he gave it his attention. "Yes, I did, 'Stafa. Are you close enough to stop by my quarters anytime soon?" he asked, rubbing his hands together almost gleefully.

"I believe we can make Ceres orbit in about an hour, sir. What's up?"

"How about we don't discuss it over an open channel, okay? Bring your first officer with you, and plan to take the rest of the day off. Dress is civvies. I have an offer for you."

"Intriguing, sir. I'll see how much time I can safely

shave off that estimate. Morgan out."

He stood up and held out his hand to Kitty. "Let's go change. Our guests will be arriving soon."

Mustafa Morgan arrived about forty-five minutes later with a young-looking man beside him, who he introduced as Mitchell Price. Both had the white-hair characteristic of regen treatments. On Mustafa it looked especially good, considering that he had the blackest skin Simon had ever seen. He'd been among the first volunteers, even before the *Galileo* left on her first mission to build a space dock.

"Welcome to Ceres, 'Stafa. Commander Price, we haven't met yet. I'm Simon Hawke, and this is my wife, Kitty. Why don't you two have a seat in the lounge area?" Simon and Kitty followed the two and sat down opposite them. On the table between them was a blue bottle and four glasses.

"So, how are things with your new ship, 'Stafa?"

"More room, better armaments and screens, faster, too. And she carries a crew of almost four hundred. A far cry from the first ships out of the yards," he answered. "But you didn't ask us here for just social talk, did you? Let's get down to business, Simon."

"You always were direct, old friend," Simon said as he filled the last glass with a liquid that seemed to glow a light blue. "Let's drink to old times, old friendships, and new adventures." He raised his glass and Kitty copied him, leaving the other two to stare at the glasses before slowly picking them up. "This stuff has quite a kick, guys, so I suggest you sip slowly until you get a feel for it."

"It can't be any worse than that horrible stuff you call

scotch, Simon," Mustafa said.

"Famous last words," Simon retorted with a smile. "Just promise me that you"ll remember them." When he held his glass farther out, all four touched glasses and took a drink. Simon, Kitty and Commander Price all took small sips at first, but Mustafa took about a third of his drink in one swallow.

Price let out a small, "Whoosh!" and looked at the glass with some respect. Mustafa, on the other hand, looked like he was about to suffer a stroke. After a minute of huffing and puffing, during which time the others took another sip, he finally asked in a strained voice, "What the hell is this stuff? Goes down smooth, then kicks your ass. Are you trying to poison me?"

"I warned you to take it slow, 'Stafa. But, no, you wouldn't listen to me. Maybe you aren't the man for the mission after all." Simon shook his head sadly.

"Hold your horses there, boss man. Things are getting boring around here. Maybe I want the job. What is it?"

Kitty spoke up for the first time. "Have you heard of the Overlook Restaurant? It's at the far end of the asteroid, has a splendid view of the lake, and a four-star menu. Dinner is on us, and I think Simon wants to talk about it there. We have a private table and won't be disturbed except by the waiter, who happens to have a top-secret clearance."

"Been there," Mustafa said, "but I've never turned down a free meal unless I had to. How soon do we eat, if you're going to be all mysterious about this? Commander Price?"

"I'm in, sir. I've heard about the lake but never seen it. If they're going to bribe us with food, I say let's eat and then hear the deal."

"See why he's my second in command? Knows how

to exploit a situation," Mustafa said proudly. "Trained him myself."

Kitty looked at her watch. "Then we should be leaving, gentlemen. The tube system will take us to an exit near the restaurant, and it's just a few minutes' walk from there." She stood up and the three men followed her example, Mustafa a bit unsteadily. He left the rest of his glass on the table, as did Price.

On the ride to the restaurant, Mustafa asked, "Just what was that stuff, Simon? It's got a kick like nothing I've ever experienced."

Simon smiled happily. "The Shiravans call it fire wine, and nobody has found a better name for it. Respectable, huh?"

"Respectable, hell! That stuff should be outlawed."

Kitty said, "That's why we asked you to spend the night on Ceres. We have rooms already assigned for each of you."

The tube shuttle slowed to a stop and the four stepped out. "One flight up and we're there. Think you can manage it, 'Stafa?" Simon quipped.

"Of course," Mustafa replied indignantly. "It'll take more than that to put me out. Besides, a meal will help me sober up some."

"Good. I'm glad you feel that way. We still have most of a bottle to go through afterwards," Simon gloated.

"So, you want me to take a courier ship and go replace Bob Greene at Shiravi. Is that all? What happens to my ship once I'm gone? A ship can't be without a captain for long." Mustafa sipped gingerly at his wine, waiting for the answer.

"Well, there's going to be a change in the command

structure around here pretty soon. What I have in mind is to have you take over Bob's command as Admiral in Shiravan space while he comes back here," Simon said.

Mustafa thought about it for a time while he savored another sip from his glass. "So, you promote Price to captain to fill my place and me to admiral to fill Bob's shoes. What is Bob going to be doing?"

Simon said simply, "My job."

Mustafa mulled the puzzle over for a minute. "So, what are *you* going to do?"

Simon just smiled. "You know what I've wanted all along, 'Stafa. A really long vacation." Mustafa gave Simon a vague look over the rim of his glass. Simon said, "You know—'going where no man has gone before'?"

Enlightenment dawned on Mustafa's face. "And just when will this momentous event occur?" he asked, smiling brightly. He had long known of Simon's displeasure with staying behind while so many others were able to step out of the solar system. "You know," he said before Simon could answer, "I remember you saying at one of the first dedication ceremonies that you were the first husband to really give his wife the stars. Congratulations. You finally get to do it. But who's going to become Herald?"

Kitty joined the conversation because Simon was halfway through a sip from his glass. "We have to wait for Bob to get back and let him get acclimated first. As for the Herald's post, I have someone in mind, but I have to go slow."

Simon nodded and added. "You know that new ship coming out of Taurus Base? That's going to be my ship unless something better comes along in the next year and a half. We're finally going to have a ship called

Enterprise, and *I'm* getting the ulcer seat. There's no rule that says an admiral can't be captain of a ship."

Mustafa shifted position on the couch. "No rule that you didn't make up, right? So, when do I leave? I've got a few things to wrap up, and I'd like to some spend time with my family if I'm going to be away for several years."

Kitty asked, "Both of your kids are grown, aren't they?" Mustafa nodded. "Why don't you take your wife along with you? I know she's gone through regen like most partners have."

"True," Mustafa agreed. "And she's been working on learning Shiravan for quite some time now since she's right here on Ceres, along with a lot of other service-connected personnel. She just might go for it."

"So, let's say you leave in about a month, then," Simon said. "Right after I promote you to admiral and Mitchell, here, to captain. Sound okay to you?"

After the two men agreed, the foursome returned to the lounge and got down to the serious business of finding the bottom of the blue bottle.

Sitha kep Parrasine stepped out of the suborbital ahead of her Matriarch, and they both looked out on the ruined land that had been Cho-An, the ancestral home of the des Harras clan for more generations than could be counted. Huge dirt movers were busily moving material from all around the plain to fill the gaping hole left by the Garmon assault.

The wound was nearly repaired and ready for the city to be rebuilt from ancient records kept in Quillas, as well as other places. Redundancy was nothing if not normal for Shiravans in almost all things. "The new city will have an added feature the old one didn't," Linnas noted almost absently.

"And what will that be, Your Grace?" Sitha asked.

"'All the bits of gava stone that can be found on the surrounding plains will be incorporated into the outer grounds of the city," Linnas answered. "It will be scattered along the top of the soil to give off a diffuse glow all around the outer walls."

Sitha finally noticed workers slowly going through the piled-up dirt, pulling out bits and pieces of stone from among the dirt and ordinary rocks. "Aren't you worried about theft?" she asked with an eye toward the value of the amazing stone.

"Only about the biggest pieces," Linnas answered. "If it's obvious, it stays here. There's no reason the people can't have a small bit of Cho-An to treasure, sell, or turn into a piece of jewelry. Until the job is done, the workers revolve regularly so they have a chance to find some small bits for themselves. In some ways it will be an economic boost to Shiravi in general."

"I see," Sitha said simply as she reached down and picked up a shard almost the size of her hand, passing it to her Matriarch.

Linnas weighed it in her hand before giving it back. "It is yours. Let's go. The sight still causes me nightmares."

Their return to Quillas was one that Sitha didn't really want to happen. The new human admiral was to be given an audience today by Linnas.

At least he won't get the title of Sister-kin, she mused to herself. In her private moments, Sitha was still a bit disturbed by the fact that two humans had been awarded that honor. At no other time in recorded memory had an alien been accorded such an honor. *Of course*, she kept reminding herself, *the only other race we've ever met has been the Garmons.*

She sat at the left hand of her Matriarch as Admiral Robert Greene was ushered into Linnas's formal reception room. The two had met once before, at the going-away party just before Marsha left. This more formal meeting was to judge the level of interaction possible with human males. Linnas's Sister-kin Kitty had personally chosen him for the position, so it was to be expected that the two would get along.

Admiral Greene, for his part, was all graciousness, to the point of speaking perfect Shiravan, although with a slight accent that made him seem all the more mysterious. He waited to sit until after Linnas and Sitha had sat down and observed all the proper formalities, if a bit stiffly. This would go away as he became more used to them.

During their conversation, Linnas said, "I hear you're getting along well with the Shiravan captains, Admiral. Do you have any problems to report?"

"No, Your Grace," he answered. "I've had the pleasure and honor of meeting and serving with many Shiravans, including Minister do' Verlas and his aide, Maratai kep Parrasine, who I'm told is related to you?"

This last was directed at Sitha so she had to join the conversation, if only for a bit more. "Yes, Admiral," she said almost reluctantly. "Maratai is my older sister."

"She brings honor to your clan. Yet you hold a higher office than she does. Is that because she's spent so much time away from home or for some other reason?" he asked pointedly.

"Maratai has been of invaluable service to us in her time among humans," Linnas answered. "She was among the first to work with Dom Carter and Doma

Spencer after their rescue from Garmon hands. This was before Shiravans and humans had even met, if you will recall, and she volunteered her services even before Manura sel Garian retired from her third vocation."

"Is there some reason for these questions, Admiral?" Sitha asked self-consciously. She'd always felt that Maratai would have made a better Second Voice than she did and wondered at her continued stay in human space. Could she really be enamored of do' Verlas? Yes, he was a decisive male, as so many weren't, but still…

"Only to get to know the persons involved better, Madam Second Voice," the admiral said. "The more knowledge one has, the better one is able to adapt to a situation."

Sitha felt that he spoke Shiravan a bit too well for her taste. Linnas had told her once that to know a culture one had to be able to think in their language. She was afraid this human was able to do just that.

"Tell me, Admiral, what do you think of the situation in Shiravan space now that you've had time to assess it?" Linnas asked, changing the subject—whether on purpose or not, Sitha didn't know. "My Sister-kin Kitty has called you one of her best tacticians. I would be grateful to hear your ideas."

Robert took a few seconds to collect his thoughts. "Well, Your Grace, this isn't only my opinion, but the opinion of others I keep close to help me make decisions. There's an old human saying—two heads are better than one. There have been no Garmon incursions in over a full turning, and you have reclaimed several worlds that had been taken from you. Instead of fourteen worlds, you are now twenty.

"Earth still has one world, though plans were going forward for our first colony worlds. You have one set of yards to turn out ships; we have four. I think it's time for you to start building more yards in other parts of your domain. Do you realize that if the Garmons had hit your yards instead of Cho-An, you'd have no ability to build ships at all? I suggest that you build at least two more yards, putting that many more ships into service that much faster. Your expansion more worlds would happen more quickly, and you'd soon be totally independent of the need for human ships in your space. I mean no disrespect, Your Grace, but it is better to have your industries spread farther out. The more worlds you hold, the more yards you will need. It will be up to you to determine the ratio.

"Also, your economy depends on your paying laborers to build and maintain these facilities. We still have volunteers who are willing to work for free just to be in space, though we're now able to pay them."

Linnas sat silent for so long, Sitha thought she was going to be angry, but she was surprised.

"I see that you've given more thought to our situation than I'd expected, Admiral. These are very good points, and I'll bring them before the Council, giving fair voice to where they came from, as well as my personal recommendation."

"Thank you, Your Grace. You know your people better than I do. If there should be the possibility of resistance to these ideas because they come from a human, please feel free to omit my name."

"It seems," Linnas retorted with a wan smile, "that you know our people as well as you do our situation. I shall keep that in mind during future talks. Do you have anything more to add?"

The Admiral had no more to say other than his good-byes, and after his departure, Linnas turned to Sitha.

"Tell me, how do you feel about his assessment of us?"

Sitha answered her Matriarch honestly. "I think he's completely correct in all respects, Your Grace."

Linnas looked surprised. "You resort to formality when we are alone? Do you have other thoughts?"

"I feel the humans have come to know us much too well, Your Grace, and that might be a bad thing," was all she could say.

CHAPTER THIRTY-NINE

If Robert Greene was surprised at his early return to Earth space, he was even more surprised at the circumstances he found the Alliance in. The *Newton* had been sent to two planets on the same mission the *Dalgor Kreth* had been on when it turned up in Earth orbit almost twenty years before. Colonists were already on their way to the first, called Terra (not very inventive as it was just Latin for earth or dirt). The second was called Aphrodite. Rumor had it that a third was under consideration after the *Newton* had a refit and crew change, to be called Nike (pronounced the Latin way— nee-kay.)

With no aggressor to fight, the fleet had grown to over ninety ships, and more were being turned out regularly. Now, though, there were a few more specialized ships being built. Passenger carriers for the trips to the new worlds were based on the old carrier designs and fitted with admittedly cramped quarters, but gyms, rec rooms, two spacious dining rooms and a theater were among the amenities, along with a plethora of books. A preliminary power core and brain went along, as well as a considerable amount of personal possessions for each family.

Habitations were set up in the most advantageous spots along rivers, near oceans, near equators and lush vegetation, and no expense was spared to make sure there were no Garmons on any of these worlds. The few found had been transported to a distant world and left to fend for themselves, leaving the new colonists with nothing but native flora and fauna to contend with. Several ships were to stay in orbit or on patrol to ensure the safety of the colony from attacks from space. The commander of the small fleet on patrol was an arbitrator whenever he or she felt it necessary to intercede in planetary affairs.

All this he had found out on his inbound vector from passing ships and his first night aboard Ceres. He had found a nicely appointed, embossed letter from the admiral's office, requesting his presence for nine o'clock the next morning. Not waiting for his luggage to arrive, he helped himself to a very long and luxurious bath right off. He wasn't too surprised to find his luggage in his room and unpacked except for what were obviously personal items.

He dressed in civvies and went out to find a bar, not having to search very long. His face was not all that well known except among his fleet crew, so he had no trouble finding congenial people proud to tell him what had been accomplished during his long absence. He went to bed that night with a slight buzz, a lot of information, and questions circling each other in his mind. And he still didn't know why he'd been recalled.

Pegra Nargresh was at a total loss as to how to deal with these new cows. Two more generations had been born since the incident with the young cow who'd been determined to work. He'd had her specially impregnated as soon as she came into her first heat, hoping that pregnancy and the necessity of raising several younglings would take the determination out of her. Reports had it that it took three grown warriors to hold her down for the process. It wasn't something he was particularly proud of.

Besides, the results were anything but comforting. Three cubs she bore—two cows and only one male. At this rate, he was going to have to start leaving some of the cows out in the wilderness to die. Escapes from the compound were so frequent now that he had given up posting guards. Their morale was dropping from being outwitted by mere cows, although 'mere' no longer applied to these cows.

If the truth were to be known, the rise in intelligence frightened him more than his first krath hunt as a cub. These cows and others all over the two planets were becoming much smarter. They'd even taken to giving themselves names—simple things like Breeze, Gatherer, Forest, and more. It had become known that some few had escaped into the forests and begun returning the cowlings left out to die. All the compounds were becoming overrun with cows, and the males were hard-pressed to keep all of them fed, as well as themselves.

The latest and most trying confrontation had come when one of the younger cows, even smarter than the one who had faced him down in front of his men, took up a spear and threatened a male as he was punishing a cow for disobedience. The warrior wasn't hurt, but the damage was done. A cow with a deadly weapon! An idea began to form in the back of Pegra's mind.

Later that night, sitting in council with his chief lieutenants, he broached the subject to his men. "We have to spend too much time feeding these cows. And today's experience has shown me the way to rid ourselves of this burden. Why not give a few of them weapons and teach them the rudiments of hunting? Many will surely be killed, helping to ease our problem, and the ones that do succeed will feed their own. It's a task worth considering."

Naturally, he was met with stiff opposition, but he sat back and held his silence. Soon the council was arguing amongst itself. Eventually they arrived at the same conclusion. Only, which to choose?

"I say pick some of the smartest, especially the one who attacked Bakat, and train them in the nature of hunting. They're smart enough to understand that if they don't feed themselves, they'll go hungry." Naturally, he got Bakat's vote right off, and it wasn't long before the rest fell into line as he had suspected they would. It lifted a heavy burden from their shoulders and had the potential to reduce the cow population.

Accordingly, the next day, Pegra and three of his most trusted followers rounded up a half dozen cows, chief among them the one who called herself Gatherer, and began to explain the rudiments of hunting with a spear. A krath-hide-covered shrub was their target, and they began to stab it viciously with the dull points of the spears they'd been given. Soon, they were left to their own devices with the warning that they were now responsible for finding food for all the other cows as well.

That night, the cows weren't fed, and Pegra stood in the shadows watching to see what would happen. Soon, the six cows, spears in hand, came together to discuss the ideas planted in their enlarging brains. The next morning there was a revolting sight at the gate, now left open because it was a waste of time to lock it.

The six cows walked out of the compound and off into the forest, spears in hand to find food for the rest. It was also astonishing. One day of practice with worn weapons and one warning, along with one night's hunger, had impelled them into the very trap he had hoped for. When they came back empty handed enough times, the other cows would realize their place in the true order of things and return to the old ways. A naïve thought, as it turned out.

Later that evening, the six returned carrying a small forest creature big enough to fill the bellies of all the cows and cubs and began distributing it among the rest of the compound's population. In the days to follow, even more astounding things took place. More spears appeared, obviously inferior but made by the hands of the cows. One day, a cow was seen wearing a belt to which a bone-handled knife was attached.

The spears had been of the old workable-stone type, and somewhere the cows had found a supply. Copied from the original tips, the new spears were a vast improvement over the originals. When Pegra inspected one, he found it to have clean, sharp edges. The knives now worn by many of the cows showed a greater capability than he had thought they would. Obvious copies of the males' weapons, these were crafted to fit the hands of the smaller cows.

The cows had been watching as his men went about the daily chores of cleaning and sharpening their own weapons. One day, he even saw the cow, Gatherer, wearing a steel-bladed knife. Wondering where she'd gotten it, he asked amongst his men. One finally answered. "Sire, it was only a worn-out blade. I threw it away and crafted a new one to replace it." He went away from the conversation worried.

The cows thrived, and more began to engage in practicing with their new weapons. Soon, daily groups of cows headed off in different directions to hunt or gather, and they were almost always successful. One group even went down to the plains to try to kill a krath. The group returned two days later with a youngling strung between two poles. They struggled up the hill to the camp, two short of their original number.

In the coming days, more parties went toward the plains, some coming back empty handed, which suited Pegra just fine, but the others made up for those losses. Then one day, the camp awoke to find the entire compound empty. All the cows were gone, along with all the young, both cows and cublings.

Their tracks were plain to follow since they hadn't tried to hide their direction. Three males were assigned to follow and find out where they went. Their report amazed him, as well as the rest of the males. Some farats away, in a glade near the edge of the forest, a new compound had been erected. The cows had settled for the night, but sentries roamed the interior, just as the males did.

A fire had been started to keep away the chill from the area, and meat could be seen smoking over the fire. The cows talked amongst themselves at times, and the silent watchers listened. The talk was of hunting and enough food and water for the group. Plans for future expansion of the tribe were discussed as well. The next day, as all the cows came out of their shelters, many young cubs could be seen among the cowlings.

Pegra would not tolerate this. He gathered his males and stormed the camp, burning down the huts and carrying off the cubs to be reared in the old ways of the hunt and adherence to the laws of the People. Several of the cows were forcibly mated as an object lesson, and the males returned to their own encampment.

Several days later, the cow's camp was deserted, and this time the tracks were not so easy to follow. The hunters had to rely on their noses to find the new camp, many farats away. A wall had been erected and the sentries were more alert, talking less and staring out into the darkness. They learned fast, these cows. All of them now carried knives as well as spears, and Gatherer seemed to be their leader. It had been one of the ones mated as it already appeared gravid and spent more time sitting than many of the rest. Still, it issued orders, and they seemed to be obeyed. It settled quarrels amongst the cows and kept the camp in order. It also directed the hunting parties on their journeys to the plains. A fully-grown krath was seen hanging from its hind legs, slowly bleeding out before butchering. The skin was set to one side as if to keep it safe.

One of the watchers was discovered by a group of cows headed uphill for smaller game. He was beaten off with spears, but not before he had ripped out the throat of one cow. Then the blades had come down and he'd barely escaped with his life. Pegra declared that this situation would not be allowed to continue, but the damage was too widespread. All the enclaves were reporting similar actions. And what would happen to the People if all the cows were killed? The absolute worst part was that the occasional patrol ship that arrived carried the same bad news, as if all the cows had been infected by something at the same time. He looked at the skies and began to wonder.

CHAPTER FORTY

Robert Greene wore his best dress uniform as he strode down the corridors of Ceres and through its plazas. The invitation had come from the admiral's office, not from Simon personally. He walked into the secretary's office and announced himself a bit self-consciously. He hadn't spent enough time in Shiravan space to screw up as admiral of the human presence there, so he was a bit mystified as to his quick relief and the undertone of urgency that had run through the courier ship all the way home.

The secretary wasn't surprised to see him, of course. The summons had specified a particular time, but he had expected to wait a bit. Instead, as soon as he had identified himself, he was ushered into the admiral's inner sanctum.

Simon looked up and set the tone of the meeting. "Bob! It's good to see you. Come over here and sit down."

He sat in a comfortable chair in front of the massive desk and said, "It's good to see you again, too, but I hadn't expected to do it for at least another year or more."

Simon got that little smile he used to have in the early days when there were only a few ships and all those bloody-minded aliens were trying to kill them. "Well, you know that we're famous for changing our plans on the spur of the moment. Coffee?" When Bob shook his head, Simon went on. "Kitty and I were talking some time back, before the ship was sent out to retrieve you— actually, I was doing the talking. She just changed the direction of my thoughts from time to time. Anyway, we, the both of us, have decided that it's time for some fresh blood at the top of the heap."

"What kind of fresh blood are you talking about, Admiral?" he asked quietly, his stomach in knots. He'd never been given to raising his voice too much.

"Oh, hell. If you don't call me Simon, I'll demote you to ensign," came the reply.

Robert looked at the smile on Simon's face and said, "Maybe that wouldn't be such a bad idea, Simon. Michiko and I were cooped up alone way too long together on the trip back. Especially not knowing why."

"Sorry 'bout that, Bob," Simon said apologetically, "but I wanted to keep this all under wraps until I had all my pieces in place."

"And I'm one of these pieces, I presume?"

"Oh, yes, very much so," Simon said emphatically, losing the smile. "One of the two most important ones, at that. I'll cut to the chase and end the suspense. How would you like to be sitting behind this desk? She's a beauty. A gift from Freddie, almost four hundred years old and as sturdy as the day she was made." Simon leaned back in his chair and waited for him to answer.

Bob had to think a minute. "You want me to become admiral of the *entire* Alliance instead of just a fleet? I guess I can handle it, if that's what you need me to do." He could hear the disbelief in his own voice. "What are *you* going to do?"

"Did you see the new ship out of Taurus Base out there?" Simon asked.

"No, I missed it since I was more concerned about why you wanted me back so soon," he said with some asperity. "Now I find out that you want me to take over your job, and I'm even *less* worried about a new ship."

"Well, you should be worried about it," Simon said, the smile back on his face again. "That ship represents what I've wanted for almost twenty long years—to be free to go where I want and do what I want, when I want. She makes the *Raptor* look like a scout ship. Almost as long as the *Newton* and carrying six times the firepower of any other ship in the fleet. She's also capable of building a new dock or fuel depot as needed. An almost completely self-contained city of over nearly a thousand, and that doesn't count the other ships that will accompany her—I figure at least five or six, at least one a farrier. All will be fitted out with the newest technology in engine design, and they'll be able to do more than three times the speed any other ship can. That means Earth to Shiravi in just over two months instead of seven." Simon sat back again and waited for his response.

"What about Kitty? Oh, let me guess," he said. "You're taking her along with you, so another piece is someone to be Herald. I know Lucy won't take it. She's had enough of that job. So, who's your sucker?"

"Kitty finally convinced Marsha to take the job, and as for Lucy, she's going to captain one of the other ships."

"Huh!" he huffed in surprise.

Simon said, "Why don't you come to our quarters around eight. Have dinner first. Kitty and I are having a little get-together. Marsha will be there, and you two will need to talk. Gayle will be there with a new special someone, and Lucy will be bringing a date, too. Simon laughed at the look on Robert's face. Bring 'Chiko, too. Marsha has an escort, so everything will work out evenly."

Simon was happy with the way things ended. Marsha had already agreed to take Kitty's place, and now Robert had weighed in on the positive side as well. Gayle's first love was a scientist she'd recruited to become one of the First Four in the beginning. It had taken her a long time to get over Stephen's death, but she had given her love, once she'd known how, and eventually found another man to trust. He and Kitty were happy for her and both very impressed with her choice—impressed enough to consider him for captaincy of one of the other ships included in his little exploratory flotilla.

"Kitty," Simon said, "I do believe we can start making more concrete plans now. Six ships, three captains. Three more and we can leak the news that we're looking for long-range personnel."

Kitty looked at him and asked, "Why don't you tell me one more time why we just don't go to Personnel and have them fill the slots?"

"Because this is just like in the beginning, honey. I want trusted people to interview each applicant personally and send me the reports. We're looking for people with a greater sense of adventure than what passes for normal these days." He was beginning to get exasperated at Kitty's resistance to the personnel selection process. "You don't have to participate in any interviews if you don't want too, Kittyn. But I'd expect you'd like to be personally acquainted with the people who'll actually be running your ship and taking orders from you."

He stepped back in surprise as Kitty rounded on him, and the fire in her eyes was unmistakable. He didn't know what he'd said, but he knew he was about to find out. "What makes you think I'm taking a ship of my own, Simon Hawke? This damned Alliance has kept us apart for far too long. Don't you think it's about time we started spending some time together for a change?" She stormed out of the room, and if the door could have been slammed, she'd have done it.

He sat down slowly and automatically reached for the bottle of scotch sitting close by, then thought better of it. He wandered the apartment, trying to figure out what to say when she got back. Of course they had been apart a lot over the past few years. Then he realized that it had really been almost two decades of separation with occasional visits together. Unable to believe his own stupidity, he went in search of the woman he loved.

An hour and an inspiration later he found her in one of the observation domes. He knew which one it was by the Herald's guards who followed her everywhere she went outside their quarters. He nodded to the guard commander, who put a hand on his arm. "Careful, sir. She's in a pretty foul mood."

"Thanks, Commander. I know. I'm the one who caused it," he said. A look of understanding and pity crossed the officer's face as he stepped aside and Simon slowly climbed the stairs into the dome. Kitty was alone when he came in. When she turned around at the sound of his steps on the deck, he raised his hands in surrender. "For once, I know what I've done, and I'm sorry, hon. We can be on the same ship together if that's what you want."

Kitty's face didn't even change expression. "Or," he added, "if you don't want to go, we'll stay here. Or on

Earth or wherever you want. You're right. We've spent entirely too much time apart." He stood there, several feet between them, and waited for her reply. When it didn't come, he hung his head and turned to leave. "I'll be in our quarters if you want to talk."

He hadn't made it to the first step when her voice came from right behind him. He hadn't known she could move that quietly. "Do you mean it, Simon?"

He turned around and looked down into her eyes. "I said what I meant, and I'll stand by it, Kittyn. From now on, things will be the way *you* want them. That's not to say that they've always been the way I wanted them, but circumstances dictated a lot of what has gone on for the last twenty years. It's time you had your say in things, so I'll do whatever you want."

"Simon, we've got about two hundred more years ahead of us. It can't be the way I want it all the time, but I'd like to have blue skies over my head for a while and to walk in the rain if I want to. Did you know that I missed the funeral of one of my aunts because I was in another solar system? And your folks are getting on, too. Don't you want to see them before we go somewhere else? I know you haven't been home but once for almost twenty years yourself."

He turned his head at the memories she dredged up. The last time he'd seen his parents had been during a rescue from government troops before the Alliance had been recognized as a separate political entity. He still had issues with his authoritarian father that would probably never be resolved, but his mother was another matter. "Sure, hon. Let's take a holiday. We'll go visit my parents and do whatever you want."

"We'll do something you want to do, too, dear. Anything you think of," Kitty answered, melting into his arms, all her anger forgotten.

He looked down into her face and an idea occurred to him. "How about the camping trip we never got to finish? It's been waiting a long, long time. Don't you think it's time we finished it?"

EPILOGUE

Life seemed to have come full circle for Simon and Katherine Hawke. Almost twenty years before, they had been in this same secluded valley when what they thought was a spaceship landed.

Now, they were taking the camping trip that had been so precipitously interrupted by that event. This time, though, they had arrived by way of a clone of that very ship. One month. That's what they wanted, and that's what they got. They had spent some time in Texas visiting Simon's parents, both of whom were getting on in years. Simon had offered them a trip through a regen chamber, but both had refused, saying they were satisfied with the life they'd lived and had accepted the inevitability of time's passage.

For his part, Simon had finally gotten some closure with his father. Sitting on the porch one muggy summer night, the two had talked for hours. Simon had related all the adventures of his life since finding the ship and forming what became the Terran Alliance, and his father had at last broken from his distant attitude enough to say that he was proud of the accomplishments of his only son. Simon was stunned. He had, in his own mind, never felt that he had lived up to the expectations of the old man. Now, he could put that ghost behind him.

The night sky of their one-time sanctuary was clear, though it was cold enough to need sweaters even around the fire that was slowly dying behind them. The couple had dragged their sleeping bags out of the tent and put them together into one. They slid into the bag and stared quietly at the stars above their heads. Stars they'd once only seen through a telescope were now places they had actually been. Kitty was trying to find Shiravi, but it was, she believed, not visible from their latitude. A few could be seen, though.

She nestled in her husband's arms and asked, "Which one are we going to see first?"

Simon ran his hand through her hair, an old, comfortable gesture she hadn't felt or seen in years. As they lay entwined, she could feel the difference in him, almost like he was a different man from the one she'd married—more relaxed, less tense, less driven. It had been this way ever since they'd left his parent's house, and she found that she liked it. The steel resolve was still there, but it was now hidden behind something new, and she thought of it as a vast improvement. "I'm not sure yet, hon. The idea is to go where no one else has been yet, and there are plenty of those. We'll decide when we get back, I think."

Kitty watched a falling star blaze across the heavens as she thought about the idea as well. "Could we stop by Shiravi first? I'd really like to see Linnas before we take off for such a long time."

They had prepared their little fleet already, and most of the personnel had been chosen from the myriad volunteers. Some of their oldest and best friends were going along. Gayle would captain the carrier ship, of course. She had turned down a chance at one of the cruisers in favor of the post she'd become accustomed to after so long. The captain she had taken up with was going along as part of her crew. The Hawkes had finally met him and thoroughly approved the match. Kitty saw how they looked at each other and realized it wasn't a rebound romance for her dearest friend. She'd silently given the couple her blessing.

Lucy Grimes had agreed to go along as captain of another cruiser, and the other slots were filled to everybody's approval. She did wish that Shirley Dahlquist had signed on, but her name hadn't been on the volunteer roster.

Simon, after a long silence, said, "Of course we can. I would have been surprised if you hadn't asked. That course has already been laid in, and plenty of time set aside for a nice visit. Shiravi is a good jumping off point for parts unknown. We have so many stars charted around both Earth and Shiravi that we have a pretty good idea about almost every star between here and there."

Kitty snuggled closer. "Good. Now, let's just enjoy ourselves for a while. I have an idea for a nice hike tomorrow." That night they made love under the stars with nothing between them but a little atmosphere.

The month passed pleasantly enough for the two Alliance icons. The pity was that it just wasn't long enough. When Kitty complained, Simon asked, "Well, what else would you like to do? Our schedule is flexible. It's not like the fleet will leave without us."

She said, a bit hesitantly, to Simon's mind, "I want to go shopping. This is going to be the last time I have a chance to do any real shopping for I don't know how many years."

Simon considered it and came to an instant conclusion. "You pick the places and we'll go shopping."

"We?" Kitty asked coyly. "When have I ever been able to get you into a store without you bitching and moaning the whole time?"

"To the best of my remembrance, I'd have to say never, hon," he said, smiling. "I don't have to be in the same store with you to go shopping with you, you know. I have a pretty good idea what you're going to do—pick out some things for yourself and a bunch of stuff for friends both going and staying behind." He shrugged. "I have the same thing in mind myself now, though if you hadn't mentioned it, I wouldn't have thought of it," he said, finishing with a small bow.

Simon could already see her thinking about a shopping trip. It was in her eyes, and they'd been married too long for him to miss the signs. "How much can I spend?" she asked, more out of habit, he thought, than anything else.

"My love, the entire Alliance treasury is at your disposal. Just leave a little bit for me, okay?" Her grin was fiercely exuberant.

"Okay," she agreed, teasing, "but just a little. So, are we through here?"

Kitty looked around her at the camp that had been home for the past month. "I guess so. There are a few things I want to keep, but the rest can go into the recyclers."

Simon walked into the tent and came out with two fair-sized bags. "One for each of us," he said, dropping one at her feet. He had strapped on his old .45 and had his M-1 over one shoulder. "It'll take me about five minutes to get my keepers," he said, leaning the rifle against a tree. "How about you?"

"About the same. Are you going to change clothes

here or back on the ship?"

"I think I'll wait," he said. "I'm still gonna smell like smoke and pine trees unless I shower first, and I want to either get out of here or stay another month."

"Same for me," she agreed. "Shall we call down a ship?"

"Two," he answered immediately. "A gig for us and a shuttle and crew to clean up the campsite for the recyclers." He dug into a pocket for his comm link, and twenty minutes later a small ship appeared above the treetops, then settled to the ground, door opening almost before the gear touched down.

The pair picked up their bags and boarded the craft. Simon felt a slight twinge as he set foot on the ramp. It had been a month without any sight of Alliance technology, aside from the laser Kitty kept strapped to her hip. Now they were going back to the world, the culture they'd started from nothing and watched grow until it now no longer needed them. A couple of shopping trips and then it was off into the black.

Kitty followed Simon to their quarters and set her bag down beside his. Before she could get out of her jeans, hiking boots, and flannel shirt, she heard the shower running. Simon was already standing under the pulsing showerhead, washing off the smell of wood smoke and insect repellent.

He stepped aside and she let the water, hot enough to turn her skin red, wash through her hair first, then let it stream down the rest of her body. She changed places with Simon, and he rinsed off while she soaped up. He stepped out, leaving the whole stall to her. She took advantage of it and stayed for several minutes after all the soap was gone, letting the warmth ease the aches she had borne for a month. She'd been behind a desk for far too long. A training schedule was going to be somewhere near the top of her list once the fleet got under way.

She came out to find Simon splayed out on the bed, letting the air dry what the bedspread didn't. She joined him for a few minutes after toweling the mass of her hair dry and spreading it out to finish drying on its own. Finally, they got up, and by mutual consent, dressed in civilian clothes. She slid her ID and a platinum card stamped with the Alliance logo into a zippered pocket.

Civilian dress meant no weapons, but it had been years since there had been an incident of any kind concerning police and Alliance personnel. After a quick meal, the pair went to the docking bay, along with the Herald's guard, all armed, and settled herself into the pilot's seat.

She jockeyed the shuttle out of the bay and headed for atmosphere. As she came into range of Los Angeles, she radioed a request for a position in the landing queue. By this time, most controllers knew the capabilities of Alliance craft, and almost immediately she was ordered to a lower altitude and assigned a spot away from aircraft moving about the airport in normal fashion.

Soon, a limo from a local Alliance affiliate pulled up and the group moved from the shuttle to the automobile. Kitty noticed that this model had no wheels but floated about ten inches off the ground. *So much for traveling incognito*, she thought. Of course, her hair and the Alliance car were dead giveaways, along with the black-clad armed security team that surrounded her.

Hours later she had spent an obscene amount of money on clothes, mostly for herself since she was getting tired of the standard black among Alliance crews. She had several gifts for her closest friends, too, especially an intricate necklace for Marsha. She and Simon made quite a stir on Rodeo Drive, considering the floating car and the stern-faced armed guards. This time she had called the mayor and local law enforcement, apprising them of her presence, and a few cars dogged her own, their officers helping to keep the crowds moving along without incident.

Finally, exhausted, she slumped into the back of the limo and told the driver to head back for their shuttle. It took three men two trips to carry everything aboard.

The fleet Kitty's shuttle was coming up on was a diverse group. First and foremost, there was the *Enterprise* herself. Painted an electric blue, her name wasn't the only thing paying homage to the various TV incarnations she'd stemmed from. Simon, maybe for laughs or maybe bowing to pressure from all the mail received after the name had been announced, had christened her with the Alliance code number NCC-1701.

Her crew was over a thousand, and she carried six massive engines powered by oversized cores, able to transfer power to three times the number of weapons of any two other ships in space. There were tractor and pressor beams, plasma bombs, stronger torpedoes of various kinds—photon, antimatter, nuclear, and long-range plasma—and lasers that outreached any ever before built into a mobile battle platform. Shields that were orders of magnitude stronger than any before them and an entire computer core had been devoted entirely to battle control. The five destroyers assigned to the fleet had been specially constructed with much of the same technology already built in rather than retrofitting older model cruisers.

The final two ships were Gayle's carrier, the *Eightball*, rechristened the *Close Call*, and a new ship altogether—a farrier. This vessel was in essence a flying repair facility for the rest of the fleet. It came equipped with a detachable fuel depot especially designed for this occasion. Once on station, the depot would be deployed after a *Sundiver* was launched into the local sun's corona, and the farrier would back away some thousands of miles. A small atom-stripper was built in, and various factories packed her interior. In all, almost five thousand people were scheduled to leave the solar system in the seven ships.

Kitty had her acquisitions delivered to the captain's quarters and stored temporarily in the adjoining conference room. There was still a week to go before they were scheduled to leave orbit, so she did an immediate turnaround and headed back to Ceres via short-jump to spend time with those she wouldn't be seeing for who knew how many years. First, she dropped into the Herald's office and asked if Marsha was in. The same secretary sat behind the desk and announced her arrival.

Marsha lost no time coming to the door herself and ushering her friend into the room. Kitty settled into one of the overstuffed chairs in front of the desk.

"So, this is what it looks like from the other side!" she exclaimed, laughing.

Marsha looked at her and muttered, "Lord deliver me from my enemies because I'm not sure I'll survive my friends. You know this is a lot harder than you let on, Kitty. I should quit on the grounds that you misrepresented the amount of work involved."

Kitty smiled wickedly. "I already told you how to

handle it, Marsha. I learned the hard way, but I gave you the tip for free—delegate. Read the reports of your department heads, and only call them in if you either don't understand or don't like something in the report. I was usually done with the paperwork by my third cup of coffee and any face-to-face meetings within another hour. I'd take an early lunch and spend the rest of the day touring facilities, quads, parks, and generally inspecting random areas of the base or meeting with whatever group managed to get past Diana's replacement out there." She cleared her throat. "You're smart, or you wouldn't have all that wood in front of you. I'll bet that within two months, you'll be doing just what I said, or a fair imitation."

Marsha got up and led her to the cozy little nook reserved for more intimate conversations. "Drink?" she asked.

"No, thanks, unless you've still got a Pepsi in there. I've got too much to do today to start drinking now."

A Pepsi soon sat on the table before her. "So, what makes you stop by, Kitty?" Marsha inquired bluntly.

She didn't detect any anger in her friend's voice or face, so she just said, "You know we leave in a week, give or take a day, and I've got something for you. A going away present."

Marsha looked a bit surprised, saying, "Going away presents usually go the other way around, you know. But thanks anyway." She reached out and took the small package, looking over the gaily wrapped box. "Now?" she asked. Kitty just nodded.

Marsha ripped the paper off and was left with what was obviously a jewelry box. "I had to guess at your size, but I think you'll be pleased. It'll go with anything you have in your wardrobe except those horrible black uniforms."

The box opened to reveal a four-strand diamond choker. "I can't keep this," Marsha protested instantly, breathing hard.

"It's bad form to refuse a gift, friend-o-mine. Besides, I threw the receipt away," Kitty said, lying through her teeth.

Marsha was almost in tears. She couldn't take her eyes off the glittering expanse of ice and platinum lying on the black velvet interior. "I've got one for you, too. It's just not in the same league with this." A tear rolled down her face.

Kitty misinterpreted the tear. "Don't you even worry about the cost difference. The money came straight out of Alliance funds."

"It's not that, Kitty. It just makes me realize that I won't be seeing you for what... five, ten years?" Now tears flowed freely down her face.

"Marsha, think about it for a minute. We've got a nearly three-hundred-year lifespan now. Just how much of your life is ten years? It always seems much longer from the front end than the back." Kitty tried to reassure her friend but wasn't sure how well she'd done. "So, what do you have for me?"

"Well," Marsha said slowly, "it's more for you and Simon both. Here." She reached behind the couch she was spread out on and pulled out a fair-sized square box.

Kitty ripped through the paper almost as fast as Marsha had. When she opened the box, she found two sweaters and two t-shirts inside. All four were jet black with star patterns in all the varied colors ever seen by even a small telescope. Emblazoned on the front and back in iridescent green embroidery were the words, "To go where no man has gone before." Kitty's had a small difference. Hers said "woman" instead of "man."

One week later, the final preparations had been made and they'd said all their goodbyes. A small group of humans and Shiravans had come to see them off and Simon had been surprised to see Rentec and Maratai holding hands in a surprising show of human affection. He'd heard rumors that the two had been spending a lot of time alone together lately.

Good for them, he thought with a smile.

Finally it was time. All hands were at their stations. The captains of the other ships in their small fleet reported that all was ready, and Simon sat in the command chair of the *Enterprise*. He looked at Kitty, who just nodded calmly, a twinkle in her eye.

"Nav," he asked, "is the course laid in?"

Helm responded, "Sir, course set for Shiravi."

He looked back to Kitty as she stood with a hand on the back of his chair.

"A few weeks to visit and bring Linnas up to date, and then it's off into the unknown," she said as she looked at Earth in one of the view screens.

This time, he saw a tear roll down her cheek, though her face showed pure joy. "Okay, Kittyn, here come the stars I promised you." He turned back to the bridge crew. With a channel open to all ships. "Nav, course is laid in for Shiravi as first port of call. Helm, you may take us out."

And another door opened...

ABOUT THE AUTHOR

Bob lived in Montana for over thirty years, since late '85. He fell in love with the state almost instantly (who wouldn't after spending the previous twenty or more years trapped in Houston, Texas). Out in the Big Sky Country, he found the "elbow room" he didn't even know he was looking for. He lived quietly with his two cats and library of nearly two thousand books—about 95% Sci-Fi. He discovered that he liked to write as well and could often be found doing just that. Bob passed away in November of 2019 and is survived by his younger brother. Before he passed, he finished his writing project of more than a decade, The Stellar Heritage series, and he will live on in the hearts and minds of his readers.

Learn more at:
bladeoftruthpublishing.com/bob-mauldin

MORE FROM THE PUBLISHER

Blade of Truth Publishing Company specializes in science fiction and fantasy stories that change the way you view the world.

To find more great books head over to:

bladeoftruthpublishing.com/books

Bringing truth into the world, one story at a time.